Frozen Lands

STATE OF
MATHURA

Patliput

STATE OF
MORIYA

Samnal
River

STATE OF
CHALAMBA

STATE OF
SATVA

Mountain of
Rebirth

Taksila

KINGDOM OF
MAHVO
The Unconquered Lands

Vihara
Mountain
Ranges

CW00735098

THE
PRINCE
WITHOUT
SORROW

THE
PRINCE
WITHOUT
SORROW

MAITHREE
WIJESEKARA

HARPER
Voyager

Harper *Voyager*
An imprint of
HarperCollins*Publishers* Ltd
1 London Bridge Street
London SE1 9GF

www.harpercollins.co.uk

HarperCollins*Publishers*
Macken House
39/40 Mayor Street Upper
Dublin 1
D01 C9W8
Ireland

First published by HarperCollins*Publishers* Ltd 2025
1

Copyright © Maithree Wijesekara 2025

Map and interior illustrations copyright © Julian De Narvaez/Folio Art 2025

Maithree Wijesekara asserts the moral right to
be identified as the author of this work.

A catalogue record for this book is available from the British Library.

ISBN: 978-0-00-867204-1 (HB)
ISBN: 978-0-00-867205-8 (TPB)

This novel is entirely a work of fiction.
The names, characters and incidents portrayed in it are
the work of the author's imagination. Any resemblance to
actual persons, living or dead, events or localities is
entirely coincidental.

Typeset in Adobe Jenson Pro by Palimpsest Book Production Ltd, Falkirk, Stirlingshire

Printed and bound in the UK using 100% Renewable Electricity by CPI Group (UK) Ltd

All rights reserved. No part of this publication may be
reproduced, stored in a retrieval system, or transmitted,
in any form or by any means, electronic, mechanical,
photocopying, recording or otherwise, without the prior
permission of the publishers.

MIX
Paper | Supporting
responsible forestry
FSC
www.fsc.org   FSC™ C007454

This book contains FSC™ certified paper and other controlled sources
to ensure responsible forest management.

For more information visit: www.harpercollins.co.uk/green

For Comet –
you made the beginning easy and the
ending hard.

Simha
Golden City
Odhi Ocean
STATE OF DEVRAM
Trikalinga
Luth
KINGDOM OF KALINGA
The Sea Dragon's Wall
Kolakola

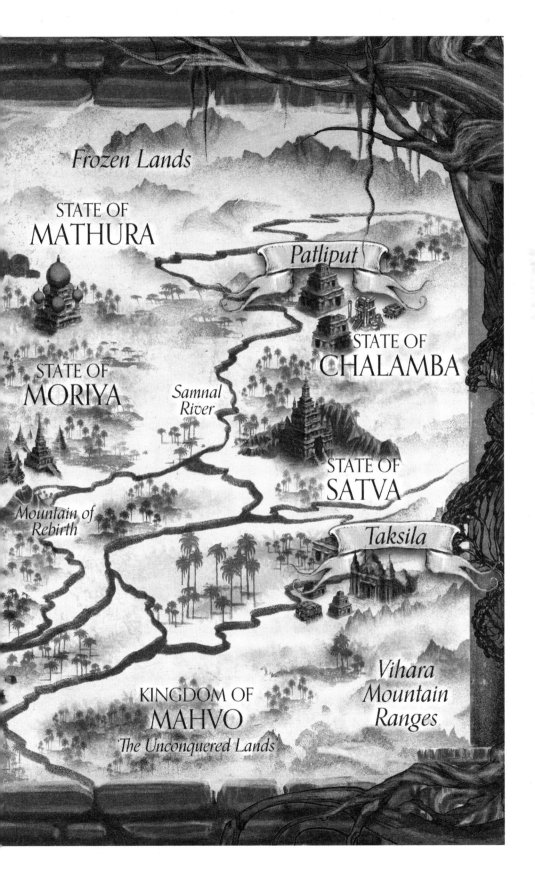

PROLOGUE

Jaya

SHE HAD EXPECTED HER LIFE TO END THIS WAY.

Bound, gagged, and paralysed – waiting for the sweet release of death. Such was the fate of all mayakari – witches – under the reign of Emperor Adil, ruler of the vast Ran Empire.

She squeezed her eyes shut, unwilling to turn her head to her side. Two other mayakari were already burning next to her, their bodies almost unidentifiable now, a blue flame engulfing their remains. She smelled cooking flesh and tamped down nausea that came raging up her throat like a river snake through a stream. At least they had only caught three.

She prayed to the spirits that her niece had escaped the village with her life. It was better to die old than young, and they needed the next generation of witches to live.

'Open your eyes, mayakari.'

A deep, rough voice stirred her out of her fervent prayers. A man stood before her, tall and muscular, carrying a longsword, a golden circlet decorating his head.

Emperor Adil.

She was surprised that he was here in person, visiting a small, insignificant town like theirs. But then she remembered why soldiers were here in the first place: the extensive mines to their village's east, its iron ore crumbling upon touch, unable to be used and sent to the capital to make steel.

It sounded as if mayakari magic had been at play, and it rarely was.

She could almost *sense* his loathing, a seething darkness in him, as if the sheer hatred of her and her kind coursed like wildfire through his veins.

'Don't be a coward,' he drawled. 'I want you to gaze upon the world as you burn.'

She did not want to give him this. She didn't want to give him anything at all. Yet, she opened her eyes and found herself staring into his as they gleamed. He was gleeful, triumphant in the face of all this death.

She wanted to curse him. To use her abilities to gift misery to the Ran Empire's ruler. But she could not. It was not the mayakari way. They were women who used their power to maintain peace, not sow seeds of destruction, it was their code, a mark of their livelihood. Their ability to speak to nature spirits, curse the living, and raise the dead were already powers that humans were wary of, and had kept an uneasy balance between fear and respect when it came to the mayakari. But being blamed for the disastrous Seven Day Flood over a decade ago had been the tipping point.

Emperor Adil's doing had caused them to be seen as nothing more than terrors in the night that deserved to be burned. How typical – the powerful fearing power they didn't understand.

Even at the end of things, she wished for nothing against him. Karma would find him one day; such was the inevitable, endless cycle of retribution.

As the emperor grasped a flaming torch and prepared to toss it at her oil-soaked body, she listened to him. She gazed at the world she lived in, understood the violence with which she would die and accepted it. Death would be easier than this.

She thought of her niece, a little bird in this brutal landscape, and she hoped she would remember, despite everything, the lessons she had given her. That anger solved nothing, that violence hurt those who wielded it as a weapon.

Find peace little bird, she thought as the tendrils of flame licked at her toes. *Find peace and let me go.*

CHAPTER ONE
Ashoka

'Kill it, Ashoka.'

Hands tingling with nervous anticipation, Prince Ashoka Maurya drew his bow tight. His target, a deer with large, curved antlers, stood a few feet away. Their footsteps had been so quiet that it hadn't yet noticed, munching away on a patch of grass with gusto.

To his right, his guard – and oldest friend – Rahil watched him expectantly.

'No time to dawdle, Ashoka,' he whispered, tone urgent. 'Hurry, before it escapes.'

Before you lose your nerve, was what Rahil left unsaid.

Steeling himself, Ashoka aimed the arrow tip at the deer's head. His body turned to lead, heartbeat running as fast as a fleeing animal as he gazed at the thick fur and spindly legs. Everything was perfect, from his stance to his lock on the deer. All he had to do was let the arrow fly.

He couldn't do it, couldn't force himself to let go. This was an innocent creature who had done nothing to harm him or Rahil, yet here he was about to take its life.

Let go, he told the part of himself that wouldn't listen. *Let go.*

A soft chittering erupted around them as he continued his silent struggle: a beautiful, soothing lullaby that echoed from everywhere and nowhere all at once.

The air around the deer began to shimmer as a figure appeared out of thin air. A round pink body atop a round head with grey sticklike arms and legs and pitch-black triangular eyes. As it opened its large circular mouth, that same melodic language he had heard floated into his ears. The creature looked like an apparition, a friendly ghost of sorts, but Ashoka knew all too well what this being was.

A nature spirit.

He rarely saw them unless he ventured out into the forests. They were notably absent in the stark, nature-less palace; the result of his father upending his grandmother's gardens and replacing them with unassuming manmade ponds and white-stone pebbles where even weeds were unable to grow.

The spirit began to chatter to the hungry deer, whose head perked up before turning its attention back to the grass. This was a picture of innocence, and he had to destroy it. This wasn't *right*.

'Ashoka,' Rahil repeated. 'Don't become distracted. Shoot.'

'No,' Ashoka said loudly, before realizing his mistake. The deer startled, its wide black eyes turning in their direction. Rahil swore.

'Shoot it, *now*,' he ordered, just as the deer began to flee and the nature spirit disappeared.

Ashoka let his arrow fly, watching it brush past the deer's ear before wedging itself firmly into the trunk of a tree. Within seconds, the creature had disappeared into the wilds of the forest, and he had failed his task, no match for a moving target.

He knew what his father would've said if he had been here, he'd heard it one hundred times before:

Weak. Pathetic. How can you not kill a simple animal, child? Your siblings would do it without hesitation.

Emperor Adil always sent him on hunts to prove himself, as if killing an animal demonstrated anything. If he could not come back with a successful hunt, he was a failure. If he came back with his kill, his father would be pleased. That kind of pride was the last thing Ashoka wanted.

Beside him, Rahil stood up.

'I've taught you to fight, but I can't seem to teach you to kill,' he said, but his tone wasn't admonishing. The afternoon rays filtering through the canopy lit his skin a glorious golden brown, the colour of precious sea glass brought in by Ridi traders from the west.

'It's an animal. It's an *innocent*,' Ashoka said, setting down his bow.

Rahil appraised him for a moment. 'Innocent?'

Sensing that Rahil was about to launch into an impassioned argument, Ashoka quickly uttered his defence. 'It does not harm others,' he said. Unlike his father, who destroyed without mercy, without care for anything else but his own ego.

'But is it an innocent when it abandons a defective newborn? When it ventures out into farmland and destroys a farmer's crops?' Rahil began before letting out a beleaguered sigh. 'You're hanging onto a warped version of innocence, and you know it.'

Ashoka chose to ignore him, but it seemed that Rahil was intent on ruffling his feathers today. 'You would make a terrible emperor,' he added, after a prolonged silence.

Ashoka felt his lips tilt downwards. 'Why do you say that?'

Rahil's crow-black hair swished at his shoulders as he held out his hand for Ashoka to take. 'You don't have the willpower to kill when it's needed,' he said matter-of-factly.

'It was a deer,' Ashoka said incredulously. 'You think *that's* what constitutes a great ruler?'

'No, that's what your *father* thinks,' Rahil corrected, absent-mindedly adjusting the dual broadswords strapped to his back as they made their way to the winged serpents that were tethered some distance away. Venturing into the forestland that lay to the north of the Maurya palace was arduous by foot, so Ashoka had convinced his friend to take the winged creatures instead. 'Why do you think he sends you out here?'

They both knew why. In a few years, he was to be sent off to govern like his eldest brother, and his father needed a gauge of his mettle. In his father's mind, performing a simple kill equated to having the aptitude to conduct a complex one.

Ashoka shot Rahil an exasperated look and rubbed at his close-cropped hair. 'Are you trying to vex me?'

Rahil shrugged in response. 'No,' he admitted, 'I was thinking about Sau's summary of the last council meeting. Aarya and Arush had a lot of opinions about the southern expansion. You'll be there with them in a few years, and you can't be entertaining ideas that'll have you laughed out of the council.'

Ashoka winced, thinking of his two brash older siblings. Alone, they were mildly threatening. Together, they were a recipe for destruction.

'You know as well as I do that nothing good ever happens whenever Arush and Aarya put their heads together and think,' Rahil continued.

Ashoka knew it well. When he was nine, Arush and Aarya had freed ten giant water bugs into his bedchambers while he slept. Deathly terrified upon waking, he had yelled for his mother over the large insects skittering around his room. His siblings had found the entire affair to be amusing, stifling their cackles as Empress Manali reprimanded them. Ashoka had hated water bugs ever since.

'Nothing particularly *good* came out of that council meeting,' Ashoka said reproachfully.

'I was surprised he took Aarya's suggestion into account,' Rahil murmured.

'Convincing father to burn Kolakola entirely was an insane proposition,' Ashoka agreed, thinking of the small, unassuming southern township that had only ever been a blip on the map until his father had learned that the iron ore being exported from the nearby mines crumbled the moment they were extracted, and it had temporarily halted the retrieval process. That, and reports of mayakari living in the village had been brought to his attention.

Unnatural deterioration of iron ore coupled with the existence of mayakari in Kolakola? It had not been a far-fetched assumption to correlate the two.

It didn't stop Ashoka from viewing his father with contemptuousness. He did not understand why the man failed to register the merits of peacekeeping like he did. To Emperor Adil, more power meant expansion. His father was relentless in his desire to grow the borders of the Ran Empire to the natural resource-rich south. The northern half of the continent was all his, save for the snow-laden mountains that separated them from the blue-eyed people of the Frozen Lands. The icy tundra was a far cry from the warm, monsoon-prone seasons of the Ran Empire.

The south, however, was a different story.

Slowly but surely, Emperor Adil was advancing downwards, annexing kingdoms he dubbed the unconquered lands and slaughtering the largely peaceful mayakari population as he did. From each annexation came scores of iron ore for steel production, and ironwood to build weapons for the military. The south was also abundant with precious stones, ripe for trade, and used as gaudy decorations in the Maurya palace, but ironwood was his father's focus. More weapons gave them a better chance in annexing the powerful sea kingdom of Kalinga, thus granting him control over the largest maritime trading hub in the known world.

'You don't think Emperor Adil would really do that, do you?' Rahil asked.

Ashoka let out a laugh. 'What, burn the township? I think you underestimate him.'

His father had departed for Kolakola yesterday. It was unusual for him to make personal trips, but the situation had piqued his interest. Mayakari so rarely fought back against his persecution, and if they did, resorted only to minor disturbances where little was harmed as humanly possible.

'He listens to Aarya like she has somehow hung the stars,'

Ashoka continued. 'I can only hope that one day he becomes receptive to my ideas, but I won't hold my breath.'

His father saw his pacifist ideas as a deficit. And, perhaps most importantly, hated that he did not see the mayakari as the ominous threat he'd made them out to be.

Women of death and shadows, able to speak to nature spirits, curse the living, and raise the dead. From what Ashoka had read of the historical records kept in the palace library, the Ran Empire had not persecuted the witches during his grandmother's reign, nor during the monarchs who preceded her. In fact, the mayakari were largely peaceful, tending to veer towards scholarly pursuits. They had a towering library built on the outskirts of the Golden City where they studied their own magic, trying to help balance societal advancement with the maintenance of wild lands and its spirits.

The distrust and hatred of the mayakari originated under his father's rule.

He could trace it back to the Seven Day Flood that had impacted the Golden City over a decade ago, a year after his grandmother's death. Rebuilding efforts had been slow. The young Emperor Adil was the one who made a proclamation asking the mayakari for help in using their abilities to force the nature spirits to regrow the rice crops devasted by flood waters. It was he who had berated the witches for denying his appeal and accused them of gatekeeping their knowledge. It was under his father's vicious reports of dissenting mayakari that the library had been burned, known witches following the same fate.

It was a point of pride for his father, the destruction of the library. He always wore the same boastful expression when he recalled that event.

If Rahil noticed Ashoka's bitter tone, he didn't comment on it. 'Then learn the middle path,' he said.

'If this "middle path" of yours involves acknowledging my father's cruel methods, then I won't do it,' Ashoka scoffed. 'I could never endorse killing like him.'

Rahil only stared at him, nonplussed.

'I won't kill,' Ashoka added, gritting his teeth. 'I would *never* kill.'

Rahil eyed him curiously. 'I'm inclined to believe you,' he said. 'You can't even kill a deer, for spirits' sake.'

'It didn't deserve to die!'

'Ashoka, I swear you would catch a fish and then apologize for cooking it.'

'I would. So what?'

Rahil snorted. 'You're insufferable,' he said, turning to lock eyes with Ashoka. His eyes were soft and fearless, the colour of smoky quartz. They were set against lashes that his sister Aarya used to painstakingly wish for in her adolescence. Rahil's handsomeness had always been the inviting kind; warm and magnetic.

Ashoka's heart jumped uncontrollably. 'And yet you have not left me,' he said.

'Then I must be mad,' Rahil replied. The ghost of a smile graced his lips as they trudged through patches of overgrown grass. 'Imagine if you *were* the emperor.'

Wishing for his rapid heartbeat to slow, Ashoka shrugged with an air of pure nonchalance as he listened to the soft cooing of myna birds above. 'And you call *me* idealistic,' he said after a while. The gleaming opalescent head of his winged serpent, Sahry, came into view. 'Once my siblings decide to have children of their own, the title will still evade me even into my next life.'

Arush. Aarya. Ashoka. That was the order of the Maurya children. Arush would claim the throne, and Ashoka would slink behind them as an infrequent council attendee, wasting his life away in a palace of luxuries.

It was not a life he would find fulfilling. No, he'd long since decided that he needed to be in the thick of things. By being part of the council, he would at least be able to temper the flood of murderous jubilation from his father and siblings. But at twenty-two, he was considered too young. Ironic, since Aarya was not yet twenty-five either but had still been allowed to join. Clearly his age was just an excuse. What a privilege to be father's favourite.

No matter. Once he was of age, his father would not be able to argue against royal decrees.

Rahil opened his mouth to respond before he tensed. He held out a hand, forcing Ashoka to stop in his tracks and turned slowly towards a rustling sound coming from the undergrowth just beyond them. Ashoka watched curiously as four spindly legs and a dark brown nose emerged, sniffing the grass curiously.

Another deer.

Ashoka heard Rahil shuffle next to him, heard the soft *twang* of his bowstring, and realized too late what he was about to do.

Rahil didn't even blink. His bow was in his hands within seconds, the arrow flying from its hold with dangerous precision. Ashoka looked away and heard a dull *thunk* followed by a pained whimper. An agonizing silence followed as they waited for the deer to take its final breath. He squeezed his eyes shut.

Weak, his father's voice, ever the thorn in his mind, echoed in his head.

'You won't even look at it,' he heard Rahil's soft voice next to him.

'I won't,' Ashoka whispered. He couldn't bear to.

There was a pregnant pause before Rahil remarked, 'You have to learn to be cruel before you can learn to be great.' It was something Emperor Adil repeated often, and it only ever made Ashoka see red. 'Just tell your father that you killed the deer. Make him think positively of you, for once.'

His comment forced Ashoka to open his eyes. Rahil was gazing at him with an expression of utmost sympathy.

Ashoka scowled. 'I would much rather disappoint him,' he said. 'Come, we need to burn it.'

'That is a waste of meat,' Rahil gestured to the deer. He appeared flummoxed by the idea. 'We should—'

'Not have killed it? Yes, you are correct,' Ashoka finished for him. When Rahil shot him an exasperated glare, the fire in his chest dimmed. He had only been trying to help.

'I'm sorry, but it did not deserve to die for me to prove my father wrong,' he said. Unlike Rahil, he had no qualms about burning it, as he forsook meat like the mayakari were known to do. 'So please, help me. An innocent requires a cremation it didn't deserve.'

CHAPTER TWO

Shakti

Late at night, the paddy fields resembled a swamp.

Moonlight reflected off the water in pieces, broken by the rice stalks that stood neat and tall like a squadron of soldiers. The smell of mud was pervasive, and the scent of water buffalo lingered even after they had been taken in for the night by the farmers. Or perhaps it was their droppings; Shakti couldn't tell. They smelled the same.

The ground beneath her slipper-clad feet was soft. Ready to crumble. She stood on a thin paddy bund, toes creating an indent on the damp earth. Despite the coolness in the air, her forehead was dusted with a light sheen of sweat and her hair stuck to her cheeks like tree sap to bark.

Opposite her, the town's weapons-master, Hasith, pointed to her back foot.

'Careful,' he warned. Coarse-looking grey streaks dotted his long beard and tied-back hair. 'Slip, and you'll be helping smelt my weapons this entire week.'

The thought of being constrained inside an arid room with burning metal made Shakti scrunch her nose in distaste. Though she loved using weapons, making them was not a process she enjoyed, and Master Hasith knew that. It was why he peppered challenges into her combat lessons. The threat of hard labour made Shakti more determined to win.

'Can't you think of another punishment?' she complained. 'My arms are still hurting from last week.'

Master Hasith lunged, his feet maintaining perfect balance of the bund. 'Then don't slip,' he said. His right foot swung out in a neat arc and hit the side of Shakti's waist. More dank ground powdered beneath her as Shakti wobbled. Her front foot lifted off the ground and she quickly twisted, placing it behind her other foot to hold steady.

'Good,' Hasith called out. Then, 'There's no use in mastering long-range weapons if you can't hold your own in close combat. You won't always have your arrows with you.' He nodded towards her bow and arrow that lay across from them.

She could argue that was what her sword was for, and she reminded him as such.

Master Hasith chuckled. 'I'm surprised your aunt hasn't tried to curse me yet,' he said. 'A smart woman like her would surely realize that you keep traipsing out of her house in the late hours of the night to practise combat.'

'Please,' she scoffed. 'If anything, she would curse *me*. Aunty knows that I leave. She just hates that I like using weapons. Hates it even more that I'm good with them.'

Weapons were a tool for violence, and her aunt Jaya maintained that mayakari should not favour them. It was a tale Shakti had heard often when she had been informed of her witch blood. Pacifism was their way of life, a well-established philosophy that Jaya had tried to instil into her but failed. One could argue that she had given Shakti too much freedom and not enough education on the doctrines of the mayakari. They were two different person-alities living in a small wooden house, and although Shakti tried to emulate her aunt's gentle disposition, her penchant for explo-siveness was difficult to set aside.

It had been that way since she was young, and she blamed part of it on Rohan.

Rohan was their next-door-neighbour's son, two years older than she was. He used to tease Shakti to her wits' end; her hair was pulled, her beloved drawings torn, her flute-playing ridiculed. He made fun of her long nose and two-toned lips as if they were the worst thing in the world. Shakti hated him. Despite Jaya's insistence that she empathize or turn the other cheek, Shakti couldn't manage to do so. She so badly wanted to curse him, to send a nature spirit after him like a malevolent ghost, but she couldn't. After all, the mayakari had their code. Cursing bred nothing but negative karma.

'It's about safety, too, little bird,' Jaya had declared. 'Let it be known you're a witch, and our lives are forfeit.'

Forfeit. As if they were in some sort of children's game. It was why Jaya had them keeping their heads low, making sure they didn't cast suspicion on themselves. Their existence was made known to a trusted few that Shakti could count with one hand. She'd learned to be cautious.

So, instead of cursing, she'd punched Rohan's nose hard enough to break. Jaya had been horrified all the same, since violence was violence. However, Shakti had long since forgotten to care. If she couldn't curse, she could defend.

Master Hasith recalled the story better than she did. According to him, a furious adolescent with short, heat-frazzled hair had come into his shop demanding that he teach her how to punch an irritating pest in a proper fashion.

It started out as a way to learn basic throws, but Shakti had ended up taking to it more than she thought. She became fascinated with the glowing silver daggers and swords that were hung carefully for appraisal at his store and was drawn to the elegant ironwood bows used by the archers that ventured out to hunt.

She'd asked Master Hasith to teach her how to throw a dagger with perfect aim. He'd complied.

For a while, it became a well-kept secret that she hid from Jaya. The story that she told her aunt was simple – that she'd gone to paint nature spirits in the wild forest. Unfortunately, Shakti's perfect façade broke sooner than she thought.

Rohan had been the reason she came to Master Hasith, and he also became the reason her aunt found out about her combat lessons. The insufferable boy had sauntered over to her aunt's back garden where Shakti was trying to scrub dried turmeric paste from a clay pot. He had jeered. Called her a pathetic little girl.

Shakti didn't give him the chance to blink. By that time, she'd become accustomed to keeping a small dagger on her person. Within seconds, she'd thrown her weapon and it had lodged itself into the pinna of Rohan's ear.

She still recalled the sound that came out of his mouth with fondness, a half-bray, half-squeal that sounded part donkey, part pig. To this day, she mocked the sound to his face whenever he mustered up the gall to throw verbal barbs at her.

When Jaya found out, she'd barred Shakti from picking up a weapon.

'I shouldn't have been so lenient with you,' her aunt admonished. 'Back in my day, elder mayakari drilled the four precepts into our heads.'

Do not curse. Do not manipulate. Do not harm. Do not kill.

Precepts were rules and she'd broken the third. Her aunt had taught her they were a way to keep a mayakari from using their powers to their full extent. The elder mayakari could blather on about how it was their code, their *laws*, but Shakti saw them for what they were: shackles; self-imposed restrictions on women more powerful than the ruling monarch. Despite her own beliefs, however, there was one thing she hated most in the world and that was seeing Jaya disappointed in her. It was a looming, itchy feeling that dulled everything. And so, to absolve her guilt, Shakti had promised not to respond to Rohan's taunts with calculated violence.

It did not mean that she kept away from her secret lessons.

Lulled back into the present, Shakti refocused on Master Hasith, whose hand was outstretched. 'Asking me to dance?' she smiled.

Master Hasith chuckled. 'You know, Jaya's wife was very much like you.'

Not that Shakti would know. Her other aunt had disappeared on a trip to the Vihara Mountains when she was a baby. Jaya never spoke of her, and the only reminder she kept was a slim gold chain with an emerald pendant that had been given to her on her wedding day. Jaya never took the necklace off.

Sometimes, Shakti wanted to ask Jaya why she had not followed her wife. They did not have to stay here with the shadow of death looming over them, but Jaya's response was always the same. Fleeing the empire was just as risky. The journey to the kingdom of Kalinga was heard to be guarded by Ran soldiers, and the icy north was a death sentence. The next viable option for a mayakari was to cross the Vihara Mountains in the east to Anurapura, but therein was the problem. The mountain region was notoriously dangerous and hazardous to cross. That, and the kingdom of Anurapura was not their terrain. They had their own mayakari with their own customs and ways of respecting the land.

In response to the weapons-master's comment, Shakti splayed her index and middle fingers, and brought them towards Master Hasith's eyes. When he moved to block, she diverted her attack, instead using the opposite arm to push his open chest, hard. The older man faltered, caught himself, and looked up as if he were about to say something to her when his stance shifted. Dark eyes narrowed as he peered over Shakti's shoulder. She saw his nostrils flare as he took an audible sniff. Curious, Shakti craned her neck to see what had caught his eye.

Nestled in the lowest portion of the fields, they couldn't see much of the township on the hill above them. Large and rectangular planks of wood cordoned off homes from agricultural land and the wild forests beyond it, but Shakti could see what had captured the weapons-master's attention.

Smoke.

'What on earth . . .' Master Hasith said as they watched faint grey plumes drift into the berry-black sky.

'Someone must be cooking a late meal,' Shakti supplied. She turned back to continue their lesson, but it seemed that Master Hasith was no longer interested. Rather, he appeared worried.

'That's too much smoke,' he replied, frowning. 'Something isn't right – come, Shakti.'

Both took off uphill, Shakti pausing only to gather her bow and arrow.

The climb uphill was harder than expected. Shakti's calf muscles were aching by the time she sped past the open wooden gate that led into town, Master Hasith's footsteps right behind her. The moment she passed the back entryway, the smell of smoke hit her hard.

It became stronger the closer she approached the town square: ripened fruit and chilli mixed with animal odour and burned wood, an unpleasant concoction. But that wasn't all – there was another smell that she couldn't identify, an unknown aroma that gnawed at her intestines like a hungry leopard tearing into rabbit flesh. She tried to place it. Something was being cooked. Roasted. It was like a slab of meat had spent too long in the sun before being thrown in a furnace. But it didn't smell like animal meat.

Kolakola's main business hub was small, and the market stalls had long since closed for the night, but the area was packed with people by the time her feet hit the limestone pavement. They were gathered around . . . a fire? Shakti was still not close enough to tell. Other than the full moon, torches were the only source of light, so it took her a moment to identify the unfamiliar men and women encircling the town square like guard dogs. Once she saw their red and black armour, her breath hitched. Dread pooled in her stomach when she spotted the grim-looking swords attached to their sides.

Soldiers. Emperor Adil's dogs.

For the normal citizen, the Royal Guard represented safety. To the mayakari, they were a merchant of death.

Jaya, her thoughts raced to her aunt. *Where's Jaya?* There were soldiers at Kolakola, and she had no idea why. The township had been taken by the Ran Empire years ago. They had no reason to be here.

Unless . . .

No, Shakti told herself firmly. *No, this must be something else.*

Voices played over each other as she edged closer, scraps of information being fed little by little:

'*. . . how terrible . . .*'

'*. . . well, what did you expect, the mines . . .*'

'*. . . wonder who accused them . . .*'

Acutely aware of Master Hasith voicing his caution behind her, Shakti pushed her way into the throng of townspeople. Sweat and rhododendron perfume, clean soap, and ash overpowered her senses. Elbows dug into her ribs and backs bumped into her chin, but Shakti pushed through.

She saw the blue flames first before she realized what she was seeing in front of her.

Burning bodies. Three, to be exact.

Bound. Gagged. Tied to thick wooden poles. *That* was what the smell had been.

Gasps and murmurs echoed all around her as Shakti huddled with the townspeople around the main square. Forcing back the tears that were threatening to spill out from her like a poorly built dam in the monsoon season, she assessed the three bodies in front of her. They were almost unrecognizable now, body parts reddened and blackened to a crisp, but she needed to appraise them closer. Shakti edged nearer to the front, straining to see above the heads of the men and women around her.

The malicious glint of a green object winked at her from the neck of one of corpses in the middle. Her heart sank.

'No,' she whispered. The contents of her dinner threatened to regurgitate. 'Please, *no.*'

Flames licked Jaya's distorted corpse in glacial blues and whites, a definitive sign of her mayakari lineage. Witches' bodies burned hotter than the orange-yellow flames that engulfed normal human ones. That meant—

One of the bodies had to be Dharvi, the bookseller. She was a mayakari with a daughter of her own, Nayani. Well into her thirtieth year, Nayani had long left Kolakola for Taksila, only visiting her mother in sporadic bursts, and she'd arrived some weeks ago. Shakti spun, looking for her in the crowd and coming up empty. The other body then had to be Laila's; the elderly mayakari who lived alone. Where was Nayani, then? Had she escaped, or was she still here, watching just like her?

Run, she told herself. *I need to run.*

Shakti found that she couldn't move. Her feet were rooted to the spot, her mind still attempting to make sense of what she was seeing.

How did this happen? Who told them?

'No,' Shakti repeated. This had to be some sort of nightmare. This wasn't real. Her aunt couldn't be dead.

But she was, and Shakti was very much awake. Her entire body wound up tightly like the strings of a sitar as the world closed in around her. Squashed against so many bodies, claustrophobia set in. The tears welled up so much that her vision blurred, and she was left with no choice but to let them fall, cringing at the cold sting of salt against her flushed skin.

Hours ago, she had helped Jaya mix a herbal tonic for a client whose mouth ulcers refused to heal. Hours ago, she had hugged her aunt goodnight. Hours ago, she had no idea that the person she loved most in the world would be taken away in a flash.

The shocked murmurs of the townspeople rose to a crescendo as eyes widened, postures went slack, and backs bent into deep, hasty bows.

Shakti craned her neck upwards to spot the source of the crowd's surprise. She noticed the sword first: a blade that was viciously long, cruelly curved, and adorned with gold at its hilt. It was attached to a man, tall and lean, his light brown skin gleaming under the moonlight. His hair was tied neatly behind him, fastened by a beautiful circlet embellished with rubies.

She knew without question the man who was gazing upon them with a secret smile.

'My dear subjects,' Emperor Adil remarked loudly. He had the powerful, guttural type of voice that caught the attention of anyone who listened. 'Witness before you the death of these dangerous witches.'

Dangerous. She'd heard his disparaging lies spewed from many mouths a hundred times before.

Shakti swallowed. Her throat was as dry as sandpaper. Emperor Adil's lies had cost Jaya's life, and now, she was nothing more than a molten lump of flesh.

'These mayakari have tampered with your mines,' Emperor Adil continued. His voice was loud and insistent, dripping with conviction. 'Weakened iron ore, caused the collapse of tunnels, caused death in the process.'

Tampered? Collapsed tunnels? She'd heard miners returning from the mountains complain about crumbling iron ore but had chalked it up to being a natural fault.

There was a stunned silence, before—

'*They were good women.*'

She stilled, as did the crowd around her. Master Hasith.

She couldn't see him; he wasn't within her line of sight. The old man had been right behind her.

Emperor Adil's posture stiffened, but his smile remained intact.

'Who said that?' he called out to the crowd. No one answered. She silently hoped that Master Hasith would keep his mouth shut. At the loud silence, Shakti saw the smile briefly slip from the emperor's mouth.

'I do not take kindly to cowardice,' he said. 'Face me or watch your people face punishment on your behalf.'

There was another long beat of disquiet before she heard footsteps shuffling. From her right, Master Hasith emerged from the crowd.

Shakti could sense something ominous in the air. It crackled and spun its silent threads in the dark sky, waiting. Anticipating. Running was the safest option for her. It was too dangerous to stay. Jaya's soft voice echoed in her head:

Giving up is still an act of courage, little bird.

Shakti knew the voice was right but, somehow, she could not find the courage to run. She chose foolishness; she chose to stay.

'Your name?' Emperor Adil inquired, assessing the weapons-master emotionlessly.

'Hasith, Your Highness,' he replied, unflinching as he bowed. If he was scared, he didn't show it.

'You believe these mayakari to be *good* women?' Emperor Adil nearly spat out the words.

'Without question, Your Highness.'

When murmurs of agreement arose from the crowd, her hands trembled. Shakti squeezed them together to calm herself down. Emperor Adil eyed Hasith with an expression of utmost pity and disdain.

'You knew they lived here, and yet you reported nothing?' Adil questioned.

Stop talking, Master Hasith, she wanted to scream at him. For a moment, his eyes flitted through the crowd until she swore they latched onto her.

Run, they seemed to say, *before they find you.*

He's not being reckless, Shakti realized. He was buying her time.

'Some of us understood that long-standing prejudices were built on nothing but lies, Your Highness.'

The crowd gasped. How bold. Brave. *Stupid.*

'A mayakari sympathizer,' said Emperor Adil softly. 'I cannot stand your type. You understand that words spoken for the mayakari are words spoken against *me*, and yet you do it anyway.'

Hasith only had time to blink before Emperor Adil plunged the sword into his heart.

Screams erupted from the crowd as they edged away. Shakti could only stare in horrid fascination as blood blossomed through Hasith's dust-plagued shirt, his eyes wide open, frozen in shock.

23

He fell to the ground with an unceremonious *thump*, the sword still wedged firmly into his skin.

Emperor Adil's gaze was unfeeling as he glanced up. At that moment, Shakti caught his eyes. They seemed to be alive with a dreadful delight.

'It appears this town is plagued with sympathizers,' said Emperor Adil. 'Plagues must always be eradicated.'

The thread being spun in the sky above her finally revealed its finished tapestry: an array of death and destruction.

They were in danger. This had been his plan all along. They never had a chance.

'Soldiers,' she heard the emperor's clear voice in the din, 'spare no survivors.'

CHAPTER THREE

Shakti

IN SEVEN PAINFUL HEARTBEATS, THE WORLD BLED INTO violence around her.

Soldiers unsheathed their swords and charged towards the crowd. Shrieks erupted around her as people scrambled to get back, to run and hide away in their homes. To burrow into a place where they couldn't be found. Bodies shoved against bodies, parents stopped to hurry along a fallen child while others stopped for no one, abandoning bravery for the need to survive.

Shakti was quick. She scampered into an alleyway, wanting to unhear the sound of metal slicing into flesh, and shuddered at the screams that were silenced under the gleam of a sword.

'I won't die,' she whispered as a hiccup burbled from her throat. 'I *won't* die.'

Clambering past a fruit vendor's stall emptied of its usual ripened mangos and furry rambutans, she held her breath as she ran. The bow and arrow were a crushing weight against her back. She wished she had her sword, too, but it was hidden in her room, locked inside an intricately carved wooden chest. She was almost tempted to rush in the opposite direction to find it but that same soft echo of her aunt's voice in her head stopped her from making a grave mistake.

Any sensible person would flee, little bird.

Flee. Yes. That was what she needed to do. There was no way to escape from the northern gate. The soldiers had arrived from there and it would be heavily guarded. Escaping out into the empty roads served no purpose, either. Likely, she would be shot down by arrows like a deer wandering out into open plains.

No, the only haven for a mayakari was the wild forest.

Back to the paddy fields, she willed herself forward. Her legs were still sore from combat training, but fear made her body forget. She skittered between small dirt paths, hands slapping against wood as she careened past the entrance to the rice fields. The steep decline made it easier for her to increase speed. Sticking to the grass was the smartest option, otherwise the stone-scattered path would create more noise. She could still see Master Hasith's face, the exact moment the light vanished from his eyes. It was impossible to believe that he had just been training with her.

The smell of smoke became ten times more pungent. Shakti turned to see that her tiny mountainous community had quickly become a landscape painted in hellfire. Houses and buildings were being set alight, the smoke rising into the tepid night. Within minutes, she had seen more death than in all her twenty-two years combined. She could only hope some got away.

Muscle memory continued to drive her legs forward. Stalks of rice trampled beneath her feet and water soaked her slippers – there was no time to worry about running along the bunds to keep the plants undisturbed. There would be no one to care for them when the morning came.

The forestland grew bigger the closer she came. Populated by towering Na, Ironwood, Banyan and Sal trees, the wild forests covered a vast stretch of land. Within it, there roamed nature spirits, almost all minor, and three Great. No one – man, woman, or royal – would dare burn it.

When she reached the edge of the forest, Shakti turned just in time to see two figures coming the way she had. Others had thought to flee here, too. They were almost halfway there, so achingly close.

Shakti blinked and, in seconds, the running figures were shot down by a barrage of arrows.

Stumbling back, Shakti's outstretched hand slapped against the bark of a tree trunk. She pressed her palm to her lips and retreated further into the forest. She was out of range to shoot the emperor's men, and there was no taking chances. Terrified cries continued to batter the night, ricocheting like echoes in an underground cave. And with each her chest tightened.

Shakti didn't stop running until the screams became part of the din. She found herself beneath a Banyan tree and slumped against one of its hefty buttresses. Roughness scraped against her back, but she hardly registered it as pain. A minor inconvenience, at most. True pain came from her shattered heart. It was still rampaging, like an ox trying to break free of its enclosure.

Her breath came out in strained puffs. Leaning back, she allowed her body to relax as best as it could. Her mind was still an ongoing explosion of fireworks, so Shakti decided to close her eyes. Meditate. The first deep inhale did not come clean; it sputtered. On the second, it reduced.

Shakti focused on her breathing until she felt the rapid rise of her chest give way to something slower, more assured. Her tears had long since dried. They didn't spring to her as easily as anger did. And though her breath settled, Shakti's mind continued to taunt her. Her aunt's burned sockets stared back like an angry demon. They screamed at her, asking why she had left her alone. Why did she leave her late at night to *fight?*

Because not fighting would have had me end up like you, *aunty.*

The truth hurt, only because it had taken casualties with it.

'Human.'

Soft. Sweet. Tinkling like a wind chime and jittering like a baby robin. The voice that spoke to her came out of a gaping black mouth with shimmery white eyes. Perched on the buttress above her was a pale blue creature with a spherical head and no neck. It bobbed like a raft on ocean waves atop a miniaturized infant's body. A minor spirit.

'*Hello,*' Shakti replied. Anyone who was not a mayakari would hear birdsong or flutes during their conversation. Such was the language of the nature spirits. They were not made to be understood by humans who never learned to appreciate the natural world. '*Forgive me, spirit. I seek shelter by your tree.*'

The spirit answered by stretching its mouth into a half-moon and moving to perch on her shoulder. She felt a sudden flash of fear, the aching of foot soles, the warmth of a hollow. Heat. Relief. Minor spirits preferred non-verbal conversation, but that tended to vex her. Words were blunt and sure, but images contained too many possibilities.

From this spirit's answer, she gathered that it promised safety and she welcomed it.

The spirit's body cast an eerie blue glow that shone on her slippers. Shakti reached down to wipe away speckles of mud and grass but that did little to get rid of the uncomfortable feeling of water sluiced between her toes. Her navy cotton trousers were also damp at the hems.

The glow turned brighter. Images of a forest followed, burning. Unable to be revived. Dark tunnels closing in around her. It could sense that she felt despair.

'*Yes,*' Shakti said hoarsely. She cursed herself for the hitch in her voice. Meditation should have worked. It should have stopped the shattered pieces of her heart from cutting into her skin. It should have blunted her misery. Sitting here with the nature spirit, however, did nothing to assuage her. The little creature was a reminder of her aunt. The *forest* was a reminder of her aunt, of what she had taught her. That the world was not anyone's to claim, that it was not theirs to possess. Memories of days and nights spent shaded beneath the towering canopy made Shakti hug her knees to her chest.

She was a mayakari. Such misfortune was expected in the Ran Empire. Danger was a promise. Inevitability did not make it any easier to swallow.

Irritably, she rubbed her eyes, lashes stuck together, teardrops clinging for dear life like a drowning man holding onto a rope. She was crying. Again.

This is no time for tears, she reprimanded herself. She fought with her mind, with that part of her that wanted to curl up into a ball and die. Or hide. She couldn't just give up. She knew how to fight.

'*The emperor killed my family*,' she told the nature spirit. Red-hot rage pooled in the pit of her stomach, and she welcomed it. Sadness had no place in her heart. It would only make her weak, and weakness would get her killed. Complacency would get her killed. '*And here I am, hiding*.'

Its response was a flash of grey. A question: *what is the alternative?*

'*I could run away*,' Shakti said. She could travel further east to the vast stretch of the Vihara Mountain ranges that separated the Ran Empire and the kingdom of Anurapura. It would take weeks to get there, and the terrain would be treacherous, but safety could be guaranteed at Anurapura. At least, that was what Jaya had told her. '*I could keep myself alive*.'

But as she said it, something felt wrong.

Running away is still an act of courage, little bird.

It made perfect sense. It was logical, given her circumstances. But what was courage to Shakti? Surely, it wasn't running away. Hiding. Lying low.

'*Or I could fight back*,' Shakti said, feeling a little foolish. What could she fight – an army? A monarch? An empire?

The minor spirit finally retorted verbally, and in sentences. Perhaps it disliked her response. '*Mayakari do not fight*,' it fussed. '*Mayakari should not fight*.'

Abilities to speak to nature spirits, to curse the living, to raise the dead. Three great powers but only one regularly used. Jaya had always asked her to avoid using mayakari abilities to harm others. They were more sinister than simple weapons; they brought on bad karma and an unpleasant rebirth. To Shakti, it made no sense. If humans attacked with fire and swords, she could equally attack them with curses, karma be damned.

Why did she have to follow rules that seemed ridiculously antiquated? What was the point of limiting themselves like this?

This reality was a desert where nothing could thrive. It forced her to bury her sadness in a clay pot. It made her hands itch for her weapons.

This was Emperor Adil's doing. This was *his* fault. Her aunt, Master Hasith, Dharvi, Laila – all were dead, and the townspeople suffered the same fate. Shakti only wished she could force that same fate on her so-called emperor.

Do not curse. Do not manipulate. Do not harm. Do not kill.

Jaya was wrong; violence should be repaid with violence. Doing nothing was the mayakari way, but it would not be Shakti's way. She couldn't sit here knowing that justice was left to time. She could resist. She could fight.

She could curse.

If she didn't there wouldn't be any mayakari left. The emperor wouldn't stop until they were all dead. She'd seen the fire in his eyes. Pettiness might not have been in Jaya's nature, but it was in Shakti's. Perhaps it was time to use the cursed language. And who was a better target for her venomous grief than the man who had so casually ruined her life?

Around her, fireflies flickered in and out of existence like miniature suns. Like ideas, they materialized and disappeared in the blink of an eye.

Shakti could not imagine being a harbinger of death. How could she take a life and do right by Jaya? But how could she not? Jaya had been loyal to the mayakari ways, she had been faithful and now even her corpse was lost, cinders at the bottom of a mass grave. How was that right? How was that natural? How was that *fair*? Was that the reward for obeying the precepts?

Do not curse. Do not manipulate. Do not harm. Do not kill.

No. No longer.

'Curse,' Shakti whispered. The word came out soft and unsure like a freshly birthed calf struggling to walk on its awkwardly long legs. She had never cursed, had only been taught the language and its basic rules, but that was all she needed.

She curled her hands into fists. *Curse.* The words needed to mature faster and saying them aloud with conviction helped. *'I'll make myself a promise,'* she told the nature spirit. *'And you, little creature, will bear witness.'*

Another image, this time of flowers suffocated by weeds. For a moment, she felt her breathing stall as if the same vexatious weeds had wrapped around her throat, pressing against the skin until she was black and blue. The feeling vanished when the spirit jumped from its place upon her shoulder. It fell like a feather, slow and gentle, and she watched as its pale feet touched the ground. There were no footprints left behind. It tilted its head at her, expectant.

Shakti took a deep breath. Held it. *'I will curse Emperor Adil for his crimes,'* she said, this time with more force. *'I will welcome vengeance where others have not. My aunt, Master Hasith, the mayakari, the people of Kolakola – their deaths will not be in vain. That is my promise.'*

The spirit offered her a sad smile before it vanished.

Shakti stood up. Her body felt less wracked, more jittery. The night air was still tinged with smoke, the quiet as stifling as a head cold.

Bow clenched between her hands, Shakti set off through the forest, listening for the sound of soldiers at her heel.

CHAPTER FOUR
Ashoka

'Prince Ashoka, I come bearing gifts.'

Glancing up from his texts on the Ridi Kingdom's language, Ashoka spotted Saudamini sauntering into his chambers with several books clutched to her chest. Her frizzy black hair was tamed into a bun, glistening with streaks of oil. Ashoka watched as Rahil closed the door behind her, looking amused.

'Sau,' he greeted her, smiling. 'Come to harass me?'

'How dare you accuse me of harassment,' Sau replied good-naturedly. She was his mother's youngest political advisor, and one of his closest friends aside from Rahil. They had suffered under the same tutelage in their adolescence – Sau's own aunt, Lakshini.

When she stopped at his desk, Sau took a curious sniff. 'You've already bathed?' she asked. 'It's only mid-afternoon, so why – *ah*. Did you manage to kill this time?'

Sau's voice wasn't filled with vitriol. Like Rahil, she never teased him for his softness. He was a weed growing among sunflowers; they had long since understood that he lacked the ferocity of his siblings.

After failing his father's supposedly simple task, he and Rahil had returned to the royal palace in silence. Both arrived looking like they had been subject to a heinous battle in the mud, baffling much of the palace staff. Their bodies had been covered in ash, fur, and a smattering of blood.

He told the staff he'd taken an unfortunate tumble. There was no point in telling them he and Rahil collected kindling, cremated a deer, and that he had cried watching it burn. Such stories would reach his father eventually, and he would be subject to another one of Adil's harangues. No matter. Once his father returned from Kolakola, his failure would be known anyway.

Though Ashoka did not care to tell his staff, he did tell Sau. 'I didn't,' he replied, 'but Rahil did.'

Rahil's response came quick. 'And Ashoka could have lied to appease the emperor, but he chose not to.' When Ashoka tilted his head to the side, he found Rahil watching him with his arms crossed. Was he upset with him? Surely not over something so minor.

'Are you mad at me?' he called out.

The answer came in a series of gestures. Rahil uncrossed his arms, placed them behind his back. His posture relaxed. 'No, Ashoka,' he responded. 'I simply thought you would accept a lie before I realized who you are.'

Not mad, then. Exasperated, perhaps, at his lack of action.

With a flourish, Sau set the books down on his desk. Ashoka examined them idly. The spines were old and battered, the paper yellowed with age. The titles were written in a curlicue script that he recognized but could not read fluently.

'This is from Anurapura,' he remarked.

'My father sent me a few more books on the mayakari,' Sau replied. Born and raised in the kingdom of Anurapura, she had relocated to the Golden City with her mother after her parents had separated. 'And look – two of these are on Great Spirits and their abilities. The artist has sketched them to perfection.'

A thrill shot up Ashoka's spine as he bent closer to view the sketches. He could never find books in such detail like this.

His father had removed all books pertaining to the mayakari and their abilities from the palace library before he was born. In fact, he'd given orders to have any texts detailing mayakari history banned within the Golden City. Such books were difficult to find now, as rare as a kept promise. Still, there were some left behind. When he was eight, Ashoka had stumbled upon a book on mayakari philosophy in his father's study. It detailed their adherence to non-violence, their commitment to preserving the natural world, and keeping a balance between humans who expanded their lands and the nature spirits that dwelt in them.

The stories in that one book negated everything his father had ever preached about the witches. How were they dangerous if their code was passivity? How were they dangerous if they lived as nomads, beholden to no kingdom? No empire?

It was forbidden knowledge. His father removed the book when he realized Ashoka had been going into his personal study to read it, and then punished him for it.

Patting the books fondly like they were a favoured child, Ashoka bumped Sau's elbow with his own. 'Thank your father for me,' he said. Though he had never met him, his willingness to send often difficult-to-find information to his daughter – and therefore, the prince – was admirable. These days, when he had any inquiries, he tended to ask Harini, one of his maidservants. Unbeknownst to anyone but himself, Rahil, Sau, and one other staff member she refused to name, she was a mayakari. It was Sau who had found her work in the palace, an action that caused Ashoka to question her sanity when he'd first heard. After all, what kind of mayakari would agree to work in the palace, of all places?

Sau had given him an answer befitting a lunatic: that it would be the last place his father would think to look. Nonetheless, Ashoka couldn't refute that idea entirely.

'I can thank him all you want, Prince Ashoka, but these books are useless here,' Sau replied.

'Not only that,' came Rahil's deep timbre, 'but I fear your father will castigate you if he ever finds these in your possession.'

Instinct made Ashoka touch his scarred earlobe. He didn't want a repeat of what happened last time. One burn was enough.

'Rest assured, I will keep these books somewhere safe,' he said. They could very easily be hidden in his cabinets or tucked away into the false bookends he'd commissioned. Sau's room would also function as a storage space if she ever allowed it.

Allowed? His father's voice came rushing in immediately. *You are a prince, foolish child. You do not wait to be allowed. You command and expect to be obeyed.*

He forced the voice away. 'Besides, what do you mean by "useless"? I can use this information for when father allows me to assume a governorship role. Rules of land preservation and nature spirit contact are advantageous.'

Arush was the only one of his siblings who had spent the last year governing the state of Chalamba east of the Golden City. He'd returned at the start of the New Year, having neither depreciated the area nor transformed it, but that was unsurprising. Nothing revolutionary would happen under Arush's rule.

Ashoka, however, thought differently. When it would come time for him to govern, he planned to cease mayakari burnings and the unnecessary culling of forestland for ironwood, even if temporarily. It would provide a respite, however brief, to the non-stop destruction his father had inflicted since he had come into power.

And besides, there was only so much that humans could take away from Great Spirits before they retaliated.

Sau scoffed at his response. 'In this empire?' she asked incredulously before her sharp eyes narrowed in challenge. 'Want to make a bet on it?'

'I'm not interested in furthering your gambling habits for petty reasons,' Ashoka remarked. Sau's wagers never went in his favour, he couldn't lose any more gold coins or books to her.

Sau tutted. 'Too safe,' she said. 'What about you, Rahil?'

'Absolutely not.'

Ashoka grinned. Even Rahil knew when to draw the line. 'I wanted to ask you – have you heard any news of my father?' Being privy to conversations with his mother and the advisors, Sau would likely know how his father had fared in Kolakola. Ashoka fervently hoped that by some stroke of luck, his father had decided to turn back.

Unfortunately, Sau did not give him the answer he hoped. 'Last I heard, he was still on route to Kolakola. He would have reached the township last night, but we are yet to receive word from messengers.'

Ashoka's heart sank. The witches would surely have been murdered by now, and the town . . .

He didn't want to think about it, but the thoughts came prickling in like needles. Emperor Adil held no mercy for mayakari or mayakari sympathizers; Ashoka could only imagine what sort of horrors they would face. Or *had* faced.

Suddenly, there came an insistent knocking at his door. Sau immediately moved in front of his desk to obscure the books from view.

When Ashoka had Rahil open the door, a tall, muscular woman stepped inside. Ishka – one of Arush's personal guards. Strands of her hair had come free of her plait, and her twin daggers jostled in their leather scabbards. Her tapered black trousers were coated in dust.

'Ishka,' he greeted her. 'What brings you here?' Arush rarely sent for him, which made this barge-in rather unexpected.

'Prince Ashoka,' she said with a bow. 'I am terribly sorry to interrupt, but your presence is needed at the serpent pens – Sahry has gone out of control.'

He stood up quickly. 'What happened?' he asked. His winged serpent rarely turned recalcitrant, and if she did, it was due to someone else's wrongdoing.

'Prince Arush visited the pens,' Ishka began, 'and he tried to—'
'Say no more,' Ashoka interrupted firmly. Sahry had been provoked, then, which was infuriating. His instructions regarding the winged serpent had always been to leave her alone. By some anomaly, he was the only person she obeyed. It was why Ashoka was the only one allowed to saddle her, ride her, and sometimes even feed her. 'Let me calm her down.'

Sau rapped her knuckles on his desk. 'I'm going to stay here,' she said. 'You will never find me approaching those terrors.'

'Be my guest,' Ashoka replied. 'Rahil, Ishka – come with me.'

He was out the door in moments.

The serpent pens were tall wooden structures, each built to twice the height of a coconut tree, and wide enough to accommodate three dozen soldiers. Winged serpents were at least five times the height of a grown adult. The floors were covered in straw, dead leaves and rotting bark, with inbuilt stone caving to help the cold-blooded creatures maintain warmth during the cooler nights. There were twelve serpents present altogether, all imported from Kalinga as the species was not found in the Ran Empire.

Three personally belonged to the Maurya children. The remainder were reserved for select soldiers and messengers to relay communications to controlled provinces quickly. Out of his siblings, Ashoka was the one who spent the most time with his serpent. Flying with Sahry gave him a freedom that went beyond what he was usually afforded. Up in the clouds, there was no one to obey. Up in the clouds, he bowed to no master.

When he arrived just outside the pens, he was greeted by pandemonium, with soldiers rushing about. Ashoka spotted his older brother immediately. He towered like a giant over the guards that surrounded him. Arush's thin gold circlet threatened to dislodge itself from his hair as he ducked, narrowly avoiding Sahry's left wing that would have sent him flying. The serpent's eyes were paper-thin slits, forked tongue slipping threateningly in and out. She'd somehow been freed from her bonds, and was trying to attack anyone within sight.

Arush saw him and pointed to Sahry. His eyes were wide open. 'Control your beast, little brother!' he yelled.

The soldiers were giving her a wide berth, some moving to protect Arush with shields while the others trained a nervous eye on her fangs. Despite being drained of venom every month, Sahry was the only one of the palace's winged serpents that continued to replenish her stores. At her most violent, she could sink her fangs into flesh and paralyse within seconds. It made approaching her difficult for anyone that wasn't Ashoka.

Why is she so agitated now?

'What did you do?' he asked Arush as he came to a halt in front of him, disconcerted by Sahry's agitation.

Arush had the gall to appear confused. Unbothered, even. 'I was merely appraising her scales,' he said. 'This is not my fault. The beast couldn't control itself.'

Frustration threatened to erupt like an earthquake, but Ashoka compressed it without a second thought. 'Sahry would not become so agitated at a mere *appraisal*,' he replied as her ferocious hisses filled the air. There was a slight *whoosh* and a rattle of chains as her membranous wings flapped about. Her fangs began to drip a honey-coloured liquid. 'What were you doing, Arush?'

At first, Arush did not reply. Only when Sahry's chains clanged again did he flinch and shake his head. 'I wanted to study her blood,' he admitted. 'It was a harmless experiment.'

Ashoka forced himself to calm. He guessed that Arush had somehow taken an interest in the serpent's continuously replenishing store of venom. At times, Arush lacked all common sense. Anyone with a working brain in the palace knew not to rouse Sahry – had he forgotten? Knowing Arush's penchant for recklessness, he wouldn't put it past him.

'Stay back,' he ordered the guards who appeared all too happy to obey. All except Rahil. Even though he of all people knew how temperamental Sahry was, he moved in front of Ashoka to guard him.

Gently, Ashoka grabbed Rahil's wrist. When he turned around, he shot him a wry smile. 'How do you expect to save me?' he asked. 'From my own serpent, no less.'

Something flickered behind Rahil's eyes like he just remembered what sort of situation this was. 'Apologies,' he said. 'I forgot for a moment that you do not need my protection.'

Lies. He always needed Rahil's protection – just not here. For once, he was in control.

'Stay back,' he repeated, watching Rahil's posture tense despite his acquiescence. He would be watching Ashoka like a hawk, that he knew, ready to step in should he need to.

A preternatural calm took over Ashoka as he approached Sahry. Careful not to stand beneath her venom splatter, he called out her name and an order.

'Sahry, peace.' She would recognize his voice. Winged serpents had poor eyesight, only sensing the world through vibrations in the air, and with their tongues.

Sure enough, at the sound of his voice, the venom dripping from her fangs slowed, but she was still agitated. Ashoka craned his neck up, examining her from head to tail. It was only when his eyes strayed to the underbelly that he found that it had been scored. Sahry was bleeding.

Why was Arush intent on causing him unnecessary trouble?

'You hurt her,' he said loudly. As Sahry retracted her fangs, he made a slow path, sidestepping puddles on the ground. They'd need to be cleaned after he got her to calm down. Her tongue flicked out, and he felt it skim his arm quickly like a bird had just flitted past him. 'Sahry, it's Ashoka.'

Sahry froze the moment he stood under the shadow of her head and placed his palm over the wound. It wasn't deep, but he could understand why she had become disturbed. Arush's apathetic curiosity had hurt something and now Ashoka had to fix it. Typical. He rubbed his serpent's underbelly in slow, circular motions, feeling her relax bit by bit. Good – no one was hurt, and she could be looked after. He continued his ministrations until he was able to guide her back into her pen.

'Bring me a salve, please,' he called out to the guards. Absently, he noted the awestruck expressions on their faces. 'Do not approach me with it. Place it exactly where you are, and I will retrieve it myself.'

When two of Arush's guards ran off to bring him the medicament, Ashoka turned his attention back to his brother. 'You're lucky Sahry didn't kill you or your guards.'

'She needs to be tamed,' was Arush's only reply.

Ashoka gritted his teeth. 'She was perfectly docile until *someone* decided to study her blood.'

His brother shrugged listlessly. 'Simple curiosity, little brother,' he said. 'The amount of antivenom Sahry could make is very profitable.'

Profitable. Ashoka couldn't believe it. 'Is this what you've learned from father?' he shot back. 'To prioritize profits?'

'Don't be foolish,' he replied. Fast. Short. It made for difficult verbal spars. Ashoka wanted to retort *'You're foolish'* but it would only make him appear childish. His siblings already saw him as a naïve young man, there was no point in furthering their beliefs. Whatever anger Ashoka held, he let it vanish. He didn't want to bother with Arush any more, not when Sahry needed his attention.

'Leave us, brother,' he said. 'Let me tend to my serpent, and *never* attempt to hurt her again.'

His tone hardened at *'never'*. The word came out with the lethality of a hunter. He saw Arush's cool mask break for a moment, saw Rahil's lips tilt upward.

'How will you govern well if you do not understand the importance of an asset, little brother?' asked Arush. 'It seems you are the one who should learn from father.'

Ashoka had half a mind to ask Arush what exactly *he'd* done during his governorship that was of consequence but held himself back.

'Leave us, brother,' Ashoka repeated. Shooting him a contemptuous glance, Arush turned and motioned for his guards to follow. Ashoka waited patiently until he was sure they'd gone before he squatted, hugging his knees to his chest. Above him, Sahry was quiet. Perhaps she sensed his frustration gathering like storm clouds, for she ducked her head until they were face-to-face, filmy green eyes watching dark brown ones.

'I'm sorry he hurt you,' Ashoka whispered.

In response, Sahry flicked her forked tongue over the crown of his head. While Arush and Aarya sometimes struggled to control their winged serpents, he had found a sense of satisfaction at being able to understand his. She was just as much his master as he was hers. It did not serve him well to assume that an intelligent creature such as this would be submissive.

'He infuriates me,' Ashoka muttered when a pair of footsteps approached him.

'Then fight back,' said Rahil. His sandalwood scent was a sensory balm.

'No, I won't.'

He wasn't surprised when his father's voice badgered him immediately after. *You won't fight back? Pathetic. How will you ever be exemplary when you cannot do something so simple?*

His brain felt ready to explode from the confines of his skull. Emperor Adil's voice was always at the back of his mind, lying in wait like a panther to criticize him for even a simple mistake. Ashoka pressed the heels of his palms to his forehead, the pressure allowing him a moment of respite.

Little things like this had the tendency to fray his sanity. Sometimes, he wished that he was not born a prince, a Maurya. Having to deal with chaos-causing siblings and a violent-tempered father for the rest of his life was a nightmare.

Rahil handed him the salve, and Ashoka began to lather it over Sahry's wound.

Being able to live a peaceful life was not something he envisioned, not when he knew his duty to be the sparest of spares. Like the mayakari, he needed to use impermanence to justify his existence. He needed to be better than these petty fights.

CHAPTER FIVE

Shakti

HER BOW AND ARROW FELT LIKE A PROMISE.

Shakti tore through forestland, trailing alongside the emperor's contingent as leopards huffed and carriages jostled on the otherwise silent road. Her limbs ached as tiredness stole into her bones, but she wouldn't stop. Every so often, she would get a whiff of smoke, of burned meat that seemed to have settled over the group like dust, and it just hardened her resolve. The scent forced unwanted images of Jaya's skin turning red from heat, then forming fluctuant boils before they popped and overcooked the flesh, turning it charcoal black.

She forced down the urge to vomit.

They had long since left Kolakola, though she could still see grey wisps in the distance, the evidence of the army's wrongdoing visible for anyone to see. They journeyed north, which meant that they were likely returning to the Golden City, their job seemingly done, the slaughter over. The road they would take was paved through the forest, which gave her the opportunity to follow them undetected as she did now.

Shakti expected the emperor to be safely tucked away inside one of the carriages but was surprised to find him riding a giant leopard with practised ease. Hatred came like lightning to her. She wished she could bottle it up and throw it at him.

Myriad curses played in her head. What would be the best one to heap upon that wretched man? Madness? Premature death? Permanent illness? Really anything that could make his suffering prolonged, but she needed to act before they entered the safety of the capital.

Her belly rumbled, pleading for nourishment. Shakti wished she could have the fried okra that Jaya had made the night before, packed into a clay pot in the kitchen. She didn't know if her home was still standing, nor did she wish to return and find out. Besides, queasiness overrode her hunger pangs. How could she swallow anything without that phantom smell of meat following her around?

Eventually – *thankfully* – the cavalry stopped to set up camp. Here was her chance. Patiently, she watched and waited as soldiers dismounted from their leopards, allowing a brief respite for her overworked legs. Emperor Adil dismounted last. He waited by his leopard as his tent was set up first, large and black with heavy gold detailing. His subordinates were quick with it, too. Once it was finished, the voice that was imprinted into her mind made her heart pound as it spoke.

'General Janak,' she heard Emperor Adil say, 'come with me.'

At his command, a tall, burly soldier stepped forward from the emperor's left, and bowed. Emperor Adil motioned for him to follow, and both disappeared into his tent. Following his departure, the soldiers began to set up their own, smaller red tents.

Not yet.

They weren't yet relaxed. Alert soldiers were a recipe for disaster. She needed to create a distraction and catch them by surprise, distract them long enough for her to curse Adil. Narrowing her eyes, Shakti glanced at the trees around her, searching for a suitable place to stay hidden. She needed a good vantage point, and that would be higher up. Staying on the ground and peering through bushes would hinder her view.

She tiptoed towards a great twisting Na tree whose thick branches interconnected with other smaller trees. With a soft grunt, Shakti hoisted herself up, finding footing on the many grooves and branches the higher she climbed. As she did, the enormous grey head of the tree's spirit appeared from inside the trunk, and Shakti fought against distraction as it chittered a welcome.

'Na spirit,' she greeted. 'Apologies, but I must find safe ground upon your tree.'

The spirit's mouth quirked upwards before it nodded and disappeared. Shakti almost laughed out loud. Safe ground. Her request had been part lie, part truth.

Shakti did not stop until she reached a branch solid enough to support her weight. She was far enough away for the soldiers not to see her but near enough to spot the emperor's tent. With some effort, she clutched a branch above her to keep balance and sat herself down slowly. Then, she observed the camp.

The scent of cooking meat and small fires lit up the dark. Men and women spoke to each other in indistinct voices, and it made her blood burn. How dare these people appear so calm when they had burned her town and its people in the name of a tyrant emperor?

Her heart pounded ferociously. Curse. That was all she needed to do. This didn't involve the piercing of flesh. These were just words, and words could only hurt so much.

This is for vengeance, she reminded herself again. This is justifiable.

Each time she reminded herself of this, the guilt lessened. She'd repeated it at least a hundred times now, and the apprehension had whittled down to the size of a gold nugget. Determined, Shakti curled her hand into a loose fist.

First, a distraction.

'Na spirit,' she whispered. 'I need your help.'

Within seconds, the giant grey head of the nature spirit appeared next to her, bobbing like a paper lantern. Its eyes were larger than the mouth, as empty as a starless night sky. Reaching out a fingerless hand, it brushed the side of her face.

Smiling, Shakti pointed to the emperor's tent. '*Surprise the man inside that tent,*' she said. '*Make it fly.*'

For a moment, she thought it wouldn't accept her request, but then the small mouth quirked up into a childlike smile. Warmth flooded her body.

Then, it vanished. Shakti waited with bated breath.

Suddenly, startled yells arose from Adil's tent as several of his personal guards and the emperor himself exited it, eyes wide open. He was without his circlet, dressed in a simple white linen shirt and trousers. His brown skin was smudged with soot, sharp and cunning eyes vigilantly searching the area around him. Without the usual regalia, he looked more human, like the common men of her township.

From inside the tent, a loud chitter emanated. The black cloth came alive with the furious white glow of the rambunctious Na spirit. Bloating like an overfed stomach, the tent stretched until the pegs that held it down sprang free and the white light continued to glow brighter. The creature was growing.

Now, Shakti told herself. She had Adil in her line of sight, alarmed and distracted.

To enact her curse, she descended into the cursed tongue. It was an ambiguous language without specificity to its words that could only be spoken by the mayakari due to its amalgamation of nature spirit and ancient Ran language. One could curse another with death, but not a specific *kind* of death. Otherwise, the curse would be void – that much Jaya had told her.

Gooseflesh erupted across her body, hairs standing up on it as if bracing for a cold front. Shakti shivered. Took a deep breath.

'*Adil Maurya, I curse you,*' she said. '*With the land and the Great Spirits as my witness, I curse you with living misfortune. May you never know peace.*'

It was as obscure as she could make it; continuous bad luck as long as the emperor remained alive. How that would take shape, only time would tell. Curses always worked, but no one could pinpoint when and how.

The moment she finished speaking, a chill descended. The world turned grey. Shakti heard screams, the cries of children, the sounds of metal grinding against flesh, and the roar of a forest fire. Then came the images: bones with muscle and cartilage still attached at the epiphysis, the gleam of a knife before it was thrust into skin, horror stories made to scare young and old, faces covered in blisters and pustules.

When the images disappeared, her aunt's voice followed:

Are you happy now, little bird?

Shakti wasn't. The victory and pride that showered her like a pleasant afternoon rain vanished.

She'd expected to feel like a monstrosity too, after cursing the emperor, but there was nothing. That small gold nugget of apprehension and fear split into another half. Now, it was the size of her thumbnail.

This isn't enough, she thought. But there was nothing more she could do.

'Thank you,' she said to the Na spirit. It would hear her, even from this distance.

As she wondered when the curse would start to take effect, Shakti was startled by the sound of a desperate yell:

'Help me!'

She resumed her gaze towards the emperor. Something was happening to him. He clutched at his shoulder as a roar of pain escaped his lips. The beginnings of chest pain, perhaps, for there appeared to be nothing wrong with his body from where she sat. Unless . . .

Shakti straightened. Her breath caught when Adil dropped to his knees and tore open his shirt. A dark stain blossomed like morning glories across his chest, spreading like vines around the left side of his body. Something that unnatural couldn't have come from the human body.

A chorus of screams and shouts followed Emperor Adil's fall. Men and women rushed to him from all sides like a tidal wave.

Is this . . . my curse, she wondered, stunned. The emperor was curled on the ground, very much alive and very much in pain. Physicians ran towards him, ordering nearby soldiers to keep him still as they examined the black mark. Meanwhile, Emperor Adil's deep, guttural scream came in intervals as his body shook.

'Stop this!' she heard him roar. 'I – my heart – it is hard to *breathe*.'

Jaya would have breathed in smoke as she died. Jaya would have found it difficult to breathe as her body was set alight. Whatever Adil was complaining of, it would not compare to what her aunt and the other mayakari would have felt. *All* the other mayakari. How many had he killed? How many families had he destroyed? After all, Shakti had not cursed him with death.

Living misfortune.

A slow, satisfied smile split Shakti's lips. He was alive and hurting – this *had* to be her curse working.

'Move His Highness into our tent,' one of the physicians shouted, directing her arm towards the closest one. They didn't dare move into the emperor's tent, even after the Na spirit vanished.

As the soldiers and physicians scrambled to move the emperor, Shakti laid her palm across her forehead. Dizziness washed over her, sudden and unwanted. The beginning of a raging headache started to make her lose focus. She needed to descend before she fell, but would the soldiers be in the woods?

She had to risk it. Her ears rang incessantly as she climbed down. Twice, she almost lost her footing, and twice she righted herself. When Shakti's feet touched the forest floor, she only had a moment of relief before her legs gave way and she collapsed.

What's happening to me, she thought blearily as the urge to sleep overcame her. If the soldiers decided to search the forestland, she would be found, interrogated, and likely killed.

She needed to hide. Her body, however, was intent on not obeying her. Sudden chest pain caused her to wince. It was too hot. She nudged away the slit of her neckline only to see a small black stain growing across her left breast, like the one visible on the emperor. Whatever was happening to her was hindering every innate function in her body. She needed help.

The spirit of the Na tree. It was still watching her. Fingers digging into the dirt, Shakti managed to raise her head and lock eyes with it. Precious creature: it wouldn't ignore a mayakari in distress.

'Na spirit,' she croaked before her eyes fluttered closed. '*Help me, I beg you.*'

CHAPTER SIX

Ashoka

Sweat soaked Ashoka's back as he aimed a blow at Rahil's chest. He took the hit and tumbled – or so he thought. As he fell, Rahil retaliated with a swipe to the leg in Ashoka's illusion of momentary victory. He had feigned his fall – *of course*. With a grunt, his knees hit the grass of the courtyard where the two were training.

'Don't let your guard down,' Rahil said, already back on his feet.

'I'm not,' Ashoka panted as he scurried back up. He arranged himself into a defensive position with his hands shielding his face before aiming a well-timed punch at Rahil's abdomen. Faces were off-limits – it was one of the few rules that Ashoka had requested early on in his training. Part of him accepted it as vanity while the other part refused to have his skull cracked in pieces if Rahil landed a blow to it.

Deftly, Rahil jumped out of his way and paused for a second before he charged Ashoka at full speed. His friend's feet moved quickly, arms reaching out to seize his waist before Ashoka regained his bearing. There was no time to think, no time to pivot. His back hit the grass with an unceremonious *thud* as Rahil tackled him with the force of a charging leopard.

'Let go!' he grimaced, twisting around this way and that to free himself. Unfortunately, Rahil was stronger. He caged Ashoka in and held him down with his weight alone.

'I hope that won't be your response in real combat,' Rahil grunted, trying to keep Ashoka's flailing arms pinned down. Realizing he was unlikely to rid himself of Rahil's crushing weight, Ashoka slapped the ground twice, disgruntled.

'I yield,' he said, watching a bead of sweat trace a path down Rahil's face. 'Let me up.'

Grinning, Rahil stood and extended a hand for Ashoka to take.

'I'll beat you one day,' Ashoka grumbled as he dusted himself off. Rahil was more muscular, more agile, more of everything that was required of a fighter. 'Mark my words.'

Rahil cocked his head to the side, smiling. 'Ashoka, if I can't beat you, then I shouldn't have been given this position at all. Besides, I'd like to keep my winning streak.'

The scent of dry grass, sweat, and frangipanis permeated the air around them as Ashoka stretched out his sore muscles. Idly, he inspected the appearance of a fresh bruise blossoming a pale red underneath the skin of his arm. It used to be that he'd got hundreds of them after his rigorous training sessions with Rahil such that his body looked like a poppy field. Now, one bruise was nothing.

A warm, calloused hand grasped his arm. Unable to stop the flush that was creeping up his neck, Ashoka glanced up to see Rahil observing his bruise in concern.

'It'll heal,' Rahil assured, shooting him a soft smile. Ashoka hoped with all his might that Rahil couldn't feel his pulse quicken, his heartbeat thud. The traitorous muscle had started to act this way several years ago and hadn't stopped since. Whenever Rahil got too close, his senses sharpened. He felt everything around him more acutely.

'I wish I had Sahry's healing,' said Ashoka. Her laceration had healed within a day. A human like him, meanwhile, took a lot longer to recover from simple contusions.

'Well *done*, little brother.'

Snapping his head up, Ashoka spotted Aarya approaching them with her guards right behind, a smug smile plastered across her face. She wore a bright red sari that was adorned with intricate gold stitching on the borders. Impossibly long earrings dangled as she walked, and a solid gold throatlet decorated her otherwise bare neck. For as long as he had known his sister, Aarya was not one for subtlety.

Ashoka frowned as she stopped in front of him. 'Well done?' he asked. 'That doesn't sound like you.'

Aarya shook her head. 'No, I meant that to be a "well done" for finding more painfully average ways to lose to Rahil in combat,' she said. Her smile was as sweet as sugared caramel, but her words were as acrid as bitter gourd.

Ashoka sighed. 'If you're here to make fun of me, you've come in vain.'

Aarya jutted out her lower lip. 'I simply came to observe how my little brother is faring in unarmed combat,' she said. 'Didn't father say that your skills were still poor?'

Ashoka clenched his jaw hard enough for his teeth to hurt. 'I've improved beyond *you*.' There was hardly a point mentioning Arush who could probably crush them both with his little finger.

Letting out a tinkling laugh that was as disbelieving as it was infuriating, Aarya stepped closer. Her eyes flicked towards Rahil who stood just behind him.

'Jealousy does not become you, *mūsī*,' she said.

He was always thrown off by Aarya's term of endearment for him. *Mouse*. Rahil thought it to be somewhat affectionate, considering Aarya's intemperate nature. Ashoka thought it signified his position as the weakest in the family and hated it with a passion.

In fact, Ashoka was so irritated by it that he almost missed the gleam of silver that appeared out of nowhere from Aarya's left hand. *Dagger*, he thought belatedly before years of combat training kicked in. He beat Rahil to action and swiftly jumped sideways. With a vicelike grip, he latched onto his sister's left hand. Aarya let out a yelp of surprise. Using her discombobulation to his advantage, Ashoka used his other hand to pin her free arm behind her back.

He saw Aarya's expression shutter. 'I thought you'd be slower,' she murmured.

'Drop the dagger, Aarya,' Ashoka ordered forcefully. He shook his head when Rahil and his guards made to step closer.

A pitying smile danced across Aarya's lips. 'Make me,' she said.

A hot flash of anger sped its way down Ashoka's body as he tightened his grip over Aarya's arm. He did not wish to fight.

'*Please*,' he said shortly. 'Drop your dagger.'

Thankfully, his sister dropped it from where she stood, albeit with great reluctance, and watched it clatter on the ground. Lapis-encrusted, the weapon bore a singular name on its hilt: *Adil*.

He let go of her arms, guilt worming in when he noticed the small crescent-shaped indents he'd left behind on her skin. 'You could have sliced my arm off!'

Despite his reprimand, Ashoka couldn't help but feel a strange sense of satisfaction at having bested Aarya. How foolish it was to consider him weak.

Aarya shrugged and she bent down to pick the dagger up. 'I wouldn't have hurt you. Nicked your skin, potentially, but not enough to gouge.'

'I could have *hurt* you,' Ashoka said, crossing his arms over his chest.

'No,' Aarya cocked her head to the side, 'you wouldn't have.'

Ashoka's left eye twitched.

'You don't know me, Aarya,' he said.

Expression brightening as if he had issued her a challenge, Aarya gave him a sickly-sweet smile.

'Don't I?' she smirked. 'How did that hunting expedition you took a few days ago fare, little brother?'

Ashoka looked away. 'It was fine,' he said.

The look Aarya sent him was full of scorn. 'Oh, so did you kill the deer like you said you would?' she asked.

His silence was answer enough.

'I knew it.' The condescending, *I-know-all* tone made him feel as if he were nine again.

'What is the point of harming an innocent?' he repeated for what seemed to be the umpteenth time that week.

The bark of laughter that escaped his sister's lips was disbelieving. '*Innocent.* Grow up, Ashoka. You say that so self-righteously, but hurting is unavoidable. Why are you so reluctant to accept that?'

Because hurting was his father's domain. Because Ashoka would not be like him.

Meanwhile, Aarya had switched her attention to Rahil. 'Ashoka's weakness comes from his docility,' she said. 'Don't you think?'

Rahil did not rise to meet Aarya's provocations. Much like Ashoka, he had learned not to react with the same energy.

'On the contrary, Princess Aarya,' Rahil said smoothly. 'What you call docility, I call pacifism, and I consider that a strength.'

Ashoka stopped himself from snorting out loud. It was only yesterday that Rahil was berating him for being *too* pacifist, but he had to admire his loyalty. Rahil had always stood by him when he needed him.

'Hmm,' Aarya appraised Rahil with a gleam in her eye, 'if only I could find someone as loyal as you.'

Sullenly, Ashoka stepped in front of Rahil, blocking him from Aarya's view. 'Don't you have someone else to go terrorize?' he asked her.

Aarya shook her head. 'Only you,' she said before her attention shifted to something behind them. 'Although, I could always terrorize Saudamini.'

'Don't you dare,' Ashoka said immediately. Unlike him, Sau could only hold in her temper so much.

'I would very much dare,' Aarya replied. 'But she already appears flustered. I wonder what sort of trouble you are in.'

Ashoka turned to find Sau rushing towards them, the blue skirt of her sari swirling like ocean currents around her. Her dark hair was almost free of its bun. Aarya was right – Sau *did* appear worried, which made *him* worried because she rarely was.

'Sau,' he called out, watching her hurry towards them, frowning. Her face was lit with consternation. 'Are you all right?'

When Sau reached them, she was huffing. She had never been one for physical exertion, always preferring to stay indoors whenever possible. Her deep brown skin gleamed under the sun, and her brown eyes were fierce as she spoke.

'I'm all right, Prince Ashoka,' Sau said in her unusually low voice. She glanced at him and Aarya nervously. 'Your father has fallen ill during his return from Kolakola.'

Ashoka made to gripe about how it had been less a visit and more of a premeditated slaughter, but the news of his father stopped him cold. Beside him, Aarya stilled.

'Fallen ill?' he echoed, sensing Rahil's own body tense behind him. 'How?'

Sau winced. 'He collapsed,' she informed them. 'A nature spirit disrupted his camp at night three days ago. He is being returned to the capital by riverboat.'

Ashoka could barely listen. His father, ill?

It seemed unbelievable. Adil had always seemed so . . . unbreakable to him. Impenetrable. So caged in by his own pride and hate that none could touch him.

'Father . . .' His sister's voice was deathly quiet as she stared dully at the ground. Warily, Ashoka glanced at his sister. By no means was Aarya the kind of person to immediately explode, but when it came to their father, she was a match ready to ignite. Aarya looked up to meet his stare, and Ashoka was shocked to spot her tears.

'I must go,' she said in a gravelly voice.

Pushing past him, Aarya very nearly sprinted away, her hair flying in the breeze. His sister was in shock, but she still possessed the vanity to hide her crying from the rest of the world.

'Well,' Saudamini remarked as they watched her go, 'that's the first time I've ever seen Princess Aarya cry.'

'If Emperor Adil has fallen victim to some type of countryside sickness, he should be healed by the physicians soon enough,' Rahil told Sau. Ashoka noticed that he sounded unsure, too.

Sau let out a haggard breath. 'He can't be healed,' she said. Her voice dropped down to a whisper. 'This is no mere illness. Reports say that the cause is from magic; a black stain is spreading across his chest, uncontrolled. The physicians are unable to slow it to a halt.'

His father had the best physicians in the empire. If they could not rectify the problem, there was little hope that anyone else could.

'Magic?' Rahil asked the question for him. 'Are you sure?'

Sau nodded. 'I've spoken to the palace physicians. They have not heard of any natural disease like this,' she replied. 'And if not natural, what else would it be?'

There was nothing else it *could* be. 'Mayakari magic,' Ashoka said quietly. But that was unlikely. Their teachings denounced causing others harm.

Sau nodded grimly. 'Ashoka,' she leaned in even closer so that only the three of them could hear, 'I don't think he will survive.'

It was a dangerous thing to say, and even more dangerous to predict. Sau stepped back. 'Your mother is awaiting further news in the throne room,' she said. 'You should go.'

Ashoka knew that his mother would be fretting with anxiety. He could just imagine her pacing the throne room, gold bangles clinking with every worried step.

'Wash yourself quickly and go,' Rahil urged him. 'I'll meet you in the throne room.'

His mother sat upon the Obsidian Throne when he entered, hastily bathed and no longer smelling of sweat, grass, and Rahil. Having changed out of his fighting gear, Ashoka was now clothed in the colours of the royal family – black and red – the shift stifling, the black sash too tight.

The throne overwhelmed his mother's birdlike figure: a large black lacquered chair whose topmost aspect was carved with the face of a leopard – the symbol of the Ran Empire, of its army that rode the beasts into battle, weapons gleaming. Beside the throne were two enormous leopards in seated positions, all carved from black marble and polished to a lustrous shine. Their eyes were beset with brilliant red rubies the size of Ashoka's palm.

Empress Manali was dressed in a pale red sari that seemed to be spun from gossamer and light. It enhanced her dark brown skin and wide-set eyes, enhancing the gold jewellery that adorned her wrists and neck. Standing in front of her was Aarya, her face a picture of anger as she gesticulated to their mother. Likely she now knew the cause of their father's illness.

His mother's sharp eyes immediately noticed him shuffling into the throne room. 'Ashoka,' she said. Her voice sounded scratchy. 'My dear, you've heard the news of your father?'

'Yes, mother.' Ashoka made his way past the royal advisors and servants who bowed respectfully after him, and for whom he bowed in return. As he came closer, he was able to spot her watery eyes and tremoring hands as she clasped the armrests.

Ashoka knelt at his mother's feet and felt her soft hands cup his chin. Her eyes resembled those of the obsidian leopards.

'He'll live,' Ashoka said to his mother, despite knowing that it was nothing but a false promise.

'He'll live,' Manali echoed, but her smile wasn't believable enough. She patted his cheek fondly and stroked his hair in a reassuring manner.

'Indeed. Our father will live, and the mayakari will burn for what they've done,' Aarya vowed. Her cheeks glistened with streaks of salt and water.

Ashoka couldn't help himself from cringing at Aarya's words of reckoning. Their mother frowned.

'Aarya,' she reprimanded. 'All we have is hearsay until the physicians arrive with the definite story. Never assume anything without certainty. Have I not taught you this basic principle?'

In response, Aarya rolled her eyes. 'Of course, mother,' she scoffed. 'How natural it is for a poison to spread like black cobwebs. It can't possibly be a mayakari's doing. My, what was I *thinking*?'

Being the only daughter had not prevented Aarya from choosing her favoured parent and it was not their mother. Empress Manali was a mediator, a peacekeeper. Aarya respected hard authority, and that was not their mother.

Ashoka would, of course, have answered differently.

Empress Manali narrowed her eyes a fraction. 'Already jumping to conclusions,' she said. 'You are too much like Adil.'

Aarya seemed unruffled by their mother's statement. 'Thank you, mother,' she smiled.

'That wasn't a compliment, Aarya.' Arush's loud voice boomed from behind them. His older brother entered, flanked by his guards. Though his voice was snide, his eyes were downcast.

Aarya crossed her arms defiantly. 'I don't see how. It *is* a compliment to be compared to father,' she said, her eyes flashing with sudden ferocity. 'He will recover and inflict punishment on the wretched mayakari who did this to him.'

Ashoka flinched. Aarya talked about murder the way Saudamini talked about the weather.

It was then that Ashoka caught sight of Rahil entering the throne room and silently taking up position just beyond the family cluster. His dual broadswords were strapped to his back, encased in an ironwood sheath. They had been Rahil's father's.

Having Rahil nearby placated Ashoka's nerves. Emboldened him.

'If this *was* the work of a mayakari, should you be surprised?' he asked. 'Even the supposedly peaceful can break after being subjected to years of oppression. Sounds like karmic retribution to me.'

The way Aarya reacted; it was as if he'd slapped her senseless. 'I beg your pardon?'

'I think you heard me well enough the first time,' he retorted.

Aarya glared at him. She was easier than Arush to argue with, but more difficult to temper. As a child, most of the fights he remembered had started with her.

Just as his sister opened her mouth to fire what would have been an acidic retort, the sound of commotion could be heard outside the door of the throne room. Ashoka saw his mother straighten and tense, her hands gripping the seat rest as if bracing herself for an emotional onslaught.

Suddenly, the doors opened with a loud groan and a woman dressed in a loose black shift and trousers entered. She was a senior court physician, and one of his father's most trusted: Lata. Dark shadows painted her under eyes, and her curls were in disarray.

'Empress Manali!' Lata rushed in, dropping onto one knee immediately at the sight of them, head bowed. 'Your Highness. Emperor Adil, I-I—'

Even before the physician uttered her next words, Ashoka guessed the remainder by instinct alone.

A terrible, gnawing feeling reached around his neck and pulled tight. He knew the next few words as if they were prophecy. Knew it as surely as he knew the constellations in the night sky.

'Emperor Adil,' the physician repeated, her forehead lightly dusted in a sheen of sweat. 'I— my condolences, Your Highness. Your husband died on the steps of the palace entrance. We suspect that it is due to mayakari magic and . . . we could not revive him.'

Your husband died.

Could not revive him.

His father, dead.

Dead.

His father. The emperor.

Dead.

Aarya was as still as a statue, and her normally cold eyes appeared glazed. Arush's stance was rigid, his lips parted in disbelief. Ashoka found himself unable to move, as if his mind and body had completely separated from shock. His hands were tremoring. His breaths were shallow.

On the throne, his mother remained still, as unmoving as the mayakari that burned in the night.

CHAPTER SEVEN
Shakti

SHAKTI KNEW THAT SHE WAS DREAMING, BUT SHE FOUND that she could not wake herself.

The last thing she remembered was dropping onto the hard forest floor. When she opened her eyes, she found herself in a throne room that seemed to have been painted by darkness. Precious jewels hung from a light fixture above her, and rubies glowed brightly in the eyes of the carved leopards that sat beside a dark lacquered throne. She knew of only one seat of power hewn from stone as black as poison.

The Obsidian Throne.

Glimmering lights cast soft shadows and lamps dotted every foot from each other along the walls worked to brighten the grim room. Impossibly tall and square glass windows allowed for the moonlight to dance along the ground.

How long have I been unconscious, she wondered. It was hard to tell. Impossible.

Shakti pinched herself only to find that she could feel no pain. It was as if all sensation had left her body. Her peripheries appeared slightly unfocused, blurred. It was the same feeling she had whenever she lucid dreamed, but at least then she could force herself awake. Here, no matter how many times she tried, her body felt stuck.

As she stared down at her arm, the sound of a sandal scraping against the floor caused her to glance up.

Where the Obsidian Throne had been unoccupied moments ago, a very much incensed Emperor Adil now sat upon it, gazing at her with a furious ire. She was startled by the appearance of that same black liquid she saw had spread across his chest, marring the white shirt in tendrils and cobwebs.

Seeing him brought a sudden and unpleasant taste in her mouth, metallic and salty. Moments later, her chest heaved of its own accord, and Shakti bit her lips hard enough to bleed. When she glanced down at her chest, Adil's marks were mirrored over her own skin, bleeding through her shift.

'You *witch*.'

The emperor's voice was hoarse as if he was suffering from a fever and had ingested sufficient poison to kill an animal. His anger terrified Shakti enough that she took several steps back.

'This is a dream,' she said aloud to herself. 'This isn't real. This is only a dream. I'll wake soon enough.'

Emperor Adil let out a bark of wicked laughter. 'You foolish *mayakari*,' he sneered. 'This is no dream. This is a part of my consciousness.'

His consciousness? Shakti thought to herself, stupefied. She shook her head, trying to wake herself up despite her own mind screaming at her that this was no ordinary dream.

'I am indeed a mayakari,' she said as her eyes met the emperor's cold brown ones. 'What of it?'

'What of it, *Emperor Adil*,' he stressed his title. 'I will be addressed as such, you wretched girl.'

'You're a figment of my imagination,' she shot back. 'I can address you any way I like, so how about I call you a fucking bastard instead?'

The stain on Emperor Adil's chest grew. The lights in the throne room flickered and, for a moment, the ruby eyes of the leopards seemed alive.

He let out an incredulous laugh. 'Watch your tongue, witch.'

'Burn me, then,' she snapped. 'I'd like to see you try.'

The emperor's scowl turned darker, but he did not respond to her taunt. 'What did you do to me, little girl?' he asked instead. 'I remember waking in fits of delirium, seeing a black cancer spreading through my veins.'

He spoke like he was real, but he couldn't be. This was some sort of sick nightmare that she had created for herself. Still, the dream emperor's haughtiness made Shakti angrier. How dare he sit on the throne and ask questions of her so dismissively. Glowering, she straightened her back and squared her shoulders.

'I cursed you,' she said.

Emperor Adil's lips pursed like he had bitten into a lemon. A grey cloud settled over him. 'No. That goes against your code,' he replied. Each word was slow and clearly enunciated, like he was still digesting her words as he spoke. 'Mayakari do not—'

'Curse?' she finished for him, slightly taken aback. What did he know of their code? 'How sorely uninformed you are. When you killed my aunt, the last thing on my mind was the code, *Adil*.'

The emperor appeared stunned. 'You . . . cursed me?'

She summoned every ounce of bravado she had. 'With living misfortune,' she said. 'I could have killed you instead, is that what you'd prefer?'

'Misfortune?' Emperor Adil repeated with a scoff. 'All that power and your kind are still soft. How useless you are. Go, leave me be.' The golden circlet glinted in the light as the emperor dipped his chin and closed his eyes.

Deep in the pit of her stomach, Shakti felt an uncomfortable pull. It was as if someone had poked a finger into her belly button, insistently and without care. It felt like she was about to bleed. Letting out a soft grunt, she clamped her hands around her sides, willing the sudden burst of pain to vanish, and oddly enough, it did.

The emperor opened his eyes. For the first time since she had laid eyes on him, he appeared nervous.

'You won't leave,' he said. It wasn't a question.

'It's my dream,' she replied. 'Why would I go?'

'This is *not* a dre—' he began in annoyance but stopped. Shakti watched curiously as he stared at his hands, the throne room, and then her. The black stain expanded once more.

'*The steps,*' she heard him say. '*The palace steps.*'

Suddenly, Emperor Adil's body seized. His eyes glazed over and rolled to the back of his head until she could only see the whites of his eyes. With his mouth hanging open, the man looked utterly demonic.

His voice was guttural as he spoke. '*I will die,*' he said. '*Please, Ashoka, I will die.*'

Die. Surely, this was her subconscious enacting some sort of twisted delusion. And why call out for his child? The name sounded like a plea, a last-ditch attempt at a bargain. What would the young prince have to do with any of this?

Something prodded the back of her head, but Shakti ignored it.

'Pleases won't help you,' she said loudly. Her voice echoed around the throne room. 'They didn't help my aunt.'

The emperor's seizures stopped. His eyes reverted to normal. 'I will die leaving this world unfinished,' he said.

'You will leave this world with a mark tainted with fear and persecution,' Shakti remarked through clenched teeth. Her mind cast back to Kolakola, the flames of orange and blue. 'Perhaps your children can rule with a gentler hand.'

Adil laughed like he found her pathetic. 'Place your deluded hopes elsewhere, witch. My children are my mirror images, though I cannot say the same for Ashoka. Spirits forbid that child sees the mayakari as anything less than people. Stupid boy.'

He sounded displeased. Hateful, even. That Adil had a child he thought to be unlike him gave her a modicum of joy. 'On the contrary,' she remarked. 'He sounds like the sane one in your useless family.'

The room blackened. 'I am your emperor,' Adil hissed. 'Do you have such little respect, commoner?'

'You lost my respect when you slaughtered your own people,' Shakti fired back.

'The mayakari are not *my* people,' Adil hissed. 'In this war, there will be casualties, and your village was one of them. It was for the good of the empire.'

'My aunt didn't die for the *good of the empire*,' Shakti growled. 'She was a peaceful woman.'

'Your powers are a plague.'

Though he saw *her* as a plague, the royal family seemed to Shakti like nothing more than parasites. They sucked the life out of innocents and ravaged everything in their path.

And parasites, in nature, required terminating.

'Even in my dreams you remain a monster,' she said. 'What will you do next, *Adil*? Will you burn me where I stand?'

Glaring hard enough to burn her out of existence, Emperor Adil let out an embittered growl. 'I very well should, witch,' he said, 'for the moment you wake is the moment I die.'

A bitter chuckle escaped her lips. 'Liar,' she said. A world where Emperor Adil did not remain alive was a fantasy.

Her remark seemed to infuriate him.

'When reality turns into fantasy, it appears that my subjects like to take liberties,' he said. 'Stupid girl, *this is no dream*. I will die. Our consciousnesses will meld. Why is it so hard for you to grasp?'

'Because that is impossible!' she exclaimed. *What was this nightmare?*

Melding consciousnesses. *Hah*. What was this dream Adil blathering on about? Such power did not exist. Mayakari could not wander into dreams, neither could they attach themselves to another's consciousness. Their powers were limited to three.

Logic told her this was a torturous illusion. Emotion told her not to judge so quickly.

He spoke about dying so surely, but it had to be a fabrication. A trick. Likely the guilt of cursing a living being was feeding this dream. In fact, she half-expected Jaya to materialize, an admonishment ready at her lips. Still, Shakti couldn't quite push away that bothersome *what if*. What if this was no dream? What if this was really Emperor Adil?

No, she shut that thought down immediately. That would mean he was dead, and she *couldn't* have done that. She couldn't have killed him. Her curse hadn't specified death, only living misfortune.

Shakti wanted to wake up.

Calm down. Think.

'How do I wake?' she asked the emperor. Asking an apparition seemed fruitless, but he was the only other person present. 'Tell me.'

'I would rather you didn't,' the emperor replied. 'You've ruined everything.'

Infuriating man.

'Shakti!'

Startled out of her anger, she turned towards Emperor Adil. And yet, it was not his voice that she had heard.

'*Shakti!*'

This time, Shakti saw Adil's mouth remain closed as the sound of her name reverberated in the great throne room. This voice belonged to a woman, and it was oddly familiar.

'Shakti,' Emperor Adil repeated aloud to himself. 'So that is your name. *Strength*. How apt.'

Shakti was unable to concentrate. Her vision had suddenly become unfocused and doubled. She felt a strange pull in her stomach and at her back, like she was a puppet being dragged away on its strings by its master.

'What's happening?' she asked aloud, clutching at her head and closing her eyes to avoid looking anywhere. Her altered vision was starting to cause vertigo.

'You are finally being called back,' Adil said, sounding rather curious. 'This is not the material world but, rather, a collective consciousness to which you do not belong. You are being wakened. Leave, for I do not wish to gaze upon your face any longer.'

Bastard.

Shakti gritted her teeth. She opened her eyes to give Emperor Adil one last dirty look and saw that he appeared to be fading away. His brown skin grew paler and paler as he, the room, and the Obsidian Throne began to wash itself white. Shakti glanced down at her hands, only to find that they were translucent, like those of a ghost meandering about in the realm of humans, invisible.

She was fading away too.

'Shakti,' she heard the voice again.

'I'm coming,' Shakti whispered.

Just as she felt herself fading away, Shakti closed her eyes to see someone else appear at the forefront of her mind. Another man.

This was a man with untied raven hair falling on his shoulders, his deep brown skin glowing in the light. His crown – a golden circlet woven with rubies – was the only giveaway to his identity.

Another royal. One whom she did not know.

He smiled pleasantly and extended his hand. Instinct drove her to clasp it and the sudden surge of raw power that she felt travel up her arm at the contact made her gasp.

She felt invincible. She felt like she had known a thousand lives – a thousand lives that were not hers.

Just when Shakti was about to call out for the man's name, he let go, and she awoke.

CHAPTER EIGHT
Ashoka

ASHOKA LAY ON THE FLOOR OF HIS BALCONY, ALONE.

The world around him was silent but he could not unhear the sound of the giant copper bell that was built in one of the palace's courtyards ring thrice, stop, and ring thrice again.

It was only ever rung that way to signal death.

In some way, it was hard to believe. His father, the all-powerful figure who loomed over the Ran Empire, who loomed over him. The man he had seen many a time in the throne room and in the war council, dead. Adil felt so omnipresent that his absence seemed like a cosmic joke. In fact, he half-expected his father to startle awake, bloodied but alive.

You dare think these mayakari capable of killing me?

Rubbing at his dry, itchy eyes, Ashoka allowed himself to observe the sky above him in silence: a pale blue dream marred by tendrils of white clouds. This was the first time he had found himself alone in quite some time. It was Rahil who was always with him, always there as a steadying, calming presence. But he was not here. At Ashoka's request, he was standing guard outside his chambers. He knew that Rahil would be worried about him, but for now, he did not want to be consoled, only to be left alone with his thoughts.

After the news of his father's death had been delivered, Ashoka left the room once his mother had been escorted to her chambers. She had tried to stand after the news but had tipped and wobbled on her feet. He and Arush had scrambled to Empress Manali's side, grabbing her shoulders to placate her shudders while Aarya remained as immobile as a statue, still in shock.

Ashoka shut his eyes. He'd heard his brother's quiet sniffles as they led their mother down the steps, his mother's harsh breaths. Admittedly, even he had felt something akin to grief at the news. Perhaps that was the consequence of being blood-related. Even from within the depths of dislike, one could manage to mine a small diamond of . . . despair? No, that couldn't be it. Feeling despair meant that love was involved somehow, and it couldn't be love. How could he feel that way for a man who had judged him for years?

A begrudging acceptance, then. Maybe that was what it was. Maybe that was why he felt this way.

The smell of incense and jasmine coming from inside his quarters corralled together like a lullaby to offer some semblance of comfort. While he was here lying in silence, the rest of the palace was in chaos. Now that his father was dead, his mother had to take his place as the acting regent, if only for a short period of time. It was she who would have to coordinate the funeral arrangements, the ordering of staff, the rallying of her children.

'Prince Ashoka.'

Ashoka scrambled to his feet at the sound of an airy voice behind him. He turned to see a young woman around his age, her dark hair gathered into a bun. Doe-like eyes stared at him, fear and relief bright like planets in the night sky. Harini – one of his maidservants.

'Yes?' he asked. How odd must he have looked, as if he were napping when his father had just died.

Whatever she had come in here to tell him, Harini did not say immediately. 'Apologies. Did I wake you?' she asked instead.

'I was not asleep,' he replied, 'only thinking.'

'Easy to think with the view you have,' she remarked with a half-smile. His large balcony looked out towards the forestland where he frequently flew Sahry to. It was here he often spent summer nights talking with Rahil or watching the rain pelt down over the greenery in the monsoon season. 'You don't seem too upset, Prince Ashoka.'

'Neither do you,' he replied.

'I have no reason to be.' She did not say anything further. Neither did she have to. Ashoka understood well enough; no mayakari would willingly mourn his father's death.

There were stray vines growing over the balcony rails. His father would have had them removed if he knew, but Ashoka had not told him. Something in this place needed greenery. At least the lack of it didn't seem to affect him as much as Harini. She could never stay in the palace for long periods of time, and often travelled to the city's outskirts where the forests were the densest. 'Are you here to comfort or to gloat?'

Harini shook her head. 'Neither, Prince Ashoka. I am here as a messenger,' she said. 'You have been summoned.'

He frowned. 'By whom?'

Harini smiled. 'Your mother,' she replied. 'She would like to meet you in her chambers.'

When Ashoka met his mother in her chambers, he found Sau there with her.

His mother sat on an ornate black chair placed atop a richly woven rug that was painted the colour of saffron, idly tapping her nails along the armrest. Meanwhile, Sau stood away from his mother, hands clasped behind her back. He did not know how long they had been here. At the sound of his footsteps, both glanced his way.

Ashoka had never seen his mother look quite so mundane. Her kohl and rouge were scrubbed clean to reveal a clear brown face with fine wrinkles around her eyes. He remembered this face from his childhood, back when she wore her painted armour less. Her clothes were dusty at the hems and her hair hung loose at her waist. Her glamour was stripped away.

'My dear,' she greeted him. She appeared tired. Worn.

'Mother,' Ashoka bowed respectfully before approaching her. 'Sau.'

Sau nodded while his mother appraised him. 'How are you?' she asked. 'Have you had something to eat?'

He shook his head. One of his staff had suggested the same, but in their haste had brought him a meal with duck. Likely that they too were rattled enough by his father's death to forget that he forwent meat. 'You wished to speak with me?'

'Indeed,' his mother replied. Her features morphed into an expression of seriousness and resignation. 'I am here to speak to you both.'

Ashoka glanced at Sau from the corner of his eye and found that she too was staring at him. Both shared a look of confusion before turning their heads in unison to the empress.

'In the three days following the funeral, Consul Rangana will read out his last written will,' his mother said. Her eyes looked defeated. She turned to Sau quickly to elaborate. 'He amended it a few years after Ashoka was born.'

Every incumbent ruler was required by law to create a will and testament in case of an unforeseen death. The will itself was usually amended around twice in the ruling monarch's lifetime, so it was not unusual for his father to have revised it following his birth.

'What of father's will?' he asked.

'I have not been privy to its contents,' his mother replied. 'Adil refused to share it with me.'

Ashoka was somewhat surprised by this. His father had the propensity to be enigmatic and untrusting when it came to highly sensitive affairs, but it always seemed as if they were discussed with his mother. Admittedly, he did not understand his mother's train of thought. Neither it seemed, did Sau.

'I don't quite understand what you are insinuating, Your Highness,' Sau remarked, her tone polite but tinged with confusion.

His mother inhaled deeply. 'I am worried,' she confessed, 'about its contents.'

Ashoka paused. Was his mother speaking in code? She did seem rather distracted.

The empress reclined in the chair and the faintest sigh escaped her mouth as she glanced at her hands, seemingly faraway. 'With Arush poised to take the throne, there will no longer be a need for me to serve as acting regent now that Aarya and you are also of age to assume temporary rule,' she said. 'As such, I will be stepping back from my duties in the council, and I will have no need for the number of political advisors that I have.'

At her confession, Ashoka noticed Sau still. Her fists clenched together reflexively before she uncurled them once more. A pitying smile flashed across his mother's lips.

'You will not work for me any more, Saudamini,' she said. 'But fear not. You will remain an advisor, but it will not be under my command. I am reinstating you as Ashoka's main political advisor before the week's end. He will certainly need you when he eventually leaves to govern, and when he begins attending council meetings. Like minds flourish when working together.'

Well. This was some positive news, at least, given that Ashoka would indeed receive a position within the emperor's council. Surely his father would have made sure of that. Sau's stance relaxed, which made him feel better. He was not his mother when it came to the skills of a regent, but he was not a complete idiot either. They could work in tandem better, considering he'd had no political advisors until this point.

'I am leaving the empire in the hands of my children,' Manali continued. 'They will each have to learn for themselves how to work seamlessly in their positions. Ashoka will need a capable, guiding hand, and I believe that to be you.'

Sau gawped. 'You do?'

Smothering a grin, Ashoka remarked, 'I think you are the only one who does, mother.'

When Sau pulled a face at him, his mother smiled. 'Other than Rahil and me, you are one of the few people who know Ashoka well,' Manali replied. 'While you have shared ideologies, you very well know that Ashoka can be a little too idealistic. You can help guide him, steer him away from any harm – and trouble.'

'Ashoka does seem likely to find himself in deep trouble entirely by accident,' Sau replied in a perfect retaliation.

When Ashoka scoffed, his mother laughed. 'Would you care to make a bet on that?' she asked. Even she knew of Sau's propensity to gamble.

'I'd rather you don't—' Ashoka began, but Sau interrupted.

'On the contrary,' she said. 'I will not. Ashoka is almost as unpredictable as Emperor Adil is.'

'*Was*,' his mother corrected Sau immediately, a grimace marring her regal features. 'Adil *was* unpredictable.'

'I—' It appeared that Sau was caught off-guard by the force in his mother's voice. 'My apologies, Empress Manali.'

'No, no – there is no need for apology,' his mother said with a sigh. The good humour he had seen in her before receded like the high tide. 'It will take time to associate Adil with the past when his memory still lives on in the present. You may take your leave now, Saudamini. I must speak to my son alone.'

Sau nodded and bowed. Just as she turned away, Ashoka caught her eye, and she winked before exiting the room quietly.

When the doors closed with a painful groan, Empress Manali reached her hands out for Ashoka. He took them, surprised by their coldness.

'Where are the others?' he asked. He had not seen his siblings since the news of their father's death had been delivered hours before.

His mother sighed. 'Arush is likely drinking his sorrows away, and Aarya . . . she is in her chambers. All of us process grief differently, my dear.'

Grief, Ashoka thought. Because this was what he was *meant* to be feeling. He didn't have the heart to tell his mother that he was the least likely to grieve their father. But perhaps, she already knew that.

'The last time that I lost someone, I became a hollow shell,' his mother said quietly. Ashoka knew that she was referring to her older adopted sister, Subhadrangi. She had travelled with his mother to the Golden City for her politically arranged marriage to his father in exchange for aid after her kingdom had suffered a dreadful earthquake. His mother had always spoken of his aunt fondly, and she had kept her from feeling completely alone in those early years. 'This loss hurts as badly yet seems less heavy on the heart.'

'Perhaps the more you accustom yourself to loss, the less pain you inflict on yourself?' he suggested. It sounded like the sort of comment a fortune-teller would make. Who was he to know such things? Who was he, a sheltered prince who knew no losses, to remark on feelings he had never felt? He'd only had one blow, and it had been today, and he was not so sure if he would label it as one, either.

But his mother appeared to have taken his words to heart. 'Perhaps,' she agreed. 'Do you feel grief, my dear?'

Suddenly, Ashoka was the deer he had seen in the woods that day, his mother the young prince with an arrow drawn and ready to release. How to respond? How to articulate his jumbled thoughts?

Luckily, it seemed as if she knew without Ashoka ever having to utter a word. 'I understand your reluctance to call it grief,' she said. 'Your relationship was complicated, to say the least.'

'*Complicated* is too loose of a word, mother,' he replied. *Strained. Antipathetic.* Those were the words he would choose.

'Given all that, he is still your father,' Manali reminded him lightly. 'Blood is blood. It is all right to feel something akin to grief, as distant as it may be.'

Ashoka said nothing. There wasn't much to say. He could not form the words. At his silence, his mother squeezed his hand gently before letting it go.

'Rest, my dear,' she ordered, becoming distracted by the appearance of two maidservants at the entrance of her room. 'You will need it. These coming days will not be easy – not for me, not for you and your siblings, and not for the empire.'

CHAPTER NINE

Shakti

SHE AWOKE IN A COLD SWEAT.

The vision of Emperor Adil and the unknown man was still freshly imprinted in her mind. Cold hands grasped her shoulders tightly to prevent her from moving. She was lying down on her back, with something warm and soft cushioning the hard ground. A blanket.

'Shakti,' she heard a voice say. It was the same voice that had pulled her out of her dream. 'It's all right. You are safe.'

Shakti's blurred vision focused on the dark brown hands clamped over her shoulders and followed their path upward to find a young woman watching her closely. Undone hair flowed loosely to her waist. Streaks of mud speckled her arms like snake eggs. Shakti knew her. This was—

'Nayani?' she managed to croak out. Sleep coated her voice, making it sound disused. Surprise pierced through her like a needle into an abscess. Dharvi's daughter *was* alive. Thank the spirits.

'Here,' said Nayani. Placing her palm against Shakti's back, she helped her to sit up. 'Slowly, now. Don't move too fast.'

Like a dutiful child, Shakti obeyed. She was light-headed and her muscles felt sore and tender, like she had been running for days on end without respite. Though her bones ached like those of an old man with arthritic knees, her thoughts were abuzz. She felt full, not in body but in mind. Pushing the odd feeling away, she focused on the mayakari in front of her.

'Nayani, what are you . . . How did you . . .'

A bitter, sad smile flickered on Nayani's lips before it vanished. She removed her hands from Shakti. 'I was in the forest that night trying to raise a dead lyrebird,' she said. 'When I saw the smoke, I panicked. Something just didn't feel right, and when I saw people being shot down . . . I couldn't leave. I'm sorry about Jaya.' Her fingers curled into her palm.

'You did the right thing by saving yourself,' Shakti said softly. Unlike her, she had run headlong into danger. 'I'm sorry about your mother.'

Blinking furiously, Nayani let out a shuddery breath and rubbed at her right eye. 'It's my fault,' she replied. 'Taksila emboldened me too much, I think. Part of me thought I could have done something to save her, but I didn't.'

Survivor's remorse. Shakti understood her guilt, the feeling that they *could have* done something. But the world would always be that way; it was an endless stream of what-ifs and could-haves. The weight of her actions would become an unremovable chip on Nayani's shoulder if she didn't learn to let it go. 'What could you have done?' she asked, hoping to alleviate her regret.

'That's true.' For a moment, they fell quiet. It allowed Shakti to assess her surroundings. Daylight shone through an alcove just in front of where Nayani sat cross-legged. The scent of wood was overpowering, as was the lit incense around them. The cooing of nature spirits filled the air as Shakti realized that she was sheltered in what appeared to be the hollowed-out interior of a Hora tree.

'How did you find me?' she managed to ask.

'A Na spirit called me,' Nayani replied. 'It said that someone needed help, so I came. Spirits, Shakti, what were you doing so close to the emperor's camp?'

Shakti was touched. The benevolent creature had indeed saved her life.

'I was observing.' The lie came unbidden. There was no reason to create falsities, but Shakti held back for the fear of judgement. She had actively cursed a living being. To admit this to another mayakari – it was shameful.

Nayani appeared disbelieving. 'Tell me the truth.'

Groaning, Shakti cradled her head in her heads. 'All right, I . . . Wait. Before you judge me, remember that the emperor killed my aunt. He killed Master Hasith. He massacred the village and has done so countless times before. I couldn't just sit there and stew with that knowledge, Nayani.'

The other mayakari remained silent, waiting for her explanation.

'I cursed him,' Shakti said.

Another beat of silence. Then—

'You *what?*' Nayani's voice exploded. Her melancholy mood vanished. 'Did I mishear you?'

'You didn't. I cursed the emperor.' Saying it felt more freeing than Shakti had expected. 'Not with death, I'll have you know. Living misfortune.'

She said it to lighten the mood but failed to have the desired effect. Nayani's eyes bugged out of her head. 'Because that makes it better,' she said. 'Your aunt always said that you were prone to volatility, but I didn't expect this level of carelessness.'

'Carelessness?'

Nayani fixed her with an adamant stare. 'That's why there was a commotion at the camp, wasn't it?' she demanded, ignoring her question. 'Something happened to the emperor; I heard the soldiers yelling. Spirits, I thought it was some sort of accident.'

'At first, I did too,' Shakti admitted. 'But it was the curse. You didn't see it, Nayani. Some sort of black liquid started oozing from his chest, and then he collapsed.'

Nayani gawped. 'The curse worked that quickly?'

Her surprise made Shakti pause. 'What do you mean by that?'

'Well,' the other mayakari appeared unsure, 'once a curse is cast, it could take any length of time to enact itself. I'm just surprised that yours worked so quickly. Did your aunt perhaps teach you something different?'

Shakti shook her head. Jaya had never gone into specifics when it came to cursing and raising the dead.

'Reverse it.'

Now, it was Shakti's turn to wonder if she had misheard her. 'What?'

'*Reverse it*,' Nayani repeated, frowning. 'You *do* know how to, yes?'

Despite herself, Shakti scowled. Part of her was quickly becoming irritated by Nayani doubting her knowledge. Yes, Jaya had limited her teachings, but not to such a detrimental extent.

She knew the basics well enough. Though a curse's enactment was left to chance, unless the victim had died from it, its reversal was immediate. Any mayakari could easily undo one so long as they knew the exact phrasing of a curse – that power did not remain only in the hands of the enactor.

At Shakti's silence, Nayani nudged her gently. 'If you don't want to, at least tell me the exact phrase you used,' she said. 'I can reverse it for you.'

'I *know* how to undo it,' Shakti replied stubbornly. 'But I won't. Adil deserves to suffer.' Besides, she'd accumulated negative karma the moment she uttered her curse. Reversal did nothing to remove it, and neither did she want to.

Nayani made a noise of frustration. 'Shakti, do you not see what you've done?'

'At least I did something instead of hiding,' Shakti snapped, guilt following her anger immediately. It was a low blow, and she knew it, but unless Jaya was miraculously brought back to life, no one on this earth could convince her to undo her curse. 'I'm sorry. I didn't mean that.'

Nayani sighed. 'I know you didn't. But, Shakti, what you claim happened to Emperor Adil – that is not a usual human disease. Anyone with half a brain will realize that there is magic at play. You may have got some sort of wretched justice, but if Emperor

Adil survives, he will just use this as more fodder for his attacks against us.'

Emperor Adil.

The moment you wake is the moment I die.

'I had the strangest dream,' Shakti murmured. She could remember it in such vivid detail too, which was unusual. Usually, she would forget her dreams or nightmares a few minutes after waking up. This one, however, remained in her mind like a lived memory.

Stupid girl, this is no dream. Why is it so hard for you to grasp?

'You were asleep for three days, so I would find it unusual if you weren't plagued by your mind's own machinations,' Nayani replied, her morose expression switching to one of concern. Her voice dropped to an unsteady timbre. 'At one point, I thought you were comatose.'

The grin that Shakti sent her was feeble. 'Thankfully, I'm alive and well,' she remarked before the weight of what Nayani had said finally registered in her head. '*Three days?*'

'Yes,' Nayani said patiently. 'I kept you alive.'

'Oh,' was all Shakti could say. That and, 'Thank you.'

Waving her hand in a dismissive gesture, Nayani reached out to tap Shakti's forehead with her pointer finger. 'I distracted you,' she said. 'Tell me, then. What did you dream in the days that you were lost to this world?'

Taken aback by her directness, Shakti could at first only stutter a meaningless dribble of words. In her mind, however, all she saw was Emperor Adil. All she heard was the wicked glee in his laughter, and all she felt was unadulterated hate.

'I-I . . . it was so odd,' Shakti said. 'I saw Emperor Adil. I *talked* to him, and he told me that he was going to die.'

'Perhaps you wanted to hear that,' Nayani supplied. 'A curse of misfortune couldn't kill him, and you wanted a more . . . absolute form of revenge.'

But it had been so *real*. That was what made her pause. Adil's personality had shone through their conversation: his hate, his pride, his egoism. A simple dream couldn't have conjured that. At best, he would have been fashioned as a towering megalomaniac with a distorted voice that she would no doubt be running away from.

Maybe it wasn't a dream, she thought.

'What if it was real?' she asked. 'What if he died and I spoke to him?'

Nayani appeared dubious, and a little concerned when she said, 'I'd say you were hallucinating.'

Shakti thought as much. No mayakari would accept her line of thinking. It meddled with their known abilities. She could have brought back some part of Adil from the dead had he died, but to speak to him in a dream was unthinkable. Three powers were all they had.

'I . . .' she began, ready to defend herself but realized that there was no viable argument. Emotions and gut feelings did not make for a sensible rebuttal.

'You really think you might have, don't you?' Nayani marvelled. Her almond-brown eyes narrowed in concentration as if Shakti were a patient with an undiagnosable condition and she the physician. 'After a great shock, it would be normal to—'

The fullness in Shakti's head returned. It was as if gallons of water had filled in the crevice between her brain and her skull, pushing and creating pressure to leak out. 'No,' she said. 'Something isn't right.'

There was weight on her arm as Nayani squeezed it gently. 'Lie back down,' she suggested. Shakti noticed that her eyes looked fatigued. Gaunt. Not only had she been hiding out in the forestland for days, but she'd also had to take care of her too. Now, the mayakari had to reckon with Shakti's frivolous blather. Guilt wormed into her, but it wasn't overpowering enough to relax her turbulent mind.

An idea came, then. Her thoughts were only theories now, but to confirm or reject it, she needed the help of a Great Spirit. They could sense disturbances in both the land and the mind, and they were more prone to verbal speech than minor nature spirits. There was at least one in this wild forest. She could only hope that it was generous enough to answer her call.

'Please.' Rejecting Nayani's attempts at laying her down, Shakti clasped her hands together. 'Great Spirit of the wild forest, help me.'

Nayani balked. 'What are you doing?'

'I want to make sure that I haven't descended into madness,' Shakti replied, 'and who better to tell me than a Great Spirit?'

'Awakening a Great Spirit to tell you if you're addled in the head?' Nayani retorted in exasperation. 'Shakti, please be serious. Lie down.'

'No,' said Shakti. 'I beg of you – let me try.'

Silent as death, Nayani gave a curt nod and placed her hands on her lap, watching.

Blowing out a deep breath, Shakti placed her hands on the ground. Soil and frayed brown leaves crunched beneath her fingers. Alive or dead, everything in the forests was connected. What was birthed eventually faded away. What was decomposed became one with the earth again and gave life and nourishment to that which came after it. This was the dominion of the Great Spirits; a continuing cycle of life and death they presided over for hundreds of years.

'Great Spirit,' she called out once more. 'Surveyor of this vast dominion, answer my call.'

Heat flooded through their little alcove. The pale sunlight turned a brighter shade of yellow, highlighting the particles of dust that floated in the air. Both gasped when moss began to enter the hollow like waves gently lapping onto the seashore. Droplets of water clung to it, glittering like diamonds.

On her hands and knees, Shakti gestured for them to exit. Moisture from the moss cooled her overheated palms. Outside, the temperature had dropped to a refreshing chill that was unusual for midday. When Shakti finally stood herself up and trained her eyes forward, she nearly toppled over in disbelief.

A giant black tiger stood in front of her. Its stripes were liquid silver that shifted and changed position every few seconds. Young green leaves and blue flower buds hung off its long white whiskers. Kaleidoscopic eyes that shifted from red, green, brown, and yellow watched them carefully.

It had answered her.

Shakti bowed deeply, as did Nayani next to her. 'Great Spirit,' she greeted. '*Thank you for answering my call.*'

The blue flower buds on its whiskers blossomed, wilted, and dropped to the ground before being replaced by another bunch. '*Mayakari,*' it said. The voice was deep and comforting, so unlike those of the minor spirits. Powerful energy radiated from the tiger in waves. This being was ancient, she could tell. '*You are unsettled.*'

It could already sense her.

'*My mind,*' she said. '*I am troubled by what I have dreamed. Am I going mad?*'

The Great Spirit observed her, blinking slowly. With a swish of its tail, it stood and stalked towards them. Every time the tiger blinked its eyes changed colour.

'*Mad is not what you are, little witch,*' it said. Like a pup, it trailed around her in circles, examining her like she was a curious new toy. '*You are not one, but instead multiple.*'

Shakti's heart stopped. '*What do you mean, Great Spirit?*' she urged.

'*You are many,*' it said. '*A collective. Multiple minds. Gift or curse, that remains for you to decide.*'

Adil's words rang in her head: a collective consciousness.

'*Is my consciousness melded to Emperor Adil?*' she asked.

The tiger shook its head and leaves fell as it did so. '*The emperor's consciousness lives on inside you. Connected, but not yet melded. You are a new part of The Collective.*'

It hadn't been a dream, then. Adil was right.

Spirits. He was *right*.

She glanced at Nayani from her periphery. The other witch looked ready to faint. Out of surprise, Shakti switched to human speech. 'The emperor's consciousness is in my head,' she echoed.

'I heard,' she replied weakly.

'*If his consciousness is connected with mine, what has happened to him?*' Shakti turned to ask the Great Spirit. A part of her knew the answer already; she just wanted to hear it from someone else.

'Dead,' said the tiger. '*The physical body is gone, but the cyclical nature of rebirth is halted.*'

Shakti's knees buckled. Sweat began to bead above her upper lip. Her body was heating up, palms clammy with moisture.

Emperor Adil was *dead*. Really, truly dead, and she had been the executioner. She had been the one holding the weapon: a litany of ambiguous words that doomed him from the first syllable.

Do not kill. Fuck. She'd broken the fourth precept, and quite spectacularly at that.

You've ended a life, little bird, came Jaya's voice. *I wish you hadn't.*

Shakti almost wanted to laugh. *Living misfortune.* Alive, but not dead. Dead, but not alive. A consciousness attached to the very people Adil hated the most. The curse *had* worked, just in its own roundabout way.

So, this was why Jaya had been hesitant to teach her.

Nayani's trembling voice followed the Great Spirit's. 'What do you mean by multiple minds?'

With a start, Shakti realized that she had skipped over that phrase entirely.

The Great Spirit let out something that sounded like a laugh. '*Generations of minds existed inside Emperor Adil,*' it said. '*Now, many minds exist inside you.*'

Shakti's eyes met Nayani's. That wasn't possible. Impossible, really, unless . . .

'Was the emperor a mayakari?'

Saying it aloud made her feel stupid. No, that was not possible. Mayakari were always female. That was what she had always been told. Men were carriers. They could not manifest any powers but carried the potential.

'*It is ancient magic twisted into something unrecognizable,*' said the Great Spirit. Its silver stripes changed once more. '*A carrier but not. A witch but not. I know no more.*'

Adil was something else, then. What exactly, she did not know and the Great Spirit could not tell her. All she knew was that in a moment of terrible luck, his ability had been transferred to her. *Stupid curse.* It may have hurt Adil, but now she carried its burden alone.

It was a burden she did not want.

Nayani appeared more agitated. 'I . . . I can't wrap my head around this,' she stuttered. She looked at Shakti like a second head had sprouted from her neck. Like she was a newly found specimen fished from the depths of the sea. 'The emperor . . . is dead? And you – he – is here. In you?'

Processing such information would take some time. Hearing from a Great Spirit that Emperor Adil had died was not the usual method of receiving news. Knowing that, somehow, the emperor's consciousness had transferred to a mayakari of all people, made it harder to digest. Still, Shakti could not help but utter a sardonic retort in human speech. 'You had ample opportunity to believe me the first time.'

'Hah! Any rational person would think you to be stark raving mad,' Nayani said crossly. 'It's insanity. I mean . . . what did you speak to him about?'

'When I spoke to Adil, he was angry,' Shakti admitted. 'He was bitter at dying by the steps of his palace and—'

Nayani made a derisive sound. Shakti did not blame her for it. Her mind cast itself back to the brief image of the man she did not know. The one with the golden circlet. The one whose hand she had grasped.

'*What is it, little one?*' The tiger's knowing eyes focused on Shakti's. She knew that she was fidgeting, restless. Shakti decided to tell them about the man she had seen – perhaps the tiger could give her some insight.

'I *saw someone else,*' she explained, quickly describing the man in the golden circlet. '*He held out his hand for me to take, and I did. The moment our hands touched, I felt this rush of power.*'

'*Part of The Collective,*' it replied.

'But who was the man?'

'*I cannot read your mind,*' the Great Spirit sounded like Jaya at that very moment with its chastising tone. '*That man's identity is yours to discover, and yours alone. Perhaps he may tell you as to how Emperor Adil kept such power inside him. I can only tell you that it is ancient magic.*'

The mysterious stranger; the one with a beautiful face. He held the key to Shakti's questions, and the only way to find the answers she sought was to find Adil again.

'*How do I get back there?*' Shakti asked, this time in spirit-speak. '*How do I return to the place where I saw Emperor Adil?*'

Talking to the man who killed her aunt was the last thing Shakti wanted to do. But this was a power she did not want. What use was it to have a warmonger's thoughts inside her head? Were her dreams to be filled now with thoughts of violence and memories of burning witches?

'*Only you can take yourself there. It requires a certain amount of mental concentration and meditation. Or alternatively, a state of deep sleep.*'

Sleep? Shakti could not bring herself to sleep at this moment. Her mind was abuzz, fluttering like a flock of doves in mid-flight. To sleep would be a nightmare.

'I'll meditate, then,' her voice rose in pitch. 'I'll call Emperor Adil to me.'

Nayani's voice reached the same high-pitched ting of a humming-bird. 'What on earth for?' she asked. 'What do you seek from him?'

'To get *rid* of him!' Shakti gesticulated angrily. 'I didn't expect this to happen, Nayani. I can understand why we don't often curse others when it could affect us, too.'

Meanwhile, the ghostly tiger watched them with detached fascination. '*Come towards me, little witch,*' it ordered, '*so that I may help you.*'

Slowly, Shakti ambled towards the Great Spirit until she stood right in front of it. Its long, snakelike tail swished leisurely on the blanket of leaves. Standing so close, she could smell its breath, musty like an underground cave. Shakti cast her eyes upward to meet its variegated ones. She trusted it the way a child naturally learned to trust a good parent. *'Your time is precious,'* it said.

Then, the Great Spirit unhinged its jaw and swallowed her whole.

Or at least, it looked like it did. Nature spirits were not corporeal. At best, they felt like a sunbeam hitting skin during a torrid cold snap. The tiger's body turned translucent as its neck extended in an unnatural fashion and its jaw lunged down to cover her entire body. Fascinated, Shakti only had a moment to realize that her body was ensconced by a dark grey ectoplasm before her thoughts turned blank and she closed her eyes.

It was as if she were meditating, and so, so desperately close to having her mind completely still. She startled at the sensation of lightning inside her body, crackling and dissipating into a thousand different bolts. It felt like magic was flowing in her veins.

Somewhere in the recesses of her mind, there was a deep, visceral *tug*.

She saw the tug as a thread of blue and white sparks coiling and winding around a dark, empty space and began to follow it. Up and down, left and right, twisting sideways and under until she felt her chest constrict and she was blinded by shining lights.

When Shakti opened her eyes, the Great Spirit was not standing before her. Nayani was not behind her, either. No longer was she in the wild forestland.

Shock overtook her when she realized that she was back in the throne room, the same as it had been when she fell unconscious. Emperor Adil sat on the Obsidian Throne, clothed in white. No black stain marred his chest this time. He looked clean. Purified, almost. A taunting smile formed upon his lips when he noticed her appear a few steps below him. And when he spoke, his voice was filled with nothing but loathing:

'Do you believe me now, stupid girl?'

CHAPTER TEN

Ashoka

Ashoka had never witnessed death on such an opulent scale.

The funeral ceremony for Emperor Adil began on the third day following his death. The entire palace had been swathed in white, the colour of death, rebirth, and peace. The colour of innocence.

A shame then, to associate it with his father.

White muslin cloth was draped over the Obsidian Throne. White roses and frangipanis scattered the garden pools. White doves were set free into the roaring blue sky. Today, his father's body would be carried from the palace to the Golden City below, and from there to the Mountain of Rebirth. Following prayers, his body was to be cremated and scattered.

Ashoka himself was adorned in white clothing, free of all the customary royal jewelleries. Only the singular gold stud on his burned ear remained, a small act of rebellion on his part.

'How do I look?' he asked Rahil before they joined his mother and siblings in the throne room.

'Untainted,' Rahil had replied.

The response had given Ashoka a brief pause. *Untainted.* That was what white signified. That was the colour his father's body would be dressed in. How hypocritical.

With Rahil behind him, Ashoka joined his family in the throne room. It was jarring to see so much disparity in the colour scheme of the crow-black hall. His mother and siblings, all dressed in simple clothing, stood in front of the throne while the palace officials bustled about with hushed whispers and furtive glances.

In the crowd, Ashoka suddenly felt insignificant.

'Can you stay beside me?' Ashoka asked Rahil quietly. Rahil gave him confidence when he didn't have it and, at this moment, he needed him. 'I . . . I need—'

Rahil laid a gentle hand on his shoulder. 'Yes, Ashoka,' he said. It was all he needed to say for Ashoka to relax. They had become so attuned to each other that sometimes words were useless. Ashoka would notice Rahil's consternation in the slight pursing of his lips, sense suspicion when his hands reached for his dual broadswords, see happiness when his eyes crinkled and shone like a thousand lanterns. And Rahil, in turn, knew Ashoka's mannerisms by heart.

As always, his mother noticed him first and offered a comforting smile.

Ashoka wondered how his mother felt.

His parents' personalities had always clashed; the hateful emperor and the sympathetic empress. As a child, he'd heard the arguments in their chamber, the heated discussions in the war council rooms, and the dismissive glances around the palace. No marriage was without its arguments – that he knew – but it felt as if his parents had more disagreements than most.

He was pulled back into his memories to the time he was six years old. He and his siblings were playing in the palace gardens. Their mother was keeping watch beneath a marquee, along with a dozen of her servants. Arush was fidgeting with a slingshot that he had fashioned. His father had been in the tent with their mother. A rare occasion, Ashoka remembered. Sitting beside him on a teal-coloured spread of cushions had been Aarya, while Ashoka squatted on the grass and observed his brother.

The *snap, snap, snap* of Arush's slingshot was consistent. Then came a high-pitched *squawk*.

Ashoka's head snapped up when he heard the stone being released from its sling. He saw it hit Arush's target: a myna bird perched on a wispy tree branch. Ashoka remembered its descent clearly; the black wings flapped uselessly as it tried to slow its fall.

Before the bird's body hit the ground, Ashoka had turned away. He stared at the shoots of grass for a moment and was hit with the image of the myna bird, dead. Its body began to decompose in front of his eyes, the flesh eaten by maggots, sinking beneath the shifting earth until all that remained was a shard of bone and a smattering of feathers.

Innocent.

His mother had echoed his thoughts. While their father praised Arush's impeccable aim, she had raised her voice. Clear disapproval coloured her sharp tones before they were shushed by their father.

Ashoka could not summon such admiration for a cruel act. Instead, he had run towards the fallen creature. Blood coated its head. He could still see its small chest rise and fall, but it was slow.

You're still alive, he thought, relieved. He could still save it.

He picked up the bird and ran to his mother, pleading for her to save it somehow. As if her adultness came with power that knew how to save a dying creature when his child-self couldn't. But by the time a servant came with a cloth to wrap the myna up in, it had died. A piece of Ashoka's own heart had died with it.

While Manali was sympathetic, Adil had scorned him.

'You will never be a warrior with that manner, son,' his father said. 'Never cry for the weak. They are that way for a reason.'

'But it didn't deserve to die,' Ashoka had refuted. An exciting idea sprang into his head. Surely his father would appreciate his creative thinking. 'Maybe a mayakari can fix it! They can bring it back from the dea—'

Pain spread across his right cheek. His father had slapped him.

'*Adil!*' Manali had screamed.

'Hush, Manali,' his father had replied. 'You dote on him too much.'

Ashoka had felt complete and utter surprise. He had never been hit before. Heat emanated from the area of skin that had contact with his father's palm. Before he could stop himself, the tears came, and embarrassment along with them. *How shameful*, he thought, blinking furiously, *to be viewed like the poor bird, helpless and pathetic.* Aarya had been observing him throughout the entire ordeal. Her expression had been blank. There was no sympathy in her eyes. Adil's, meanwhile, promised a lifetime of punishment.

'Throw away that stupid bird,' his father's voice boomed, ignoring his tears. 'And never speak of such things again.'

Rahil's insistent prodding at his arm brought Ashoka out of his thoughts. 'Go,' he urged, 'play the prince.' It was what Rahil always said when Ashoka was obliged to attend royal ceremonies that made him want to bludgeon his own skull.

'But I . . . the ending ceremony,' Ashoka said, face creasing into a frown.

'I know,' Rahil patted his back reassuringly, 'you'll be all right.'

Comforted that Rahil would be close by, Ashoka made his way towards his family members who were all standing side by side.

Arush frowned as Ashoka found a place beside him. 'You're late, brother,' he remarked.

'What could I possibly miss?' Ashoka replied. 'Father remains dead.'

Arush flinched.

From the other side, Aarya turned to him, looking scandalized. 'Ashoka!' she scolded him. 'How dare you speak in such a disrespectful manner.'

He had the sudden urge to incense Aarya further. 'Draping him in white seems hypocritical,' he said. 'Father and the word "peace", I would argue, are mutually exclusive.'

'Ashoka,' Aarya began, frost seeping into her voice, 'this is the height of contempt.'

At that moment, all Ashoka wanted to do was to rain hell upon his sister's indignation. Father's favourite be damned. He was soon to be cremated, and here she was trying to act like he was a benevolent god instead of a malicious monster. 'It is not contempt if it is the truth.'

The look she threw him would have matched the icy tundra of the north. Then, her eyes flickered to the side of his face, and her eyes narrowed in disgust.

'Take that stud out, Ashoka,' she ordered coolly. 'Be respectful.'

Ashoka stiffened. How unsurprising; Aarya was trying to order him around even during a funeral. 'I'd rather not,' he replied nonchalantly and tugged at his burned ear. 'Think of this as my own special way of remembering him.'

'Children, please,' their mother's voice snapped the siblings out of their terse exchange. 'Stop this squabbling – you're like a murder of crows. Compose yourselves so that we can begin the funeral procession.'

At their mother's warning tone, the three Maurya children sewed their mouths shut. Even the tempestuous Aarya, who was more likely to pick a fight with their mother than agree with her, quietened down. Moments later, the sound of a lone flute broke the sombre silence.

The procession had begun.

The officials inside the throne room formed a parallel line in an orderly fashion from the steps of the throne to the entrance of the room, effectively wedging the small Maurya clan between them. Their heads bowed low as Ashoka and his family passed out of the throne room and the long palace corridors onto the palace steps. His mother led the three of them, her head held high and her eyes devoid of tears.

His father's ornate black casket lay surrounded by wreaths of red and blue flowers, crushed gold flecks, and gossamer white cloth. Ashoka's heart pounded like mallets at the sight of the open coffin. He had not seen his father since the day he had left for Kolakola. In fact, he had avoided gazing upon his father's dead body in the last few days with the knowledge that he would be forced to look upon his face on the day of the funeral ceremony. Now that it was here, he wanted to run away. But running was seen by his father as an act of cowardice, and Ashoka could not be a coward in front of a dead man. After all, what was there to fear?

A priestess stood beside the coffin, her hair braided with white jasmines and her arms folded together. As the royals approached, she bowed and took three steps back, allowing them to surround the casket like a flock of birds and gaze upon its sole inhabitant.

Ashoka's breath died in his throat when his eyes rested upon his father's body.

Adil looked almost . . . peaceful. His eyes were closed. Ashoka half-expected to see the rise and fall of his chest, as if to prove that his father was not dead and simply asleep. His harsh features, the sharp nose, the hard angles of his jaw, and his razor-sharp brows were more relaxed than Ashoka had ever seen them. In his death, they had erased his anger and made him human. This was magic that not even the mayakari could achieve.

Staring at his father's face brought forth a wild rush of emotions. It was everything that Ashoka had felt for him since his childhood days. Embers of affection. Blind respect. Wildfires of anger. Whorls of distrust. A lifetime's worth of disappointment.

Aarya was watching him curiously.

'You've gone pale,' she remarked. Her gaze flicked briefly towards the gold stud in his ear again, lips thinning in disapproval. 'Are you all right?'

Ashoka found himself nodding and taking a step back, feeling dizzy. He needed to steady himself; the youngest prince could not be seen observing his dear father's casket with such vehemence.

His eyes sought Rahil's, who was standing with his guard a few feet away from them in their midnight-coloured armour. Rahil's features appeared indifferent and emotionless, but his umber eyes spoke a clear message:

Play the prince, Ashoka.

Steeling himself, Ashoka hardened his features and straightened his back. The cacophony of drums began to permeate the air, beating fast and angry under the mid-morning sun. They were the sounds of war drums, traditionally used before an army left for battle. It was unusual to use it in a funeral procession, but for his father's passing, it made more sense than not. He supposed that his mother had authorized their use.

Ashoka watched silently as his father's coffin was delicately loaded onto the back of the carriage, drawn by four beautiful leopards. It was first to be taken in a viewing carriage through the Golden City so that citizens would be able to pay their respects.

As the children began to search for their carriages that would similarly take them through the city to the Mountain of Rebirth, their mother stopped them.

'Once we reach the base of the mountain, I have advised there to be no carriages to take us up,' Manali remarked firmly. 'Today, we walk.'

Ashoka balked but was unsurprised. Coming from their mother, it would likely be some sort of lesson in humility. His father may receive a grand farewell through the city streets, drawn in leopard and carriage, but they were still alive. They were still present with beating hearts, sound minds, and able feet.

'Mother!' Aarya's outrage was palpable. 'You will let us travel like commoners? For what?'

'A lesson in humility,' Manali echoed Ashoka's exact thoughts. 'If you do not agree with me, stay where you are, Aarya. That decision belongs entirely to you.'

'Father would not have us travel like *peasants*,' Aarya seethed, her brown eyes sparking with barely restrained fury.

'I do not doubt that,' their mother replied coolly, 'but this is an old custom of my kingdom, and I wish to see it executed. It serves as a sign of respect for the departed. Do not argue with me, Aarya.'

Ashoka saw a muscle twitch in his sister's jaw and thought she would lash out with some choice words of her own. He knew Aarya was hurting more than him or his brother over the loss of their father. The golden child had lost her favoured parent. Thinking he ought to prevent another acidic retort from his older sister, Ashoka spoke at the same time his brother did to cool the waters.

'I will aid you if you feel too weary to walk,' Arush pacified.

'We all have our customs – let mother grieve in her way, and you grieve in yours,' Ashoka added.

Though Aarya scowled, it was in defeat. 'Fine,' she agreed, moving towards their carriage, 'but I do not require your help, Arush. I am perfectly capable of trekking up a mountain – I simply loathe the fact that we are to travel like the common people. We shall be subject to the heat, the dirt, and the sweat. What a bother.' She shot a contemptuous look at their mother who pointedly ignored it.

Their carriage took the steep downward slope of road that connected the hilltop palace to the Golden City. At the base of the hill, the main road diverged, one towards the city centre, the other towards the Marble Stupa and the Mountain of Rebirth several miles south. While their father's carriage took the former route, the Mauryas took the latter.

All four of them were quiet, each lost in their own thoughts. They passed a large, destroyed stone building singed black near the outskirts of the city where trees, weeds, and wildflowers grew from the ruins. The old mayakari library. A shame, Ashoka thought. Centuries' worth of knowledge and innocent bodies destroyed by hate.

Aarya's statement soon proved correct. After reaching the Mountain of Rebirth, the royals and their guards took the trail that was barely paved, brimming with overgrown tree roots and the occasional birdsong of nature spirits. Dressed as they were in their long saris, Aarya and their mother must have found the task of climbing past rubble and giant stepping-stones arduous, but the two took it in their stride. Aarya's glowering features had morphed into a determined expression, as she staunchly refused Arush's hand to climb over ledges. By the time they arrived at the top of the mountain, and from the position of the sun in the sky, Ashoka guessed that they had spent a good half hour walking to their destination.

The Mountain of Rebirth was an odd place. Like the royal palace, it was situated on the extremities of the Golden City, east of the city centre and several miles south of the palace. Standing alone like a giant, its peak perpetually covered in a thick, grey mist, the summit was a marriage of life and death. Greenery scattered the area from tall twisting Hora trees to poisonous purple petals, but it was intermingled with flora that were withered and lifeless. Some trees had lost their leaves, leaving dried-up branches and rotting roots behind. Some flowers remained wilted. It was unusual – they did not decompose but instead continued to flourish in a permanent state of death. Hundreds of years ago, during the reign of his namesake, Ashoka the First, the mountain had been as natural as any other, until magic – either mayakari or Great Spirit, not even the empire's greatest scholars could deduce – caused half to deteriorate like a necrotic limb. This reason was the most well-known, but later stories for the mountain's current state often veered into downright fantasy.

Officiants and the head ascetic of the Marble Stupa – the largest in the city – were already present by the time they arrived. They stood with flaming torches in their hands and the oil-slicked coffin behind them, ready to burn.

'Empress.' The ascetic bowed as they approached. 'Princes, princess. I hope the trek to the mountain proved to be without complication?'

'Indeed, ascetic Venya,' Manali nodded. 'We are ready to begin the cremation.'

The ascetic bowed once more, stepping back to murmur something to the other officiants beside her. They all turned their backs to the royals, and the ascetic began to chant a verse for luck and good rebirth.

'Emperor Adil of the Maurya clan, of the glorious Ran Empire – may your rebirth be plentiful.'

Ashoka clenched his jaw at the ascetic's stanza. He wanted nothing more than for his father to get his karmic retribution. Senseless slaughter did not warrant a bountiful rebirth.

If I could tear your legacy apart, father, I would do so without question.

The words came to him like lightning. Uttering them aloud would be seen as treachery. Uttering them aloud would see him removed from the throne line and exiled to the north.

With a final prayer, the men and women silently threw their torches onto the coffin, which burst into frightful angry flames. Ashoka heard the slight hitch of Aarya's breath, Arush's sharp exhale, and his mother's light gasp.

This was the end.

And so, they watched. Watched and waited patiently as the coffin and the man inside it burned into ashes. The flames licked ever higher, and Ashoka swore that he almost saw the spark of bluish white flames erupting from the yellow-orange glare.

Following the burning, the painting of the ashes began.

From the still-smouldering pile of grey matter, the head ascetic dipped a spindly, damp hand into the ashes, allowing his father's ashes to be glued to her skin like a mixture of paint and wet sand. Slowly, the woman approached his mother who knelt on one knee, her face angled towards the sun. Ashoka watched as the ascetic gently drew a circle on his mother's forehead – signifying the never-ending cycle of samsara: the beginning that would never end – observing the grey ashes that were once his father stick to her like a second skin.

He remembered Sau telling him that this tradition had come from the mayakari. He forced himself not to heave out a dry chuckle at the irony of it all.

One by one, the Maurya children were painted with the ashes of their father. When the ascetic finally stopped in front of Ashoka, he felt ill. He half-wished that he were not here, having to kneel only to have an old ascetic draw a circle on his forehead with paint made from his father's cremated remains. This was all that was left of Adil, and yet, Ashoka was unable to escape it. His father's presence followed him even after his death, and now, his ashes would be branded onto his skin.

The touch of her hand was warm, but the sensation of the crumbled fragments of ash made Ashoka feel as if he were frozen in ice.

You will follow me to death, father, he thought to himself. *I can never escape you. But, for all this, I will never become you.*

CHAPTER ELEVEN
Shakti

SHAKTI DROPPED INTO A MOCK-BOW AT THE SIGHT OF Emperor Adil.

'My condolences,' she said. 'For your death. I would have wished for an unpleasant rebirth but alas, it appears that you have been punished in kind. Rebirth will not claim you.'

Emperor Adil stared at her like she was a dung beetle. 'Does your kind not teach basic manners?' he responded.

'My kind teaches *vipāka*,' she retorted snidely, watching with satisfaction when Adil cast his eyes skyward. He would know it – the ripening, the maturing of karma. Its result escaped no one, not even a royal.

'*Teaches*,' he said with a derisive snort. 'And what do you do with these philosophies, witch? Nothing. All that power to use, and you store it away.'

Shakti bristled at his comment. Of course he didn't understand. Not having grown up learning a pacifist code made him apathetic to the mayakari ways. 'You're like any power-hungry monster,' she replied. 'You don't understand that simply because one holds greater power does not mean it has to be used. Sometimes, power is best left alone.'

This was the same spiel Jaya had given her. Even as she said it,

Shakti knew how hypocritical she was being. Preaching the careful use of mayakari power was worthless when she had used it based on anger and grief. That, and she felt vindicated after using it.

The emperor seemed to be thinking as she did. 'A false ascetic then, aren't you?' he asked softly. In the gleam of his eyes was a panther waiting to kill.

'You know, I don't understand your motive,' Shakti said, tapping her foot on the floor in a slow rhythm. 'You despise the mayakari and wish to eradicate them from the face of this earth. And yet, this power that you have – is this not the power of a witch?'

Emperor Adil's answering smile reeked of wickedness. 'What do you know about power, child?'

'Power?' Shakti echoed. 'It is something that can be taken.'

'Indeed,' the emperor looked oddly surprised by her answer. 'Power always has the potential to be taken away. And who better to stand a chance in taking away the legacy of the great Maurya dynasty than the vile mayakari with their atrocious death magic?'

'You're paranoid,' Shakti said, scoffing. 'Delusional. The mayakari have lived peacefully for thousands of years. Why slaughter a race that has done nothing to deserve it?'

'Power like yours was made for war,' said Emperor Adil. His dark eyes looked hungry at the mention of mayakari magic. It was intermingled with another emotion; one she couldn't identify. 'But you abhor it in favour of peace. I have lost to pacifism once, and I will not lose to it again.'

Before she could ask him what he meant by that, the emperor delivered yet another barb. 'Only the deserving should wield such power, and your kind is not deserving.'

Shakti snorted. The powerful lusted after power. What a surprise. 'How fortunate that you will not be reborn, Adil,' she replied.

The emperor glowered at her informality. 'You know, rebirth will not claim you either, mayakari,' he said. 'Those who hold The Collective do not.'

A cold prickle spread down Shakti's spine. 'What did you say?'

'Power cannot be held without consequence,' the emperor replied. He seemed pleased by her shocked response. 'Whatever it is that makes up your consciousness will be tethered to the next holder. You will be denied a rebirth, mayakari.'

Surely, he was lying to scare her. Was such a thing even possible?

It was as if Adil sensed her distrust. 'It is true,' he said. Even now, he made it sound as if she were a child who could not understand basic writing skills. 'If it is not, I would not be here.'

There was an unpleasant lurch in the pit of her stomach.

No rebirth. No chance to die naturally, to have her ashes scattered to the winds. To find their place at the bottom of a riverbed, to sink deep into forest soil and become part of the earth once more.

If his claims are true . . .

Tears threatened to spill but Shakti held them back. Adil's claims promised an eternity of loneliness. Of attachment. Of suffering.

No, she told herself. *I do not deserve suffering.*

'Tell me how to get rid of this, then,' she demanded and gestured to the throne room.

'You can't,' came the swift reply. But it was too quick.

'You lie, *Adil.*' Hoping to spark annoyance in him, Shakti addressed the emperor without his formal title once more. 'If this is a collective, there are others here, and that means there is someone who has the answer to my question.'

'How will you know if I lie or not?' he questioned in return. 'Perhaps this is all I know. Perhaps I am a fool.'

The emperor was lying through his teeth and they both knew it. Adil did not seem like the type of person to willingly call himself a fool. There had to be a way to get rid of this affliction. Shakti couldn't imagine having to spend a lifetime with the emperor in her head. She'd summoned a Great Spirit, of all beings, to help, and if this were to end as a fruitless endeavour, the shame she would inflict upon herself was endless.

'Fuck you,' she spat.

'You *dare*—' he began, incensed. With a practised anger, he stood and raised his left hand high as if about to come down and slap her. Panicked by his towering figure, Shakti cast her eyes downward and imagined his arm slipping back down, unable to touch her. *For spirits' sake.*

When she glanced back up, she found Adil frozen in place. His arm was still raised but it quivered like a plucked bowstring. It was as if he were trying to move but his brain and joints were disconnected. Was this her doing, or his? Surely, it wasn't Adil's. No doubt, he would have slapped her without hesitation.

Suddenly, the landscape changed. The Obsidian Throne vanished, replaced by a vivid blue sky and scorched ground. The environment wasn't clear; it was as if she were stuck in that pesky stage of opening her eyes after sleep and finding the world blurred. The only sure thing Shakti knew was that she was overlooking some sort of mountain cliff. The hazy blue of the sky was too vast for it to be forestland. Adil, too, had disappeared. Another figure had taken his place.

Shakti gasped as her vision cleared. This was the man from before. The beautiful one, with glossy black hair, the charming smile, and the golden circlet that mirrored Adil's.

'Who are you?' she asked him.

The man smiled in response and shook his head. 'You are not . . . connected,' he said. '. . . must ask Ashoka . . . wisdom of past rulers . . . first . . .'

His voice broke with every word, becoming disjointed and faded the more he spoke. Shakti frowned, unable to understand.

'Ashoka . . .' he told her. 'Ask . . .'

'Prince Ashoka?' Shakti was confused. What would the young prince know about The Collective? She made to ask this mysterious man about his cryptic remarks, but he had disappeared altogether. Only his deep, husky voice remained in her mind:

Ashoka.

Ashoka.

Ashoka.

*

Shakti felt warmth again.

The moment the mysterious man vanished, the real world appeared. She looked down at her feet. The ash-grey ectoplasm surrounding her started to retreat. Gentle like a baby's breath, it swished upward, releasing itself from her legs, then torso, then head, until the jaw of the tiger snapped back into its original position. The extended neck shortened, and the tiger became visible again.

Ask Ashoka.

She had heard of him, the youngest prince, from both travelling merchants from the Golden City and from Adil himself. Merchants dubbed him to be soft, and from the way Adil had described his son, the rumours were likely true. Yet, how was Prince Ashoka Maurya the answer to her problems?

'Shakti!'

Nayani's voice shook her out of her trance. Carefully, she took a few steps back from the tiger and bowed deeply.

'*Thank you, Great Spirit,*' she said. '*You have my gratitude.*'

As Nayani followed her bow, the gentle beast let out a deep, satisfied roar. It made the ground vibrate; the tree leaves tremble. '*I wish you luck, little witches,*' it replied. A gold glow emitted from its body as it turned from them and walked away. Where it stepped, moss grew, and when it removed its foot, the moss disappeared. Quietly, they watched it disappear into the forest, until the pleasant warmth that surrounded them a moment ago disappeared entirely and the usual humidity took over once more.

'Did you see him? Emperor Adil?' were the first words out of Nayani's mouth. 'You seized up for a few minutes.'

Pursing her lips, Shakti looked away. She was still trying to decode the unknown royal's words, but the mere mention of Adil brought an unpleasant taste to her tongue.

'He was present, and as unhelpful as I remembered him to be,' she said.

Eyeing her like she was an illness, Nayani furrowed her brows. 'I know the spirit told you to decide what kind of power this was,' she began, 'but is this not something cursed? To have that monster's consciousness in your head is cruelty.'

Yes. Too late, Shakti realized that she had forgotten to ask the Great Spirit *why. How.* Arguably the most crucial set of questions, and in her haste to make sense of herself, she'd forgotten. No matter, she didn't need to know the how if she didn't want to keep this ability.

'He couldn't – *wouldn't* – tell me if there was a way to get this blasted added consciousness out of my head,' she told Nayani. 'The other man, though . . . I saw him again. He – he asked me to speak to Ashoka.'

'The prince?' She wasn't alone. Nayani's line of thinking was the same as hers. 'He's as young as you are, isn't he? What could he possibly know?'

Another idea was hatching in Shakti's mind, itching to be birthed. 'I'm not sure,' she said as smoothly as she could, 'but I need to find him to get my answer.'

She saw Nayani still. Saw the few seconds it took for her to chew over what she had said. Visible confusion came first, followed by horrific realization.

'*Find* him?' she echoed. 'You don't mean—'

'I do,' Shakti interrupted her, firm but gentle. 'I'm going to travel to the Golden City, find my way into the palace, and then speak to the prince.'

It looked as if Nayani wanted to induce Shakti back into a comatose state herself. 'This is the same prince whose father killed our families.' The tone was flat. Dubious. Judgemental.

'Haven't you heard the stories?' Shakti added. 'He is said to be quite unlike his father. Some say a mayakari sympathizer.'

Both knew that she was hedging her bets on the tales of merchants, which could range from the exact truth to a complete and utter lie. 'I have nothing left, Nayani,' Shakti pressed. 'My only family is dead. Our village is gone. It's all Emperor Adil's fault and now he's stuck inside my head. I want him out.'

'Do you realize what you are risking?' Nayani asked softly.

Her future. Her life. But there was no use in living a future where she would be stuck with a tyrant emperor. It was an insult to her existence, to Jaya's existence. To any mayakari's existence.

Impassive eyes stared back at her when she asked, 'Come with me. Help me. They killed your mother; they killed our people. It may not be the justice that is good and righteous, but it is the justice that Adil deserves. If you ever had a fire, this is not the time to lose it.'

She'd struck a nerve. 'It was never lost,' Nayani said, lips thinning. 'Did my mother mention why I left for Taksila? Why I rarely visit her?'

From memory, Dharvi hadn't. She'd remained uncharacteristically tight-lipped and chagrined whenever Shakti asked after her daughter. When she shook her head, Nayani sighed.

'I'm part of their resistance,' she replied. 'We . . . fight back against the governor there.'

Fight? With weapons, curses, or both?

Nayani seemed to read her thoughts. 'Not in the way you imagine,' she clarified. 'The governor there is insistent on destroying the wild forests. We don't harm the way soldiers do, but we cause minor disturbances with the help of minor spirits to protect the land and ourselves. Though I can't say that the younger mayakari don't dream of picking up swords and cursing him to death. The older generations preach peace, but when you grow up persecuted, there's only so long you can abide by the code.'

For once, Shakti didn't feel alone. Others shared her fury then, too.

'Then, will you help me?' she asked again.

An excruciating pause followed. Shakti felt as if she lived through seven lives before Nayani finally answered.

'Fortunately for you, I might be able to,' the mayakari replied. 'But if you want to find your answers, you must act without rousing suspicion in the palace.'

Even the furthest reaches of the Ran Empire knew of the great palace that belonged to the Maurya clan. From what she had heard, it was a towering white beast of a structure built atop a hill, almost devoid of nature – a nightmare for a mayakari.

'How do I find a way into the palace, then?' Shakti asked Nayani.

'Easily enough, I hope,' she replied. 'I know someone who can let you in.'

CHAPTER TWELVE
Ashoka

CONSUL RANGANA, THE PALACE'S OFFICIAL SCRIBE, STOOD in front of Ashoka's family in the throne room. 'The reading of Emperor Adil Maurya's will shall now begin.'

Lifting a hand to his forehead, Ashoka felt the phantom graininess of ashes and dirt on his skin. The funeral procession was well and truly over; the pressure in his chest was relieved. He'd bathed himself immediately after they had returned, scrubbing desperately at his body and his forehead like a madman attempting to rid himself of an uncontrollable fever.

'Please, Rangana – omit the granting of material possessions,' Empress Manali ordered with a wave of her hand. She sat on the Obsidian Throne with a rigid posture. 'I know Adil enough to know that he favoured granting power over possessions, and that is what I wish to know instead.'

Ashoka raised an eyebrow at his mother's bluntness. Lounging beside him on the steps beneath the throne, Aarya straightened up with interest.

Rangana cleared her throat. 'Very well, Your Highness,' she said before opening the scroll with gentle movements. Ashoka and his family were silent as they waited for her to speak.

'I, Adil Maurya of the Maurya dynasty, hereby decree my will as thus. Upon my death, I grant Arush Maurya, my first-born son, the throne of the Ran Empire. As written by the ancient laws, you shall be crowned emperor. The lands, both conquered and to-be conquered, are yours.'

Ashoka did not even flinch at this proclamation. The eldest inherited the land and the power first, after all. Briefly, he wondered then, what had changed. His father had altered it for a third time a few years ago and he remembered hearing of yet another stifled argument with their mother about it.

'To my wife, Manali, I grant you the power to continue as the acting regent prior to the coronation of Arush Maurya, acting in the best interest of myself and the empire. Your ways may be far removed from mine; however, your strength and judgement have earned my respect.

'To my golden daughter Aarya, I assign you control of the empire's armed forces as their leading general. Your cunningness renders you fit to lead the nation's finest men and women under the guidance of your brother. Furthermore, if Arush is deemed unable to rule, you are given the crown to assume the role of empress as the second-in-line to the throne.'

Ashoka was next. He waited with bated breath to see what was to be assigned or taken away from him.

Rangana's voice sounded unsure. 'To . . . Prince Ashoka,' she paused for a moment, eyes scanning the page as if making sure the will was written correctly, 'I command thus: shadow your elder siblings as they assume their positions of power in the royal court. Learn the makings of a good ruler. You will then be sent to govern Taksila to prove your worth. Attempt your ways of peace talks if you must but know that you will soon find my teachings to be true: to maintain control, blood must be spilled. My hope is that you return understanding my desire to eradicate the witches entirely.

'As the rightful sovereign, I, Emperor Adil Maurya, decree my will as written.'

There was a stunned silence after Rangana read out Adil's final line. Ashoka sensed his hands unconsciously clench. He felt everything and nothing all at once. His father had shot him with a metaphorical arrow to the heart while he already lay bleeding on the ground.

There was no mention of him being third-in-line to the throne. Surely, it was a mistake. Both his siblings had their succession mentioned except for him. Even his participation in the council hadn't been allowed, only the chance to shadow.

That meant *nothing*.

'Shadow the siblings? Govern Taksila?' Manali echoed, looking startled. 'Are you sure, Rangana? Ashoka cannot be the only child being ordered to govern, not when Aarya is yet to do so herself?'

'I do not make mistakes, Your Highness,' Rangana said firmly. 'What I have read out is what has been written by Emperor Adil.'

Even Aarya seemed mildly put out. 'No year of governorship?' she said aloud to the silent group. 'What a shame.'

'I too am unsure of certain . . . peculiarities regarding the emperor's will,' Rangana said, eyes flitting towards Ashoka for a moment. 'I understand your concerns, but the laws dictate that the will must be executed at the time of death, despite the circumstances.'

Ashoka did not understand it. Where was his acknowledgement of succession? And why had his father asked him to govern Taksila?

Ashoka knew of the infamous capital in the state of Satva. It had been one of his father's most arduous conquests. Originally a hub for mayakari to gather and provide their assistance to its people, the city overlooked a vast forestland rich in ironwood and iron ore and housed a considerable number of Great Spirits, who now, due to the destruction of their forest for materials, continuously razed the city. They had ravaged the area for years following its annexation.

Karma, really.

Taksila was also the first city to have a resistance of both mayakari and civilians who operated against his father. Ashoka had been too young to know what truly happened in Taksila, but

Adil had eviscerated much of the mayakari population within months. Whatever way the witches fought had not been enough. Without their advice, soldiers plundered forestland without proper rites, causing the Great Spirits to retaliate in anger. Even now, pockets of the resistance remained, causing minor troubles for the current governor.

Not once had his father attempted to rectify the situation in Taksila. Or perhaps, he couldn't.

As far as Ashoka knew, the situation in Taksila remained complicated. Why on earth, then, would his father have thought his youngest son would fare any better than a seasoned governor?

The answer came like lightning: *he didn't.* The only way his father had maintained relative stability over the area was by quelling dissent from the mayakari and their sympathizers, and largely ignoring the razing of land. Not even the elected governor had been able to stop the spirits in the several years that he had been appointed. His father was only commanding Ashoka to govern so that he was forced to use brutal tactics. So that his idealism could be tempered.

How unbelievably cruel.

'May I read it?' he asked as Aarya continued to complain about the absence of a governorship. He did not doubt Rangana's literacy, but he wanted to see the will for himself. The consul's posture stiffened, and she cast a questioning look towards his mother, who nodded her assent. Gently, she handed him the will.

Tuning out the noise in the room, Ashoka read his father's will. He recognized the clear and sharp handwriting in a heartbeat and, almost immediately, he noticed a glaring disparity in his father's writing.

In his last written will, Emperor Adil had referred to his children as *my first-born son Arush, my golden daughter Aarya.* And yet, Ashoka's name was written without any form of endearment. It was written simply as: *Ashoka.* Beside it, as the consul had read out, was the order to govern Taksila without a mention of his being third-in-line to the throne. Godlike fury spiralled into him, working its way into his head, twisting into the deep trenches of his heart.

'Did father hate me that much?' Ashoka asked bluntly, turning to his mother. 'Why am I not mentioned as the third successor?'

'Ashoka,' Arush warned. 'Calm yourself.'

'Your father didn't hate you, my dear,' his mother's voice was soft as she answered him. 'You frustrated each other, yes, but he didn't hate you. You are his child.'

An untruth. 'Children aren't always loved.'

'And your cynicism is not always appreciated,' his mother replied. 'It is likely a mistake, Ashoka. It was the third amendment your father made. Perhaps he simply forgot.'

Ashoka bristled. 'He can't *forget* that I'm third-in-line to the throne. He can't ask me and *only* me to govern Taksila as if he wants me to fail. Why would he do this to me?'

His mother sighed. 'Ashoka, he was a complicated man,' she said half-heartedly.

'*Mother!*' Ashoka found himself practically shouting. Empress Manali appeared visibly shocked by his sudden outburst. His siblings fell silent, amazed too at the anger in his voice. It was the first time he had raised his voice towards their mother, and it wracked him with guilt to do so. 'Can you stop defending his actions, just for once?'

Her silence was all he needed for an answer.

'Ashoka,' his mother said again, a note of grief tingeing her voice. 'You do not understand.'

'Then *make* me understand!'

More silence.

Enraged, Ashoka threw the scroll onto the ground, watching his mother flinch as it hit the floor. Aarya made a sound of disdain and barked out an order for the consul to retrieve the fallen scroll.

Ashoka watched with wary eyes as Aarya turned to him. The clean, precise lines of kohl around her eyes made her seem more catlike than ever. 'Stop being a child,' she said. Beside her, Arush nodded in agreement.

Ashoka found that at that moment, he simply did not care. He let himself relish in his father's death, thankful that the man who once sat upon the throne of the Ran Empire was gone.

Arush's voice held a note of pity. 'Taksila, little brother,' he said. 'I wish you luck. If your governorship fails, I won't be surprised.'

'Arush!' their mother scolded.

'What?' his brother shrugged in response. 'I am not blaming Ashoka. If father could not fix it, I do not expect him to, either.'

His mother gazed at Ashoka with beseeching eyes. 'You don't *have* to go, my dear,' she said. 'Shadow your siblings until you feel comfortable enough to leave.'

Perhaps his mother had a fledgling suspicion that he would fail, too.

He thought of his father. Of how he had been so insistent that he learn his ways of brutality. Funnily enough, his father had cared enough to try to force him down a bloodied path to victory.

Glancing at his siblings, Ashoka realized that he had no interest in shadowing them in their newly instated roles. They were akin to ducklings taking to water for the first time: unsure and hasty, poised to make decisions based on emotion rather than logic. There was no sense in watching them blunder about like fools.

His family glanced at him with sympathetic eyes, even Consul Rangana, and he hated it. Before he had even stepped foot into the blasted city, they had made their minds up. Ashoka clenched his fists.

His father was wrong. He *could* govern without force or death. He *could* rely on peace talks and politics. And when he returned, he would ask for more than mere observation.

He wanted the chance to lead.

'I will do as father says, mother,' he said loudly. 'I will govern Taksila.'

Not just govern. The final thought he did not say aloud to his family. Under his governorship, he could make sure the mayakari remaining in Taksila would be protected. Safe. With Arush, he knew he could evade any consequences with more ease than if it had been their father still on the throne.

This can be good, he realized. *I can safeguard innocent lives.*

At his announcement, his mother's eyes widened. Aarya's mouth fell open. Even Arush appeared mildly impressed.

'But Emperor Adil's will stated that—' Rangana began, but Arush cut her off politely.

'I don't believe that Ashoka needs to shadow us first,' he said, shooting Ashoka a sardonic smile. 'If he wants to make a fool of himself in Taksila, I say we let him.'

Ashoka rolled his eyes despite the backhanded agreement. Their mother still appeared unwilling. He reached out his hand to clasp hers that gripped the throne. 'Let me go, mother,' he said quietly.

'You're still a child,' his mother whispered. 'You're all still *children*.'

Every one of them knew it. However, a ruling monarch's final will had to be followed. There was no refuting it.

'I think we are well beyond being children now, mother,' Arush said in gentle tones.

Empress Manali closed her eyes. Took a deep breath. She was silent for a long time until she opened them again. Ashoka's heart lifted when he saw her wide eyes drowning in resignation.

'All right, Ashoka,' she said, nodding her head in agreement. 'You have your wish. You will travel to Taksila.'

From his place upon the steps, Arush stood up and appraised the room coolly. 'Well, now that this matter is settled, let us begin preparations for my coronation,' he remarked. A euphoric grin was plastered across his lips. 'Let the people greet their new emperor.'

CHAPTER THIRTEEN

Shakti

IT TOOK SHAKTI AND NAYANI NEARLY THREE DAYS TO arrive at the capital by riverboat. The Samnal River was the major body of water that ran through the continent, used for fast travel by commoner and royal alike. They'd replenished their food when their chartered boat anchored at a stopover town for one night, but Shakti's stomach was still rumbling when it made a final stop on the docks outside the walls of the Golden City.

Shakti had never seen the capital, only heard of it. It lay sandwiched between two mountains inland, with the west looking out over the Odhi Ocean that the Samnal River eventually emptied into. The northern mountain was where the royal palace was built, with the infamous Mountain of Rebirth lying on the southernmost point.

Dead centre of the city was said to be the Imperial Gardens, commissioned by the first Maurya emperor, Ashoka. Thought to be the first and last of his name until the young Prince Ashoka was born to Emperor Adil, he'd ordered a breath-taking natural wonderland to be built in homage to the mayakari and Great Spirits.

In this day and age, Shakti was surprised to hear that it was still standing.

The descriptions she had heard of the Golden City didn't do it justice though. Once they left the busy docks and entered through the southern wall, she didn't expect such a hubbub of bright colours and deafening noises. People hustled about, bartering at markets, putting on stage displays for children or carting stock from vendor to vendor. As they passed by a merchant selling skewered roasted chicken coated in a mixture of spices, Shakti's stomach rumbled again.

As if she had heard her thoughts, Nayani – who was leading them decisively through the crowded streets – turned her head. 'We have no time to stop, Shakti,' she said. 'You can eat later.'

The two passed through winding alleyways, superbly tiled buildings with glass domes and intricate mosaics, bridges built from dark brown Na wood that crossed over small riverways, and a menagerie of shops selling everything from soft gold to counterfeit pearls. Almost every nook and cranny was covered with white cloth of various makes: cotton, canvas, silk, linen, and cashmere. Remnants of a grand funeral, Shakti realized, likely for the emperor. In the huge maze that was the Golden City, she felt very small indeed.

In the distance, she could easily spot the blinding white palace that sat atop the mountain. A straight stone-paved road cut through the centre of the city up to the royal palace. Nayani had said that between the mountain base and the palace were three thousand steps and a separate upward sloping road paved with granite. Those who made the journey by foot tended to take the former method of transportation, while carts and horses took the latter route.

Shakti scowled as they passed by a mural of Emperor Adil that had been painted in chalk along the outer walls of a house. Flowers and tealight candles were laid in front of it. Someone had written along the wall in hasty script: GLORIOUS EMPEROR FELLED BY MAGIC; YOUR DEATH WILL NOT BE IN VAIN.

'The emperor dies and it's a tragedy,' Shakti said, glowering, 'while our people die and we're nothing but a statistic. A plague.'

Leaning close to her, Nayani pinched her arm. 'We're not just a plague now,' she whispered. 'Did you not see the signs in front of the eateries; do you not hear the whispers? The people know that he died by mayakari magic. We're the enemy.'

Shakti felt sick. Word truly travelled like wildfire.

There were already no favourable impressions of mayakari here, and the knowledge that the emperor died from magic meant that the rage against them would only intensify. This was all her fault. Vengeance praised her but recklessness punished her.

As they passed through the streets, Shakti made note of various prints plastered on walls and windows. They were very similar in their makeup. All had a woman – either young or old – painted with bug-like eyes framed by delicate lashes, burgundy lips, and ridiculously long painted nails. Spirits and grey shadows hovered around them. The drawings were made to look beautiful but dangerous, interesting but unsettling. These women's mouths were usually open wide, curlicue letters in a free space stating: A CURSE ON YOU! A CURSE ON THOSE YOU LOVE! Others had similar instructions or threats: MY SPIRITS ARE MY ARMY, or NONE CAN HELP YOU WITH A MAYAKARI LOOSE – REPORT SIGHTINGS TO THE RELEVANT AUTHORITIES IMMEDIATELY.

Report sightings. Hah. There was only one way that a mayakari could be identified without being burn-tested, and that was if they were to use any of their abilities openly. No mayakari in the Golden City, or even the empire, would be foolish enough to take such a risk. Though, she supposed, there were more incidental ways of being discovered. Minor spirits, for one, had the tendency to gravitate to or seek out mayakari and follow them around. There was never any malicious intent behind their actions, only innocent and simple ones. Sometimes, the little spirits simply wanted to chatter. Then, there were the baseless accusations. Anyone could just accuse, and the suspect be burn-tested for grievously petty reasons. She wondered how many human women wandered the streets with burns that never recovered.

It took perhaps another hour of walking until Nayani stopped in front of a small, nondescript brick house in a modest residential area. Two stone animals stood at either side of the doorway: a winged serpent and a leopard, their faces worn from weather and age.

Nayani rapped sharply on the door, stepping back to whisper in Shakti's ear, 'Follow along, all right?'

As Shakti nodded, the wooden door swung open to reveal a middle-aged woman dressed in a forest-green sari. Her curly hair was piled neatly on top of her head and her face was bare. She looked to be around her aunt's age. Shakti noted with a lurch that the woman also wore a *nula* around her wrist– a white thread to commemorate an almsgiving.

The woman's eyes narrowed in confusion as her eyes first sought Shakti's before widening in recognition when she saw Nayani.

Nayani's face was a picture of relief and nervousness as she smiled at the woman. 'Ruchira,' she greeted. 'It has been a long time.'

'*Nayani?*' Ruchira's tone was one of pure disbelief. 'What on earth are you doing in the city? Come in, come in – both of you.' She ushered them inside, patting their shoulders as they passed, giving Nayani an additional smack on the back of her neck as she did so.

The smell of burning incense assaulted Shakti's senses the moment she stepped into the room. Her mind harkened back to its scent smothering the temples, mingling with the sweetness of decorative flowers. She coughed, trying to dispel the sudden burning sensation in her throat.

'My apologies,' Ruchira said. 'Admittedly, I have burned more incense than I had planned to.'

Shakti waved away Ruchira's apology. 'That's all right,' she said. 'Sorry to disturb you. My name is Shakti. I am a friend of Nayani's, from Kolakola.'

'Ruchira is one of the palace cooks,' Nayani informed Shakti. 'She makes an excellent curried carp.'

'Ah.' Ruchira observed her for a moment. 'A mayakari as well, I gather?'

'I—' Startled by the woman's frankness, Shakti could only nod, shooting Nayani a furtive glance.

'Ruchira is a friend of my mother's,' Nayani replied. 'She knows what I am. Don't worry.'

'Oh yes, I'm no accuser, but I must ask what the two of you are doing here?' Ruchira asked. 'The *capital* of all places – tensions are high enough as is after the emperor's death.'

'Shakti and I fled Kolakola after Emperor Adil murdered our families and burned the town to the ground,' Nayani replied, glowering.

Ruchira appeared taken aback. 'You were in Kolakola? Last I heard from your mother, she told me that you were in Taksila,' she remarked before her expression turned into an apologetic one. 'About Dharvi, my dear, I'm so s—'

'Please don't,' Nayani interrupted flatly. 'My mother will have a good rebirth – that is the only thing that pacifies me, though I cannot say the same for Emperor Adil. Thank the spirits he is dead.'

Ruchira's eyes widened. 'Not here!' she hissed, her eyes flashing towards the half-open windows. 'Never speak ill of the emperor here.'

'It is no lie,' Nayani muttered, more quietly this time. 'Is that who you are burning incense for, Ruchira? For that depraved killer?'

Ruchira lowered her eyes. 'For him, but also for those who had their lives taken there. Innocent women never deserve death, but Emperor Adil was still the nation's monarch. You know, his funeral procession passed by a few days ago. The royal court made it known to the public that the mayakari were to be blamed, and the rage that followed was . . . terrifying. A great many women were burn-tested without tangible evidence. Accusations were flying left and right, as if finding and burning more mayakari would avenge the emperor's death. If a mayakari was living here before, they have to take great care in not rousing suspicion for themselves.'

'Greater,' Shakti corrected. When Ruchira glanced at her in confusion, she added, 'they have to take greater care than before.'

A sad smile flitted across the cook's face. 'And who did you lose, my dear?' she asked quietly.

'My aunt,' Shakti replied.

'Listen, Ruchira, I came to ask a favour of you,' Nayani said carefully. 'Something I hear you've done before.'

Ruchira stared at her for a moment. 'Anything within reason, I can do.'

Seemingly satisfied by her answer, Nayani grinned. 'Good,' she said and nudged Shakti forward. 'Are you able to find my friend Shakti a job in the palace? Perhaps as a kitchenhand, or a maid-servant? She has no place to go, and no way to earn a living wage.'

The true purpose of her employment would remain a secret between them. No one else needed to know. Shakti couldn't risk a slip of the tongue turning into a rumour that would cost her life.

At first, Ruchira said nothing. Then, she carefully made her way towards the half-open windows and shut them. Once the latch was fastened, she turned to them with an incredulous stare.

'There's already one mayakari in the palace,' she said. 'It'd be a risk making it two.'

Shakti perked her head up in interest. *Another mayakari?* 'Then why work there at all?'

'Because it'd be the last place Emperor Adil would think to look,' Ruchira replied. 'What kind of mayakari would actively put herself in such danger? And imagine having to burn-test half the palace staff – no woman would work there if they did.'

Shakti put on her best doe-eyed, pleading expression and aimed it at Ruchira. 'Then please help me, Ruchira. I have nowhere else to go.'

Pinching the bridge of her nose, Ruchira sighed. 'At least Harini will have a friend . . .' she heard her mutter. That must be the other mayakari. 'Are you skilled in any particular field, Shakti?'

Archery, Shakti thought wryly. *Combat*. Instead, she informed an expectant Ruchira of her middling sewing, cleaning, and animal-rearing skills. She figured that the palace would have its fair share of creatures bred for battle, and being around them rather than people would allow for a welcome reprieve.

'You may be able to find work in the stables,' Ruchira sounded satisfied with her answers. 'Not many people enjoy being in the vicinity of leopards and winged serpents.'

'It's settled, then,' Nayani said as she shot Shakti a knowing look. 'I will take my leave.'

Shakti frowned. 'So soon?' she asked her.

Ruchira reached out a hand to cup Nayani's chin. 'If you ever need a haven, remember that you have one here,' she said quietly. The gesture reminded Shakti of Jaya. Everything loving and motherly did.

A small smile found its way across Nayani's lips as she stepped back.

'Your kindness is much appreciated,' she told Ruchira before heading for the door. 'My part is done, Shakti. I hope you . . . find what you need.'

'Wait!' Shakti exclaimed. 'Nayani, please. You should rest before you leave.'

Nayani turned. Dropped her voice to a whisper. 'I won't stay the night in this hateful city,' she said, her voice sad and urgent. 'I'm returning to Taksila.'

The resistance. 'Be safe,' Shakti replied. 'You're risking your life there.'

Nayani's response was brief. 'Coming from you who risked and *continues* to risk her life? That's rich.'

'You could die,' Shakti hissed.

'Perhaps,' Nayani replied, after a minute pause. 'Maybe then I might be reborn as a human, and there will be no need to fear for my life.'

'How depressing,' Shakti said.

Nayani's laugh was melancholy, tinged with blues and greys. 'Oh, I can't believe I almost forgot,' she said with a snap of her fingers. Reaching into her knapsack, she began to sift through it. 'I thought I packed it – here.'

Shakti's vision tunnelled as Nayani fished out an achingly familiar emerald attached to a thin gold chain. Suddenly, she couldn't breathe, couldn't move, couldn't *think*. For a second, she thought she was hallucinating.

'Is that . . .' she choked on the last few words, unable to get them out. Nayani's answering smile was as sepulchral as they came.

'It is,' she confirmed, grabbing Shakti's hands and tilting her palm upwards before dropping the chain onto it. 'I returned to the village before I found you. It . . . it was a mass grave, but I found –' Nayani's breath hitched, '– my mother. Your aunt. The necklace was still attached. The chain is bent, but the emerald is unbroken. I . . . I'm sorry for removing it but I thought there was a chance that you may have survived.'

Shakti just stared at her.

'Shakti?' The mayakari waved her hands in front of her face. 'I haven't broken you, have I?'

'No,' Shakti said hoarsely before she launched herself at Nayani, embracing her in an iron grip. 'Thank you.'

Nayani patted Shakti's hair affectionately. The tears came hot and fast, and before Shakti knew it, her whole face was drenched, her lips tasting the salt of her tears. Letting go of Nayani, Shakti gazed down at the emerald nestled in her palm, felt the weight of her aunt's death in the stone's lustre, and shuddered at the thought of it having touched her burned, crisped skin.

'Thank you,' she whispered.

Nayani only grimaced. 'You should have something to remember her by,' she said before gesturing towards the door. 'I must go now.'

'Nayani,' Shakti said again. She was starting to feel a storm of butterflies brewing in the pit of her stomach at the thought of

Nayani leaving her to her own devices. 'Write to me if you can, please. And promise me that you will stay safe.'

Nayani smiled. 'I will,' she agreed, 'write to me too.'

With a final wave, she turned to leave Shakti alone in a foreign city, with only her dreams of retribution and the voice of Emperor Adil in her head for company.

CHAPTER FOURTEEN
Shakti

Two days later, Shakti made the bothersome trek to the royal palace.

Shakti had rolled her eyes at the sight of the opulent white building visible from the base of the mountain when they reached it. It was too grandiose to exist.

She listened to Ruchira's stories about the palace: its absolute lack of nature, its thirteen jade and lapis pools, its stable of pure-bred winged serpents and two hundred sleek black leopards bred for battle. Its uninterrupted views of the wild forests to the north where the elder prince and princess went hunting. The hundred or so ornately decorated rooms, the famous Obsidian Throne and, of course, its five main inhabitants.

Well, four.

'I was able to pull some strings,' Ruchira was saying. 'The head matron will decide where you're rostered. I assume you'll be assigned to the kitchens, or maybe the stables. It's highly unlikely you'll be assigned to the royal children or empress – their staff hardly ever changes.'

Ask Ashoka.

Shakti blinked furiously, banishing the sound of the man's voice from her head. She wondered if she had been thrown a trick or a riddle. From Adil's description of his son, Ashoka wouldn't know about The Collective. So why then had that mysterious man asked her to do the opposite?

She needed to find a way to speak to the youngest prince.

The stark white palace looked imposing from a distance and magnified tenfold once Shakti arrived in front of its gates. They were impressive, hewn from iron and spiralling towards the sky. Guards were stationed every two feet where the gates encompassed, looking stoic and dangerous with their khandas. Master Hasith had made a few of those double-edged straight swords in his forge.

Kolakola seemed so small then, an anthill next to a den of lions.

This palace, this space . . . all for five people, Shakti thought to herself. *Yet there are people who live in squalor, their homes lost due to Emperor Adil's conquests.* Anger wove itself anew in her veins at the thought.

'Come,' Ruchira said and tugged Shakti's hand. 'We must go through the staff entrance.'

Shakti followed Ruchira through the separate entrance, where she was immediately greeted by an expansive central hall that adjoined multiple rooms. A large painting of two black leopards graced one of the stark white walls as the staff bustled in and out of corridors like ants.

Ruchira led Shakti into the main kitchen, where she met the head matron: Avasthi. She was a short, hawklike woman with delicate hands and sharp features.

'Ah, the new girl, I assume,' Avasthi remarked when she saw Shakti lagging behind Ruchira. 'Welcome to the royal palace.'

'Thank you for allowing me to work here,' Shakti replied.

'It wasn't my order,' the woman replied before directing her towards a storage cupboard. 'Here. You will find a suitable uniform inside. You're lucky to get this position, child. Two of my staff have elected to take a period of rest – they are close to birth.'

Immediately after donning her uniform – a long-sleeved black tunic and trousers that covered her ankles – Shakti was sent to weed the area outside the training courtyard. It wasn't as if there was much to remove since plants did not seem to grow here. The sheer lack of greenery was unnerving; if trapped here forever, a mayakari would easily descend into madness. She wondered how the other elusive mayakari withstood it.

The palace was a maze, but she was able to orient herself quickly. Remembering directions was easy for her; it always had been. Behind the main building was where the stables, the training ground, and gardens were situated. During her trek, she found herself in a large, fenced area with low roofs. Other than the training courtyard, this was the only other part of the palace with a hint of greenery.

As she approached the area inspecting for pesky weeds to pull out, Shakti heard a chorus of loud snores coming from the stables and she came closer. The sudden flash of a long black tail swishing over a wooden gate made her gasp.

Holding onto the basket she had been provided with, which contained a multitude of shears, Shakti made her way into the shaded stables. She fought hard to contain the excited squeal that threatened to erupt from her mouth when she entered. All she could hear were the contented purrs and snores of a dozen or so giant leopards, ranged in various shades of black.

They were quite curious – docile, even – as she approached the one closest to her. Unlike the rest, it was awake. Wide eyes held irises that were a shocking green as it appraised her slowly before padding over and hanging its head over the gate.

'Hello,' Shakti said softly, reaching up to rub the underside of its silky soft jaw.

The giant leopard's eyes closed contentedly as she petted it. *What a beautiful animal.* Shame, though, that these creatures were bred for battle. They were innocents that did not deserve to partake in the conflicts that humans created for themselves.

She was so enamoured by the creature that she almost didn't hear the heavy thud of paws to her right. Turning, she saw two giant leopards standing side by side, watching her. Sitting atop them were two young men, their heads obscured by deep brown cloaks. They too, assessed her curiously.

The one saddled on the smaller leopard pointed to her basket. 'I wouldn't advise trying to shear them with gardening tools,' he pointed out.

Shakti flushed and stepped away from the leopard. 'I was only petting them,' she said.

'My apologies,' the young man replied. 'I assumed you were in want of a quick death.' With the grace of a dancer, he swung himself off the leopard and rubbed its neck fondly.

'If I wanted a quick death, I would have sliced my own head off,' Shakti said before wincing. What an unpleasant way to start a conversation, and with palace staff, no less.

Oddly enough, the young man chuckled as if he were amused. She couldn't observe him properly as the hood of the cloak draped over his hair and forehead, but she noticed the doe eyes, pouting lips and sharp jaw beneath. 'How direct,' he replied.

'Better than bleeding out on the floor after a leopard tears your abdomen into strips,' she said.

'You do raise a point,' he mused.

They were stableboys, perhaps. Or not, she amended as the taller one hopped off his leopard and removed his cloak. He was ridiculously handsome, with brown skin and shoulder-length black hair half-tied behind his head. Strapped to his back were a pair of vicious dual broadswords, and she was quite sure stableboys didn't saunter around with weapons of this size by their side. He was dressed in plain clothes, but his rigid posture and muscular frame were easily discernible. He looked trained.

Still, she couldn't help herself. 'Are you both stableboys?' she asked.

The young man with the dual swords frowned at her question. He opened his mouth as if he were about to reprimand her but was stopped by the boy with the bright doe-like eyes who placed a hand around his wrist. With a mischievous smile, he turned to Shakti.

'Not quite. My friend here is a soldier,' he told her. 'He was granted a day of rest, you see, so we paid a visit to the city markets. He tried bartering but failed. Quite miserably, too.'

'I hope you didn't buy anything valuable,' she told him. 'Jewels are sold for more than what they're worth in the city, I hear.'

The doe-eyed boy turned to his friend. 'See, I *told* you that lapis was too expensive,' he complained.

The soldier rolled his eyes. 'How was I supposed to know that?' he countered. 'Do you want to keep the present or not? Otherwise, I'll throw it away.'

'No, I'll guard it with my life.' The young man pushed back his cloak, revealing close-cropped black hair and a near-flawless face that radiated a boyish charm. The only imperfection on him was a notable burn on the left ear that left it a dark, puckered pink. Then, he turned his attention to her.

'Are you new?' he asked. 'I don't recall seeing your face anywhere.'

'I started working at the palace today,' she told him, 'but as you can see, I got distracted.'

'Ah.' Something close to understanding dawned on the taller boy's features, and he grinned. Whatever tension she had seen in him vanished. 'What's your name?'

'Shakti,' she replied, finding his slow smile oddly endearing.

'Shakti,' he repeated. 'It's a pleasure to meet you. My name is Rahil. I guard Prince Ashoka.'

Shakti stilled, wondering if she had heard him incorrectly. 'Prince Ashoka?' she repeated. 'That's quite an honour.'

Before she could ask the other young man his name and status, he nudged Rahil with a smile. 'The greatest of honours, wouldn't you agree, Rahil?'

The scoff that Rahil let out held no malice. Rather, it was fond. Shakti studied him for a moment. 'You must be well trained, then,' she said. 'I'd be quite poor in comparison.'

The comment slipped out without much thought. It had been an offhand remark, but Rahil pounced onto it immediately.

'You can fight?' He looked impressed. 'Who taught you? Where did you grow up?'

'Mathura,' she said. It was the empire's largest state five days' journey from the capital, famous for its weapons-makers and weapons-masters – Hasith included. 'A . . . friend taught me how to fight.'

'Which weapons are you trained in?' Rahil asked. He seemed genuinely interested in her background, which only served to confuse her. Meanwhile, his friend shook his head, muttering, 'Now you've got him started,' loud enough for both to hear.

'The bow and arrow,' she confessed. No sense in fabricating a lie. 'Although I can handle a sword quite well.'

A glint appeared in Rahil's brown eyes. 'Show me,' he said.

Taken aback, Shakti could only stare at him, flabbergasted. 'Excuse me?'

'Show me,' he repeated before unsheathing one of the broadswords on his back. 'Here, use my sword. It won't be well-adapted to you, but I want to see what you're capable of.'

'What on earth for?'

'It's not often that we have palace staff who know how to wield weaponry,' Rahil replied. 'Will you spar with me or not?'

'I suggest you don't,' his friend told her.

For Shakti, his words were a challenge to be accepted. A grin made its way across her face as she took Rahil's broadsword, a magnificent weapon with a name engraved on its blade: *Indran.*

'My father's,' Rahil said as he watched her read the inscription. 'One of the few things of his I'd rather keep.'

'It's beautiful,' Shakti commented as she traced an arc through the air. 'This must have been specially made.'

'It was,' he said and took out the second broadsword. 'It was made in Mathura, in fact.'

'Are there any rules to this?' she asked him, avoiding any further conversation on Mathura. She only knew the barebones information about the state, and any further interrogation would reveal her lies immediately.

'No killing and no serious bodily harm seem fair,' Rahil said calmly and gestured for them to head outside. Shakti nodded her assent and followed. That was easy enough. Besides, she didn't want to be known for harming the prince's guard on her first day at the palace.

His friend trailed behind them. 'Good luck,' he told her. 'Stay alert.' Then, he retreated beneath the shade of the stable. She watched Rahil track him before turning his attention to her.

Shakti stepped back, as did Rahil, circling each other like vultures around a carcass. She was studying him, and he in turn was studying her. Arrogance told her that years of Master Hasith's training would serve her well, perhaps even better.

It took only a split second before Rahil made the first move.

Shakti's pride took an immediate battering when she found Rahil to be a menace. With strength, speed, and agility at godlike levels, he whirled, sliced, and jabbed, hellbent on destruction like an enraged Great Spirit. She couldn't imagine what havoc he could cause with two swords.

Her best option was defence, but she could only use it for so long. Rahil easily broke through her defensive holds, but she sensed that he was holding back. She could feel the force with which he slammed the blade of his sword against hers, brutal and unyielding, but it always retracted in the last few moments.

'You should attack,' he called out, echoing her own sentiments.

What impressed her most was his demeanour. There was neither a pinched brow nor a clenched jaw in sight. In fact, he was expressionless, and it terrified her beyond belief. Here was the look of a soldier who thought nothing of a kill, who thought of battle as a mere playfight.

It was no wonder that he served a prince, but he would have been fit enough to serve the emperor himself.

Shakti took his advice to heart and shifted her position to an attack. Gripping the sword tightly, she charged, trying to skitter out of the way before Rahil could plunge his sword into her ribcage. She wasn't fast enough.

The tip of his sword sliced a thin line through the material of her clothing and into the outer layer of her skin. Grimacing at the sharp flash of pain, Shakti sidestepped out of the way.

'You're good,' she said, gritting her teeth.

'Of course I am,' he replied. He blocked her second attack like he was slicing through water.

From her periphery, Shakti noticed that a crowd of onlookers had appeared, but she barely paid them any attention. The broadsword started to feel heavy in her hands. Likely sensing her weariness, Rahil took his final blow and aimed a swift kick at her chest that was forceful enough to send her tumbling down.

Time slowed. It was as she fell, half-incensed and half-impressed, that Shakti saw an opening. Just before she felt her back hit the grass, she dropped the sword to her non-dominant hand, catching it neatly by its hilt. Like lightning, she managed to slice through Rahil's free arm cleanly enough for him to recoil. She registered his surprise before he recovered. Then, she was on her back with his sword pointed at her throat.

Shakti lifted a hand up. 'I concede,' she said, panting like a dog on a hot afternoon. Rahil grinned. Retracting his sword, he held up a hand for her to grasp. Her cut traced red rivulets down his arm.

'Colour me impressed,' Rahil said quietly. 'And it seems like I'm not the only one.'

A slow clap descended upon them as she pulled herself back up and glanced around them. The onlookers turned out to be soldiers, dressed in the typical red and black uniform she should've seen on Rahil, who watched with interest.

Two in the crowd stood out in stark contrast to the rest. One was a young woman who appeared to be around Shakti's age, with sharply lined kohl around the eyes and severely burnished cheekbones. The shrewd eyes and haughty countenance that seemed strangely familiar were offset by the soft draping of her purple sari and gold jewellery. Next to her was another young man older than her; a tall, hulking giant who looked like he could snap her in pieces. Dressed in such ostentatious garb, these two could only be—

'Prince Arush. Princess Aarya,' Rahil greeted them with a bow and Shakti followed suit, standing beside him wearily.

No wonder they looked so familiar. Both had inherited at least one feature from Emperor Adil, from his thick brows to the tilt of his smile. It made her want to curse them where they stood.

Rahil's friend had made his way towards the group. The princess noticed him approach and raised an eyebrow. 'Another unannounced trip into the city, little brother?' she asked. 'Mother was worried you'd get lost.'

Mother?

Shakti's heart stopped beating. Eyes widening, she turned her attention to the young man who noticed her burning gaze on him.

'You never asked me who I was,' he said with a sympathetic grin.

Ashoka.

She wouldn't have guessed that he was Adil's son, for the youngest prince appeared the least like his father. But spirits, he was here, right in front of her: the potential answer to her problem.

If only she could ask what she wanted to. Alas, informing him – and subsequently his siblings – of her current predicament would leave her dead.

'My apologies, Prince Ashoka,' she said with a bow. 'I meant no offence.'

'None taken,' the prince replied. 'I should apologize for tricking you.'

Rahil laughed. 'I would hardly call that a trick, Ashoka,' he replied. He addressed the prince without his title, and in front of his family no less, but the royal siblings didn't even flinch. Whatever rapport they had was deeper than that of a prince and his guard. 'It was a deliberate omission at best.'

'Says the one who could not barter for his life.'

Meanwhile, Prince Arush cocked his head at her like a curious puppy but addressed Rahil. 'Training a new guard?' he asked.

'No, Prince Arush,' Rahil said with a bow, 'I was simply inviting

Shakti to spar with me out of curiosity. She is very well trained in weaponry, it seems.'

'*Emperor*,' Arush corrected Rahil immediately.

'Until the official coronation, you're still the prince,' Princess Aarya reprimanded, jabbing her brother's side. As Arush winced, she turned to Shakti with the same sense of self-importance she had seen in Emperor Adil.

'You adapted to Rahil's broadsword quite quickly,' she remarked. A sly grin wormed its way into her lips. 'Where did you come from?'

'Mathura,' Shakti replied.

A moment of awkward silence followed her answer. Shakti spotted Prince Ashoka now fighting to contain a smirk, while the soldiers around him wore expressions of faint horror. Princess Aarya raised an eyebrow.

'Well.' She let out a forced laugh. 'That may be the first time someone has addressed me without a title.'

Too late, Shakti realized her mistake. 'My apologies, Princess Aarya,' she corrected herself. 'My name is Shakti. I hail from Mathura.'

'I gathered,' Princess Aarya said dryly as her neatly lined eyebrows finally descended. 'You fought well, Shakti.'

'Oh,' Shakti muttered, 'it's nothing, really.'

'Nothing? You managed to scratch Rahil,' the princess replied. She sounded impressed. 'Few people can get through him, you know. It's why my little brother is rarely injured.'

'I fight too, you know,' Ashoka muttered. This earned a chuckle from both Arush and Aarya.

'Of course, little brother,' Arush's toothy grin was nothing short of condescending.

Shakti watched them in fascination. The sudden urge to fracture their silly little lives grew from the pit of her stomach, unwarranted. The children were Adil's pride, were they not? As he had so brazenly razed her town and killed her aunt, why not heap a thousand curses upon them in kind?

No, she admonished herself. *You are veering too far into destructive thoughts. Remember why you're here.*

'You're not a soldier?' the princess asked.

'Palace staff, princess,' she replied, shaking her head. 'Ruchira was kind enough to find me work here.'

In her periphery, Shakti saw Prince Ashoka still. Worry spiked her heart rate; had she said something wrong?

That, or she was irrationally anxious.

'General staff?' the princess queried. 'Well, let me relieve you of that job—'

'Shakti was hired as a new addition to *my* staff,' Prince Ashoka interrupted coolly, coming to stand in front of Rahil, 'so there will be no relieving of positions, sister.'

The prince sounded assured. Confident. Meanwhile, Shakti was attempting to conceal her shock.

His staff? What on earth was happening?

'She can fight,' Princess Aarya replied in disbelief, 'and you're keeping her on as *general staff*?'

'Correct,' said Prince Ashoka. 'This little revelation was simply a happy surprise.'

'Don't contest him,' Rahil whispered to her as the Maurya siblings argued. Shakti made to argue but was stopped by his beseeching gaze. 'Just agree.'

Well.

Getting on the prince's good side wouldn't hurt. Shakti wracked her brains, wondering what she'd said to trigger him into an argument with his sister. She came up short.

Princess Aarya turned to her. 'Would you prefer to clean linens for Ashoka, or fight, Shakti?' she asked, ignoring Prince Ashoka's protests.

Shakti almost blurted out *fight*. However, Rahil's order made her rethink. Logically, her best bet would be to go along with Prince Ashoka. Agreeing with whatever Princess Aarya had in mind was risky.

Out of the two of them, only one was known as a mayakari sympathizer.

'I was brought in to aid Prince Ashoka,' she replied, watching the tension dissipate from the young prince's shoulders. 'Thank you for your kind offer, but I must decline, princess. I'm happy to clean his linens for several decades, if need be.'

CHAPTER FIFTEEN
Shakti

WHEN GRANTED A DAY OF REST, SHAKTI CHOSE TO wander the Golden City by herself. She could have asked for company; she'd finally met the other mayakari working under Prince Ashoka – Harini. A nice, well-mannered young girl, but Shakti wanted to be alone.

She left the palace at mid-morning, traversing the steep down-hill path from the palace to the capital. The walk was ridiculously long, but she supposed that invaders would also have a difficult time attempting to reach the top. A disadvantage for the masses but an advantage for defensive purposes, at least.

Coins jingled in the drawstring purse she kept in her satchel as she reached the base, winded. Her destination was the Imperial Gardens in the city centre which, if travelling by foot, would take a good two hours. To avoid an arduous trip, Shakti hailed a horse and cart driven by a gruff but friendly vendor heading in the same direction.

Market stalls upon market stalls materialized as they neared the central business district. Noise, too, increased to a consistent, loud buzz. Crowds wandered around like those in an ant colony. Flute music drifted from a nearby travellers' inn, melodic and sharp. Around her, the people of the Golden City were also setting up for Prince Arush's coronation in two days' time. Banners were hung, leopard masks sat in piles next to stalls, and chalk murals decorated walls. Official signs bearing the date of his crowning obscured noticeboards.

An acute metallic taste coated Shakti's tongue. She'd bitten the inside of her lip hard enough to bleed. All this fanfare for a young man who would continue to perpetuate a cycle of violence. The world was deeply, cruelly unfair.

Her mood shifted when she spotted the towering figure of a Na tree coming into view. The Imperial Gardens were close by. Tipping the vendor, Shakti hopped off the cart and merged into the crowd eagerly. Even after a few days spent in the nature-less palace, she had felt her energy diminish and needed a reprieve.

Inspired by the infamous Mountain of Rebirth, the gardens were a testament to its architect. A circular stone wall enclosed them from the outside. Flowers of every colour imaginable dotted the grass and hung like lanterns from wooden lattices and bronze poles. Native Hora trees provided shade to visitors. White stone gazebos with their domes studded in gemstones looked out into a manmade lake, in the centre of which stood the largest statue of a leopard that had been constructed in the empire. And, unlike those in the Obsidian Throne room, this leopard was lacquered in gold.

Grand, Shakti thought to herself, *but gaudy.*

She could see the minor spirits appear and disappear like hallucinations as she walked. They weren't as prominent as the ones in Kolakola, their colours not as vibrant. A side effect, perhaps, of thriving in areas with limited natural land. People wandered past the little spirits, unafraid. She wondered why she had not expected them to be.

When Shakti finally exited the gardens, she felt much lighter. Stomach rumbling, she made a dash towards the expansive market area once more. Kolakola had only its locally sourced foods and whatever limited options traders brought with them from the capital. Here, she was spoilt for choice. Sliced sugarcane. Deep-fried glutinous rice balls drizzled in honey. Bitter plum juice exported from the Ridi Kingdom. Her mouth watered.

Greediness made her buy both the deep-fried rice balls and sugarcane. She continued to meander about, stopping to stare at a store selling dozens of herbal tonics before a cloud of despondency hovered over her. Jaya would have liked them.

The flash of red and black in her periphery caught Shakti's attention, and she made to cover her head with the hood of her cloak before thinking better of it. Soldiers couldn't tell if she was a mayakari just by appearance alone. All this fear would turn her grey in weeks, and—

'Mayakari!'

Shakti started, head swivelling left and right like those of the others around her, albeit for different reasons. Had someone spotted her? How? She had been perfectly commonplace, blending into the crowd without suspicion.

When she realized that no one was looking at her, Shakti relaxed. She was safe, but that meant someone else wasn't. Where had the shout come from?

'Quick – get her!'

Like pigeons towards rice grains, the crowd surged forward. Taking her neck scarf and tying it around the lower half of her face, Shakti let herself be dragged along by the current. She pushed her way through to see what had caught the attention of the masses.

In front of a seedy-looking inn, a young woman was being held hostage by two soldiers. Shakti's breath caught. The woman's face looked terrified as she tried to wrench her arms free, eyes darting around in panic. A short, stout man with a long, oiled beard stood with his arms crossed next to the soldiers. Disgust radiated like waves as he spat at the young woman's feet. 'Fucking *mayakari*,' he ground the word out like a curse. 'I don't need scum entering my business.' Turning to the soldiers, he said, 'Caught one of them little spirits following her around last night when she came back to my inn. She was trying to shoo it away.'

Shakti's stomach dropped. *I'm going to watch another mayakari die*, she thought before her resolve kicked in. Jaya had died before she could do anything. She couldn't let something like this happen again.

Meanwhile, the young woman started to cry.

'No need for your tears, girl,' one soldier said loudly. 'If you're human, there is no need to fear. Ravan – a match, please.'

Desperately, Shakti looked around for something, *anything*, she could use to cause a distraction. The crowd wouldn't even blink if she started to throw pots and pans on the ground like a madwoman, not when they were more invested in watching a mayakari be discovered. Just when she was seriously considering summoning a minor spirit, Shakti spotted a stall selling fire-crackers.

Perfect.

Its owner was absent, likely too preoccupied with the sudden turn of events like everyone else. It gave her the perfect opportunity to borrow from it. Throwing her hood over her head, Shakti edged over to the cart, catching stray conversations as she went.

'Poor thing,' she heard one woman in a group of three whisper sympathetically. The remaining two stared at her, scandalized.

'*Poor thing?* Have you gone mad – that's a *witch!*'

'You're all fools,' Shakti muttered to herself, tucking a handful of small red cylindrical fireworks up her sleeve. Hopefully the vendor also kept – *yes.*

Adding a matchbox to her list of stolen goods, Shakti picked up her pace. She needed to find a clear enough space to throw the fireworks into, and a place to exit during the commotion. Quietly, she stepped up into a set of upturned wooden boxes adjacent to the cart. An empty alleyway to the north caught her eye. That would work well enough.

Heart thundering with trepidation, Shakti lit a match, and with it, the fuses of three fireworks.

Do not harm, little bird.

Jaya's voice came too late. By that time, she'd already aimed and thrown them in front of the soldiers.

A loud *pop* came first. Then – *bang*.

Startled yelps followed as sparks flew and plumes of grey smoke obscured the view. The crowd began to scramble back. The soldiers had their swords raised, attention no longer on the mayakari as they searched for the perpetrator. Undeterred, Shakti lit another four fireworks and hurled them before making a mad dash towards the young woman.

She saw her through the haze, hands wrapped around her head to shield her eyes. There was no time to hesitate.

'Get up!' Shakti yelled, grabbing the crook of the young woman's elbow. She screamed and tried to wrench herself free before their eyes locked. Shock was written all over her face.

'We need to go,' Shakti said, tugging her arm forcefully, '*now!*'

Survival instinct must have kicked in, because the young woman scrambled to her feet. Her eyes were red-rimmed, hair matted.

'You there – stop!'

Fuck.

'Run!' Shakti screamed and ran towards the alleyway she had spotted. The young woman followed. They melded with the confused crowd of onlookers, but not well enough. When she turned behind her, she could see the soldiers gaining on them. At this rate, they would be captured within moments.

Her breathing strained. The presence of people didn't help; they only slowed their escape. They were so close to the alleyway . . .

I'm not going to die like this.

You will die like this, little bird.

'Stop!'

Just as they squeezed through another stall, another high-pitched shriek filled the air. A deafening roar erupted. It was so loud that Shakti couldn't help but glance back one more time. Before she could comprehend anything, a pair of large, blurry black objects came speeding towards them, crashing into the vendor stalls and knocking over the approaching soldiers like they were flimsy toys. With a squeal, the mayakari dropped to the ground, Shakti crouching down to shield her out of instinct. Screams and yells followed as trinkets fell and scattered, potato sacks tumbled and rolled.

It took Shakti a moment to realize what had caused the chaos: giant leopards.

They shook themselves off, emitting growls loud enough to cause any bystanders to flee. The two soldiers who they had pounced on were on the ground, unmoving. *Spirits, were they dead or unconscious?* However, any momentary concern for them vanished when Shakti recognized just whose leopards they were.

A shadow fell over her. When Shakti glanced up, she met a familiar pair of brown doe eyes and nearly fainted from shock.

'Take her and run,' Prince Ashoka ordered, his mouth settling into a grim line. Behind him, Rahil surveyed the carnage, glancing back at them for a moment before he let out a shrill whistle. At the sound, the leopards snapped to attention and bounded forward, blocking the small alleyway from any onlookers. 'Down the alleyway and to your right – it will lead you back to the canal. Follow it south.'

'I—'

'This is no time for you to have an epiphany, Shakti,' the prince interrupted her, 'go.'

Shakti? How did he—

Terror resurfaced when she patted her cheek only to feel that her mask had slipped. Fuck. *Fuck.*

'Go!'

His insistent tone snapped Shakti out of her reverie. She didn't need to be told again. She needed to react, and quick. 'Thank you,' she muttered hastily before hauling the slack-jawed mayakari up. 'We need to run.'

There was no time to sit there and wonder if he was leading them into a trap. A window of opportunity to escape had presented itself, and Shakti was determined not to miss it. She grabbed the woman's hand and they raced down the alleyway. She looked behind her to see Prince Ashoka mount his leopard just before they turned sharp right and he vanished from view.

The young woman let out a ragged breath as they arrived at a waterway. 'The canal!' she exclaimed. So, the prince hadn't been lying to them.

Follow it south.

Panic clouding her orientation, Shakti used the position of the sun to determine south. Why had he suggested – *oh.*

The Mountain of Rebirth loomed like a giant in the distance. He had been trying to lead them to forestland.

'This way,' she urged. Away from the centre, this area was mostly quiet. A few people passed by them, throwing an odd look here and there at their dishevelled appearances. Shakti barely paid attention. Her focus was getting to the base of the mountain. Fewer people. Fewer *soldiers.*

Part of her wondered if she had slipped into a strange dream before dread came knocking and settled in like an unwanted parasite. *He knew.* Well, at worst, he knew. At best, he suspected. How had her good deed gone punished? Was karma flaying her hide for enacting a curse?

But he had helped them. Ashoka Maurya had *helped* them. Willingly, and without even a second thought. He could have stood there and done nothing, like most bystanders did. Nor was he obligated to. After all, why would a child of Adil go to such lengths? Out of the former emperor's poisonous children, Prince Ashoka seemed to be the antidote.

The rumours of him being a mayakari sympathizer were well and truly correct. Saving her kind instead of having them vilified? He could be the one to do it.

'My name is Priya.'

The crisp, accented voice shook Shakti out of her thoughts. The young woman was staring at her with a tired but grateful smile.

'Shakti,' she said. 'Are you—'

'A mayakari? I am,' she confirmed. Her voice started to tremble. 'Thank you for helping me. I-I thought . . . it was – that I . . .'

'You're welcome,' Shakti replied gently. 'Are you all right? They didn't hurt you?'

Priya shook her head. 'No burns, just sore arms and a few bruises,' she said, wincing as she stretched her right arm. 'I don't think I can go back there for quite some time. I'll have to lie low in the outskirts.'

'Do you have someplace safe you can stay?'

Priya nodded. 'I do,' she said. Then, 'Who was that? The ones who helped us?'

'Erm—'

'Soldiers, no?' the mayakari determined. 'They had to be if they were controlling those leopards. But that's *impossible*, so who . . .'

She trailed off, looking stupefied. Shakti couldn't blame her. The crowd would come to the same conclusion as her. She had no doubt that this would have caused an upset in the palace by the time she returned.

Ask Ashoka.

Yes, now was the time. He had seen enough, and she had nothing to lose. As she and Priya walked towards the mountain, a single thought appeared and lodged itself like a splinter in Shakti's mind:

He would make a better emperor than his father.

CHAPTER SIXTEEN
Ashoka

'A MAYAKARI ESCAPED IN THE MIDST OF YOUR ANTICS, little brother.'

Arush stared down at him as he stood next to their mother who sat upon the Obsidian Throne. Next to him was a smug-looking Aarya. To his mother's right were several consuls, all wearing the same stern expression. Consul Rangana, especially, eyed him with a sort of puzzled exasperation. The ruby eyes of the leopard statues seemed to be judging him as if he were a failure. A useless young man who would never be able to prove himself by enabling violence as a form of rule like his father.

Ashoka shot Arush a defiant grin. 'How terrible,' he retorted, not caring that he sounded the least bit remorseful.

Behind him, Rahil snorted. 'Sound more regretful, why don't you,' he muttered under his breath.

Ashoka could not find it in himself to do so. Though he had caused panic in the central business district by unleashing Rāga and Māra, he had also saved a life. He had stopped a violent death from happening. Objectively, he had done the right thing.

Pathetic boy.

With practised ease, Ashoka pushed his father's voice aside.

Sometimes, it was harder to will away. Other times, when he was surer of his thought and actions, it was easier to quieten.

'Ashoka,' his mother said. 'You have caused a great deal of damage. This is no small matter; reparations must be made.'

'I know, mother.'

'And you left for the city again without an adequate number of guards,' she continued, a worried dint appearing between her brows, 'you were being unsafe.'

Guilt pierced through him. 'I'm sorry, mother.'

Palming his face in a haggard manner, Arush cast his gaze to the ceiling. 'My coronation is in *two days*, Ashoka,' he said. 'Why must you create such chaos? Are you intentionally trying to vex me?'

'Yes, brother. Because every decision I make revolves around you.'

Arush didn't seem to grasp the basics of sarcasm when he replied, 'Be better than that,' but Aarya caught onto it. She always did.

'Why go alone – are you stupid?' she asked.

'I had Rahil,' Ashoka replied.

'"*I had Rahil*,"' Aarya mocked him. 'You took royal leopards into the city and caused unnecessary destruction. What was all this for?'

Shakti's gobsmacked face came to mind. He'd seen the moment she recognized him, and he her. What humbled him was the shiver of abject fear that had run through her. His father called the mayakari monsters without a second thought but, in that instance, Ashoka felt as though the monster was him.

'My apologies,' he said airily. 'I must have forgotten to tether Rāga properly.'

The surrounding consuls looked confused. His mother appeared disbelieving. Both his siblings' eyes twitched, moments apart. All three shared the same habit when driven to vexation.

'And what about Māra?' Aarya retorted icily, her gaze passing over him. 'How did you manage to lose control of *your* leopard, Rahil? That is quite unexpected. And disappointing.'

Before Ashoka could defend him, Rahil's assured, steady voice filled the room. 'When Rāga became spooked and bolted, Prince Ashoka ran after her,' he said. 'Since it's my duty to protect him, I followed. In my haste, I too didn't bother to check if I'd tethered Māra – and as you all know by now, I hadn't. I apologize for my carelessness, princess.'

His words sounded more convincing than Ashoka's. Nobody needed to know that Rahil had willingly followed his plan to let loose the giant leopards to create a distraction.

'The *damage*—' Arush began, but Ashoka cut him off.

'No one was hurt,' he said defensively. 'It was not as if I commanded Rāga to kill.'

Arush snorted. 'As if you ever would.'

Arms crossed behind her back, Consul Rangana nodded in agreement. He expected no support from them. This public harangue was a form of punishment against him, after all.

'You aided a witch, Prince Ashoka,' she said.

'Did I, consul?' Ashoka refuted, shrugging. 'Rāga simply misbehaved. She must have got spooked by the crowd. Can you blame her?'

Aarya appeared unconvinced. 'Rāga was trained to withstand such overstimulation,' she replied. 'If she fails at something so basic, perhaps she should be put down.'

Ashoka dropped his smile. Of course Aarya was attempting to rile him up. Make him take back his words. 'I did not think you to be the type to waste a valuable asset,' he said. 'Will you order every animal of ours who spooks occasionally to be killed? It seems a rather foolish choice.'

'Don't be impudent, little brother.'

'Don't be an upstart, sister.'

'Enough, you two.' Empress Manali let out a long-suffering sigh. 'Ashoka, you will not step foot into the city again till you leave for Taksila.'

Ashoka balked before he and Aarya opened their mouths to refute their mother in unison.

'Mother, no, you cannot expect me to—'

'But that's hardly a punishment! Because of him, a parasite continues to roam free in—'

'This discussion is over,' their mother said firmly. 'Now, I must speak to Arush – alone.'

That was the signal for all others in the throne room to depart. Tension Ashoka did not realize he harboured in his body lessened when Rahil stepped closer and placed a reassuring hand on his shoulder. Aarya stalked down the steps towards Ashoka, head held high. As she passed him, she pursed her lips and leaned in.

'Mother always takes it easy on you, *mūsī*,' she whispered, 'but when Arush takes the throne, you and your sympathizer antics won't be tolerated any more.'

CHAPTER SEVENTEEN
Shakti

PRINCE ASHOKA WAS LOOKING FOR HER.

At least, that was what Harini told her the next morning while Shakti was collecting fresh linen sheets to be brought to the young prince's bedchambers.

Anxiety spiked her heart rate. Spirits, it was too early in the morning for this.

'Why?' she asked.

'I'm not sure,' Harini shrugged, glancing at her shrewdly, 'perhaps it has something to do with your little escapade.'

With practised ease, Shakti threw a dyed-blue sheet at Harini's face. The mayakari let out a shrill squeak and tugged it away. 'Why must your first response be violence?'

'Where is Prince Ashoka?' Shakti asked, ignoring her jab.

'He's left for the serpent pens,' Harini replied.

Murmuring her thanks, Shakti set down the linens and prepared to leave, wondering what fresh horrors awaited her there.

'Shakti . . .' Harini called out. She paused for a moment, as if stringing together her thoughts, '. . . I admire you for helping that mayakari. But please be more careful – there are a hundred more ways to die out here than you would find in Kolakola.'

Shakti sent her a sad, knowing smile. If anyone knew about her unusual ability, there would be a hundred and one more ways to meet a grisly end. After the audience with the Great Spirit, she'd tried to re-enter The Collective, but to no avail. It was hard to still her mind when anxiety came as easily as breathing.

She headed towards the serpent pens, palms sweaty. No matter how many times she wiped them on her blouse, her hands seemed to be permanently damp.

There's nothing to be afraid of, she told herself. *He helped you. Surely, he won't betray you.*

Repeating the thought like a mantra, Shakti found herself calming down when she entered the pens. Dead leaves and bark crunched beneath her feet. Her breath caught as she observed the serpents.

Spirits, she'd never seen one in real life.

One at the furthest end of the courtyard caught her eye, curled up into its pen and dozing with occasional contented hisses. It was larger than the others, with beautiful opalescent wings that glinted in the light. Its scales were a mesmerizing amalgamation between soft pink, silver, and white. Cautiously, Shakti approached it, noticing the thick leather bonds that it was tied to with disappointment. Chained like a prisoner, the poor creature.

'Careful with Sahry,' said a voice behind her. 'She'll bite.'

She hadn't heard the footsteps. Alarmed, Shakti turned to see Prince Ashoka. He'd appeared out of nowhere along with Rahil — *were those two ever apart?* — staring at her with interest.

'Hello, again,' Rahil greeted her with a smile. Meanwhile, the prince moved closer towards the serpent.

Gold and jewels did not adorn him the way they did Princess Aarya. She wore so much that Shakti thought it was armour. The prince was a minimalist: two gold rings on his right hand, a ruby pendant dangling from his neck to match the deep red of his robe and sash, and circular studs. That left ear was truly a nasty burn.

'Prince Ashoka,' she greeted. 'Good morning.' In her haste, she forgot to bow. Fortunately, the prince didn't notice or, if he did, he paid it no attention.

'They're magnificent creatures,' he agreed, 'but perhaps you should step away from this one.'

'Why?'

'Sahry is my winged serpent,' he explained. 'She does not allow anyone else to approach her alone. One handler was bitten and died from the poison. Some got flung several feet, suffered from broken bones, concussions – the lot. Rahil here tried to ride her once and ended up breaking his leg.'

'A truly riveting experience,' Rahil deadpanned.

Interesting. Said serpent seemed quite non-threatening as it dozed. Meanwhile, the prince eyed Shakti curiously. Those cavernous brown eyes held the inquisitiveness of a tiger cub venturing out into the forest for the first time. 'How are you?' he asked.

'I— sorry?' Shakti had been ready for an interrogation, a deep probe into her history. Being asked how she was in such a casual manner was not what she expected. 'Fine. Relieved now, Prince Ashoka, that the mayakari is safe.'

'Good. You managed to travel to the mountain without delay?' he inquired. Beside them, Sahry stirred. Her filmy eyes opened as she let out a low, lengthy hiss.

'Yes,' Shakti replied. 'Thank you.'

Her thanks seemed to confuse the prince. 'Not necessary,' he said. 'There is no glory to be had in watching the death of an innocent.'

The more he spoke, the more Shakti relaxed. There was something about his manner, the slight lilt to his speech, that lowered her defences. Authority did not ooze out of him like it did with Princess Aarya or Prince Arush. He appeared more grounded, more approachable.

Unlike his father.

Shakti watched as Sahry hung her impossibly large head over

the gate. Tongue flicking in and out, the serpent ran it over Prince Ashoka. In response, he rubbed the underside of her jaw.

Ask him.

'Why did you help me?' she asked instead. It was hard to concentrate with the serpents here. 'Help us?'

'I helped you because two witches would have burned in the city otherwise,' he responded. 'You do not need to be scared – I won't turn you in. I'm offended you think I would.'

His quasi-harangue astonished her. It also brought her attention to the fists she was clenching so tightly. 'Forgive me for holding a modicum of distrust against a Maurya,' she replied, 'but how could you tell?'

'Tell what?'

'That I'm a mayakari?'

'Oh, I couldn't tell based on action – there was nothing to suggest it. It was what you said,' Prince Ashoka answered. When she shot him a look of confusion, he elaborated further. 'You said that Ruchira was able to find you work here. Sau had told me a few days ago that Ruchira came to her asking for some strings to be pulled because she wanted to find work for another mayakari in the palace. Admittedly, I was slow to connect the two that day at the stables. I panicked when Aarya nearly got her hands on you.'

Stunned into silence, Shakti could only look elsewhere. *He'd known all this time?* That was why he'd been so insistent in declaring that she worked specifically for him.

'How chivalrous of you, Prince Ashoka,' she replied.

'Not really. I would call it plain common sense,' he said. 'You will only suffer a painful death if she ever finds out what you are.'

He's the safest bet.

Sahry hissed again, chains rattling as she shifted, this time towards Shakti. Unafraid, she craned her neck to lock eyes with the serpent. Ignoring the prince and his guard's worried expressions, she placed a gentle hand on the animal's underbelly. The mayakari and wild creatures naturally didn't fear each other; they had a stronger connection to the land than humans did. After all, it was always humans who drove and killed creatures out of fear or the need to urbanize.

As expected, Sahry didn't react violently to her touch. Prince Ashoka raised an eyebrow.

'Interesting.'

Shakti frowned. 'Why?'

'You are not dead,' he replied. 'Do you want to ride her?'

He didn't have to ask. The 'Yes' tumbled out of her without a second thought. It was only Rahil, who had been listening along to their conversation in silence, who started. 'Ashoka, I beg you, *don't* perform any death-defying tricks in the air with someone who hasn't been on a winged serpent before,' he chastised.

'Why?' the prince teased. 'Afraid you'll lose me?'

Rahil snorted. 'Hardly. I'm afraid we'll lose a competent new staff member.'

'I'll pretend I didn't hear that you don't care about me,' Prince Ashoka replied, laughing. 'Shakti, I promise you will not die.'

She wasted no time helping Prince Ashoka saddle Sahry, though it took some time. They led her out of the pens and into the open air before placing a two-seater saddle between her iridescent wings. It was odd; very different to a regular horse. Sahry's scales were dry and cold to the touch. Prince Ashoka hauled himself up first before extending a hand for Shakti to take. Careful not to tread on Sahry's wings, she found footing on the stirrup, accepted his hand, and swung herself over.

When they were properly saddled, Prince Ashoka tugged at his reins. Sahry's wings flapped loud and insistent as she responded, body twisting and rising from the ground to keep herself steady as she began her ascent.

'Hold onto the saddle horn,' the prince yelled when Sahry picked up speed. Shakti complied, not wanting to risk a premature death. A strong gust of wind hit her face, and she squinted. Her stomach muscles tensed until the winged serpent stopped her ascent and maintained a steady pace in the air.

Shakti looked down. The prince had directed them towards the forestland that lay to the north. For once, she could see the world how a Great Spirit would in its enraged form. Lush shades of green sprawled the hills and brown-yellow grass flooded the flat plains.

She grinned. Flying was phenomenal.

The prince kept his promise to Rahil. No death-defying stunts were performed; they simply flew in a leisurely manner in the quiet, still air. Eventually, she saw him loosen his grip on Sahry's reins.

'What are you doing, Prince Ashoka?' she called out.

'Giving her control,' he replied and looked over his shoulder. 'You don't appear concerned.'

'Why would I?' she asked, confused.

He grinned. 'Yes,' he said. 'Why indeed.'

A lengthy silence followed, with only the steady beat of Sahry's wings to fill it.

Ask Ashoka.

'I don't believe I have ever offered my condolences to you,' she raised her voice hastily, trying to keep the conversation afloat. When Prince Ashoka shot her a puzzled glance behind his shoulder, she added, 'For the loss of your father.'

He offered her a small, tight smile. 'Of course,' he said.

Interesting. The response was too blunt, like there was no love behind it. She thought back to Emperor Adil, of how he spoke about Ashoka with disappointment. Maybe the feeling was mutual between father and son. But why?

An interesting question, but one that she couldn't ask; it seemed far too personal. Besides, she was not here to hear stories about emotional neglect. She was here to get her own answers.

'I had the chance to visit the palace library, Prince Ashoka,' she began, 'and I found there to be a distinct lack of texts on the mayakari and our history.'

Prince Ashoka outwardly winced. 'My father burned most available texts on the mayakari before I was born, but he did have a private collection that he kept. I used to read them too, until he found out.' The stud on his left ear winked as he fiddled with the burn.

She eyed it curiously. 'How did you burn your ear, Prince Ashoka?'

He gave her an odd look, as if this was something she should know. 'I'm surprised the palace staff haven't told you yet,' he said. An arid chuckle escaped his lips and, for a moment, his bright eyes dimmed. 'When my father found out I was reading mayakari texts, he was furious. As a punishment, he showed me how the soldiers tested for signs of a witch.'

Spirits.

The emperor had burned his own son's ear as punishment. Picturing a young Ashoka mewling in pain as Adil hurt him was shiver-inducing. More disturbing was that the prince recounted the story without much feeling. He stated it like it had been some sort of forgettable memory, like this was something he had learned to expect.

Not just witches had suffered under Adil's hand, then.

'Tell me.' He changed the subject. She didn't blame him. 'What is something true of the mayakari that my father says is a lie?'

'He claims that the mayakari raise the dead to cause havoc, but that is not true,' she said without thinking. 'We do not like to raise the dead. There are stigmas. Rules.'

She wanted to kick herself in the foot following that comment. There was a price in letting others know such knowledge. But instead of interrogating her like she was a criminal, the prince appeared to be genuinely interested.

'Stigmas?' he asked.

'When mayakari raise the dead, they're bringing something back,' she explained. 'A fragment of a consciousness that once was. Not a soul, but not nothing, either. Perhaps it is because they are forcing a halt of samsara when they *do* raise the dead, I do not know. I do, however, understand why it is looked at with such apprehension.'

Shakti was telling the truth this time, because she too did not know what was being brought back. It was the great mystery that had confounded mayakari scholars decades before the persecutions began and continued to confound to this day.

Meanwhile the prince had been listening to her, enraptured. 'I suppose, you are harming something in the end,' he added, 'and the mayakari do not hurt.'

Such a sure admission. Guilt burned her like fire. Despite members of older generations like her aunt refusing to partake in harmful action, Nayani's admission that younger witches like her would likely not keep their heads down and suffer remained. Mayakari were not atypical; they were still human.

Shakti changed the subject, not wanting to think about Jaya. 'There have also been discussions on a . . . group consciousness of sorts. A collective. Have you heard of it?'

Disappointment came swift like a butcher's knife against meat. The moment Prince Ashoka's brows crumpled, she knew that he was lost. 'I don't believe I've ever heard of such a thing,' he admitted.

Ask Ashoka. Did this blasted consciousness lie to her?

'Neither have I, Prince Ashoka,' she replied. 'Much of mayakari history remains a mystery these days.'

The prince rewarded her with a bitter smile. 'Yes,' he agreed. 'My father declaring a war against innocents – I do not expect this was what Ashoka Maurya foresaw when he first founded the empire.'

The hostile sentiment against his father did not escape her notice. However, all thoughts of Adil flew away when she digested his last few words.

Her mind cleared. A key turned in a lock. A door opened.

Ask Ashoka.

She was so stupid. That was why she had doubted the ludicrous message of asking the youngest prince for help to remove a curse. It wasn't *Prince* Ashoka that man had referred to. It was the *Emperor* Ashoka Maurya. Ashoka the First, the founder of the Ran Empire. The ultimate predecessor of Adil Maurya.

This is a collective; a gallery of consciousnesses past and present.

The answer had always been there; she had simply failed to listen to it. To speak to Emperor Ashoka, she needed to find him inside her head.

CHAPTER EIGHTEEN
Ashoka

PROUD OBSIDIAN-CARVED LEOPARDS WATCHED WITH
bloody eyes as Arush was crowned emperor.

The monarch's ruby-studded circlet was placed atop a stone
pedestal in the throne room, the surface draped in red silk.
Seated at the front of the hall with his family, Ashoka watched
as a solemn-faced Arush took the circlet in both hands and
slowly placed it on his head. Then, he made his way to the
Obsidian Throne, got down on his knees, and placed both hands
on the seat as a sign of respect before he stood up and then sat
upon it.

Coronations in the Ran Empire were a relatively simple affair.
Monarchs were crowned with the royal family, consuls, advisors,
and other important officials in attendance. Meanwhile, citizens
in the Golden City and throughout the empire celebrated the
occasion with much greater fanfare, with festivities and song, with
dance and drink. Public rest days tended to bring out the more
jovial side of people.

On the outside, his older brother appeared dignified and
composed, but Ashoka knew that he was fighting glee deep down.

What is the point of his excitement, he thought, *when he will keep
things exactly the same?*

Beside him, Aarya sat with her hands in her lap. She smelled overwhelmingly like a pink lotus and, with her gradient sari, she looked like one, too. Like him, she appeared uninterested, but perhaps for different reasons.

'Where is your new guard?' she asked suddenly, not taking her eyes off the circlet upon Arush's head.

'Who?'

The look she shot him was one of utter irritation. 'The one who fought Rahil. *Shakti.* Have you not sent her to be trained as one yet?'

Ashoka eyed his sister with mild distrust. *Why the sudden interest*, he wondered as he shook his head.

Aarya tsk-ed. 'Having her do such mundane tasks when she was able to make *Rahil* bleed,' she said with a maddening air of superiority. 'You are wasting her talent. How will you govern Taksila when you cannot organise your own staff?'

The urge to commence a full-blown verbal sparring match was strong, but Ashoka forced himself to calm. As usual, Aarya was trying to get a rise out of him. Why she resorted to such measures when peaceful existence remained an option was beyond him. It was as if his father's ideals had sunk its claws so deeply into her that she had become infected, unable to be treated.

'I am being sent there to *learn*, yes?' he replied, keeping his tone nonchalant. 'No need to worry for me, Aarya. I am sure that I will manage.'

Shaking her head with an irksome smile, his sister turned her attention back to the ceremony. Ashoka was left wondering whether he should take Shakti as part of his travelling party to avoid Aarya's interest. Knowing his sister, she would poke and prod until her identity was revealed and then . . .

The mental image of witnessing his first mayakari burning made him shudder. The memory was deeply etched into his mind, unable to be erased. Blue flames, horrifying screams, burning meat, and smoke. His father, watching without guilt.

He never wanted to see it again.

After the official coronation ended to thunderous applause and the crowd in the throne room slowly departed, Rahil escorted him back to his wing. Ashoka was silent, lost in thought about Taksila. Only a week remained till he was set to depart. A strange sense of overconfidence was starting to take over him. He had Rahil. He had Sau. He had Harini. The latter was the most important in terms of brokering some kind of negotiation with the mayakari resistance in the city. If he wanted to solve a nature spirit issue, he needed the backing of a mayakari to obtain support from those who did not trust his family.

Once he was safely inside his study, Ashoka let himself slump against his chair, squinting from the sunlight streaming through the giant windows.

Rahil watched him with a wry smile. 'Why so woebegone?' he asked.

'I am simply drained,' Ashoka murmured. 'Infuriated.'

He closed his eyes. *Infuriated* didn't even begin to describe his well-deep emotions. Aarya would inherit two official positions following the coronation: commander of the armed forces, *and* chief strategist of the war council under the authority of the emperor. Meanwhile, he was relegated to governor. It was ridiculous. Though Aarya was trained in military and warfare strategy like the rest of them, she followed their father's guiding principles. Extricating her thoughts from his would be nigh on impossible. It was a shame, considering the war council had the utmost authority on where and when soldiers were dispatched. For as long as he was alive, his father had concentrated his forces to the south. Here was a chance for redirection, and it would not happen.

'Ashoka.'

He cracked one eye open. Rahil stared at him, as if peering into a soul that did not exist. Ashoka's heartbeat jumped. Firecrackers exploded in his head, bright sparks and smoke overwhelming his ability to think.

'I'm sorry,' he blurted out. Embarrassment quickly followed. *What was that?*

The sudden proclamation also seemed to baffle Rahil. 'For what?' His eyes narrowed. 'Did you make a bet with Sau?'

'No,' Ashoka replied quickly. 'I'm sorry for dragging you into my antics that day.'

'Don't be sorry when you saved a life,' Rahil said. 'You did the right thing.'

Ashoka sighed. 'I know I did the right thing,' he said. 'I just . . . I'm sorry. Thank you.'

Rahil's broad shoulders shook as he let out a deep, amused laugh. 'Why are you fretting?'

'I may need to take Shakti to Taksila with me,' Ashoka replied. Rahil was never one to let a concern go. 'Who knows, two mayakari may be better than one when attempting to speak to the resistance.'

'Do you think Arush will approve of trying to contact the resistance?' asked Rahil.

Pinching the bridge of his nose, Ashoka audibly exhaled. 'The hope is that I can convince him at the general council meeting,' he said. 'It baffles me that they'll likely see my plan as idiotic. It's like they don't *want* peace.'

Deep down, Ashoka knew he would rule better than his siblings, his father. If the Obsidian Throne were his, there would be no more unnecessary violence, because what was the point of it? All it did was create suffering. It was an erroneous way to rule. If each rebirth happened to place them in the same position over and over again, he would do it better each time. Too bad he would never be given the chance. At this stage, the current Mauryas would destroy innocents along with the empire.

Spirits knew that Aarya would continue to concentrate soldiers to the south the moment she began her new duties. If only he could be there to redirect in some way, to temper.

'They could have given *me* the chance to lead the war council,' Ashoka said aloud to himself, picking at his burned ear. What he wouldn't do to prove his dead father wrong.

Rahil coughed. 'Ah, well . . . as much as I admire your ideals, do you think you would be suited to make the required decisions for war?'

'My purpose wouldn't be to start wars or maintain them,' Ashoka replied, his tone fierce. 'It would be to stop them, or, better yet, make sure they do not begin at all. There is no sense in an empire that continues to perpetuate violence. Is that not an objective truth?'

There was no reply from Rahil. Of course there wasn't. Even Ashoka knew that his ideas were lofty and optimistic. His were the dreams of an ignorant child, that much he knew. That much, he was forced to digest.

Ashoka's mood soured and Rahil, as he always did, noticed.

'You could work with Aarya,' he suggested helpfully. 'Lessen her workload.'

Hah. Him and Aarya working together was akin to two crows battling for the same scraps. One would fly away with more and leave the other destitute. Opposite personalities on a war council only spelled disaster and in a battle of egos, she was the winning horse. Besides, he would never get the chance to be in the war council.

'Are you sure you aren't the wishful thinker out of the two of us?' Ashoka asked Rahil.

He ducked as Rahil's arm swept out to smack his neck and smiled. Although Rahil's heart was in the right place, he had the wrong idea. The only way to win against Aarya would be to make sure he never faced her as an opponent.

And thus, a near-impossible idea sputtered to life.

Night fell when Ashoka found Arush in the throne room.

His older brother stood at the bottom of the steps, gazing up at the Obsidian Throne. With his back to him and his arms crossed it looked as if he were appraising a painting; an unlikely pastime for his brother.

At the sound of Ashoka's footsteps, Arush turned.

'Little brother,' he greeted.

'Arush,' Ashoka replied and looked around. 'Why are your guards outside?'

Several had been posted outside the entrance when he arrived, and they'd let him in with baffled expressions.

'I could ask you the same thing,' Arush responded. 'Where is Rahil?'

'Asleep.' He'd sent Rahil to his quarters early, feigning tiredness. And he'd evaded the remainder of his guards by escaping from the balcony. This was a conversation that did not require others to be present. 'I came to make two requests of you, brother.'

Arush didn't answer him. Instead, he gestured to the Obsidian Throne. 'Strange, isn't it?' he questioned. 'To take father's seat.'

'Plenty of Mauryas sat upon the throne before him, and you will not be the last,' Ashoka replied. He did not want to descend into conversation about Adil's legacy at this hour. 'You are not him. You can create your own legacy.'

Ashoka meant it to be a throwaway comment, but he did not expect Arush to consider it so seriously. In fact, he stood there for a good while, mulling over his words.

'You are right, little brother,' Arush finally replied. 'Then, let me hear your request as an emperor should: upon his throne.'

'You really don't have to—' Ashoka began but was stopped by Arush as he made his way up the steps and sat himself down on the throne with a look of newly filled purpose. 'There was no need for such melodramatics.'

'What are your two requests, Ashoka?' his brother asked, ignoring his jibe.

Spiders crawled up Ashoka's legs. There was a price in his request, not just a simple *yes* or *no*. A larger imbalance of power rested between him and Arush now; everything he said had to be carefully constructed.

'This pertains to my role in father's will,' Ashoka said. 'I understand that you may be reluctant to change it, but I was hoping you would allow for a change in positions.'

He was hedging, and they both knew it. 'Out with it,' Arush commanded, 'and try not to blather on.'

Confident. Direct. That was how Ashoka planned to sound, and already he had failed. Shoving the anxiety down deep, Ashoka cleared his throat and wrung his hands together behind his back.

'My first request is that I want you to acknowledge that I am the third-in-line to the throne,' he announced. 'It was never explicitly written in father's will, and by now the entire council will have heard its contents.'

'Vanity?' Arush smirked. 'I did not expect that from you, brother.'

Good. He hadn't denied him yet. 'On the contrary,' Ashoka replied. 'It is to make the council aware that I am a valid successor. You know how strictly they adhere to written laws, brother.'

Thankfully, his point seemed to get through. 'That I do,' Arush remarked. 'I can certainly do that for you, little brother. Although, I don't know how this will benefit you. There is no chance you will ever lay claim to the Obsidian Throne once I have a family of my own.'

'Father as many heirs as you would like, Arush,' Ashoka replied. 'I simply want my legitimacy confirmed.'

Leaning back in his chair, his brother drummed his ring-studded hands on the armrest. 'What is your second request, then?'

Behind his back, Ashoka wrung his hands tighter. Here was perhaps the trickiest entreaty. 'I want to lead the war council,' he announced.

Silence drowned the room following his proclamation. Arush's expression was akin to a fish realizing it was out of water. 'Are you insane?' he asked, tone disbelieving.

Ashoka found his footing. 'I don't believe so,' he replied.

Arush laughed. 'Little brother,' he said. 'Surely you realize that you are the least suited for the job. What will you do? Bludgeon the concept of pacifism into the council's heads until they listen?'

'If that works, yes,' Ashoka replied tersely. Arush's pitying smile vanished at his serious tone. Their father's ruby circlet glinting in the moonlight made Ashoka feel a jumble of confusing emotions.

'If I return from Taksila successful, I want to lead it. Aarya can focus on her command of the armed forces. Would it not be less of a burden for her?'

His brother's response was nothing short of insulting. 'Little brother, this is not the time for jokes.'

'This is not one.' This was perhaps the most solemn he had ever been in his life, yet his brother thought him the equivalent of a court jester.

Arush eyed him like an abstract sculpture he could not quite decipher. 'Oh,' he said. 'You are . . . quite serious?'

'I want it, Arush,' Ashoka let himself say. 'I want to lead it.'

A slow, devious smile arose on his brother's lips. 'Well,' he remarked, 'I certainly can't leave my little brother disappointed, can I? All right, Ashoka – your request is granted.'

Half-pleased, Ashoka took a step back to evaluate his brother for a moment. But Arush was a watered-down version of Aarya, which meant that he too always had a trick up his sleeve.

'What is the condition?' he asked.

'It is as you said,' Arush replied. He cracked his knuckles, the sound of bone popping against bone oddly satisfying. 'You can participate in the war council . . . *if* you return Taksila to its original glory; a city without its land dying and spirits rampaging the north. All these conditions must be met.'

He still thinks I can't do it, Ashoka raged. *I'll show him.*

'Deal,' he said.

Arush's incredulous smile only inflamed Ashoka's fierce need to prove him wrong. Arush spread his hands out, inviting a challenge.

'It's settled, then,' he said. 'I shall let Aarya know of our agreement, though I doubt she will be happy to hear it. I wish you the best of luck, little brother.'

CHAPTER NINETEEN
Ashoka

'Taksila is father's greatest failure.'

From his periphery, Ashoka saw Sau's eyes widen to owlish proportions. Seated around them at a large, circular table, the remaining council members gazed at him with thinly veiled shock. His father was rarely – if ever – criticized for his tactics. Such was the way of a monarchy. This, he had realized in his adolescence.

He and Sau sat beside each other as they presented their joint plan to the general council regarding Taksila. They had holed themselves in his study for days on end following the reading of his father's will, poring over local maps, the governor, and civilian reports on the nature spirit rampages. His brother's main goal was to stop them, and perhaps reverse the slow death of the land in the process. This was not for altruistic reasons, however. Ashoka knew that all his siblings cared about was the unimpeded access into forestland to obtain iron ore.

Aarya's face pinched at his open accusation.

'Ashoka,' she replied forcefully, 'be careful of what you say and who you accuse.'

'Yes, Prince Ashoka,' Saudamini dropped her voice low enough that no one except him could hear, 'ideally I'd want your sister in a more forgiving mood.'

'Then resurrect my father,' Ashoka replied and slumped back in his chair.

Sau raised her eyebrows at him. 'When he's already ashes in the wind?' she queried. 'My chances would be quite slim.'

'Anything to add, Saudamini?'

Sau jumped at Arush's voice. From his seat at the head of the table, he threw them a suspicious look. His hulking figure cast a brooding shadow over the room.

Arush had settled quite comfortably into his new role as emperor, but Ashoka could tell that his interest waned during council meetings that weren't focused on expansion. His eyes began to droop, his posture slackened, and his gaze became distant. Up until Ashoka had insulted their father, he'd appeared quite uninterested.

Sau cleared her throat. 'Forgive my impertinence, Emperor Arush,' she said smoothly, 'but I agree with Prince Ashoka. Taksila was annexed without preparing for the consequences.'

'Being an advisor to Ashoka doesn't mean you can parrot him, Saudamini,' Aarya replied with a haughty expression. Ashoka shot his older sister an exasperated look which she ignored. She was trying to irritate him by needling Sau, and they both knew it.

Aarya had become especially thorny once the news of his deal with Arush had been relayed. Maintaining power was important to his sister, so losing it would have grated at her. Still, she could not argue against Arush now; a sentiment that brought Ashoka some comfort.

'It may be upsetting to hear, but it's true,' Sau replied. 'Emperor Adil left the region unchecked. Land in the north is dying and no one knows why, ironwood is plundered in areas absent of Great Spirits, and the mayakari resistance is retaliating over these forests being cut down. Frankly, I am surprised that the city is not in worse shape than it already is.'

'I think you forgot to breathe during that harangue, advisor,' Arush told her.

Next to him, Councillor Hiranya, one of his father's closest aides, nodded along. 'The mayakari resistance is not an issue, advisor,' she contested. 'These "retaliations" you speak of are mere nuisances for our soldiers. They are quickly taken care of, I assure you.'

'*Nuisance* is too tame a word,' piped up another councillor. 'The witches have asked minor spirits to guard ironwood and ward off suppliers in undamaged forestland. They are not Great Spirits but . . . it makes the extraction more troublesome.'

Ashoka locked eyes with Sau. Their attitudes would make the next suggestion even more unpalatable, but he had to hold firm in their position. This was no time for diffidence.

'My most pressing concern is to stop the rampaging of the Great Spirits and uncover why the land continues to die,' Ashoka stated loudly. 'For that, I will need to enlist the help of the mayakari resistance.'

The subsequent silence was thunderous.

Ashoka had expected it. The idea itself was plausible in theory but putting it into practice would be difficult. No intelligent mayakari would willingly choose to aid the crown – not when they knew of its history. Not when they valued their lives. If he was a mayakari, he wouldn't have gambled his life either – not even for a thousand gold coins.

Aarya's voice rose two octaves. 'You wish to *enlist* the mayakari?'

'How else am I to solve a problem that we don't have the answer to?' he retorted. 'If we come to some sort of agreement with the resistance—'

'No,' Arush interrupted, thumping his hand on the table. 'That goes against everything father stood for.'

'What father stood for was violence,' Ashoka replied, keeping his voice as calm as possible. 'We have a chance to right his wrongs. We don't have to be like him.'

'Right his wrongs?' Aarya repeated in disbelief. 'Little brother, you're the only one who sees father as the villain. You and your rotten ideas of mayakari and *peace*. They will destroy us all if that little resistance overwhelms you.'

'Oh, please,' Ashoka replied. 'You're spitting out the exact same spiel father gave me. You're just his copy.'

'You think that's an insult?' Aarya hissed, her lips curling into a sneer. Before he could retort with words that pierced like needles, Sau jumped in to help.

'What Prince Ashoka means to say, Princess Aarya,' Saudamini began hastily, 'is that we cannot speak to nature spirits, so there is no way to reverse the damage without a mayakari. It cannot be done by our own hands. Like it or not, we need them.'

The tension in the room was high. Aarya was still seething, and Ashoka needed to defuse her. He turned his gaze to Arush.

'Brother,' he pleaded.

Though Arush appeared less unconvinced than he had before, he poured salt over Ashoka's wounds.

'I know that the two of you would've made multiple plans on the very issue,' he said. 'So, find an alternative. One that doesn't use the mayakari resistance as an aid. I will not have father's legacy ruined this way.'

It was as if a thousand rocks were piled onto Ashoka's back. His chest suddenly constricted, as if it were being caged in without a way out. *There is no other way*, he wanted to scream. Pride and stubbornness were the reigning vices of the royal family. They wore them as proudly as they wore their silks and jewellery.

Sau's voice hitched, 'But, Emperor Arush—'

'*Silence*, advisor,' Arush's voice was a pair of footsteps crackling on eggshells. 'My commands will not be refuted. And, Ashoka, I will have the governor correspond with me to make sure you follow my orders.'

Ashoka shook his head at Sau. There was no point trying to convince Arush any further. Meanwhile, he sensed Aarya's gaze on them. Ashoka knew that look. It was the same one Aarya had when she first realized she could not separate Rahil from him. She had understood something; gathered information and tucked it away for later use. It made him unsettled; nothing was worse than Aarya having an idea.

'Ashoka.' Arush's voice broke him out of his reverie. 'You will do as I say. Go against me and your request will be denied – do you understand?'

Underneath the table, Ashoka clenched his fists, his left foot tapping irately on the wooden floor. He didn't answer. If he did, he knew that it would only lead to another argument. Spirits, did they want him to fail? Did they not want the land restored or did they simply not care?

'Ashoka?' Arush raised an eyebrow. 'Have you finally gone silent, brother?'

He felt a swift kick on his shin. Sau's foot had found him. Ashoka started, the rage vanishing like grey mist in the morning.

'I understand,' he said. 'I will do as you say.'

'Good.' Arush rapped his knuckles on the table. 'The matter is settled, then. You will depart for Taksila in two days. Now, I must discuss this vexing matter of the Ridi crown prince wanting to remove his soldiers from our northern and southern borders.'

'The Ridi prince, yes,' Aarya piped up, 'but I want to put forward a new proposal, brother: sending soldiers out to locate deadlands.'

Arush raised an eyebrow. 'Deadlands?' he repeated. 'Father stopped looking for them decades ago, sister. Why the sudden interest?'

Why indeed. Deadlands were uncommon: vast stretches of land where a Great Spirit had died from unnatural causes. What did Aarya want with them?

'If you listen to my ideas, you will find out soon enough,' Aarya replied.

'All right,' Ashoka's brother agreed, shrugging before turning to him. 'You are not needed here, Ashoka, although you may observe if you wish.'

He saw Sau sag in her chair. Since she was now his advisor, it meant that if he was not privy to this meeting, she would not be either. He knew that she would rather him stay and observe, but he didn't. The Ridi prince and the deadlands were not his concern – Taksila was.

As he stood up, the chair made an unseemly scraping sound. 'No need, brother,' he said. 'I will retire from this meeting.'

'I hope you govern better than I think you will, little brother.' Aarya offered him a sweet smile. If that smile was a fruit, the flesh would be bitter to the tongue.

Before Ashoka could utter a response, Sau stood up with him. 'You underestimate him, princess,' she said to his sister, polite as usual. 'Prince Ashoka shall govern exceptionally, and I will aid him in doing so.'

'Together,' Aarya murmured. 'Yes, of course you would.'

Ashoka's left eye twitched. 'I beg your pardon, Aarya?'

Aarya shot him an impish smile and waved her hand dismissively, topaz-studded bracelets clinking. 'It's nothing that concerns you, Ashoka. Off you go.'

Gritting his teeth, Ashoka turned and stalked off towards the entrance where Rahil waited with the other guards. When his eyes met Rahil's warm brown ones, Ashoka felt his stomach swoop. He had been observing them quietly from his post – what would he say about his conduct?

You are a prince, the logical side of his mind reminded. *Why do you care what your guard thinks?*

His sentimental side was quick to respond. *Because it is Rahil.*

He thought no more of it until he spotted the small smirk on Rahil's lips after they exited the hall. 'Admirable work there, Ashoka,' he said.

'Did you expect me to adopt the patience of an ascetic?' Ashoka responded, running a hand aggravatedly over his close-cropped hair. 'They are ridiculous.'

'For what it's worth,' Rahil began, 'I think you did well despite the circumstances.'

Ashoka flushed. 'Yes. Well. Would Sau agree with you, though?'

Sau's voice came from behind them. 'I most certainly would *not*,' she huffed as he turned around. 'You need to learn not to enrage your siblings, Prince Ashoka.'

He groaned. 'The very thing that inflames them within seconds is the very problem I'm trying to fix, Sau.'

'I know,' she said. 'In the future, try not to insult Emperor Adil while doing it.'

Rahil harrumphed. 'Asking this one to remain polite about his father is like asking you to stay away from playing cards and a bet.'

Both he and Sau spun to face Rahil with similar expressions of incredulity plastered on their faces.

'I can stay away from bets,' Sau remarked.

'I can be *polite* about father,' Ashoka refuted.

Rahil sighed.

'Of course you can,' he said sardonically before ruffling Ashoka's head. The action caused his spine to feel as if it were dislocating without pain. 'Let's take our leave, shall we?'

'Yes, let's,' said Sau before snapping her fingers sharply. 'Princess Aarya is up to something. She was staring at me far too hard.'

The statement was about as unsurprising as seeing rain during the monsoon season. Nonetheless, Ashoka agreed with her observation.

He had not liked that look at all. It spoke of a thousand sharp paper cuts and a world of disappointment.

Ashoka's gold-hilted dagger hit the wooden shelf with a dull *thunk*.

'Try not to kill me, will you?' Sau muttered sardonically as she adjusted a thick stack of parchment between her hands. They had retired to his quarters after the meeting, trying to think of a solution to the spirit rampages that didn't involve the mayakari. Unsurprisingly, both had hit a wall.

'*Don't use the mayakari for help,*' Ashoka put on Arush's low growl, '*you will do as I say.*'

'If you're trying to imitate Arush, you're failing,' Rahil told him.

'How else am I supposed to resolve a problem that needs the witches?' Ashoka thundered. 'Pathetic, the both of them.'

'Careful,' Rahil joked. 'Aarya hears insults about her like a cat and she'll come running at full speed to scratch you.'

'Ah, yes,' Saudamini said. 'We'd all love to see you be chastised by your serpentine sister.'

'Be louder, why don't you?' Rahil remarked pointedly as Sau poked her tongue out at him. Ashoka ignored their repartee.

Why did his siblings refuse to see logic? He had the ideas, he had the strategies, but they closed the door on him so quickly he didn't have time to think of an alternative. Though he needed to prove himself in Taksila, Arush had given him an unsolvable puzzle.

Playing by such narrow rules would end in disaster for him. Winning the bet and taking leadership of the war council was paramount, so he needed to go against Arush. He had to break the rules.

'There's no alternative,' he said aloud. 'I need to ask the mayakari for help, even if it goes against the grain. I can't have nature spirit rampages continue during my governorship. How useless I would be.'

Rahil's face went slack. 'Go against Arush?' he asked. 'Do you *want* to lead the war council or not?'

'Perhaps we can do it in secret.' Ignoring Rahil's incredulity, Sau jumped in to offer her own thoughts. Unlike Rahil, who had law-abiding tendencies, Sau was more likely to tweak the rules. 'Contact the mayakari resistance without alerting the governor. He'll be watching you closely if Arush wants regular correspondence about your activities.'

'We might have to operate in the dead of the night, then,' he mused, moving to remove the lodged dagger. 'There are so many soldiers stationed there, I cannot risk wandering during the day. It will be safer for Harini to accompany me at night then, too.'

'I see that my scepticism has gone unnoticed,' Ashoka heard Rahil mutter.

'It hasn't,' he promised. The dagger finally tugged free. 'Arush's original bet was that I restore Taksila to its former self. He didn't provide stipulations then.'

'You're arguing on a technicality,' said Rahil. 'Doing that will leave you in trouble.'

'Must you be so pessimistic, Rahil?' Sau asked.

A sigh escaped Rahil's lips. 'You're thinking of how to succeed,' he replied. 'I'm thinking of the likelihood of the plan leaving this idiot –' he jabbed Ashoka's arm '– dead.' Ashoka watched, amused, as Sau considered Rahil's remark, agreed with it, and return to her reading.

Ashoka found himself focusing on a flat macule on Rahil's neck, off-centre at the base of his throat. 'Potential trouble is a small price to pay if I can work with the mayakari and right Taksila,' he said softly. 'A period of peace created by a child of Adil Maurya – is that not worth something?'

Creating peace through destroying everything father has achieved, was what he kept to himself.

The rigidness that possessed Rahil seemed to vanish.

'Worth is subjective,' he said, shooting a half-bemused, half-defeated smile, one that sent Ashoka's thoughts scattering into a hundred different directions. 'So, make yours count.'

CHAPTER TWENTY
Shakti

SHAKTI LAY ON HER BED, FIGHTING TO SLEEP.

She was trying in vain to enter The Collective, something she had been unsuccessful at since the Great Spirit's intervention. All she needed was to enter a state of profound concentration, meditation, or deep sleep. The latter evaded her often these days, as she found much of her resting period to be lucid. Worse still, simply willing herself to keep her mind clear did not seem to work and only served to make her feel more agitated.

'Don't think too hard,' she whispered to herself. 'Concentrate on the breath.'

Squeezing her eyes shut once more, Shakti let her head sink into the pillow and mind relax. She thought about nothing and everything. Nothing. Her village. Jaya. Nothing. Death. Emperor Adil.

Concentrating hard, she imagined the same tug she had felt in the forest, that thread made from blue and white sparks. When her breathing felt slow enough to warrant lifelessness, there was that same *tug* she'd felt that day with the Great Spirit. *Finally.* Then, she followed it until the darkness turned into a blinding light and, behind her eyelids, her vision turned an odd mixture of brown, red, and white.

When her eyes opened, she was in the throne room. Emperor Adil sat on the Obsidian Throne. His gaze was equal parts curious and dismissive as he gave her a callous smile.

'Adil,' she greeted him without the formal bow. Excitement radiated through her – she had *arrived*.

'She still knows not how to address the emperor.' Adil's features contorted into one of vexation. 'You're a stain that cannot be removed.'

Shakti clenched her teeth. 'It gives me no pleasure to see you either, you vainglorious bastard,' she replied. 'Fortunately, I am not here to speak to you.'

His response was akin to that of a violent child being asked to keep their emotions in check. Emperor Adil balked. The dark shadow of his beard failed to cover his astonishment. 'Why are you here then, witch?'

'Since you so graciously informed me of your complete and utter lack of knowledge, I have found someone who can help me,' she replied with a sneer. 'I hope it means that I can get rid of you.'

'Who on this earth could help you?'

'The other man,' she said.

With slow, careful movements, Adil stood from the throne. Looking up at him, Shakti felt like an ant. He exuded a horrific enchantment the way a cobra mesmerized its prey. She could see why the common people had been drawn to him and his lies.

'What other man?' he asked.

'You told me that this was a collective,' Shakti replied, 'which meant that the consciousnesses of the other monarchs were present. One informed me to ask Ashoka. I thought he meant your son, but he denied any such knowledge. That left the first Maurya – the *first* Ashoka.'

'You spoke to my son?' the emperor thundered. 'How?'

Pettiness overrode the need to aggrandize herself, so she refused to answer him. After all, Adil had refused to help her. Why should she explain her current predicament?

'How?' he asked again. This time, it sounded like a command.

'How did you convince yourself to burn his ear?' she retorted instead.

'What convincing?' Adil replied. Not a hint of remorse graced his features. 'Ashoka needed to be taught a lesson. No good would come from him reading texts that spew lies.'

Lies. As if her existence was one.

She scowled. 'Why do you hate us? What have the mayakari ever done to you?'

As he so often did, the emperor snubbed her question. He turned his head away, refusing to look at Shakti like she was some sort of cockroach he would ask someone to dispose of. Deep down in her gut, Shakti knew he had an answer. Hatred was not born, it was made.

But for now, it did not matter. She was here to solve her own problems, not let herself become bogged down by arguing. She wanted the emperor Ashoka.

She took two steps towards Adil. 'Bring me Ashoka Maurya,' she called out to the void, 'the first of his name, the progenitor of The Collective.'

As she uttered the final word, the atmosphere in the room changed. Shakti only saw Emperor Adil's eyes widen in panic before he vanished from the Obsidian Throne completely.

Confused, she swivelled around, trying to see if the emperor had reappeared in a different area but he had not. It was then that the ground began to tremble beneath her feet and the throne room descended into colourful chaos. Garish reds, sombre blues, and poisonous greens blinded her enough to squeeze her eyes shut. When she felt the tremors dissipate and the faint pangs of colour vanish behind her lids, Shakti reopened them only to find the mysterious man she had seen before sitting atop the Obsidian Throne.

His beauty astounded her. The shining black hair, the gleaming brown skin, the bright eyes. This man radiated a power that was unlike Adil's. His felt ancient. Potent, like that of a Great Spirit.

Shakti tilted her head. 'You again,' she remarked.

'Hello, Shakti,' he said. His voice was calming. Peaceful. It was like a cool breeze on an arid day; like the gentle caress of Jaya's hands running through her hair as she oiled it.

'You know my name,' she replied stupidly.

He raised an eyebrow. 'I would be remiss if I didn't. You are the newest user of The Collective, and I believe that you now know mine.'

The answer came to her, slow like the sunrise. 'Emperor Ashoka.'

Shakti didn't know what she had expected. Some part of her had expected a lookalike of Prince Ashoka, but this one looked nothing like him. For starters, he was far more handsome, more matured and grown into a set of rugged features. Unlike the prince, there was no trace of softness to be found.

Emperor Ashoka nodded. 'The first,' he said. 'The original. I could not speak with you for long because the consciousness was not fully melded to you. The moment you summon me and accept The Collective is the moment your ability manifests.'

He spoke in short, swift sentences that were laced with ambiguity. For a moment, Shakti lost her eagerness to rid herself of the consciousness. For a moment, she indulged herself in asking a question that not even a Great Spirit could answer.

'Your lineage holds a power that not even mayakari can wield,' she said. 'How?'

Emperor Ashoka smiled. 'How else, but with the aid of a Great Spirit? How else would it be possible?' he replied. He didn't expand on it, which Shakti took as a clear sign that he wasn't interested in explaining his story, which was infuriating. Men could not wield their power, and yet, here was an emperor telling her the opposite.

'My story is not what you are here for, Shakti,' he said. 'Tell me – what do *you* want?'

'How do I get rid of this power?' she asked, gesturing to her head helplessly. 'I don't want Emperor Adil in my head. I want a rebirth.'

The look he gave her was sympathetic. Guarded. 'I understand your desire to rid yourself of The Collective,' the emperor said, 'especially when Adil represents all that was taken away from you. You will not be happy to hear it, Shakti, but there is only one way to rid yourself of this curse.'

'Let me have a guess,' she said. 'Must I die?'

His face turned grave. 'Yes,' he said. 'You are now part of The Collective. If you wish to transfer it to another, you too must die. Do you want that?'

A small part of her wanted to scream *yes*. Maybe then, she would finally be free of this forsaken world and its hateful ways. Maybe then, she wouldn't have to suffer through life alone. Except—

'I cannot be reborn if this power is transferred,' she said. Misery pounded her chest like a frightful wind against a ramshackle home. She didn't want to know how the process was done. 'I will never know peace. So then, what happens if I die as is, without giving this power to anyone? There will be no host, so will I be free?'

His answer was disappointing. 'I do not know,' the emperor admitted. 'Do you wish to find out?'

Do you want to die? Do you want to swallow poison, tie a noose around your neck?

No. The answer came without hesitation. Death was the natural way of life, but it was not what she wanted. Attachment was the root of all suffering, and her attachment to living would bring her misery, no doubt. But dying solved nothing. 'I do not wish to die. Not yet,' she said. To offset her ever-dampening mood, Shakti fed her curiosity instead. 'What does this ability allow me to do?' she asked.

Emperor Ashoka's eyes gleamed like he was finally satisfied with her line of questioning. 'Not only can you speak to one dead monarch, but you can also call upon any of the past rulers of the Ran Empire who succeeded me,' he explained. 'You may call out their name, seek their advice, and view their memories. Access to their minds is limitless. There is no corner you cannot touch – all past monarchs knew this before they bound them-selves to The Collective.

'And you can do what witches cannot, Shakti. You can invade others' dreams, tamper with them, and assume any form you'd like in them given that the past rulers have them in their own memory. You can influence the actions of others in the real world. That is the true power of The Collective.'

Shakti's eyes widened. 'All Mauryas who held The Collective could invade dreams?'

Emperor Ashoka shook his head. 'No. Only those who identify as female can access this power, similar to how witches are only female,' he said. 'Except for myself – I am the genesis, after all. You have an added advantage in that you are also a mayakari, Shakti. This power could be limitless for you.'

Dream invasion. No wonder the Great Spirit had called it ancient magic – this was unheard of. If wielded with cruel intention, it would breed negative karma. It would be a more intimate form of torture than curses. To invade a dream was to see someone's darkest desires and fears, to manipulate them.

I've cursed myself, she thought. According to the emperor, there was no feasible way out of this predicament, no easy way to remove this problem from her head.

Unless she decided to stop thinking of it as a problem.

She thought back to her escapade in the Golden City. Of how Prince Ashoka had helped her and Priya flee, and the relief in his eyes when she later returned to the palace confirming the mayakari's safe getaway. One blistering thought had wormed itself into her mind in the days since, unable to be silenced.

He would have made a good emperor.

Rule under Prince Ashoka Maurya would not be painful. The mayakari wouldn't have to fear for their lives and hide away. They wouldn't have to burn. Perhaps they could return to the old days when they were respected. When they were allowed to continue scholarly pursuits so that nature spirits and humans could live in harmony.

He will be a good emperor.

Here she was, with a power seemingly unknown to the mayakari, the common people, and the royals. Here was a power that not even a Great Spirit could place the origin of. Adil was a man; he could not have been privy to the full benefit of this power, and she, a *mayakari* at that, was now able to wield it.

The Collective would only be what she needed it to be. Treating it like a hindrance was unwise; she needed to wield it as a weapon. If she could somehow use The Collective to place Prince Ashoka on the throne . . .

No, the righteous side of her mind retaliated quickly. *Do not even think it.*

A useless attempt to pacify and reconsider the moral implications. As usual, Shakti's more avenging, unforgiving side won over.

If I could invade the dreams of Emperor Arush and Princess Aarya, *influence their actions in the real world enough to make them appear* *inept and incompetent to lead,* she surmised, *it will pave the way for* *Prince Ashoka to be seen as the better option. He could sit on the* *Obsidian Throne.*

'I could drive someone to madness,' she didn't mean to say it aloud.

Emperor Ashoka tilted his head, assessing her as if she were some strange new weapon. 'You could,' he said. 'You can.'

Tamper with dreams. Influence actions. A reckless emperor and a *mad princess.* Who would care to be led by incompetents when the capable Ashoka Maurya stood on the sidelines?

Yes. Yes. She knew there was no sense in watching a monarchy fall without a failsafe. It would only lead to a power vacuum, posing the risk of putting others who had learned to hate the mayakari in positions of power to continue practising some iteration of Adil's laws. Crowning a royal sympathetic to the mayakari plight was the better gamble.

Even better, this power could be manifested away from its victim. She could just as easily conduct these dream invasions elsewhere.

Like Taksila, she thought. *I can convince the prince to take me* *with him. It's safer than staying in the palace.*

But you will be tethered to this world if you venture down this path, Jaya's voice arrived like a gentle breeze. *You will do what you should not by halting samsara. Is vengeance worth it?*

Her aunt's corpse flashed in her mind's eye. To undertake a burden for the sake of others – was that not selflessness? Good karma? And, after all, was selflessness not what her aunt had preached?

This is for the greater good, she reminded herself. If there was even a small chance that she could use this power to alter the lives of the mayakari, she needed to take it. But this didn't simply have to be played as a malevolent, twisted form of altruism. Retribution still fuelled her, and she wanted to witness Adil's older children tear themselves apart, driven to madness by dreams. She could kill two birds with one stone.

This is exploitation, little bird.

This is justice, she told Jaya's voice. *For you. For me.*

'Ah.' Emperor Ashoka's calming voice drew Shakti from her ruminations. 'Have I changed your mind?'

She would use The Collective for her benefit. She would help place Prince Ashoka on the Obsidian Throne for the greater good of her people.

Shakti smiled.

'Yes,' she said. 'You have convinced me, Emperor Ashoka.'

CHAPTER TWENTY-ONE

Shakti

The day before Prince Ashoka left for Taksila, Shakti knocked on his chamber door.

The muffled voices she'd heard when she arrived stopped. 'Come in,' came the prince's voice.

Upon entering his chambers, Shakti found Prince Ashoka seated in his study, texts and various pieces of paper obscuring the wood. Rahil was there, as usual, standing guard by the door. The prince's advisor, Saudamini, was leaning against the window. All three stared at her in silence.

'Shakti,' Prince Ashoka hurried to stand. 'What brings you here?'

'I . . . er . . .' *I'm going to help you sit on the throne*, was what she wanted to say. Instead, a strange sense of wariness subdued her initial bravado. 'May I speak to you alone, Prince Ashoka?'

By accident, her eyes flitted to Saudamini.

The advisor seemed to notice her disquiet. 'Oh, I won't report you,' she said cheerily. 'In fact, you should probably thank me for getting you this job. When Ruchira said she pulled some strings, she meant me.'

'*Sau*,' Rahil griped.

'What? If anything, Shakti should be more wary of the rest of your guards,' the advisor argued. 'You should've seen the way they reacted once they learned that Emperor Adil's death was due to mayakari magic.'

Shakti flinched. *If they only knew.*

No point in speaking to the prince alone, then. 'I want to help you,' she said, squaring her shoulders. 'In Taksila.'

Rahil and Saudamini gave her equal looks of bafflement like she was a lotus flower growing without water. The prince, however, appeared unsurprised. He moved from his desk and sauntered towards her. 'You do?' he inquired.

Unable to gauge his tone, Shakti continued her spiel. 'Harini told me that she's accompanying you to help communicate with the resistance there,' she remarked. 'I can help. Two mayakari are better than one, and I have an added advantage.'

Interest flickered behind Prince Ashoka's doe eyes as he asked, 'Which is . . .?'

'A connection,' she replied. 'I have a friend, a mayakari. She's part of the resistance in Taksila. I can find her out, plead your case. Have them help.'

Saudamini whistled appreciatively. 'Karma is good,' she remarked, clapping her hands together.

Prince Ashoka was silent. He was looking at Shakti, but she could tell he was unfocused, thinking of other things. Up close, she could see the dark shadows under his eyes. Had he not been sleeping?

She'd heard the palace gossip of the council meeting where the prince proclaimed his intent to utilise the mayakari resistance during his governorship. That Emperor Arush had struck him down without hesitation. That the legacy of the great Emperor Adil would remain unchanged. That the prince was clearly not his father's child, rather a shadow of his mother's.

Adil Maurya was an obstacle not only to her, but to his own son.

When the prince refocused, his expression was one of resolution. And elation. 'You have given me some hope, Shakti. A direct link can allow for better communication.'

Shakti could only hope that Nayani would see reason once she found her.

'I planned to have you join the travelling party nonetheless,' he continued. 'My sister has shown far too much interest in you becoming a soldier for me to consider leaving you here to your own devices.'

Jubilation washed over her before it was quickly replaced by confusion. *The princess?* 'Why the interest?'

Prince Ashoka tsk-ed. 'She believes it to be a waste of your talents,' he supplied, 'especially since you can fight.'

An uncomfortable shudder passed through her at the thought of working for Princess Aarya. She reminded Shakti of an elephant creeper: able to smother and destroy trees if left unchecked. Thank the spirits she could enact her plans away from the palace and its utter lack of greenery.

Another knock sounded on the door.

'Popular today, aren't you?' Rahil quipped.

'Who is it?' Prince Ashoka called out. Moments later, Harini's head peeked out from behind the door. She cast a quick, confused glance at Shakti before bowing.

'Princess Aarya wishes to speak to you, Prince Ashoka,' she announced.

Saudamini rolled her eyes. 'You aren't acquaintances, for spirits' sake,' she said. 'Why does Princess Aarya need to announce her presence like some stuffy old dignitary?'

The prince smiled. 'Tell my sister to come inside,' he informed Harini, who nodded and shut the door.

'What does Princess Aarya want?' Shakti asked.

'Perhaps she heard Sau calling her a serpent,' Rahil said in deadpan.

'Or perhaps she's here to gloat about my impending failure?' Ashoka countered. 'I don't know. She's about as unpredictable as the weather.'

'What a compliment, little brother.'

Shakti startled. Princess Aarya stood at the door, watching them with mild amusement. The bangles around her wrists clinked together as she moved to cross her arms over her chest. Her yellow sari made her look like a tulip that needed to be trampled.

'Aarya,' Prince Ashoka greeted. 'What are you doing here?'

Princess Aarya pouted. 'What? Can I not visit my little brother without a reason?'

'No,' he said. 'You always have a reason.'

The siblings levelled each other with a stare. *There is so much of Adil in Aarya*, Shakti realized with venomous distaste. Heredities were truly unfortunate. Sensing that whatever natural disaster the princess brought would end up in an argument, Shakti cleared her throat, dragging the royals' attentions to her.

'If you'll excuse me, Prince Ashoka, Princess Aarya,' she bowed, 'I'll take my leave.'

Perhaps noting her apprehension, the prince nodded his assent. However, Princess Aarya held up her hand in a motion to halt.

'Oh no,' she said sweetly. 'Stay. I have such good news to tell you, Shakti.'

CHAPTER TWENTY-TWO
Ashoka

AARYA HAD SEVERAL SMILES.

He'd learned to interpret them early on, knowing which ones to dismiss and which ones to make note of. When his sister's smile turned wolfish as it did now, Ashoka's guard was up.

'What news?' he asked as Shakti stilled.

'Several noteworthy articles,' she replied. 'The first being that Shakti here is relieved of her duties.'

Shakti let out a soft gasp, looking like a dog that had finally been chased into a corner. Ashoka refused to give her a reaction. His heartbeat pounded in his ears.

Does she know?

'No,' he refuted immediately. 'You have no authority to let her go.'

'Let her go?' Aarya's surprise was genuine. 'Little brother, how crassly you think of me. I am advancing her. Shakti is to join my personal guard.'

Rahil let out a sound of discontent. Meanwhile, Ashoka struggled to silence his newly surfaced anxiety. This could not be happening at a worse possible moment.

Just when I got my hopes up.

'Shakti is part of my staff,' he retorted. 'You can't simply move people around as you wish.'

Seemingly unbothered by his vexation, Aarya inspected her nails. 'Unfortunately, you cannot dismiss the directive of the emperor,' she told him.

There was an unpleasant lurch in his stomach. Ashoka clenched his jaw. *The emperor.* Hah.

'Was this really Arush's own order?' he asked in disbelief.

'He is capable of seeing logic, you know, and his order has simply turned out in my favour.' An answer that was not an answer. Ashoka did not believe this was simply a lucky turn of events for Aarya. He had an inkling that she orchestrated this somehow but infuriatingly enough, wouldn't admit it. Turning to an unmoving Shakti, his sister shot her a triumphant smile. 'I know an asset when I see one.'

'Shakti isn't an object, princess.' Rahil finally spoke. He sounded irked.

'I did not suggest it,' Aarya replied. She looked rather affronted by the accusation. 'She is an asset in the same way you are. Besides, working under Ashoka tends to keep one complacent, no? You could have guarded our father just as Indran did, but you chose not to.'

It was getting too hard for Ashoka to control his riotous thoughts. *Spirits.* Under Aarya's command, Shakti would be in constant danger. His sister was no fool; if the mayakari made even one slip, she would notice.

All this work just to prove a point. Aarya was too petty for her own good.

But what was Ashoka to do now? His brother had issued an order. To fight it would be to infuriate Arush and risk him backing out of their deal.

Regrettably, Aarya was not finished with her blows.

'Arush has additional instructions he wished me to relay to you, little brother. It's about Taksila.'

All four of them straightened up at the mention of Taksila. Aarya chuckled.

'You're still leaving, don't you worry,' she smirked, 'but unfortunately for you, you'll be losing a treasured member of your party.'

'What?' Ashoka ground out. His first thought was Rahil, and he almost cried out in anger. But as his gaze followed Aarya's, he realized that she was pointedly staring at Sau.

Oh no.

'Sau?' Ashoka exclaimed. 'No, she comes with me. I won't have it.'

Sau was important. Aside from himself, she was the only other person who was well-versed in Taksila's issues within his small travelling party. It was between themselves that they'd strategized on everything from preventing the Great Spirits from razing the northern communities to returning Taksila to one governorship that reported to Arush in the manner of decentralized governance. He couldn't do this alone. He needed her to make sure his plans wouldn't regress into bloodshed.

Aarya couldn't take her away.

His sister didn't seem to care. 'You can argue with Arush all you want, but he has given an order,' she said. 'Saudamini will not leave with you.'

First Shakti. Now, Sau. What karma had Ashoka committed in a past life to deserve this?

'Where will I go then, Princess Aarya?' Sau asked.

'Makon.' Aarya clapped her hands together delightedly, ignoring Sau's shocked face. His sister seemed far too cheerful delivering this unfortunate news. The Ridi Kingdom's capital. 'I hear you're almost fluent in their language – it would help you immensely while you're there.'

'What for?' Ashoka shot his sister a distrustful look that she ignored.

'This is your chance to prove your worth, Saudamini,' Aarya said nonchalantly. 'To prove whether you deserve a place in the royal council. Ashoka is not yet allowed into these meetings, and since mother has moved you from her advisory, you've effectively become redundant.'

Ashoka caught a glimpse of Sau's face. It was pale.

'But I'm meant to assist Prince Ashoka in Taksila, princess,' Sau's voice was reedy, high-pitched.

'That isn't my problem,' Aarya smiled sweetly. 'Arush has given you an order. *He* is your emperor, not Ashoka, so I suggest you follow him.'

'Princess—'

Aarya tsk-ed. 'He simply wants to offer you an opportunity,' she said. 'One that doesn't come your way often. You're the most capable in speaking the Ridi language out of anyone in the political court, and you are well-versed in the country's politics. All you must do is travel to the Ridi Kingdom and convince the current prince to uphold the agreement our father made with his mother – to keep the Ridi soldiers at the northern and southern borders. I would rather have you try than not at all. It would be a waste of your talents otherwise.'

'The Ridi prince is not his mother,' Ashoka jumped in, fully vexed. He'd heard of the conflict-averse regent succeeding the ill queen. 'He will not approve your request.'

Sau nodded in agreement. 'And what if I cannot convince him?' she asked Aarya.

'Then you are useless to Arush,' Aarya said with a straight face. 'The Ran Empire's political advisors never fail, and if you do, you will be relieved of this position immediately. Not even Ashoka can save you.'

If possible, Sau's face paled even further.

'Did you not hear me, Aarya?' Ashoka said loudly. 'You're giving Sau a task that's doomed to fail.'

'And I will tell you again: it doesn't concern me,' Aarya said. 'We need the Ridi soldiers at our borders, and the only way to do that is to convince Prince Ryu to keep to that old agreement. Saudamini seems the most obvious choice. She isn't as set in her ways as the older advisors, which would have made nego-tiations with the prince difficult. We plan to continue the annexation of the south. Arush and I agree that our end goal is complete control of the continent, including Kalinga. We are keeping father's legacy alive.'

'You could never take Kalinga,' Ashoka said, thinking of the isolated island kingdom. The third biggest landmass in the known world, its naval fleet was the largest among the dominant monarchies. Its army rivalled theirs, such that a battle would only end in a pyrrhic victory. 'We do not have the resources to take control of it.'

'Soldiers and weapons are our resources,' Aarya shrugged, 'and what better access to material than the south?'

Every trek into the heavily forested south and its small states carried the risk of angering the Great Spirits of the wild forests. Collecting resources was doable in moderation, but his siblings would remove more, relying on old maps of the continent that detailed approximate locations of the ancient creatures.

'You cannot remove too many natural resources without creating problems for yourself,' he told her. 'There is power in keeping an empire contained and strong.'

Aarya snapped suddenly, losing her patience. 'Don't argue with me any further, Ashoka. You can choose to take this up with Arush if you wish.'

Ashoka could hardly believe that his brutish older brother was solely responsible for sending Sau to Makon. This reeked of Aarya's puppetry.

Ashoka drew himself up to his full height. 'You're right,' he said. 'I will go and speak with the *real* ruler and not the lackey who acts to relay his messages.'

He knew he had stung her effectively when Aarya – who was brilliant at keeping a composed countenance – flinched. Lips curled back into a tiger's snarl, she scoffed, turned her back to them, and stalked out of his study.

'Oh no,' Sau said as she scrambled up hastily. 'I need to ask her – Princess Aarya! A moment of your time, *please* –' Ashoka watched as she hurried out the door, nervousness evident on her flushed face.

The silence that blanketed the room after Aarya's departure was stifling.

'This wasn't Arush's idea,' Ashoka growled. He closed his eyes, trying to calm himself down, and felt the pressure of Rahil's hand on his shoulder.

'It's an unexpected change,' Rahil confirmed, 'but it's nothing that can't be handled. I'm sure another advisor can come with you.'

Ashoka shook his head. 'I can't trust them,' he said. 'They'll report everything to Arush. They'll tell him that I'm failing, and that I can't govern a region to save my life.'

He cared too much about how he would appear to his siblings and the remainder of the court. More than anything, he needed to look capable. How else could he argue his way into the war council? There was a price to pay when he wanted to be respected by others, and it was his old friend, anxiety.

Shakti had not yet moved. For all he knew, she could have gone into a catatonic state. He felt nothing but pity for the mayakari. It pained him to know that he was unable to help.

'Lie low,' he told her. 'Do what is required, but nothing more. And never let yourself be lulled into complacency during conversation with Aarya.'

She didn't seem to be listening to him. 'This wasn't . . .' she began before her words petered off. 'I suppose I can't leave with you in secret, Prince Ashoka?'

'You could,' he replied, 'but then both of us will be reprimanded. For you, the consequences will be worse. Are you willing to take such a risk?'

He couldn't imagine that Shakti would. Neither did he want her to. People would only wonder why a newly admitted member of the palace staff was so insistent on staying by his side.

To his relief, she shook her head. 'I don't want to die just yet,' she said. With a heavy sigh, she craned her head to the roof as if in begrudging acceptance of her situation. 'Seek out a mayakari named Nayani in Taksila. I'm sure she can convince the resistance to help you in some sense.'

Nayani. He stored the name away.

'I'm sorry,' he told her.

Shakti offered him a bemused smile. 'I doubt your father would ever apologize,' she replied, 'but thankfully, you are not him.'

Bewildered by her sudden mention of his father, Ashoka could only say, 'I try not to be.'

'Good,' she replied. 'If you'll excuse me, Prince Ashoka.' With a bow, she turned on her heel and left. Moments later, Sau re-entered, her eyes wide and glassy.

'I don't have a choice,' she said stoically. 'I must depart for Makon tomorrow. The chances of succeeding . . . even I would bet against myself. Ten gold pieces would do, I think. I cannot help you, Ashoka – I'm sorry.'

In his sympathy, Ashoka had an idea.

'You won't go alone,' he said firmly. 'Rahil will travel with you to Makon.'

Sau gaped. 'What?'

'*What?*' Rahil thundered. His grip on Ashoka's shoulder turned to iron. 'As much as I would like to help Sau, who will protect you?'

Ashoka raised an eyebrow. 'My guards are perfectly capable of protecting me from any threat,' he said, 'and, I hope you haven't forgotten, I can defend myself quite well.'

'Prince Ashoka.' Sau shook her head so vehemently that he was sure it would fall off. 'I cannot ask this of you.'

'Good, because you didn't,' Ashoka said bluntly. 'I will have Rahil escort you to Makon, whereafter he will depart for Taksila. You should at least have someone you know with you, Sau.' This last part he reminded her in a gentle tone. She had very few friends, and those who were, were mostly maidservants under the orders of Aarya and his mother. They would not be departing for the Ridi Kingdom, and she would be all alone.

Rahil frowned. A muscle clenched above his glass-sharp jaw. 'Ashoka.'

'Rahil.'

'*Ashoka.*'

'Look at it this way,' Ashoka told him, suppressing a shudder at the deepness of Rahil's voice. 'You get to travel beyond the empire like your mother did.'

Rahil shot him a look of utter incredulity. 'I can't leave you,' he sputtered. 'I *cannot.*'

Not even Rahil's bottled-up dreams to travel the known world would sway his sense of duty, it seemed.

Ashoka stepped closer. 'You once told me that you were afraid that your position would prevent you from leaving the Golden City,' he whispered. 'Why are you reneging now?'

'I—' Brows scrunching, Rahil tilted his head back. Paused, as if searching for an elusive answer. 'I cannot abandon you like that.'

'You won't be. I can ask Sachith to take over your position in your absence,' Ashoka reminded him before letting out a snort. Rahil's second-in-command was just as capable. 'Besides, do you think me so incapable that I cannot fend for myself?'

'I don't, but—'

Ashoka pinched the bridge of his nose between his fingers. 'Don't argue with me, please, Rahil,' he interrupted. Having to ask him to leave was hard enough. Of course, he had the option of throwing this idea away into the breeze, but it was better for Sau to travel with someone she knew. 'Visit Makon. Wander around the capital and bring me back something. I hear bartering is not allowed, so there is no chance of you inadvertently paying more for anything cheap.'

'And we can try their pickled plum juice,' Sau interjected, clearly trying to dispel Rahil's unwillingness as she clung to his arm like a dejected child. 'Besides, I did not think I was such a terrible travelling companion.'

Under their coordinated attack, Rahil softened. 'You're not terrible,' he told Sau gruffly. 'I'm wary, is all.'

His sentiments were shared. Ashoka could not recall the last time he'd been without Rahil for longer than a day. Still, this was a good opportunity to find footing on his own and not be so dependent on him.

Suddenly, an idea struck him, bright like lightning against the pitch-black of the night. Aarya may have thought that she had thrown a wrench in his plans, but she had inadvertently given him a golden opportunity. 'Sau, I want you to do me a favour,' he said.

Her response was quick. 'Anything within reason, I can do.'

Ashoka smiled. His request risked punishment, so it was a good thing that Aarya was not around to hear it. 'Arush wants the Ridi soldiers stationed in our border extremities, but I want you to convince the crown prince to have some of his forces relocated to Taksila instead,' he said.

As expected, Sau's eyes went as wide as a night owl's at his request.

'Did I mishear you, Ashoka?' she asked. By her side, Rahil assessed him like he was some sort of broken doll.

He shook his head. 'You did not,' he affirmed. 'Sau, if we can get foreign soldiers who have no bias to the emperor into Taksila, I can use their numbers to enact my own changes without challenge. Father's soldiers will be of no help to me.'

'You're not the emperor, Ashoka,' Rahil pointed out, ever the pessimist. 'What makes you think this can work?'

'Because the mayakari in the Ridi Kingdom are safer than the ones here,' Ashoka argued. As far as he knew, the Ridi did not persecute mayakari the way his father had done. Perhaps its crown prince could be swayed with empathy. 'This way, I can enlist the mayakari for help, and have Ridi soldiers to protect them from our own. They won't report me to Arush – they only answer to *their* monarch, not ours.'

Sau shook her head. 'I understand, but you are asking me to create a new deal without express permission from Arush,' she said.

'I know,' he replied. 'It is a gamble; one that you will have to attempt in secret if you are to succeed. I would hazard a guess that the prince would prefer sending a small contingent of soldiers to Taksila than have them all freeze to death in the north.'

Sau palmed her face, wearied, but her eyes had brightened when he mentioned 'gamble'. 'I'll try to convince him,' she said, her tone cautious. 'At least now I have something that I will be willing to argue for.'

Ashoka stood up. 'Good,' he said. One problem was more or less fixed, and now he needed to talk to someone else. 'I will take my leave.'

'Where are you going?' Rahil asked curiously.

'To find Arush,' he replied.

In the throne room, Ashoka found Arush in conversation with their mother.

It still jarred him to see his older brother sitting on the Obsidian Throne. Arush was bigger than their father, rippling with corded muscle from years of fighting. He filled up the throne by size alone, but he did not command the room. Not like their father had. Perhaps with time, Arush would come to do the same.

Arush's eyes snapped upwards to meet Ashoka's. 'Brother,' he called out to him. 'I assume Aarya has relayed the news?'

'You relocated two of my staff. Why?' Ashoka asked. If Arush was truly behind this, he would have an immediate answer, but his brother hesitated. He paused long enough for Ashoka to know that he was scrambling for a coherent answer, for him to realize that this idea was not entirely his own.

'Never mind that,' Ashoka cut Arush off before he could answer. 'I can't go against an order from the emperor, so I will do as you wish. But I request that you do not provide me with a political advisor during my time in Taksila.'

Arush looked surprised. 'You truly want to go without one?' he asked. It was an unusual request, and a stupid one.

His mother, too, seemed astonished. 'My dear,' she began, 'an advisor is of paramount importance. I do suggest you rethink your request.'

'No,' said Ashoka. 'I can manage without, or eventually seek one out on my own. I will correct Taksila under my own principles, not anyone else's.'

Arush rested a hand on his chin, watching Ashoka without

batting an eyelid. 'And I would call that political suicide, brother,' he sounded half-amused and half-vexed, 'but do what you must. Just don't come crying back to me when this show of bravado fails.'

Not *if*, but *when*. No matter, he would prove him wrong.

'I won't,' Ashoka promised loudly, 'and when I return, Arush, you had best keep your promise.'

CHAPTER TWENTY-THREE

Ashoka

'THAT'S THE YOUNGEST . . .'

  '. . . looks nothing like Emperor Adil . . .'

  '. . . those leopards are magnificent creatures, aren't they . . .'

  '. . . heard he's the mayakari sympathizer . . .'

The murmurs floated like dandelion seeds in the air, rife with accusation and wariness. As Ashoka had expected, curious heads and tentative whispers fluttered out onto the streets like moths towards a flame. The people of Taksila wanted to see the prince who had come to govern them. Did he share his father's face? His countenance? His temper? Or was he just a sad counterfeit of a man they associated with power?

Neither, he thought. *I am none of those things.*

Heartbeat quickening at all the eyes that were placed firmly on him, Ashoka adjusted the reins on Rāga, his leopard. Rāga let out a displeased growl when he tightened her muzzle, and he instantly loosened his grip.

'My apologies, Rāga,' he leaned down to whisper in her ear.

Rāga simply huffed.

His small travelling party rode behind him as they passed through the streets of Taksila's affluent half on their journey to the royal estate. Determined to avoid the confines of a stuffy ship for much of the journey, Ashoka had first elected to ride Sahry from the air. He only chose to return to the boat when she tired and they needed to dock for the night. That, and to ascertain Harini's mood occasionally. Her nervousness had doubled the day he'd told her of the loss of Sau and Rahil, tripled when she heard of Shakti's new position.

'She shouldn't be alone, Prince Ashoka,' she'd told him. 'Once I help you negotiate with the resistance, I want to return to the palace.'

He'd agreed without argument.

Sahry now flew freely above them, an additional marvel for the people to gaze at if she ever descended from the clouds. When he'd first seen Taksila from the air, its inharmonious contrast surprised him. The city lay at the base of a mountain range. Areas close to the wilderness, the north, were nothing but rubble, a muddied wasteland. Further south, where stretches of flat plains met the river, was a bustling metropolis. A clear demarcation was made between the northern and southern areas, the former of which were lined with drab, rundown houses tightly packed together, and the latter with more spacious, multi-storeyed palatial residences and well-maintained courtyards.

The royal estate where he was to reside was built on the affluent side, sticking out like a white peacock among its more colourful counterparts.

Despite knowing that there were a dozen solid bodies behind him, there was an ache, a gaping hole in his chest. The one person he'd wanted in Taksila more than anyone else was on a ship, sailing to Makon, and he'd been rash enough to send him there.

Sau needs Rahil more than I do, Ashoka repeated the phrase in his head like a mantra. Some part of him had been entirely convinced that he would be fine without Rahil, that he would be perfectly at ease for a few weeks without him.

How foolish.

Ashoka had met Rahil and Sau before they left for Makon with Sachith by his side. Since Rahil would not be with him for his journey to Taksila, his second-in-command had taken his place. It was odd to have anyone else beside him and Ashoka was sure that even Rahil had felt the same.

'Be smart,' Ashoka had told Sau before she had departed, 'and remember – get those soldiers to Taksila if you can.'

If Aarya wanted to ruin his plans, he would ruin hers in return.

Having soldiers without unequivocal loyalty to his brother follow his orders instead was a gamble, but one Ashoka was willing to take. It now rested on Sau to successfully convince Prince Ryu to agree to their plans, and he trusted her like a blind dog trusted its master.

'Don't die,' Rahil had told Ashoka, grabbing onto his arm tightly before he climbed into the leopard-drawn carriage with her. 'I'd be vexed at having to attend your funeral.'

Ashoka's smile had been paper-thin. 'Funny,' he replied. 'I was going to say the same thing to you.'

He hadn't missed the way that Rahil's sharp gaze had settled onto him. How his brown eyes darkened, and his posture became stiff. 'Play the prince, Ashoka.'

Ashoka had squeezed Rahil's arm tightly and let him go. After a moment of hesitation, Rahil climbed into the carriage and then, the two people he trusted most in the world had disappeared from his sight to the Golden City's port.

Only an hour had passed before Ashoka turned to mutter a joke to someone who wasn't there. That was all it had taken, and whatever coin-sized piece of misery he'd held in his heart grew exponentially.

No, he berated himself, *what sort of prince are you, wallowing like some sad jackal?*

'Your Highness,' Sachith called out from behind, distracting Ashoka from his ruminations. 'The royal estate is just ahead of us.'

Glancing up, Ashoka spotted the tall, balconied building with wide archways painted in a milky white. This was where his father had stayed during his brief tenure in the region, and it had remained uninhabited for years. Despite the years of disuse, it was still being maintained by staff who resided in Taksila. Both grandiose and minimalistic, the three-storeyed building featured intricately carved illustrations of nature spirits at the entrance, with the front pillars recounting in the Ridi script his father's annexation of Taksila and the slaughter of the mayakari.

Upon his arrival into the expansive courtyard, Ashoka spotted a lone figure waiting by the steps of the royal residence.

The governor, Kosala.

After dismounting Rāga and giving her nose a quick rub, Ashoka approached the governor with his soldiers behind him. Tall and burly, the governor bowed low when Ashoka stopped in front of him. He was dressed in fine red garments, black beard neatly trimmed, and thick silver rings adorning his pale brown fingers. 'Governor Kosala, Prince Ashoka. Welcome to Taksila,' he greeted. 'I hope that your journey was pleasant.'

'Quite, Governor Kosala,' Ashoka replied. 'I flew much of the way here.'

The governor's eyes widened at the mention of the word 'flew', his eyes shifting upwards. The moment he did, a dark shadow appeared from a break in the clouds before it vanished again.

'Yes, my winged serpent is up there. Frolicking, I assume,' Ashoka said cheerfully. 'Do try not to pet her after she descends – she'll bite.'

Kosala's face contorted, as if the last thing he would do was pet a winged serpent. 'My condolences on the loss of your father, Prince Ashoka,' he said instead. 'It is truly tragic to have lost one of the Ran Empire's finest monarchs.'

Ashoka was about to dismiss Kosala's condolences when he was reminded of Rahil's constant imperative.

'Thank you, Governor Kosala,' he replied. 'It's been a trying time for my family. But I'm here to govern, not fall into a depression at the mention of my father.'

Kosala looked surprised at his answer but played along. 'Of course, my prince,' he said smoothly. 'I think you will find that

Taksila is under control. I fear that you may not have much to govern.'

The undercurrent of condescension made Ashoka smirk. 'The rioting nature spirits haven't escaped my attention, governor,' he replied with a tight-lipped smile. At his pointed glance, the governor flushed a pale red.

'It's an unfixable problem, Prince Ashoka,' Kosala finally found his voice. 'If a problem cannot be fixed, then it's best to leave it alone. No amount of money or aid can help the razed lands. Unless . . . you have any knowledge on how to remove the Great Spirits?'

None, except ask the mayakari for help, which you refuse to do, he thought, frustrated.

'Unfortunately, I come bearing no information,' Ashoka said, smiling politely. 'But rest assured, governor, that I will attempt every possible option.'

'I see.'

Governor Kosala looked unconvinced, like he knew he would fail. Unconvinced like Aarya, like Arush.

Unimpressed, like his father.

White-hot fury sparked in his chest. Usually, Rahil would sense when his anger overwhelmed him, would place a reassuring hand on his arm to calm him. But Rahil wasn't here, so Ashoka forced himself to quell his temper, allowing it to simmer beneath the surface like a crocodile waiting silently beneath still water.

He let the governor take him on a tour of the estate, surprised to find that behind it was a large, formal garden with multiple, symmetrical garden beds enclosed with hedges and flower borders of orange jasmine and jungle geranium, oleander, and anthurium. Meticulously maintained, the framework was dotted with topiaries. At the centre was a water feature; the body of a minor spirit from which liquid spouted. It was hard to believe that his father had resided here without ever asking to uproot the garden when he had taken great care to make sure the palace was without.

One area in particular caught his eye: a cobblestone pathway that led to a hedge off to the side. Whatever was inside was closed off by a white wooden door. Wondering what sort of indescribable feature would be behind it, Ashoka opened it and stepped inside.

He found himself staring at a sprig of abnormally sized, glimmering flowers erupting from the ground. It took Ashoka a few moments to realize that they were not real. Rather, these flowers appeared to have been crafted from gold. They were at odds with the natural flora present elsewhere in the formal garden.

Kosala, it seemed, had been tracking him. 'Ah, that is one of your father's most ingenious ideas,' he said appreciatively. 'He had the flowers made with all of the leftover trinkets.'

'I beg your pardon?' Ashoka questioned. His father had never been the type to melt down precious family heirlooms.

'Trinkets,' Governor Kosala repeated, albeit with mild confusion. 'I was told that the gold belonging to those in the mayakari resistance here were melted down and resculpted into this. Amazing, isn't it?'

Bile rose in his throat. *Amazing?* These pieces of gold were stolen from the dead. Wrenched away from snapped necks, violently torn away from slashed, bloodied wrists – this was a picture of life created from destruction. Of course, his father would have revelled in this sick and twisted form of art. Ashoka couldn't bring himself to imagine the screams of torture that would have echoed in the months following Taksila's annexation. Of children weeping, of mayakari burning, of families torn apart by a sadistic monster deluded by dreams of grandeur.

You cannot erase me, son.

The crocodile stirred. It opened its filmy eyes, widened its jaw. Ashoka now saw a different scene in his mind. It was one of a battlefield, littered with the corpses of Ran soldiers, the battered flag of the Ran Empire burning in blue flames while the mayakari and the nature spirits reclaimed their land, his father's legacy destroyed. An odd little spark ignited in his chest.

Pathetic boy, his father's harsh voice taunted him. *You will amount to nothing.*

For a moment, Ashoka wanted nothing more than to see blood staining his hands. *No, father,* he thought, *I will amount to everything you never thought I would be.*

CHAPTER TWENTY-FOUR

Shakti

SHAKTI'S FIRST FEW DAYS UNDER THE EMPLOYMENT OF Princess Aarya were spent training before she was able to follow closely behind her like a watchful dog. Combat with Ran soldiers gave her energy; Master Hasith's teaching had allowed her to be on par with them without too much strain. The thought gave her an inflated sense of pride.

What she despised was having to shadow the princess, especially since much of her days were spent in council meetings. Yesterday's had been a particularly mind-numbing affair, with the princess proposing a decrease in the cost of textiles.

Often, Shakti wondered if Princess Aarya could sense her distaste: the grudge she harboured for plucking her away from Prince Ashoka and the promise of Taksila. The answer was always a resounding *no*. It took little time to discover that the princess was as vain as a peacock.

Today's topic was more disturbing: mayakari burnings. The emperor, the princess, and several council members sat around a large, lacquered table while the guards stood back in silence. This was a frequently discussed topic, one that made Shakti want to go on a rampage and attack every member present. They spoke of her people as if they were nothing more than livestock bred for consumption.

'The governor of Chalamba reported new two burnings in one of its small townships,' Consul Rangana said. 'There was some minor . . . pushback from its citizens.'

'Sympathizers?' Emperor Arush inquired from his seat at the head of the table.

'No, Your Highness,' the consul replied. 'Women and their families. Dozens were burn-tested before the two mayakari were found.'

With a nonchalance that set Shakti's fury aflame, Arush leaned back and shrugged. 'Unfortunate, but it is the price that must be paid.'

Just you wait, Arush, she thought, clenching her jaw. *My first victim will be you.*

To her utter surprise, she was not the only one who appeared infuriated by his response. One, in particular, held all the temperament of a disturbed winged serpent as she spoke:

'You have the privilege of indifference, brother,' Princess Aarya refuted, her tone cold. 'You will never be burn-tested.'

Scoffing in incredulity, Emperor Arush narrowed his eyes. 'Neither will you,' he replied. 'Why would you care? Are the mayakari not so pressing as your insane desire to explore those ridiculous deadlands?'

'Of course we need to expose mayakari,' the princess replied crossly, 'but we should act to reduce the harm of innocent human women.'

The irony of it all, Shakti thought. *Mayakari are innocent women, too.*

The emperor raised his eyebrows. 'Do you have a proposal for this, sister?' he asked. 'Or will you simply spout vague opinions without presenting a proper plan?'

'Nothing comes to mind yet, brother,' the princess replied, schooling her features into an inscrutable expression. 'Though I shall present a solution if I find one.'

Shakti wondered if the emperor picked up on the princess's

tone: polite and clipped, as if she were holding a thousand curses back.

Once the meeting adjourned, Shakti followed the princess as she took a short stroll about the palace. It was just the two of them, the silence as stifling as a cold. For the most part, the princess was quiet. She appeared faraway, lost in her own thoughts, and Shakti was only too happy to follow along quietly.

She half-wished the princess would request to wander the outskirts of the Golden City; she wished so badly to be surrounded by nature. Shakti had received her first letter from Nayani a few days prior, of Taksila's hill-laden paradise. Then came the unfortunate discovery that letters to the palace were carefully monitored. Luckily, Nayani hadn't written anything to arouse suspicion, but it made Shakti think twice about maintaining frequent communication.

To her surprise, the princess eventually made her way towards Prince Ashoka's quarters, where she stopped in front of the closed door. She seemed to be in a mindless daze.

'Do you have siblings?' Princess Aarya asked her, breaking Shakti's ruminations.

'I— no, princess. I am an only child,' Shakti replied. *Orphan* was the better word for it, but that truth would cost her. 'Why do you ask?'

Adjusting the bright pink pallu of her sari, the princess shrugged. 'No matter, then,' she said. 'You would not understand the vexation that siblings can cause.'

Interesting. 'Nonetheless, I can empathize, princess,' Shakti offered.

Aarya gazed at her for a moment, her hard eyes unflinching. Adil's face stared back at her, taunting. Mocking. Shakti resisted the sudden urge to deface the flawless face with a rusty dagger.

'Empathy is difficult,' Aarya replied. Then, 'Arush appears disinterested in any proposal that doesn't consider war.'

Anyone with half a brain could see that. The young emperor's eyes lit up when expansion was discussed, but the moment more mundane matters came to the forefront of a conversation, his eyes dimmed.

'Is expansion not what the Ran Empire requires, princess?' Shakti asked, wanting to gag at the question. She couldn't imagine how many more mayakari would burn beneath the Ran flag.

'Of course it does,' Aarya said offhandedly, 'but what good is an empire without control of its inner workings? A competent ruler must be interested in both, and it appears that Arush is not. If father were here, he would tell him the same.'

Your father is here, Shakti thought, mildly amused. *He is inside my head, and he cannot leave.*

'Not every monarch can be your father, princess,' Shakti replied.

Princess Aarya turned her head away. 'No,' she said quietly. 'He can't.'

Despite herself, Shakti felt a twinge of sympathy. She understood that demeanour, the hung head, the downcast eyes, the glazed expression. This was the picture of someone who had lost and had let that loss affect them badly. It was her whenever she thought of Jaya.

'You miss Emperor Adil,' she said without thinking. She hadn't meant to say it, hadn't meant to offer what sounded like compassion. The princess's father was a tyrant, and she a tyrant's daughter, but grief did not change its ways for those who were wicked. Pain was felt, therefore sorrow followed. 'It will take time to heal.'

When the princess spoke, her voice was croaky. 'How would you know, Shakti?' she asked. Her caustic tone still carried through. 'Have you ever known loss?'

Shakti kept her face impassive when she said, 'Yes,' she said. 'My aunt passed away from an incurable illness, I'm afraid. She died . . . peacefully.'

Each lie speared her through the chest. Shakti half-expected a phantom to tear through her skin, break through her ribcage, and rip out her heart as penance for how she described Jaya's death. She saw it being squeezed, saw the muscle deform under the pressure, and splatter on the ground like pulverized potatoes.

Some would mark her and Aarya's losses to be similar; both had lost family. And yet, the magnitude of them was different. Jaya died a senseless death. Adil's had been justified.

Who are you to justify death, little bird?

She felt her wrist being squeezed. When she glanced down, she found Aarya holding onto it lightly. How unexpected. 'I am sorry for your loss,' the princess said sombrely. 'How did you contend with it?'

'I . . .' Her immediate thought was to say *'By seeking revenge'*, but that would have been an unpalatable answer. 'I wallowed in my thoughts for a while. I liked being alone with them.'

The princess scrunched up her nose. 'I would despise that,' she replied. 'I prefer to be accompanied. Distracted.'

Distracted. The whole palace knew how Princess Aarya kept herself distracted from her grief. During her night-time posts, Shakti had seen enough lovers enter Aarya's bedchambers and leave the next morning flushed, rumpled, some with scratch marks on their arms and shoulders, to know that she had kept herself plenty preoccupied.

At first, Shakti couldn't decide whose way was healthier in terms of dealing with grief. It was only later she decided that *neither* was the correct answer.

Before she could respond, another voice cut through their bizarre exchange.

'Sister?'

A cold shiver ran down Shakti's spine. *Arush.* What was he doing here?

The young emperor had arrived with three guards by his side. Shakti had immediately noticed that he never travelled without them. She'd heard that he had them posted outside his doors when he invited court ladies into his chambers. Maybe he was afraid that he would one day fall victim to death like his father now that he was monarch, a sentiment Shakti understood. Paranoia did that to people. Aarya, meanwhile, toured the palace like a self-entitled cat who thought that nothing, not even the mighty nature spirits, could hurt her, and all but chased away guards whenever she invited men and women into her chambers.

'Arush?' Princess Aarya threw up her hands. 'What are you doing here?'

The corner of Arush's lips tilted upward. 'Are we missing our little brother, Aarya?' he asked. 'He has not yet been gone two weeks.'

Shakti observed interestedly as the princess's rouged mouth tilted downward. Did she really miss her brother? The princess presented herself to be so spiteful that it left little room to entertain the idea that she could care for her youngest sibling.

'Missing Ashoka is like missing a pathetic stray cat,' said the princess, effectively destroying all thoughts of Aarya having a modicum of empathy beneath her ruthless guise. 'I cannot wait for him to run Taksila to the ground.'

'Give him some credit,' Arush replied before he turned his gaze on Shakti. 'Do you think our little brother has a chance at success?'

Princess Aarya sneered. 'Please,' she scoffed. 'He'll come back with his tail between his legs.'

Whatever smidgen of humanity Shakti had seen in the princess had vanished. 'I'm unsure, Your Highness,' Shakti replied to Arush, adding, 'One can only hope the Great Spirits in Taksila can be pacified.'

'Such faith,' Arush commented. 'I cannot imagine that the Ashoka who sat around and read could lead well. He does not fight – he only ruminates. I will never understand him.'

'Only because the concept of thinking is foreign to you, brother,' Aarya replied snidely.

The glint in the emperor's eyes resembled that of a hound tracking a scent. 'I can only assume that dealing with my sister is like handling a pit snake?' he asked her. At his comment, Princess Aarya visibly bristled. 'Perhaps she is more aggravated because she fears she will lose her position in the war council.'

Princess Aarya's expression settled into a hard glare. 'Ashoka will lose his wager,' she said. 'Do not attempt to vex me. Why don't you focus on your duties, brother. Have you viewed my proposal to relocate our soldiers from the Frozen Lands to the south?'

Before she could stop herself, Shakti's hands went straight to Jaya's necklace. It felt like an open confession around her neck.

Arush let out a frustrated growl. 'No, sister. I will not act on anything without assurance from the Ridi prince that more of his cavalry can be sent here,' he said. 'I can only hope Saudamini is able to convince him. Are you so sure it was the best option to send her instead of an older consul?'

Shakti caught the barest trace of a sly smile on the princess's face. 'Of course, brother,' she said.

The princess's insistence on the redistribution of Ran soldiers threatened to take more mayakari lives. But the emperor . . . for some insane reason, he seemed obsessive about expansion into the Frozen Lands. A fool's endeavour, by any means. An environment unfamiliar to warmth-adapted bodies would be disastrous. For all that nature provided, it took away with unflinching brutality.

But it would be far better an outcome than having more mayakari lives lost in the south. If Emperor Arush was somehow convinced to make a sudden decision to act without consultation . . .

An idea formed; a tuberose blossoming in the night while the world slept, smothered by dreams and nightmares.

The reckless emperor not beholden to anyone or anything – Shakti knew just how to shape him.

CHAPTER TWENTY-FIVE
Ashoka

ASHOKA SAT IN HIS FATHER'S STUDY, THE HALF-MOON
bathing the courtyard below in a pale glow.

He had just finished his dinner: steaming hot rice and a variety
of vegetable curries cooked with a tamarind paste peculiar to
Taksila. The study was quiet and cold, with nary a sound to be
heard except for the occasional shuffling of soldiers outside the
room. It smelled unnervingly like his father: of moss and areca. It
had been left untouched, preserved the way it had been for years,
with maps marking pockets of mayakari populations still hanging
on the walls, the colours faded and yellowed. A handful of paper
scraps lay on a wooden shelf, all in his father's blunt script, all
with the same inscription: AS THE EMPEROR STANDS TRUE, NONE
WILL STAND WITH HIM, AS THE EMPEROR STANDS TRUE, YOU
WILL LIE WITH HIM. Ashoka had brushed the scraps aside, without
much thought. Sketches of women ranging from adolescent to
elderly littered the floor, some marked over with large 'X's. He had
torn them to shreds immediately.

He blew out a frustrated breath. The ride through Taksila with
the governor had shown him nothing; only what had been sanitized
for his own benefit. It wouldn't do. He needed to see Taksila as
it was, with the veil lifted.

'Sachith,' Ashoka called out.

A moment passed before Sachith's dark head peered out from between the crack in the door.

'Your Highness?' he asked, bowing his head.

'I'm going out for a stroll,' Ashoka said coolly, leaning back against the chair. The wood pressed uncomfortably into his back.

Sachith glanced outside. 'It's the middle of the night, Prince Ashoka.'

'I did notice that, yes.'

His guard appeared perplexed. 'Right. I can order some soldiers to accompany you—'

'No need, Sachith,' Ashoka interrupted. 'I don't see the point in disturbing them. I'll go alone.'

'Absolutely not, Prince Ashoka,' Sachith said immediately.

'That's not your order, Sachith,' Ashoka replied. 'I will go alone – no guards.'

Sachith sighed. 'Rahil told me you might do this,' he muttered.

Ashoka's stomach fluttered. 'Did he now?'

'Yes, Prince Ashoka,' Sachith said, exasperation clear on his blunt features, 'and his advice was to bargain.'

Ashoka smiled. Rahil and good bargaining skills were mutually exclusive. 'I shall entertain you, then,' he said. 'I refuse the accompaniment of soldiers.'

'And I refuse you going alone,' Sachith countered.

'Sachith,' Ashoka said. 'I would've fled into the night without informing anyone, but here I am being honest with you. Surely, you'll give leniency for my candour?'

Sachith's expression was like granite. 'No,' he said.

'I'll take Rāga,' Ashoka tried, 'no one in their right mind will approach her.'

'And then you will be recognized,' came the frank response.

'Would you rather I take Sahry?'

The mention of his serpent gave Sachith pause, as if the idea was worse than the first. 'No. We'll take the horses,' he said finally. 'That is my final offer, Prince Ashoka.'

'Honesty gets me nowhere,' Ashoka grumbled. '*All right*, Sachith, I agree to your bargain.' Somewhere in his mind, he heard Rahil cheer in victory.

He let Sachith lead him to the stable where the horses were being kept. Rāga was nearby in her own pen, likely sleeping away her tiredness. Curious glances were shot their way, but Ashoka kept his head high as Sachith quickly explained to the inquiring guards his desire for a midnight stroll.

After he saddled himself on a chestnut mare, Ashoka patted its neck. 'You seem quite friendly,' he remarked.

Sachith snorted. 'Anything is friendlier than Sahry, Prince Ashoka.'

'If I flew her into the razed lands, she'd terrify every living thing,' Ashoka agreed. Out of the corner of his eye, he saw Sachith's hands still.

'You wish to take a stroll around the razed lands, Prince Ashoka?' the guard inquired, eyes narrowing.

'Did I not mention that?' Ashoka asked innocently.

'You did not,' Sachith replied, terse.

'Well, what a surprise,' Ashoka replied before he laid out his argument. 'I'm not trying to kill myself, Sachith. I'm not travelling there to start brawls and terrorize people. I'm simply going to do as I said before: wander.'

'But . . . you are you, Prince Ashoka.'

Ashoka narrowed his eyes. What was it that people saw when they looked at him – helplessness? 'Do you think that I cannot keep myself safe, is that it?' he asked. 'Who will I be attacked by that I cannot fight against?'

'Very muscular thieves,' Sachith replied instantly. 'Children who are brilliant with knives—'

'The nerve to think I'd be bested by a *child*—'

'A world-weary, battle-hardened child,' Sachith corrected, 'and those mayakari monsters.'

This time, Ashoka snorted.

'The mayakari would only be a problem if I threaten them,' he replied. 'That does not make them monsters. That makes them human.' He had meant to be sardonic, but the intonation had completely flown past Sachith's head.

'Prince Ashoka, the mayakari are not to be trusted,' he said. 'Your father—'

Ashoka's chest constricted. 'My father is not *here*, Sachith,' he interrupted. Why did his name bleed into every conversation? Was the man not dead? 'He does not govern Taksila. *I* do, and you will not contradict me any further.'

His tone was harsh. Unyielding. In fact, it reminded him of his father. Of his forcefulness, his adamant nature. Guilt came first, but it fizzled out quicker than he expected.

Chastened, Sachith cast his eyes to the ground. 'As you wish, Prince Ashoka,' his tone had deteriorated into something meeker, less insistent. Ashoka realized that, normally, he should've felt guilty.

All that he felt then, however, was satisfaction.

The distant wailing of the nature spirits caused goosepimples to erupt over Ashoka's skin. He had never heard their sepulchral cries before, only their mellifluous chatter whenever he visited wild forestland. This, however, was something entirely different; this was a song of a thousand sorrows drowning in reverberation. How the people of the northern districts suffered through these ghostly dirges every night escaped him.

He'd left Sachith and their horses by the embankment that separated the northern and southern districts. Sachith had still been displeased at having to leave him alone to his devices, but he could not very well object. Sachith was beholden to Ashoka's word. Such was the law; such was the way of the monarchy.

The northern district was jaw-droppingly decrepit. It was as if humanity and nature had warred against each other, with both sides having emerged victorious. Dusty-looking lanterns lit the streets, patches of wild grass grew out from cracks in walls, untamed and unkempt. Tree roots broke through paved roads, smooth surfaces fractured like a tooth. Lone stragglers sat outside small eateries, conversing in soft tones, and stray cats wandered the dingy streets in search of mice.

Ashoka found himself traipsing into a backwater alley, where shrill moans and concentrated grunts filtered out of brothels. He flushed at the sounds but was also hit by the pungent smell of smoke, soil, and saltfish in the air. What a startling difference it was to the smells of the palace, its sterility, freshly made sweets, and the scent of old parchment in the grand library.

Surrounded by the faraway chirping of crickets and the muggy darkness, he had never felt so free. No midnight straggler glanced his way, no pesky sibling taunted him from the council room. It was a freedom he could never have.

In his intense ruminations, Ashoka almost missed the sound of a scuffle as he passed by an unlit, unoccupied storefront. A pained whimper came from behind the fencing that separated the back from the front of the road, from where he spotted flames emitting from a torch.

'From the resistance, are you?' a gruff voice asked. 'How lucky for us – two birds with one stone.'

'Please,' he heard a woman's voice plead. Then came the sound of flesh being hit; a sharp slap followed by a muffled cry that made him tense. Fear spiked through his blood, paralysing him the way a drug would. Part of him did not want to venture into what was an unknown, dangerous situation. And yet, someone behind the fence needed help. Who was he to turn away like a coward and run?

Careful, the logical side of Ashoka's head crooned as he approached, slowly unsheathing his sword. One hand pressed gently against the wood, Ashoka peered through a broken slat and bit his lips to prevent an audible gasp from coming out at the sight before him.

Two women were on their knees, hands bound behind their backs, surrounded by a group of soldiers. Another soldier stood in front of them, smiling viciously with a sword in her hand.

One of the bound women lifted her head up. In the dimness, he could not make out her expression. All he heard was, *'Please.'*

His heartbeat picked up. Mayakari. They had to be. And from what he had heard, potential members of the resistance.

The soldier with the sword confirmed it. 'My father lost everything in the Seven Day Flood,' she said viciously to the witches. 'His home, his crops, his mother. And while the common people suffered, *your* kind refused to help.' Spittle came flying out as she said it. Still, the bound mayakari made no move to respond. It seemed to infuriate the soldier even more.

'Wretched witch,' she hissed. 'Emperor Adil may have passed on, but we continue his legacy.'

Go, a part of Ashoka's mind urged. *Help them. Free them.*

How? the other half responded, anxious.

Talk them down, came the suggestion. *Your reputation will be sullied, but surely you will not let innocents die?*

In a moment of indecisiveness, Ashoka missed his moment. Too late, he heard a startled gasp. Too late, he snapped his head up only to watch in silent horror as the soldier picked up her sword and sliced one of the mayakari's heads clean off. The witch beside her screamed, a grief-stricken cry that pulverized his innards. He flinched as the head dropped to the ground with a dull *thunk*. Blood the colour of anthuriums spilled onto the ground in a hellish waterfall as the soldiers around her let out a loud cheer.

No.

No. He was too late, and it was all his fault.

'What should we do with the body?' one soldier asked as the cheers died.

The soldier shrugged dismissively. 'Burn it,' she suggested. 'The witches burn a nice blue. Pretty to watch.'

You did nothing. Ashoka heard Rahil's voice this time. *You stood by and let a terrible thing unfold. You let this happen when you had all the freedom in this world to stop it. How dare you, Ashoka.*

An unlikely blow, but a needed one. Ashoka clenched his teeth. Just as he heard the soldier say, 'One more body,' he leapt into action. Gripping the fence post, Ashoka found footing on the rails and hoisted himself over it, landing like a cat with its nine lives still intact. His landing surprised the group of soldiers who swiftly pulled out their own swords.

'Who goes there?' one demanded.

Ashoka refused to provide an intelligible response. 'Step away from the mayakari,' he ordered.

A harsh laugh followed his request. 'Ah – another useless resistance member?' one soldier asked. When Ashoka deigned not to reply, the soldier let out a frustrated growl before he barrelled towards him, hands outstretched and curling into fists. Ashoka had only a moment to locate his exposed neck before he delivered a swift punch to the soldier's throat that sent him back, sputtering and winded.

'You'll pay for that, scum,' the soldier growled, hands curling into fists. Ashoka barely avoided the punch intended for his jaw before he ducked and aimed a forceful blow, this time at the soldier's nose bridge. Wheezing at the impact, the man stumbled back. Blood poured from his nose. Ashoka hoped he had hit hard enough to break it.

The soldier roared, his hands reaching for his sword. Before he could unsheathe it, Ashoka withdrew his own and aimed the tip near the man's throat.

Rahil would have been impressed by his speed, though he would have critiqued his fluidity.

'Put your weapon down, soldier,' Ashoka ordered harshly. 'Before I kill you myself.'

At the sound of his voice the soldier's hands stilled, as did the others. Two holding torches came forward, abandoning the bound mayakari, causing Ashoka to flinch at the sudden flash of light. He watched the soldier whose throat was still pressed against his blade frown, and his eyes narrow as he scanned his face before they widened. Likely, he had noted the circlet. It gave him away without question.

'Prince *Ashoka*?' The soldier's voice was incredulous. A chorus of stunned gasps followed as the remaining soldiers bowed hastily.

'Correct,' Ashoka replied. He kept his weapon engaged. 'Step away from the mayakari – all of you. *Now*.'

'B-but, my prince,' the soldier who had claimed the killing blow stepped forward, sputtering like she couldn't believe her ears. Still, his order was followed. Weapons were lowered and a wide berth around the remaining witch was created. 'This woman is a *mayakari*.'

The soldier had expected him to *agree*. She had not expected pushback. It was only a mayakari, after all. Let them be tortured and killed. What did it matter?

In his death, his father had left behind monsters of his own creation. No longer.

'I could not care less,' he said harshly. 'What have they done to you?'

The soldier blinked. 'We caught one of them speaking to a nature spirit in front of—'

'Did they curse you?' Ashoka demanded. The woman shook her head. 'Did they send a spirit after you?' Again, she denied it.

'Then you had no business participating in murder, soldier,' Ashoka said. 'If they had done nothing, I believe the real perpetrator is *you*.'

A stunned silence followed. He knew that the soldiers would only be reciting one phrase in their heads: *mayakari sympathizer*. No doubt, this would be a blow to him in the future. Soldiers talked. To each other. To the people. To the governor. A misstep on his part, but at least he had saved one life. One was enough.

He lowered his weapon. 'Leave.' As he gave out the order, Ashoka straightened his back to make himself appear more commanding. 'Do not expect me to govern like my father did. You will face dire consequences otherwise.' A child's threat. How well it worked, he did not know, but he knew that the soldiers would not refute a prince's orders.

Quietly, the group of soldiers bowed before they retreated, one by one. Some glanced surreptitiously back towards the mayakari who remained alive, then at him. Just as the female soldier passed, the chains in her armour clinking like cups, Ashoka placed his hand on her shoulder. At his touch, she halted, surprise etched across her wide eyes.

'Prince Ashoka?'

He leaned in close. 'My condolences for your father's loss of property, soldier,' he muttered into her ear, 'but that does not warrant senseless death in the name of personal justice.'

When he pulled back, her face was wiped clean of any expression. With a small nod, she too, departed.

Once he saw the glimmer of torchlight vanish down the road, Ashoka relaxed. Then, he turned his attention to the mayakari who had been watching their exchange in silence – a young woman who appeared to be a few years younger than him. Her wide, calf-like eyes were red and filled with tears as she gazed at him in absolute fear.

Ashoka held his hands up, palms out in a gesture of peace. 'I'm not here to hurt you, I promise. Look.' To prove his point, he slipped his sword back into its sheath. 'I'm here to help.'

The young girl glanced at her headless comrade. When she turned back to look at him, her face was pinched. Destroyed. 'They killed her, and they were about to kill me,' her voice was devoid of all emotion as she spoke. 'What's to stop you from doing the same, *Prince* Ashoka?' She stressed his title with venom. Ashoka understood the distrust.

'You're right,' he said. 'You can't trust me. I understand that. At least let me unbind you. You cannot go far with your hands tied.'

The mayakari said nothing, but she angled her back slightly towards him in a gesture of defeated acceptance. Hastily, he rushed towards her, bent down on one knee, and unknotted the thick rope. As it fell away, he spotted the indents against her wrists.

The moment the rope was removed, the young mayakari crawled towards the dead woman's body, a sepulchral cry escaping her mouth. 'Saumya,' she sobbed, her hands squeezing the fabric across her friend's torso. Visibly trembling, she turned to the head where the dead mayakari's eyes were still open and frozen in terror.

Ashoka couldn't bring himself to focus on the head for more than a few moments before he forced himself to look away; his stomach churned when he stared too long.

'I am sorry,' he said, tone soft, 'for you. For your friend.'

The young mayakari didn't seem to hear him. Instead, she reached out and gently closed the eyelids. Her hands moved to rest on her lap once the task was complete, and for a long while, they stayed there in silence. A prince and a mayakari; the son of an oppressor and the oppressed. Then, she finally broke the quiet.

'Naila,' the mayakari said quietly. 'My name is Naila.'

'Naila,' Ashoka echoed. 'You should leave. The soldiers may come back.'

The young woman didn't move. Instead, she appraised him suspiciously. 'You really don't want to kill me,' she remarked.

'Should I want to?' Ashoka asked, exasperated.

'You are a Maurya. Forgive me for assuming otherwise.'

Ashoka paused. There was nothing he could say to that.

'Well then, if you're not here to hurt me, help me,' she said, adding, 'Prince Ashoka,' almost as an afterthought. 'I can't leave Saumya's body here. She doesn't deserve to be a feast for the crows.'

'I . . . what do you . . .?' He gestured helplessly at the body, then the head. What did Naila want to do? Perhaps they could burn it here, or even bury it. However, it seemed that she had an altogether different plan.

'I-I'll carry Saumya's head,' she stuttered first before twisting her expression into a determined grimace, 'and you look quite capable, Prince Ashoka. Can you carry the body?'

Ashoka balked. Being asked to carry a dead body was certainly not what he had expected to do in his first night at Taksila. He couldn't even look at it – how could he *carry* it? The thought made him sick, but he turned towards it. He could not stand there and do nothing.

The grass was stained dark where the head and body were separated. Small puddles of blood shone in the moonlight. Releasing a harsh breath, Ashoka bent down and gently, gently placed his arms beneath Saumya's body, lifting so that they supported the back and legs. Shifting enough to right his posture, he couldn't help but glance at the neck. Muscle, torn skin, and a distended gullet greeted him.

Breathe, he told himself. *Breathe.*

The body was warm, giving the impression that it was somewhat alive, but it wasn't. It smelled like flowers and sweat, and he tried not to inhale, afraid he would regurgitate the contents of his dinner.

He watched Naila pick up the head in complete silence. Her hands and arms became smeared with streaks of blood as she cradled it like it was a baby. Beneath the glare of the moon, she looked like an avenging warrior from a children's tale.

In this empire though, she was no hero; she was a midnight terror.

'Where do we take her?' he asked.

'To the forestland where she belongs,' Naila replied. Then, a quiet 'Thank you' followed.

Basic decency did not require a show of thanks, but Ashoka decided not to press Naila on it. After all, mayakari were likely used to receiving the bare minimum from Ran soldiers. Instead, he said, 'Lead the way.'

As they walked, death blanketing them like a stifling heat, Ashoka recalled a similar scenario: the deer. Rahil. His father's command. Here he was once again, burning an innocent. Blood from the open neck slithered down his right arm, and his skin crawled in response.

In both instances, he could have prevented a senseless death. But here, he could have steeled his resolve quicker, tempered his indecisiveness sooner. Saumya's death was his fault. He could have stopped the soldiers.

And, for the first time in his life, Ashoka wondered if violence had been the right response.

CHAPTER TWENTY-SIX
Shakti

ENTERING THE COLLECTIVE WAS EASIER THIS TIME. EYES closed, Shakti sat on her bed and leaned against the cold wall in a meditative pose and let herself relax. Having her mind become empty was near-impossible but focusing on the breath helped lessen any extraneous thoughts and outside noise. At least the hubbub of the palace was diminished in the dead night. Then, when she felt that inevitable tug and grasped the thread, she forced herself to think not of Adil, but of Emperor Ashoka.

'Well done.' She heard his voice first. When Shakti opened her eyes, she found that, for once, she hadn't arrived in the throne room. This time, her surroundings were natural: a mountaintop where grey fog shrouded her ankles, deep green foliage and bright-coloured flowers intermingled with lifeless vines and dead tree stumps with dried-out, glossy sap. The emperor stood beneath a vibrant Na tree, his dark eyes welcoming, the golden circlet blinding. 'You have called me, Shakti.'

She didn't respond at first, instead drinking in the environment around her. Being stuck inside the royal palace had deprived her of the natural world, and this was a pleasant change despite it being in her mind. Odd though, that there was such a prominent display of life and death here. 'Emperor Ashoka,' she greeted him finally. 'Where are we?'

'The Mountain of Rebirth,' the emperor replied. 'A place that holds many memories for me.'

Ah. So, this was where the Maurya family's ashes were scattered.

'What kind of memories?' she asked.

'Ones of my youth,' he replied. As usual, there was no further explanation. 'Why have you called me, Shakti?'

'I come with a request,' she said, and stepped towards him. 'I wish for you to guide me through a dream invasion, Emperor Ashoka.'

He did not hesitate. 'As you wish,' he said. 'Picture the target in your mind's eye.'

Pleased by his compliance, Shakti thought of Emperor Arush, his bulky frame and his harsh features. The same ruby-studded circlet around his head. Once his image was seared into her mind, Shakti felt a strange sensation take over her. It was like a hundred pinpricks were stabbing at her back.

When she opened her eyes, the emperor was not there. She could no longer see the Mountain of Rebirth. Instead, she was viewing a scene through something akin to a translucent globe. As if she were a teller of prophecy and fortune peering through her glass ball.

She saw Arush through this glass. He charged through a battlefield on a giant leopard, arms swinging swords that cut through flesh like they were sun-softened, bruised mangos. He held onto his saddle through core strength alone. Blood spurted from the necks and chests of his opponents in a manner that could only be described as comical. Splatters covered his brown cheeks, his armour, his leopard. Poor creature, being forced to fight battles it did not have to fight.

This was Arush's dream. Even in his sleep, he dreamed of violence. How like Adil he was.

Will yourself into the dream, Emperor Ashoka's voice whispered to her.

'As myself?' she asked aloud. That would be far too strange, even for her.

As anyone, the emperor's voice replied. *Simply will it to be so.*

Who could she appear as, that Arush would not find jarring? There was only one person. Shakti thought of Emperor Adil and thrust herself into the dream. It felt as if she were pushing through a wall of cotton. It was unsettling but posed little difficulty.

When she glanced down at her hands, Shakti was surprised to see them thicker, hairier, and corded with lean muscle. Gently, she touched her head and felt the phantom sensation of a circlet pressed against her forehead.

She was Emperor Adil.

Soldiers on giant leopards whipped past her, but she was unharmed. They were ghosts, as was she. Slowly, she approached Arush from the opposing side, arms stretched wide.

'Son,' she said loudly, caught off-guard by Adil's voice booming out of herself. That would take some time to get used to. 'How well you fight.'

The dreamscape shuttered at her words. All movement halted. Leopards paused in their charge. Atop his steed, Arush was the only one who moved. His eyes widened when he caught sight of her – no, *Adil* – coming towards him.

'Father?' he asked, voice full of wonderment. With incredible speed, he descended from his leopard. When Shakti stopped just in front of him, Arush got on his knees and touched both hands to her feet as a sign of respect. 'How glad I am to see you.'

'And I you, my son,' she replied, touching the crown of his head. It felt odd to portray herself as an elder. 'Whom do you fight?'

Even she could not tell. The Ran Empire fought against the mayakari, but these soldiers were not just women. Arush, too, appeared to be confused despite it being his own dream.

'I—' he began and looked around as if to clarify for himself. 'I fight the south. The mayakari. For you.'

Shakti tilted her head to her left to gesture to a dead man with an arrow protruding from his chest. 'This is not a mayakari, my son,' she said. 'Who is it that you fight for in my name?'

Emperor Ashoka had said the weak-minded could be easily

influenced, and it seemed that Arush was a surprisingly easy pick. At her words, she saw tendrils of white dust snake along the ground, falling from the sky and covering the dead like a smattering of powdered sugar.

'I fight . . .' Arush began to say but stopped when the terrain around them changed.

Beneath her feet, the ground was as white as the feathers of a dove, stretching to where the ground met the grey sky. Sunlight did not shine brightly here like it did in the Ran Empire. It was partially blocked by grim, ash-coloured clouds. Dark sprigs of grass jutted out of the snow, not quite dead but not quite alive. Mountains began to form, but they were blurred, half-finished. Arush could not picture it in its entirety, but she knew what this was. The Frozen Lands, or what seemed to look like them as it appeared like an unfinished painting. Arush would not have seen the terrain for himself, she realized. He could only imagine what it looked like based on drawings or from second-hand accounts.

The change in Arush's mood was potent – Shakti could sense it. There was a deep yearning here, an unshakeable desire. A want.

'You wish to conquer the Frozen Lands,' she said. Arush didn't look her in the eyes when he nodded his assent.

Focus placed to the north would relieve the south. 'Brilliant,' Shakti told him, smiling. 'A conqueror's heart.'

Snow dusted Arush's dark hair as he stared at her, appearing somewhat confused. 'Do you speak the truth, father?' he asked.

'What do I gain from lying, son?' she replied.

A smile lit up Arush's face. So unaware. So foolish. So easy to manipulate.

Here, in the dreamscape, Shakti was the emperor.

Grasping Arush's shoulder, she gestured towards the foggy mountains. 'Why follow my path when you can create your own?' she told him. 'If you wish so badly to conquer the north, there is ample opportunity for you to try.'

'Really?' Arush asked. There was a hint of tentativeness, but his voice sounded surer. More confident.

'Forget the south,' Shakti said again. 'Conquer the Frozen Lands. It does not matter how many bodies you send to their deaths. Only make me proud, my son.'

CHAPTER TWENTY-SEVEN
Ashoka

Naila took him to a wasteland to bury Saumya's body.

Even a fool could guess where they had trekked to. Rubble and dust, mud and giant footprints marred the landscape. If there had been buildings here before, it was hard to see them now. Wood was splintered, stones half crushed into a fine powder, and the ribcages of long-deceased farm animals jutted from the ground in gruesome bouquets. Everything within view was damaged.

These were the razed lands that the Great Spirits destroyed every single night. Even a distinct change in the air was noticeable, mud and decomposing food with a slight undertone of sulphur.

For the duration of their journey, Naila was silent, and Ashoka made no move to converse with her. He sensed that she needed to be in her own thoughts. Having to carry around her friend's body and head was cruel enough. Forcing her to speak at the same time would be brutal.

Unlike the remainder of Taksila, this land was unoccupied by soldiers. Even in the dingiest streets of its poorest district, they had skulked about. Humans were notably absent where malevolent Great Spirits wandered.

Naila took a path that cut straight through the rubble. It made him nervous. The land around them was open, the north bordered by mountains. An image came in his head, one of nature spirits emerging out of the forestland, their fury directed right at him. They charged like leopards, intent on ripping him apart, bone by bone, while Naila watched gleefully.

He shook his head, irate. These were remnants of his father's tales of caution. Ashamed by his own distrust, Ashoka pushed those thoughts away. He had no reason to doubt Naila. Not yet.

His back was starting to ache from carrying Saumya's body for what seemed to be an eternity, so Ashoka was relieved when they finally stopped at the very outskirts of the ravaged lands, just where destruction met nature. Even here, there was decay; the plants appeared wilted, trees leafless with bark shedding like a dog's fur in the summer months.

'You can leave her here,' Naila said. Her voice still sounded hoarse, as if the back of her throat had been scratched.

Careful not to cause more damage, Ashoka gently placed the body down on the ground, angling his head upward as far as possible so as not to have the slashed neck hit the underside of his chin. When he stood back up, he found Naila observing him.

'All this time has passed and yet I remain alive,' she remarked.

'You keep expecting me to kill you,' he replied, a little frustrated. 'I won't.'

'I see,' she said. Then, 'I'm curious, Prince Ashoka. Why were you wandering about in the middle of the night? Without your royal guard, no less.'

'I wanted to observe the razed lands,' he replied. 'I can only assume that crucial information would be kept a secret from me in order to make the city appear pleasing.'

'Mayakari killings aren't kept secret,' Naila said sharply.

'That I know,' he replied. 'I was referring to the nature spirit rampages. I want to put an end to them; see this city at peace.'

Naila let out a laugh. In that moment, she seemed like his siblings, intent on doubting him at every turn. 'How rich,' she said once her laughter subsided. 'A Maurya trying to fix what a Maurya has broken.'

'I heard one of the soldiers before they killed Saumya,' he said gently. He needed to make sure Naila did not take his next remark under suspicion. 'You are part of the resistance?'

The effect was immediate. Naila's head snapped up so fast he thought she would get whiplash. She eyed him like he was a tiger peering through foliage, waiting for its prey. At that moment, Ashoka wondered if he'd made a mistake. 'Is that a question or an accusation?'

'A question,' he replied. 'It would benefit me greatly if this were true.'

He could sense that her guard was back up again. 'I knew it. False niceties. I will not—'

'I need the help of the resistance,' he interrupted before she could spiral into a typhoon of distrust. *Spirits.* He should have brought Harini with him. 'I cannot imagine that I can stop the nature spirit rampages without them.'

'You . . . want our *help*?' Each word was enunciated with a progressive degree of scepticism.

'Given the circumstances, I understand why this would be hard to digest,' said Ashoka. 'But I think we can both agree that the Great Spirits are a problem. Understanding why they are behaving this way and stopping them would be of great benefit to everyone.'

Realization dawned on the young witch's face. 'You want to meet our leader.'

The moon hung lower in the sky than he had seen it last time. He could not stay any longer; Sachith would either be having a heart attack or preparing to send out a search party. Neither were favourable outcomes.

'Believe my intent to right my father's wrongs,' he implored. 'I want to help.'

'No.'

No hesitation; the rejection was swift and cutting.

'The Great Spirits keep—'

'We know what the Great Spirits do, Prince Ashoka,' Naila's voice turned hard. 'Despite what you believe, we are trying to solve this problem. The resistance doesn't need your help. You'll be as useless as the governor.'

And what aid could you possibly give, was the question left unsaid.

Ashoka faltered. Without another mayakari to back him, this reckless plea had been in vain. He needed to have the resistance trust him and he'd been foolish enough to assume that carrying a body would be the way to earn it. But that was hardly likely, not when the cause of death was because Adil Maurya and his propaganda had decreed it.

'What is the governor doing?' he asked, trying to ignore her jab but the insult stung more than he thought it would. *That was how she saw him?*

'Nothing,' she replied. 'That's the problem. He doesn't understand that the more he plunders forestland for ironwood, the more he risks aggravating the Great Spirit that resides there. He'll turn the northern forests into a wasteland, same as this.'

Mentioning Governor Kosala seemed to cause a shift in Naila's mood. Whatever good will she had shown him before seemed to vanish. 'You should leave,' she said quietly. 'Go back to your estate and pretend to govern. Spirits know that Kosala does.'

Ashoka had the awareness to not probe her further. He needed another way to contact the resistance, but perhaps this would alter Naila's perception of him. Ashoka Maurya, acquiescing to a mayakari's orders, leaving her alone in the forestland, not having harmed her. Not every step had to be a big one.

'What will you do with your friend's body?' he asked before turning to leave.

Naila's answering smile was a sad one. 'What else is there in life for us, Prince Ashoka?' she said. 'We burn.'

Three days later, Ashoka ordered a ban on mayakari burnings and temporarily halted ironwood logging in the north. Naila's words had haunted him till his return to the royal estate.

What else is there in life for us?

He'll turn the northern forests into a wasteland.

If such senseless deforestation would lead to another set of Great Spirits being angered, he was all too glad to halt the process. Claiming to Arush that this was part of his plan to rectify the situation without the mayakari resistance had enough merit to pacify his brother's suspicions. As far as good economic decisions went, it wasn't one. But better that Arush and Aarya enjoy knowing he was making mistakes than indirectly helping the mayakari.

Ashoka expected blowback from Governor Kosala, who wasted no time in making his feelings known. Days after his proposal came into effect, he was informed by one of the estate staff that the governor requested an audience.

'Governor Kosala,' Ashoka greeted as the man strode into his father's study. He was in the middle of drafting a summary of events to be sent to Arush. 'In a hurry, are we?'

Governor Kosala's face was schooled into a mask of cool detachment. His gold rings were thick and gaudy, studded with a ridiculous number of gemstones – a sure sign of a man with new money. 'Prince Ashoka,' he bowed, 'your order to interrupt ironwood logging – I must ask you to reconsider it.'

'Why?'

'I understand that you are still young,' the governor replied, his voice patronizing, 'so you may not grasp the consequences yet, Prince Ashoka. When you halt work, you halt the people. They do not get paid. No payment means no food on their table. No ironwood means less revenue. It is a never-ending cascade.'

'Let me paint you another scenario, governor,' Ashoka remarked, adopting the same tone. 'More deforestation without appeasement rites means more risk of angering the Great Spirit. More angry spirits mean assured destruction of natural resources. Destruction of natural resources means further limiting areas to procure ironwood. In this scenario, workers will still be unable to work; the timeline to it is simply longer. I'm delaying destruction. Work can be redirected elsewhere.'

Kosala grimaced. 'We can always find new forestland,' he said. 'Appeasement rites aren't necessary.'

'Then, are you willing to run your city into the ground?'

The governor did not respond. Instead, he fixed Ashoka with an inscrutable gaze.

'I heard the most interesting tale,' the governor said, finally.

Setting aside his ink-dipped stylus, Ashoka folded his arms neatly on the table. 'Do tell, governor,' he replied. 'I love stories.'

Perhaps the governor missed his sarcasm, for his eyes flashed with a sly mirth. 'One of my soldiers has informed me that they ran into you close to the north-western district a few nights ago,' he replied. Ashoka sensed that the governor was watching him carefully, waiting for him to show a sign of fear. 'From what I have been told, you *saved* a mayakari. I do hope this was nothing but a fanciful tale.'

Plastering on a nonchalant expression, Ashoka leaned back against his chair. 'What of it?' he asked.

Kosala's eyes widened. 'I . . . *what of it?*'

'Has ageing made you hard of hearing, governor?'

'The mayakari resistance are a nuisance, Prince Ashoka,' the governor protested. 'We try to build new roads throughout the districts – they order the spirits to grow weeds over them. We attempt to gain access to any remaining forestland with ironwood – they send spirits to guard them. We have no choice but to respond in kind.'

'By having soldiers execute them?' Ashoka asked in blunt tones. 'I would hardly call that equal retaliation.'

Kosala sounded genuinely curious when he asked, 'If not burning, what else will you have them do, Prince Ashoka?'

'Nothing,' Ashoka replied. 'They should be left alone.'

Kosala raised an eyebrow. 'The whispers are true, then,' he remarked.

Whispers. As if his ideals were not so obviously an open book lying in wait for someone to read. Ashoka had never made any attempt to align himself with his father, and those who worked in the palace knew it. If the staff knew it, everyone else in the empire would know it.

'Brand me a mayakari sympathizer if you must, Kosala, but Taksila is now under *my* governorship,' he replied coolly. Rahil's face flashed in his mind, urging him to keep calm as he spoke. 'My promise to my brother was to right the problems here. To do that, I need to work with methods you consider to be unorthodox. And rest assured that if these targeted murders continue, you will be the first to feel my wrath.'

Unused to making threats, Ashoka felt like an imposter; a child playing villain. Unfortunately, his threat didn't have the effect he had hoped on Kosala, for his face twisted into a sneer. 'You cannot threaten me, Prince Ashoka,' he said. Kosala's voice was still as he responded, but his undertone held all the malice in the world. 'Especially as your brother has given me strict orders to make sure you do not attempt any *tricks*. His own words.'

Ashoka bristled. 'That does not mean you can overrule all of my decisions.'

'When it concerns the mayakari, I can, Prince Ashoka,' Governor Kosala refuted. 'Reverse your decree before I let Emperor Arush know. I don't think you want that, do you?'

Ashoka was sure that he was gritting his teeth hard enough to crack. Blast Arush and his rules.

His silence seemed to renew the governor's good mood. Kosala straightened his shoulders and shot him a smile.

'Since there is nothing else to discuss, Prince Ashoka, I will take my leave.' His voice was nonchalant when he bowed, as if absolutely nothing had transpired between them. 'I hope my story satisfied you.'

'It was poorly told,' Ashoka replied, stone-faced.

Kosala shrugged. 'I was never one for stories,' he said before turning to leave. The way in which he departed, whistling a merry tune, held the air of a man who had never been denied anything in his life. Ashoka had the sudden urge to run after him and ram his dagger through his heart. He wanted to see the blood pooling out of his chest, wanted to see the light disappear from his eyes as he lay dying a slow, painful death.

No, he told himself. Such rage was not him. *You will not think this way.*

To calm himself, Ashoka decided to walk around the courtyard among the trees and flowers. He had half a mind to visit Sahry in her pen but decided against it. She tended to sense his moods and reciprocate in a similar fashion; if he was angry, she would be agitated.

A relieved Sachith followed him out to the courtyard, keeping a respectful distance away. Ashoka had found him that night by the embankment, worried out of his mind and ready to call in additional guards to track him down. Hearing that he only wished to take a stroll within a confined cage and not a maze-like city would have made him exorbitantly pleased.

I hope you can get the Ridi soldiers to me, Sau, he thought. Kosala was right. These soldiers would distrust him. They knew as well as he did who the true emperor was. He wandered the gardens and found himself drawn past the hedge that housed the ornamental gold flower patch. It stood out like a dead body in a barren field. How cruel of his father to place something like this here.

Stooping down, he observed the handiwork; whoever had made it certainly had a talented hand.

As he ran a gentle finger around the petals' edges, Ashoka felt a phantom brush against his left cheek. At first, he thought nothing of it, but when Sachith let out a shocked gasp, Ashoka turned to his side.

A minor spirit greeted him.

This one was a wisp of a creature; one-eyed, pale green and little. It had one arm like a human while the other was a curlicue tendril dusted with flecks of gold. It chattered to him incoherently, and the sound recalled the echolalia of a child.

Ashoka wished he could understand it. That incandescent song was as foreign to him as his father's pride. 'Hello, little one,' he said with a smile.

Hovering by his neck, the spirit tugged at his burned ear with its human hand. At first, the sensation was ghostlike; the next minute, he was doubled over, fingers grasping the dirt as his entire body went into shock.

'Prince Ashoka!'

Sachith's voice was faint, barely there. A terrible fear took over Ashoka as he clutched his throat. His lungs felt full, not with air but with something more solid. For a terrible, split second, he couldn't breathe.

What is this, he thought to himself as he let out an aggressive cough. He could feel Sachith's hands thumping against his back in a furious attempt to dislodge something. What followed the fear was dread, a dark acceptance, a vengeful promise, then—

Blood. Heat. Metals smelted. Remodelled.

With another frightful cough the paralysing distress left Ashoka's body. His spine stopped tingling, his stomach unknotted itself, and his fingers relaxed against the dirt.

Those are not my emotions.

'Prince Ashoka!' It was Sachith's voice again, this time much clearer. Clasping his shoulder in a tight squeeze, he helped Ashoka sit up. 'Are you all right? What happened? I shall fetch the physician immediately.'

'No.' Letting out a ragged breath, Ashoka lifted his head so he was eye-to-eye with the nature spirit. 'There is no need, Sachith.'

'No need?' Sachith's pitch rose a fraction. Ashoka was going to send the poor man into an early retirement, that much he was willing to bet coin on.

'I was not overcome with an affliction,' Ashoka replied. He stared at the one-eyed spirit with wonderment. 'You showed me something, didn't you? What was it – fact, fiction, or both?'

The nature spirit did not answer him with words. Instead, it fisted its human hand in the air and extended it before repeating the movement again.

'What's it trying to say?' Sachith asked, sounding baffled.

Mystified, Ashoka continued to observe the spirit. It kept performing the same motion. *A salute? A code? What was it?*

Then came the realization. The flowers were made from looted trinkets. They carried with them violent memories. Blue fire. Gold burning against salt-stung skin. This poor minor spirit likely knew the true weight of his father's cruelty and had to live alongside it.

'What else, Sachith?' he said, and stood up. Dirt was wedged into the lines of his palms. 'But that my father caused suffering.'

CHAPTER TWENTY-EIGHT

Shakti

ARUSH WAS MORE MALLEABLE THAN SHE HAD THOUGHT.

Two days following the dream invasion, he called for an impromptu council meeting, stating that it was a matter of great importance. Shakti was with Princess Aarya when the directive was given to meet the emperor in the throne room in two hours.

Aarya had rolled her eyes. 'I will not be made to wait,' she announced, 'and I do not want to be attacked with any sudden announcements.'

She'd stalked out of her quarters, leaving behind a handful of ruffled maidservants. Shakti had no choice but to follow the princess to the throne room.

'Brother!' Aarya exclaimed once they entered. Emperor Arush was sitting on the Obsidian Throne, guards lined neatly in rows behind him. Shakti bowed as was customary as they approached. Aarya, meanwhile, did no such thing and remained as she was. Arush wasn't as fear-inducing as Adil had been, but there was still something imposing about him, as if he could snap your neck without thinking twice about it. Cruel and handsome features seemed to be a speciality of the Maurya clan.

'Little sister,' Arush greeted her. 'You forgot to bow.'

Aarya stared at her brother, gaze unflinching as she came to a halt at the base of the steps to the throne. 'Well, go on, then,' she ordered. 'Tell me what it is you intend to surprise the council with.'

'Bow, sister,' Arush repeated, this time with more force. 'Being family does not exempt you.'

Still, the princess did nothing. When three of Arush's soldiers stepped forward, instinct drove Shakti to move in front of the princess. Despite her grievances about the Mauryas, she still had a role to play. Her duty was to the princess first.

She felt a hand gently press against the back of her shoulder before it disappeared. Aarya. The look she gave Shakti was inscrutable as she conceded to Arush and bowed, her gold throatlet swinging like a pendulum, lapis-studded earrings clinking like glass.

'Better,' came Arush's voice. Shakti saw Aarya stiffen as she straightened up.

'Well then, brother,' she began, 'tell me what it is you plan to do.'

The emperor's response came fast. 'I am removing all our soldiers from the southern border,' he stated.

Incredulity and euphoria worked together to lift Shakti's spirits as she recalled her commandment to Arush. *Forget the south. Conquer the Frozen Lands. Make me proud.* The dream manipulation – it had worked. Satisfaction rushed through her, cold and sharp.

Meanwhile, Princess Aarya let out an audible gasp. 'What?' she screeched. 'Brother, what on earth for?'

'My plan is to focus on the conquest of the Frozen Lands.' Undeterred by his sister's palpable indignation, Arush continued. 'Our army is currently spread thin across the four corners of our empire. We need to concentrate it on one area at a time.'

'What about the Ridi soldiers?' Aarya demanded. 'Are they not to be stationed at the northern border?'

Arush shook his head. 'I received correspondence from Saudamini,' he said. 'Apparently the crown prince was unable to be swayed completely. According to him, Prince Ryu was initially preparing to remove all remaining Ridi soldiers from the Ran Empire, but Saudamini convinced him to keep half.'

Aarya muttered something unintelligible.

'Father was intent on conquering the north as he was the south,' Arush said. 'Losing half of the Ridi military is already a blow. I'm simply going about this logically.'

Shakti wondered if his logic had come from her whispering in his dreams.

'No, you're being foolish.' Aarya curled her lip. 'We are ill-equipped to trek into the north. Our supplies are not enough.'

Arush's expression was stony. 'You disagree with my plans, then,' he said.

Princess Aarya crossed her arms. 'Completely,' she replied. 'Removing our soldiers from the southern border is madness. What about Taksila?'

At the mention of Taksila, Shakti's ears perked up.

'What about Taksila?' Arush sounded almost bored.

'*Ashoka*,' Aarya said as if that were answer enough. 'He is – how will he maintain control of the region without an adequate number of soldiers?'

A curious expression flitted across the emperor's face. 'Oh yes, it nearly slipped my mind,' he said. 'Some of the Ridi soldiers will be sent to Taksila. It would counteract the removal of our own soldiers there. I heard that Saudamini negotiated her way through that deal as well – what a good pick on your behalf.'

From Aarya's consternated expression, Shakti had an inkling that the princess had not expected this whatsoever. Pleasure shot through her at Aarya's sudden bout of misfortune.

'Why this sudden concern for little Ashoka, sister?' Arush asked, raising an eyebrow. 'I was half-inspired by him, too, you know. He sent me correspondence suggesting I relocate the soldiers in Taksila and replace them with Ridi soldiers at my behest – it seems that they are too many in number there. Rest assured; this change won't expose us. I don't see Kalinga attempting to conquer what is unconquered. Do you?'

The princess appeared not to be listening. 'Ashoka suggested this to you?' she asked.

'Are you deaf, sister?' Arush replied. 'What exactly is the matter?'

Shakti watched Aarya close her eyes and breathe in deeply. When she reopened them, they were as dull as an unsharpened sword. 'The mayakari, brother,' Aarya said. 'Did you forget them? Those monsters still infest the south, and you wish to halt your attacks?'

The urge to wrap her hands around the princess's throat was strong enough for Shakti to clench her fists together. *Monsters*. As if this privileged brat knew anything about her. Had an original thought ever crossed her mind, untainted by Emperor Adil's words?

'Temporarily,' Arush explained. 'It does not mean that we halt mayakari burnings altogether, sister. People can still report sightings, and soldiers can still investigate. I simply will not have a horde of soldiers blaze through the unconquered lands when they could be sent to the Frozen Lands.'

Hearing the two talk about mayakari like they were nothing more than a rat infestation was bloodcurdling. Shakti realized that she had perhaps become too lax here, had forgotten what kind of power the royal children now wielded. All these talks of expansion and she was forgetting who its victims were.

Aarya, it seemed, was not appeased by this. 'You are making a mistake,' she said bluntly. 'This is not out of respect for father's provision. You want some sort of glory, some sort of satisfaction for yourself.'

Arush smiled. 'Yes, little sister,' he said. 'It's called a legacy, and I intend to leave one.'

That night, Shakti stole into Princess Aarya's dreams.

Dream Aarya sat on the Obsidian Throne. She wore a crown bedazzled with jewels, hewn from gold. Swathes of men and women surrounded her, kneeling respectfully on the floor as she surveyed her subjects.

Shakti could feel Aarya's desire. This aching, chasmic want for power, to hold onto it indefinitely.

'We are victorious, Your Highness.' A faceless advisor approached Aarya and bowed. 'The mayakari infest this land no longer. They are eradicated. Your father would be proud.'

That last sentence spoke volumes. Shakti could sense the happiness radiating off Aarya like a monstrous wave crashing to the shore.

Her conversation with Emperor Arush must have enraged her enough and made her feel powerless enough to redirect her anger at the mayakari. Only in dreams could the princess get what she wanted.

Not this time, Shakti thought as she crossed into the dream as Emperor Adil. The barrier felt thicker than last time. Heavier, more resistant than Arush's had been. Once she made sure that her identity had shifted to Adil's, Shakti called for Aarya.

'Daughter,' she said loudly. Aarya turned to her, dark eyes bright.

'Father!' she exclaimed, making to sit up from the throne. 'Father, look! I've killed every last mayakari. I've accomplished your vision.'

'I see,' Shakti said, gesturing around the hall. Here was a child who waited for the parent to burst into tears of pride. 'You've killed hundreds of innocent women, my daughter. Well done.'

Shockingly enough, Aarya didn't pick up on her derision. She did, however, pounce on one word.

'Innocent?' she echoed. 'They possess power that humans should not. They are a threat to the Ran Empire, father. You taught me that. And have I not proven myself to be a great ruler? Do you not approve?'

Aarya was waiting for it. She was hoping so desperately for the crumbs of approval to fall from Adil's mouth, and he was only a dream. Shakti smiled inwardly. Her weakness was all too easy to discern.

'You're pathetic,' Shakti said, her voice like thunder. At least Adil's voice was effective when it needed to be. 'Sitting on that throne as if you deserve to be. But let me tell you now, daughter, that you will *never* be enough for the throne. You will never achieve greatness. You are a little girl playing make-believe.'

She watched Aarya's mouth fall open, her lower lip tremble. Shakti wondered if the golden child had ever received backlash from her father before.

'Father, I—'

'Arush,' Shakti let her voice drip with cruelty. 'He ought to be where you sit. You say you killed the mayakari? Foolish child, you're sitting on the graves of your brother's victories.'

For good measure, she began to laugh in earnest. 'And Ashoka. Ashoka will surpass you all,' Shakti continued to laugh, silently praising herself for her acting. 'He is the terrible. He is the great. But you? You will slip away into the shadows of history, unknown.'

The scene around them started to dull to a pale and furious red. The sound of flutes and horns screeching filled the air in a delicious cacophony. There was no sense of mercy. There was no voice in her head, Jaya's voice, to remind her that she was wrong. No, that voice was dulled to an undiscernible frequency.

To drive home her verbal assault, to twist the dagger where it was lodged in the proverbial heart, Shakti found herself uttering a dark commandment, unlike that she had asked of Arush.

'Take a knife in your hands,' Shakti spat out, 'and cut yourself, for you deserve to bleed, daughter.'

Aarya's shrill scream rang in the air as the dream shattered like pieces of glass. Shakti felt a lurch in the pit of her stomach, and in moments was whisked back to the Obsidian Throne where she was met with a still-faced Emperor Ashoka.

'You hurt Adil's child,' was all the emperor said once she fully materialized.

'That is the least I can do for what Adil did to me and my village,' Shakti glowered.

His intelligent eyes appraised her as he beckoned her forward.

'Come. I want to show you a memory,' said Emperor Ashoka. His glowing brown eyes started to dim as his gaze pinned her own. 'One I believe to be important.'

'What—' Shakti began, before the world was shrouded in darkness, as the emperor and the throne room vanished like smoke. What reappeared was a dark and moonlit night in a wide and spacious building: the Maurya palace.

It was as if she had slipped into a strange dream. She had the distinct feeling that it wasn't hers, but she was viewing the memory as if it were her own, albeit very distorted. She felt like she was drunk on spirits and had smoked enough opium to kill herself with.

'Did she name it?' she heard herself ask. Except, it didn't sound like her. This voice was a harsh baritone, one she could now discern without fail.

Emperor Adil.

'It's a boy,' a tentative voice replied, but she couldn't place it. The speaker sounded on the verge of tears. 'She has named him Ashoka.'

'*Without sorrow*.' Shakti-as-Adil's voice had turned as venomous as a viper. She had never felt this much blind hatred.

'Yes, for she bore him without sorrow,' said the voice. It lulled for a few moments before it spoke again, albeit tentatively. 'Would you rather he had died?'

'*Without question*.'

Shakti's blurred vision disappeared, just as Adil's final words rang like an echo in her ears. Emperor Ashoka reappeared, lounging on the Obsidian Throne, cognizant eyes watching her with interest.

'What . . .' Shakti felt dizzy as the world around her adjusted to its normal surroundings in The Collective. 'That was . . . I was Adil.'

'Yes.'

'And he was talking about Ashoka. *Prince* Ashoka.'

'Yes.'

'Why would that be of any importance to me?' she asked. 'So, Adil wished his son had never been born. He cannot be the only parent to feel that way about their child, I can tell you that much.'

'This memory is important,' Emperor Ashoka said again, just as he glanced up. A peculiar expression crossed his face. 'Remember that. For now, you must reckon with the consequences of your actions.'

'Reckon with my actions?' Shakti echoed, confused. 'What are you—'

Strangely enough, she could hear a bell. One ring after a five-beat interval, repeatedly. In front of her, Emperor Ashoka turned grey. She felt disconnected, then, as if not properly tethered to The Collective. The bell continued to chime until she realized what was happening.

'Wake,' the emperor whispered before he vanished.

Wake, little bird.

Shakti gasped as she opened her eyes and sat up on her bed, breathing hard and fast like she had been starved of air. That aggressive bell continued to ring, the sound reverberating through the stone walls. Outside her door, she could hear voices. Multiple. They sounded concerned. Fearful.

Blinking furiously, she swung open her bedroom door to see utter chaos.

Palace staff rushed through the corridors of their sleeping quarters. They were headed back upstairs, she noted. *What was going on?*

She managed to grab the elbow of an older man who was speeding past her. 'What's the commotion about?' she asked.

The man's expression was inscrutable. 'Some of the staff had to rush to the northern chamber, along with the physicians,' he said as his eyes assessed Shakti. 'Princess Aarya has been injured.'

Shakti felt herself still.

'How?' she asked.

The older man winced. 'I heard she woke up screaming nonsense, and then proceeded to slash her arms with a ceremonial knife.'

'What?'

Cut yourself, for you deserve to bleed, daughter.

Her commandment echoed in her head. It had been intended as a cruel jab, a thorn meant to prick the recesses of the princess's mind. A small act of psychological warfare. She couldn't have imagined that Aarya would take it as a decree.

Shakti knew without question that this was her doing. She had not just influenced a mind – she had managed to translate a hellish order into reality.

'One child wasting soldiers in the north, the other going mad from grief,' the old man replied nervously. 'Spirits know what's happening to Emperor Adil's children.'

'Do you happen to know what she said?' she pressed. 'The nonsense?'

The man was silent for several beats before he spoke. 'Apparently, she was screaming Emperor Adil's name,' he replied sombrely. 'As if it was a curse to end her very existence.'

CHAPTER TWENTY-NINE
Ashoka

Prince Ashoka,

You may thank me – I have fulfilled your request. Crown Prince Ryu has accepted the proposal to send a troop of his best soldiers to Taksila. I hope that this small victory helps to push your plan forward.

In even better news, Rahil has left for the Golden City. He will return to you in a few days. Unfortunately, I will not.

For your request to be granted, I have made an agreement with the crown prince. There is a perplexing issue regarding the sudden disappearances of the mayakari in Makon and he has asked for my help. Why he needs a Ran advisor is beyond me, but I have decided to stay to uphold my end of the bargain. Before you worry, I beg you not to. My safety has been guaranteed. I will return to Taksila once the matter in the Makon is resolved – do try not to flounder in my absence.

Yours,

Sau

SAU'S LETTER INITIALLY FILLED ASHOKA WITH HOPE. Then excitement, then confusion before being replaced by worry despite Sau's advice. He wondered the same as she did: what sort of problem required a Ran advisor to stay behind in a foreign kingdom? Sau did not have to agree to such terms, but she had. For him.

Ashoka found himself torn in two. For one, Rahil was to return. His heartbeat doubled at the thought of his friend beside him once more, but Sau would not be here. His mother's request that they work together was still paused for the time being. He could only hope that Sau kept herself out of trouble as best as she could before departing for the Golden City. There were wins today but also losses. Temporary losses, he hoped.

Right now, he had more pressing concerns. In Taksila, he'd returned to the starting line. Under Kosala's threat to inform Arush, he'd been forced to reverse his initial proposal to halt ironwood logging. Doing so had made him feel ridiculous, like he was a rambunctious child without forethought. No doubt the people of Taksila would see him as the same.

Perhaps because of that, and despite his strict orders to ban mayakari killings under the guise of preventing harm against human women, soldiers beholden to the governor refused to listen. They harassed any woman who so much as stopped to pick a wilted flower from the street. It reminded him of something Sau had told him many years ago as they had sat together and observed the dark forestland from his balcony.

'I love the night, Prince Ashoka,' she had said. 'But the night does not love me.'

These soldiers seemed intent on going against him. Prejudice clouded their actions to an unhealthy degree. In fact, he could almost hear his father laughing at him. *Attempt your useless ways,* his voice crooned. *But can you see now that they do not work?*

Useless ways. Ashoka was determined to prove a dead man wrong.

Two hours past midnight, when he was sure his guards stopped checking on him, Ashoka stole out onto the balcony. Peering over the rails, he spotted three soldiers standing guard below, their backs turned, staring out into the placid night. They were far away enough that he could just swing himself over the balcony and drop to the ground to hide among the foliage below.

Ashoka pulled himself over the balustrade, hands first holding the handrail before he crouched like a langur to grip the base rail. He dropped his feet so he was left dangling over the edge, arms supporting his body weight. Letting himself swing to gain momentum, Ashoka let go of his hands and landed on the grass without a sound.

Hiding behind the ground foliage, he adjusted his cloak. Underneath, he wore plain civilian clothes that Harini had procured for him. At his side, his dagger seemed to bear the same weight as a boulder.

'Prince Ashoka?'

He jumped and turned around. Another cloaked figure emerged from the dark. Its features were barely visible, but he knew the voice without question.

'Harini,' he greeted.

'I watched your escape, Prince Ashoka,' Harini replied in a whisper. It sounded like she was trying to smother her laughter. 'You looked like a leaf monkey.'

'Glad to provide some hilarity,' he said. 'I thought I would be meeting you outside the staff quarters?'

Harini shook her head. 'Some of the soldiers ventured into the kitchens for food and drink after their shift,' she replied. 'I wouldn't suggest it.'

He swore under his breath. What he wouldn't do to be a common man.

'Lucky you came here, then,' he replied. 'We should leave; there are only so many hours in the night left.'

Harini was accompanying him to the razed lands where he had left Naila to bury her friend's body. Mayakari were difficult to find in the city, what with the risk of their lives being forfeit upon discovery. If the resistance were to have a base of operations at all, it would be deep into forestland. With Harini present, he could have her ask a minor spirit to guide them in the direction of other witches. His plans were reasonable enough. The only problem was just how he could leave the royal estate without being seen.

Rāga was not a feasible option since she would need to exit through the front gates. It left Sahry who, thankfully enough, no one approached out of sheer fright. Since his arrival, he'd kept her in a large enclosure that was built far away from the leopards. At home, he had to keep the serpent bound, but here, he left her unchained. Unless threatened, winged serpents did not attack humans; they abstained from flying into populated areas. They were more active at night, and with Taksila's densely forested, seemingly endless mountain ranges, it gave Sahry more area to fly in. Like a domesticated cat, she always returned before the sun rose. A few times, Ashoka had visited her in the morning to find the bloodied body of an animal, usually so mangled that it was hard for him to identify.

It took little time to reach the enclosure where Sahry was kept. Green eyes turned their attention on him and Harini as they approached. She was awake, tongue flicking against his skin lazily as a way of greeting.

Ashoka saddled Sahry with uncanny speed. Once both were secure on the serpent's back, he had her rise into the sky and fly towards the razed lands.

The night was cold. Down below, lantern lights dotted the landscape, demarcating streets and waterways. North-west of the impoverished district, the razed lands spread out like an ocean, dead and flat, before they blurred into wild forestland once more. Everything there was destroyed except a giant gold-plated statue of his father, which perplexed everyone. He'd been told that it was something of a phenomenon among the Taksilan people – the indestructible figure that withstood the onslaught of the Great Spirits. It made his father seem more powerful, more omniscient.

He spotted it as they flew closer, a dark statue standing intact around rubble. Part of him was curious to see it, why it resisted damage. Beneath the gold layer was bronze, a common alloy.

There's nothing special about it, so why . . .

'Hold onto me,' he told Harini as he tugged Sahry's reins, commanding her to descend.

To his surprise, Sahry refused.

She bucked and instead rose higher. Grunting, Ashoka tried to wrestle back control. *What was wrong with her?*

'She's nervous, Prince Ashoka,' Harini called out behind him.

'Of what?' he asked. 'Sahry, *down.*'

'I . . .' the mayakari's voice petered off as she let out a gasp. He spotted the cause of her amazement quickly: a bright glow emitting from the forestland.

Thud.

Suddenly, he heard a deep rumble. Even up here, the air around them seemed electrified, as if in tense anticipation. He managed to get Sahry closer to the ground, a comfortable distance away from the unusual light that continued to turn brighter, grow larger. A chill crept up Ashoka's spine.

Harini's voice was reverent. '*Spirits,*' she said.

Thud.

Ashoka had never seen ones so impossibly large.

They came out like dancers in a procession: enormous tigers and leopards, elephants and snakes, both concrete and transparent at the same time. They weren't the usual small, undefined oblong shapes he had seen in the Golden City. Those were harmless minor spirits. These were Great Spirits that towered taller than Na trees, bodies coloured in translucent blues, reds, and yellows. Fuelled by anger, their forms had changed and evolved. Their faces were horrific; dissimilar to the animals they presented as. Blood-red eyes, demonic faces, and elongated canines dripped a sleek black liquid that turned into mist the moment it touched the ground.

Their footsteps made the ground tremble like a miniature earthquake as they stomped and crushed, destroying what was already destroyed.

The nature spirits circled his father's statue as if they had no intent to destroy it. As if they *couldn't* destroy it, Ashoka realized. Their pitiful wailing, intermingled with the howling of the wind, created a melancholic, funereal orchestration that sent shivers down his spine.

'What are they saying?' he yelled out.

His ears strained to hear Harini above the din. 'I can't under-stand them, Prince Ashoka,' she replied. 'Their voices are unintelligible.'

Ashoka could only watch and listen as the tigers and leopards and elephants continued to parade around his father's statue. Their screams went on for long enough that he started to hear them as sepulchral lamentations, like those of a parent without their child. No longer did it sound like a war cry, but the sad melody of a lost soul. They never approached the statue in their march, not even once. It was as if they feared it.

An eternity seemed to pass before the spirits finally ceased and returned to the forest one by one, their howls vanishing like smoke into the night.

With the creatures gone, he was finally able to have Sahry land by the statue.

Harini jumped down first. 'I've never seen anything like that,' she said, shock colouring her voice. 'You only ever hear the stories about angered Great Spirits, but *that* . . . their voices are lost, Prince Ashoka. What cruelty, to inflict pain upon them.'

Ashoka thought back to their demeanour, their song and dance. It was reminiscent of the pale green minor spirit in the royal estate. Both radiated distressed energies, and were not the calm, tranquil creatures he had thought them to be. Loss of land would do that, he supposed, since the natural world was an extension of a spirit; much like an arm to the torso. But intuition told him this was something else.

He glanced up at the statue of his father, begrudgingly noticing the impressiveness of the way the carver had captured Adil's usual expression of sophisticated distaste and duplicitous benignity.

This is your fault, father, he thought, *but what did you do?*

The thought was left answered when a furious shout rang across the desolate landscape:

'You there – step away before I curse you both!'

CHAPTER THIRTY
Ashoka

BLIND INSTINCT DROVE ASHOKA TO REACH FOR HIS dagger. It was only when Harini laid a gentle hand on his arm to dislodge his fingers from the hilt that he came out of his stupor.

Shame flooded him immediately. A weapon had been his first choice of defence, just because he'd heard the word *'curse'*. At that moment, he was no better than his father.

'We come in peace,' he called out to the approaching figure, a woman, letting his hands drop to his sides. It was only when they came closer, did he recognize her. He had not thought he'd see her again. *'Naila.'*

The mayakari's gold earrings shone in the moonlight as she narrowed her eyes. 'How do you—' she began but started when he pulled the hood of his cloak down. *'Prince Ashoka?* Spirits, what are you doing out here?'

'I came hoping to—'

'Find another poor mayakari to bow to your request?' Naila scoffed before turning to Harini. 'Who are you?'

'One of the prince's staff,' she replied. 'I'm a poor mayakari, it seems.'

The declaration caused Naila to still. A thunderstruck expression ghosted across her face. 'A mayakari? *Work* for the Mauryas?'

she asked, letting out a bitter laugh. 'Please. As if any witch would be both so foolish and traitorous.'

Ashoka didn't expect Harini to be so affected by her accusation. *Traitorous.* But he could hardly fault Naila for her reaction. 'I really am a mayakari,' Harini placated, 'just as you are. We just want to talk.'

'Hah,' Naila snorted derisively, 'prove it.'

Harini smiled, then opened her mouth, from which came a steady stream of birdsong and flute-like melodies. *Spirit-speak,* Ashoka noted, awestruck.

Naila's jaw went slack. Her eyes darted from him to Harini, and back again, as if confused about their presence together. Though the distrust had vanished from her face, she did not seem completely convinced. She too began to use spirit-speak, to which Harini responded. They seemed to be having a conversation. Ashoka watched, wishing he could understand them but, alas, this was a language neither he nor any human could ever learn.

When their dialogue ended, Naila turned to him. 'You brought reinforcements this time,' she remarked.

'I needed you to believe me,' he replied. 'We've just seen the Great Spirits. I want to help.'

'Why?'

'Because this is senseless destruction,' he said. 'Because the land is dying, and you and I both know it. Because the Great Spirits have been harmed and must be saved.'

Naila straightened. 'The Great Spirits aren't poor, hapless kittens left to scavenge on the streets, Prince Ashoka,' she told him. 'They need appeasement, that's all.'

'And have you been able to appease them?' Harini asked, frowning.

Naila's silence was all he needed to wheedle in. 'Intuition tells me this has something to do with my father. The Great Spirits were angered after he conquered Taksila. I likely have more information than you on my father's time here – we can help each other find the root of the problem.'

'I understand the hesitation in trusting a Maurya,' Harini said firmly, 'but Prince Ashoka is not his father, and I can wager my life on that. Both he and the resistance want the same thing.'

He watched as Naila's gaze landed first on the statue, and then on Sahry without so much as a blink. She appeared to be deep in thought.

'Follow me, then,' she ordered brusquely. 'If you attempt anything, rest assured that I will retaliate.'

Turning on her heel, she stalked towards the forest. She looked back once to gesture them forward impatiently. Buoyed by her assent, Ashoka and Harini followed.

'By the way,' he leaned down to whisper in her ear, 'what did she ask you back then?'

'If I was here against my will,' Harini answered softly. 'I said no.'

The mayakari resistance operated deep in the forest.

Wayward branches threatened to tear at his clothing and strange little hisses promised to inject venom into his skin as Ashoka, Naila, and Harini trekked through the semi-dark. The moon above them provided little to no help. Minor spirits appeared from shrubs, underneath buttresses, and dangled from vines as they walked. At certain points, Naila conversed with them, the words indecipherable.

'She's asking them to warn the others in advance, Prince Ashoka,' Harini whispered.

The others? It took him a moment to realize she meant the members of the resistance.

Eventually, Naila stopped at a hilltop where Ashoka could make out the entrance of a cave. The sheer abundance of foliage almost covered its mouth, making it pass as a typical rockface, but the dim glare of a lantern light gave it away. What a perfect place to hide. No soldier would dare venture so deep into lands they knew belonged to the very spirits that waged an endless cycle of war.

He didn't realize he had halted in his tracks until Sahry flicked the back of his neck with her tongue.

'Even your serpent is impatient,' Naila called out from in front of him. 'No time to stand and observe, Prince Ashoka.'

No time indeed.

'One more thing,' said Naila. Her gaze travelled to his side. 'Leave your weapon here. They do not enter a haven.'

Dutifully, Ashoka dropped his dagger. After ordering Sahry to stay outside, Naila motioned them forward.

One lantern light turned into two, then three, the moment they pushed past the foliage and entered the mouth of the cave. It tunnelled inwards, dry and arid. It was the perfect abode for a winged serpent if ever there was one.

'There will be multiple mayakari here,' Naila warned. 'Just remember that they're more scared of you than you are of them.'

'I am not scared of the mayakari,' he replied. For good measure, he patted his head once more, as if to remind himself time and time again that his circlet was absent. They did not need a reminder of Adil.

The tunnel opened into a large cavern, illuminated by the blue light of glow worms on the roof and walls. Hanging in clusters, they gave an illusion of the starry night sky. Lanterns were pinned here and there against the rock walls, providing better visibility.

In this vast chamber were stone and wood tables scattered everywhere. Atop them were parchments and bottled plants, maps, drawings of spirits and women, and flowers in pots that were either alive or dead.

It took Ashoka's eyes a moment to adjust to the change in his surroundings. The soft hubbub of chatter he'd heard when he'd first arrived had died down and now there was only silence. Worse, he noticed the stares . . .

The mayakari of Taksila's resistance were here, and they were watching him.

'Don't be alarmed,' Naila called out to the silent crowd. He could almost *feel* the nervous energy radiating from the witches. 'Prince Ashoka Maurya has come without weapons.'

The word *Maurya* caused a sudden uproar among the women, whose faces watched him with distaste. A clear voice rang through the murmurs:

'The Mauryas do not need weapons to kill.'

Strong and unhurried, a voice with a slight drawl echoed throughout the chamber. Ashoka turned his attention to the left where the sound had originated. From behind a handful of mayakari sequestered by a table, a woman appeared. She seemed to be several years older than him. In fact, most of the mayakari around him appeared to be around his age or younger. Older mayakari were absent here. The woman's face was clear, save for a purple bruise that stained her right cheek, just above her mandible. Long black hair was tied into twin plaits. No jewellery adorned her body, and Ashoka noted that most of the mayakari there did not wear any either. Though she only wore a plain black shift and loose trousers, she carried herself with the confidence of a queen.

Ashoka nearly forgot his manners. 'Ashoka Maurya,' he greeted. 'I am—'

'I know who you are, little prince,' the woman replied as she approached. Not once did she break eye contact with him. 'All of Taksila knows who you are.'

'Then you know what I stand for,' he said.

'I have heard of your . . . unlikeness, yes,' she retorted. 'Naila told me about her encounter with you. Thank you for saving her life and helping her carry Saumya's body back to the forest. But I must say – halting ironwood logging only to reverse your decision was a strange one.'

'My influence is . . . limited,' he admitted. 'My brother is making sure of it.'

'Hmm.' That one sound spoke volumes. 'If you're constrained, what is it that you think you can do here, then?'

'I want us to work together,' he replied, 'to halt the Great Spirits' rampage and return the land to its original state. Rebuild the northern community.'

'That is exactly what Naila told me,' she said. 'How virtuous of you.'

He heard the vitriolic undercurrent, understood it. 'May I ask your name?' he inquired.

The woman paused. 'Nayani,' she replied after a beat. 'I currently lead the resistance.'

'Currently?'

'We don't know when we'll die, Prince Ashoka,' she replied. 'Our previous head, Pushpa, was found and burned some weeks ago. This is not a permanent mantle.'

As she spoke, a chest unlocked in his mind's eye, and Shakti's voice came whispering out.

Nayani.

'Do you happen to know another mayakari by the name of Shakti?' he asked. 'She asked me to seek you out. Suggested that you might help us.'

Nayani stilled. Her posture went rigid, as if she were bracing herself for a fight. 'You know what she is?'

'Until recently, she was working as part of my staff,' he replied, surprised that she did not even attempt to deflect. 'Rest assured she is wise enough to lie low.'

Nayani let out a small, secret smile. 'You don't know her, Prince Ashoka. She's a firecracker waiting to be lit,' she said. 'But if she's told you about me, then . . .'

The mayakari trailed off, seemingly lost in thought. Silence sank and settled in like maggots over flesh. 'Tell me, little prince,' she began, 'what is it that we stand to gain from this collaboration?'

'I . . .' Her question drew Ashoka into silence. In truth, he had not expected a bargain. Some naïve part of him still thought that the mayakari would stick to their altruistic philosophies, but how could they? Suffering in a world that sought to kill them, they would have no choice but to adapt. Pacifism could not thrive in a hostile, unwilling environment. 'You will see the spirits pacified;

the region renewed. I hope to return Taksila to the way it was before my father's annexation.'

Silence greeted him, and not the pleasant kind. His dreams weren't enough for the leader. 'Anything,' Ashoka added. 'Ask me anything within reason and I will do it.'

Nayani laughed. '*Within reason*,' she chuckled. 'I do have a favour for you, Prince Ashoka, but I'm not so sure you will achieve it.'

Doubt. Misjudgement. He hated it. 'Tell me what you want,' he said.

'Something quite simple,' Nayani said, her teeth gleaming white. 'You say you want Taksila restored to its glory days before my kind was murdered, and so do I. But that can only be done by ripping out the weeds by their roots.'

Ashoka could not identify what it was that Nayani wanted, but it unsettled him to receive orders as if he were a soldier and not a prince.

'One order,' he found himself saying. 'One order that I will enact to the best of my abilities, and you will never command me again.'

Raising her eyebrows in surprise, Nayani dipped her head in the smallest of nods.

'Very well,' she said with a glint in her eye. Her grin was like a jungle cat, playful and expectant. 'My one command is that you order mayakari killings to be stopped. *Permanently*. I do not care how you do it but see to it that you do. We've been terrorized long enough.'

He wanted to tell her that the request was simple, that it was easy. And yet, Nayani was asking for the stars. He could certainly enact this order, but it would be swiftly reversed. Any resistance on his part would result in Kosala running to Arush, and then he would lose. So long as the governor played an active role in Taksila, his hands were tied.

So you agree. The governor is the problem, said a small voice in his head. *He is the weed you must rip out. He must be gone for you to grant Nayani's wish. Depose him by disposing of him.*

I . . . no. No. That is a foul thought, his more logical side replied.

You can find another way, but for now, accept her command.

'I shall do my best,' he said.

'Do not go back on your word and stab us in the back,' Nayani warned. 'Your father has done that enough.'

'I do not plan to be my father,' Ashoka said. 'I want to work together so that we can unearth the reason for the Great Spirits' distress.'

'The reason?' Nayani repeated his words with a frown. She shot someone behind him a confused glance. When Ashoka turned, he found that her gaze was planted squarely on Naila.

'You didn't tell him?' she asked. Mutely, Naila shook her head.

His intestines strung tightly into a knot. 'Tell me what?'

Nayani's voice held the airy quality of a parent forcing truth into a child's fantasies. 'We know *why* the Great Spirits are destroying the northern district, Prince Ashoka, even if you don't,' she said. 'We are here attempting to remedy it.'

Shock hit him like lightning. *They knew?*

'What . . . what is the reason?' he asked.

'Something cruel,' Nayani replied, her lips twisted into a grimace. 'Terrible. Unethical. Something done by a mayakari that we cannot yet undo: a curse.'

The world around Ashoka started to spin. Had he expected a simple answer? No, but anything would have been better than this. 'I— are you sure?'

Nayani's face was grave. 'Yes,' she confirmed. 'The reason that the Great Spirits rampage that land every night is because they have been cursed.'

CHAPTER THIRTY-ONE
Shakti

PRINCESS AARYA FOUGHT AS IF HER LIFE DEPENDED ON IT.

She was like a wet, angry cat, eyes narrowed, claws out and ready to kill anyone within her sight. Combat training with the princess of the Ran Empire was something Shakti had never entertained in her life. It would have been an absurd thought, a lunatic's daydream.

Yet, here she was, hands clutching her sword, sweat beading on her upper lip, legs heavy like iron as she deflected Aarya's brutal onslaught.

'Control yourself, princess,' said Aarya's sword-master, Kudha. She was a middle-aged woman who kept her sleek black hair trimmed short. Aarya insisted that Shakti be her sparring partner ever since her appointment. At first, Shakti realized it was a desire to test her skill against hers and Shakti had accepted. Why not since it posed an excellent way to humiliate the princess. Now, she was forced to admit that it was getting a little harder to upstage her. 'You need to show restraint.'

The said restraint and deadly precision that Aarya was known for in the palace was untranslatable in the arena. Yes, she was relentless, but Shakti had soon discovered that accuracy was not in the princess's repertoire when it came to physical combat. She struck whenever she regained a burst of energy, but she never scrutinized her opponent as much as Rahil did. She was powerful, but it was useless unless she knew how to direct it.

'Stop!' Master Kudha ordered, her voice stilling the blade in Shakti's hands. She stepped back as the weapons-master wandered over, her gaze fixated on the princess who loosened the grip on her sword.

'What is it, Kudha?' Aarya panted. 'My attacks have been relentless. What have you found this time?'

'Relentless, yes, but imprecise.' Master Kudha shook her head before turning her gaze towards Shakti. 'You defend well, and you fight well, Shakti – as expected of a student trained in Mathura. Try and mimic your guard here, Princess Aarya.'

The silence that followed her command was agonizingly long. Shakti had quickly come to realize that Aarya was no fan of criticism. She only bottled it up and unleashed her vengeance through petty, often vicious verbal assaults. But here, Shakti knew that Aarya had no choice but to stay silent. Master Kudha was superior to her in terms of skill and knowledge, and her blunt remarks needed to be tolerated.

'Try and mimic Shakti?' Aarya echoed, her expression blank.

Master Kudha nodded. 'Your guard is adequately restrained and explosive when she needs to be, princess. With more training, perhaps you can surpass Prince Ashoka one day.'

Eyes widening, Aarya huffed. 'You think baby *Ashoka* fights better than me?' Her tone was sceptical, cold. Whenever she spoke of her younger brother, it was always in a way that clearly signalled her inherent superiority over him. Ashoka was the weakling, he could never best Aarya in anything.

Shakti was beginning to wonder why Princess Aarya was determined to keep him below her for some inexplicable reason. What it was exactly, she had yet to find out.

'I've seen Prince Ashoka fight,' Master Kudha said, 'and he fights like Rahil.'

Before she could stop herself, Shakti let out a low, appreciative whistle. Fighting like Rahil meant that Prince Ashoka would be, in some degree, extremely competent with a sword. He would most certainly be better than his older sister.

Princess Aarya turned to her, eyes flashing. 'And what do you mean by *that*, Shakti?' she asked tightly.

Ah, fuck. 'Rahil is one of the best fighters in the palace, princess,' Shakti replied with a one-armed shrug. 'If Prince Ashoka fights like him, I can understand why Master Kudha would assume his superiority in swordplay.'

In truth, she'd been aiming to sting, and it worked. Aarya's whole demeanour shifted as a muscle ticked beneath her strong jaw. With rigid movements, she wiped a thin sheen of sweat from her brow, her breaths steadying as she adjusted her fighting garb.

Master Kudha shook her head. 'Rahil was trained by his father, and it was part of what made him brilliant. Why that boy refused a position under Emperor Adil, I will never understand,' she said, mystified.

Aarya let out a bitter, clipped laugh. 'Rahil has all the skill in this world and yet he will never stray from Ashoka's side,' she said, glancing at her sword. 'Why do you think, Kudha – blind devotion topples even the best of giants.'

Blind devotion?

Shakti remembered Prince Ashoka's doe eyes, the ferocious intensity with which he had observed Rahil after she had injured him. It had been nothing but a thin slice, but it appeared as if Ashoka's whole world had been on fire.

That was not blind devotion, she thought to herself with a wan smile, *it was anything but.*

Rather, it looked like deep affection. Romantic love. It was something she could never understand, never feel despite the world around her telling her how it *should*. That she *would*. Such feelings were not for her, she had long since decided.

'In any case,' Master Kudha pointed to Aarya's sword, 'if you can match the level of your brother or even surpass him, you may finally impress me.'

'Ashoka is a deer,' Aarya said dully. 'He will never be a tiger. He will never be like me.'

Never be like you? Shakti thought to herself shrewdly. *What, cowering in your room and refusing sleep for two nights?*

Ever since the night that resulted in Aarya's self-mutilation, Shakti had been more careful with her dream invasion. In her defence, she had not realized that the ability could be used to harm someone physically. Besides, Aarya only sustained a deep cut. Emperor Adil had killed Shakti's family – that was a far greater insult.

The dream invasion seemed to have scarred the princess for a short while, but her usual composure had been restored at the insistence of those around her claiming it was nothing but night terrors.

Best to err on the side of caution. It was why Shakti had found herself invading the princess's dreams, but never assuming any form or interfering with them. Aarya's dreams were fascinating, and she found herself as drawn to them as she was drawn to The Collective and Emperor Ashoka.

Aarya was a wicked little thing. Viewing enough of her dreams had soon made it clear to Shakti that the princess desired power beyond anything else. Power over her siblings, her fleeting lovers, and her father's empire.

She'd almost felt guilty intruding in such a way. But the guilt had immediately been erased when the princess had one day spoken about a group of mayakari who had been discovered in a village just beyond the Golden City. Vindictive pleasure had emanated from Aarya's eyes as she informed the council of the group of soldiers that she'd sent out to capture and kill the witches. The Ridi soldiers were yet to arrive, so the princess had ramped up investigations of potential mayakari, this time by offering gold as an incentive. And, since money drove the masses, more and more soldiers were dispatched to inspect any claims.

Shakti wanted nothing more than to drive a blade through Aarya's heart.

'Of course, he would never be like you, princess,' Master Kudha said, her deep voice jolting Shakti back to the present. 'I've never met a royal child more power-hungry than yourself.'

Princess Aarya smiled. 'I only want what is best for the empire,' she replied. Her eyelashes fluttered prettily as a sickly-sweet smile marred her features. 'And what is best is to make us stronger than anyone else.'

Master Kudha hummed. 'I cannot say that sending soldiers to the Frozen Lands is the best way to achieve it, princess,' she said. 'Seems a sure-fire way to send innocents to their deaths in the cold and unknown.'

Covering the snort that threatened to erupt from her lips, Shakti busied herself by idly scratching the hilt of her sword. Soldiers, innocents? *Hah.*

But Master Kudha wasn't alone in her sentiments. Soldiers around Shakti talked. The palace staff talked. There was an under-current of confusion in the young emperor's decision to expand into the Frozen Lands. Shakti had run into Ruchira a few days after Princess Aarya's dream invasion, and the cook, too, had expressed concern.

'Perhaps the children are traumatized by Emperor Adil's death,' she'd mused. 'Grief can lead to rash decisions and unforgiving dreams.'

Shakti had been drunk on satisfaction. Her dream invasions were working.

'I disagree with Arush's plans to divert soldiers to the Frozen Lands.' Shakti was startled out of her thoughts by the sound of Princess Aarya's voice. 'Why he chose to do this, I cannot imagine. The south is the path of least resistance – it is the most obvious choice. I hear they have deadlands that are untouched.'

There she went again with those deadlands. What an odd thing to be invested in.

'Why the fascination with the deadlands, princess?' Shakti asked curiously. 'From what I've been told, they're rare and the grounds are tainted; they're difficult to farm. Is there any use in useless land?'

Jaya had told her that deadlands were where a Great Spirit had died of unnatural causes, like a curse or extensive human-made changes to the climate and terrain. The land didn't stay permanently dead, of course. It always regrew, but mayakari could always sense something wrong. Something tainted.

Princess Aarya ran the tip of her sword along the ground, leaving a perfectly straight indent behind. 'There is a plant that is purported to grow in those areas that is of great interest to me,' she replied. 'The Ghost Queen. Have you heard of it?'

Shakti frowned. 'It may as well be a myth considering how incredibly rare it is, princess,' she said, recalling a lengthy story Jaya had once told of a translucent flower that bloomed at night and disappeared during the day. According to her aunt, the Ghost Queen only grew in deadlands and nowhere else.

'Rare and of no use other than looking beautiful,' Master Kudha added impatiently. 'Let us recommence your training, princess.'

Princess Aarya seemed to hold a hundred secrets in the upturn of her lips when she replied, 'I was told they were priceless in their use.'

She resumed her stance, but Shakti stalled for a moment, digesting the princess's words. Unease wormed its way into her intestines. On one hand, she could understand that Aarya would be the kind of person to procure an item for its rarity. On the other hand, why insist on sending out groups of soldiers to search for something so uncommon? And what priceless use was she talking about? She didn't remember Jaya giving her words of caution when it came to plants.

Let it be, little bird.

Should she?

Adil's daughter is his mirror, her inner voice rebuffed Jaya's. Intuition told her there was something else to it. Though she had never stepped foot into a deadland nor seen one in her life, Jaya had told her that to mayakari, they were adulterated. But she'd never expanded upon it, and Shakti had not pressed further. Not when she had been so invested in learning combat over anything else.

262

Where can I find more information, Shakti wondered, frustrated. She barely heard Master Kudha's order to ready themselves. Muscle memory obeyed the command, but her mind stayed elsewhere. *Where would the princess get—* ah.

Just when Princess Aarya's sword met hers, the answer came fast and sharp like the prick of a needle against skin:

Adil.

CHAPTER THIRTY-TWO

Shakti

'The wretched witch calls me again.'

Emperor Adil was lounging on the Obsidian Throne when Shakti materialized in The Collective after turning in for the night. He wore black trousers and a long jacket with a gold leopard motif sewn into the left arm. A single ruby studded its eye. One hand rested under his chin as he gazed at her with scorn.

'Adil,' she greeted, not batting an eye. 'Insult me all you want, but you're the fool that karma finally caught.'

'What do you want from me, girl?' Adil remarked.

'An answer,' she replied. 'If you're not willing to give me one, I can simply replace you with Emperor Ashoka. I imagine it must be tedious for your consciousness to dwell in The Collective without use.'

Though he scoffed, the emperor made no attempt to refute her statement. 'The Ghost Queen,' she began, watching his reaction. Interest flickered in Adil's eyes as he straightened on the throne. 'What do you know of it?'

Dread rushed into her when he responded with a smile that echoed Princess Aarya's. 'A rare flower with a dubious story,' he replied. 'How did *you* come to hear of it, witch? Was it my daughter?'

'She's insistent on exploring noted deadlands in the south,'

Shakti confessed. 'Aarya is your mirror, Adil, so there's an under-lying reason. What does she want with it?'

'How do you not know anything about your own kind?'

Because Jaya didn't teach me everything. Because sometimes, I didn't listen.

She didn't know which answer applied to his question. In truth, both statements sufficed.

Do you resent me for it, little bird?

'Tell me,' she ordered, pushing her aunt's voice away.

'How rich,' Adil smirked, 'I too attempted to locate them in my youth, but never did. I doubt Aarya's quest would prove successful. Listen carefully, witch – the Ghost Queen is purported to reveal a mayakari if they come into contact with it.'

The Obsidian Throne distorted. Around her, the room flickered, shifting from black to a dappled white-blue before it reverted to its original state. It took Shakti a moment to realize that the sudden change was a response to *her*.

Reveal a mayakari?

'You—'

'Lie?' Adil finished for her. 'What would be the point? You cannot stop my daughter when she is determined to get something.'

'I don't understand,' Shakti murmured, more to herself than Adil. 'Why would it harm us?'

'Pathetic,' he said, laughing. 'You are an embarrassment to your kind. Surely you must know *how* deadlands are formed, little girl?'

'Of course, I do,' Shakti snapped. 'They're created when a Great Spirit dies of unnatural causes. The land becomes tainted.'

'Not so ignorant, then,' Adil replied. 'Such a death causes negative karmic energy, to bleed into the land and infect what regrows. That is what you say feels "tainted" to a witch. And it is the Ghost Queen that is said to harm your kind, because it only grows from what is, for lack of a better word, *cursed*. Magic harms magic, after all.'

'But how does it reveal a mayakari?'

'From ingestion,' he responded, shrugging, 'skin contact, perhaps, though I do not know its exact mechanism. Perhaps it could reveal and kill your kind at the same time – now that's efficient. How laughable that the natural world your kind reveres the most can turn on you in such a way.'

Shakti frowned. He seemed so sure of its complications. 'How do you know these things?' she asked. For a man who claimed to hate the mayakari so much, there was information he was privy to that left her baffled as to how he knew it.

'Manali had a sister,' said Adil, sounding oddly disturbed. 'Subhadrangi. Adopted, but acted as if they were blood. Came with her from their home state to live in the Golden City. To study. Take a guess where.'

She shrugged, impatient.

'The mayakari library,' Adil replied. He was watching her closely. Watching for her reaction, Shakti realized. 'Because she was a witch. Whatever she told Manali, Manali told me.'

It was hard to stay expressionless. Jaw hanging open wide enough to swallow a hornets' nest, Shakti shook her head vehemently. Impossible.

'What – where is she now?'

'I had her burned,' Adil replied tonelessly. 'Manali decided to fill the children's heads with silly lies and told them she passed from an illness. I did not care enough to object, but the story of the Ghost Queen came from her and I in turn told Aarya.'

Shakti's breathing became laboured. Her mind harkened back to that council meeting where Aarya had countered burn-testing. Where Arush had asked her for another option. Where she claimed not to have one.

Was this her grand solution?

She's following a theory, Shakti reminded herself. *Not fact. Nothing is proven.*

But she couldn't risk the princess continuing down this path. Rare flower indeed, but that did not mean it was impossible to find. Deadlands existed, which meant that the chance of a Ghost Queen sprouting existed.

What a headache.

She needed to cast this fancy of Princess Aarya's away.

One more dream invasion couldn't hurt, she thought to herself. *Command her to cease this infernal search and have her appear indecisive in the process. She's more of a threat than Arush.*

Ignoring Adil's taunts, Shakti closed her eyes and thought of Princess Aarya. When she reopened them, Adil and the Obsidian Throne were gone, and she was looking through glass at the princess's dream.

Dream Aarya was trapped in the strangest-looking forest Shakti had ever seen.

Na and Hora trees shot up to the sky, the sky barely visible from the canopy. She had appeared in a clearing shaped into a perfect circle, but it was inconsistent. One blink, and she saw solid ground. The second time, there was mud, and then water. Seven blue lotuses were spread across the clearing, floating in mid-air. In the centre was Princess Aarya, brandishing a sword and attempting to wrench herself out of the ever-shifting ground.

Shakti entered the dream, surprised by the mild resistance she encountered, and morphed herself into Emperor Adil. It never stopped feeling like betrayal when she did.

'Daughter,' she called out to Aarya.

Clear water transformed into emerald, green moss around the princess's legs as she turned to face Shakti. Yellow-white spores fell from the sky like raindrops, dusting her skin. 'Father?' she called out.

Nothing about the natural world here seemed inviting. Everything appeared ready to hurt despite its bright colours. 'Why do you struggle?' she asked, stepping into the clearing. Unlike Aarya, she didn't sink. Instead, Shakti floated on the ground.

'I—' Aarya scrunched her brows as if she couldn't explain how she found herself in this predicament. 'I do not know. Help me, please.'

She extended her hand. Before Shakti could ponder the benefits of having the princess sink into the muddy depths of her own dream, a single spore landed on the princess's outstretched palm.

Amazed, Shakti watched as it expanded, inflated, and morphed into a clear, eight-petalled flower.

The princess sank deeper into the ground as she retracted her hand and stared at it. 'The Ghost Queen,' she murmured.

Oh, spirits.

'The Ghost Queen isn't real, daughter,' Shakti said. Taking another step closer, she plucked the flower from Aarya's hand and crushed it. 'I command you to stop your search.'

The princess stopped struggling, causing the moss to spread like mould up her legs. 'Father?' she replied, confusion apparent. 'Why are you . . .? You don't *understand*—'

Willing herself to float higher, Shakti rose until her feet were at Princess Aarya's shoulders. Without a second thought, she bent her knees and placed both her hands on the princess's head.

To Aarya, it would've appeared as though she were being blessed by an elder, for she bowed her head. Shakti smiled inwardly, relishing the power she held over the princess in the dreamscape, and pushed.

Aarya let out a startled shriek.

Paying her no mind, Shakti continued to place pressure over the princess's head, watching her sink deeper into the ground.

'No empire will respect you if you chase rarities, daughter,' she whispered. 'Power comes from creating fact, not fiction.'

'*Father!*' Aarya screamed, arms flailing like a baby bird unable to fly. '*Stop, please!*'

Little bird, stop.

Jaya's voice gave Shakti pause for a moment, forced her to look at what she was doing.

I'm not harming her, she told her aunt. *This isn't real. She's not being burned alive.*

There was no response. The guilt that came with her actions was not so strong any more, perhaps that was why.

Just as Aarya was up to her neck in moss and mud, Shakti saw her hands change. Corded and muscular one instant, thinner and veiny the next. *My hands*, she realized, before they shifted back to Adil's.

Glancing down, she met the princess's frightened eyes. Shakti felt no remorse. Mayakari had died under much worse conditions; at least Aarya would wake up to a new dawn sky.

'You dream of it, but you don't deserve the throne,' she told her softly. 'Struggle, daughter. Struggle and drown.'

One final push, and Princess Aarya's head sank like stone beneath the moss.

CHAPTER THIRTY-THREE
Ashoka

To rectify the wounds inflicted by the Great Spirits of Taksila, he had to lift a curse.

Ashoka wanted to laugh. Of course, this wasn't going to be easy for him. Complications followed him like a hound after a peahen. Once it sank its claws into him, it would hold on until it bled him dry.

Spirits, he wanted someone here to help calm his racing thoughts. He wanted Rahil.

Ashoka imagined a ghostly apparition of him, gentle and handsome, clasping his shoulder as he always did when Ashoka descended into his anxious ways. The thought relaxed him until his heart steadied into its usual rhythm, and he focused his attention on the expectant Nayani.

'A mayakari willingly cursing a spirit?' he remarked. Beside him, Harini appeared shellshocked by the revelation. 'A *Great* Spirit, at that? Who would do such a thing?'

'Usra,' Nayani replied. When Ashoka shot her a confused glance, she elucidated. 'The original leader of Taksila's mayakari resistance. The one who pushed back against your father.'

'If you know who did it, and how, are you not able to placate the Great Spirits?'

Nayani shook her head. 'Not quite,' she replied. 'A mayakari's curse can be reversed but there are only two ways to do it. The first is if the original curse-maker undoes it. The second way to remove it is—'

'If you know the true intention of the curse,' Harini finished quietly. 'But that assumes the mayakari in question has told you.'

Ashoka sensed their problem without any further explanation. 'Then, I gather that Usra is dead. Burned?' he asked.

After a lengthy silence, it was Naila who answered. 'Even worse,' she replied. 'Missing.'

'Missing?'

'She vanished during the final days of the burnings here,' Nayani replied this time. Her face contorted. 'Older mayakari have told me horror stories of those days, Prince Ashoka. Things that they never want to remember. Can you imagine your own mother being burned alive while you hid and watched? And when the only person they held hope in vanished . . . the resistance crumbled without its leader, and it stayed defeated for a few years before some of us decided that we could not stand our circumstances any longer.'

Missing. In his father's reign, that could have meant anything from hiding to being murdered behind closed doors.

'If your only hope of reversing the curse is gone, what can we do?' he asked.

Extending a hand to gesture at the mayakari around them, Nayani let out a long exhale. 'We are experimenting with curse magic,' she replied, shrugging as if this were not earth-shattering information. 'To see if we can undo Usra's work without her. So far, it has been unsuccessful. We have tried to communicate with the Great Spirits when they embark on their rampage, but we cannot understand them, and they in turn do not listen to us.'

Ashoka had never heard so much new information regarding the mayakari in his entire life. The scholarly part of him that remained interested in the witches and their ways itched to hear more of Nayani's explanations, but he forced himself to focus.

'I cannot imagine why Usra would curse nature spirits,' he said aloud. The mayakari he had read of did not mirror the ones he met.

Nayani scowled, and Ashoka realized he had spoken out of turn. 'Perhaps you can imagine how Usra would have felt at the time of enactment,' she replied. 'Scared. Maybe upon the brink of death with no hope of salvation.'

'Fear can make a person act without reason,' he acquiesced.

Nayani scoffed. 'To you, it may seem that way, Prince Ashoka,' she replied, 'to a mayakari staying alive through fear, perhaps it *was* within reason.'

'My mistake,' he apologized quickly. An idea had started to take root in his head. Both he and the resistance lacked the access to information. If a mayakari had gone missing, he suspected that his father would have recorded it somewhere. The man had kept meticulous records on alleged witches and death counts, and there was only one place in Taksila that housed them.

'I might have a way of tracking Usra,' he said. 'My father's study. When I first arrived, it was filled to the brim with maps and lists of names. Portraits, detailed notes of mayakari sightings – perhaps we can find information related to Usra there. If you can meet me in front of the estate tomorrow morning, we can begin immediately.'

Nayani visibly shuddered. 'A good idea,' she agreed, 'but one you should carry out on your own. I will not step into that monster's home, not if my life depended on it.'

Beside him, Naila raised her hand. 'I can help you,' she said. 'It is not the most pleasant of situations to be in, but if we are able to find anything related to Usra, it would be a start.'

Grimacing, Nayani tilted her head in acceptance. 'As you would like it, Naila. Keep yourself safe,' she said before turning to Ashoka. 'Please, see to it that she is not harmed, Prince Ashoka. Each time a mayakari dies, I lose more hope.'

When they returned to the royal estate, Ashoka walked Harini back to the staff quarters, avoiding soldiers on their way. The mayakari was unusually quiet, arms crossed over her chest and staring at the ground.

'To curse Great Spirits is near blasphemy, Prince Ashoka,' she remarked out of the blue, 'but I can understand why this Usra did what she did. I hope you and the resistance can release the spirits from their misery.'

Ashoka stopped, and she mirrored him.

'That sounded like a goodbye,' he said. 'Will you be returning to the Golden City?'

Harini nodded. 'I'll be taking a riverboat in the morning,' she replied. 'You've reached an agreement with the resistance, so I consider my job done, Prince Ashoka. Besides, I cannot in good conscience leave Shakti alone now that she works for your sister.'

Guilt wrangled him again at the reminder that he had been unable to do anything about Shakti's reassignment. Being powerless to a sibling was oddly humiliating.

'I shall have some of the guards accompany you to the docks tomorrow,' he advised. 'Please be careful.'

With an amused smile, Harini bowed and left, closing the door quietly behind her.

Stifling a yawn, Ashoka departed towards his balcony. The excitement of the small hours was starting to wear his alertness down. Fighting fatigue, he silently hoisted himself up the rails and entered his room.

Sleep greeted him quickly. He dreamed of an open field, of the pink dawn sky, of an amorphous and translucent being that morphed into a tiger – a Great Spirit of the jungle. He dreamed of the Obsidian Throne, of the royal circlet encircling his head, of the mayakari he'd watched die come back to life.

And, of course, Ashoka dreamed of Rahil.

He dreamed of hard muscle and gleaming broadswords, of promises and umber eyes, of skin touching skin with breathless anticipation.

'I'm waiting for you,' he told the Rahil in his dream. 'Are you waiting for me?'

'Always,' Rahil had replied, his answering smile like a gentle caress.

And when he awoke, Ashoka was flushed, twisted in his sheets. He stared up at the ceiling exasperated that his own body and mind had revealed his want so clearly. The dream had felt so real, yet its reality was impossible.

It was with bleary eyes that he readied himself, struggling to swallow the milk rice and delicately cut fruits that had been laid out for him in the morning. Harder still, was trying to ignore Sachith's confrontational stare. At first, Ashoka said nothing, having Sachith follow him through the halls back to the study, but it soon became unbearable. Though his guard was quiet, his silence was deafening.

'What is it, Sachith?' he finally asked.

The man's response was immediate. 'Do you take me for a fool, Prince Ashoka?' he sounded agitated. 'Sahry was gone in the middle of the night.'

Undeterred, Ashoka crossed his arms. 'Out for a hunt, I think,' he replied.

Sachith snorted. 'Did you accompany her, too, Prince Ashoka?' he retorted. 'I didn't think that would be something you'd willingly do. You're lucky I didn't send out a search party.'

Spirits.

'Why didn't you?'

'You were with Sahry,' the guard responded. 'She terrifies more than a soldier does.' He thought of her as a weapon, like many did. She wasn't one.

'Regardless, I am expecting someone today,' Ashoka changed course. 'See to it that she isn't harmed.'

Throwing him a confused glance, Sachith bowed. 'Of course, Prince Ashoka,' he replied. 'But . . . why would she be harmed?'

'Because she is a mayakari,' said Ashoka. When his guard's eyes widened and he opened his mouth to no doubt spew protestations, Ashoka stopped him with a wave of his hand. 'I will not hear it. Those Great Spirits must be pacified, and the witches are the only answer. I am letting you know because, sooner or later, you would have discovered it; make sure news of this arrival does not go beyond the estate walls.'

'A *mayakari*, Prince Ashoka.' Sachith's distress was acute. 'Is that why you left the estate last night? *Spirits*, they can curse you, curse us all! Oh, Rahil will murder me for this, I'm sure of it.'

'He won't, because which one of us would tell him?' inquired Ashoka. 'If you want to avoid a quick death, just follow my command. This is the easiest, most logical plan. My siblings may not see it the same; inherited hate clouds judgement that way, but my idea is the correct one.'

Naila arrived to heightened suspicion.

Ashoka left to greet her when Sachith alerted him to her arrival. However, once he arrived at the palace steps, he found his soldiers surrounding her like a pack of leopards, weapons drawn.

'Stop!' he yelled, shaken by the sight. 'Drop your weapons, *now*.'

At the sound of his voice, the men and women complied. One piped up nervously, 'But Prince Ashoka – she's a *witch*.'

Ah. Sachith must have notified them. Dressed in a nondescript blue shift and black linen trousers, Naila looked like any other common citizen. 'Prince Ashoka,' she greeted, then jerked her thumb towards his guards. 'They initially thought I was a lover of yours.'

Ashoka let out a beleaguered sigh. 'What nonsense,' he told his guards, who looked down guiltily. 'I am here to govern, not invite a lover into my bed every night. Naila is here to assist me, not sleep with me.'

He saw a small grin paint itself across Naila's face at his words. 'What a way to let down a woman,' she remarked, her eyes laced with mischief. 'If I were more hot-headed, I would have cursed your entire existence.'

The word 'cursed' was like a trigger. Within seconds, his guards had drawn out their weapons – longswords, broadswords, rapiers, and dangerously curved sickles – and were pointing them at Naila who yelped in fright and ducked behind him.

'This is ridiculous,' Ashoka muttered to himself, before grabbing Naila's wrist and steering her closer towards his guards, all of whom muttered and took cautious steps back, as if Naila were a volcano ready to erupt.

'Stop where you are!' he ordered. 'We have a mayakari helping us – helping *me*. It gives you no reason to treat her like some sort of contagious disease. I trust Naila, and I need her help to solve the nature spirit rampages in the northern communities. If you disagree with any of my actions, you are free to leave. Do not expect what you've been accustomed to under my father's reign.'

He saw Naila's surprised face and ignored Sachith's astonished one as his soldiers remained quiet. He noted with some satisfaction that, despite the crowd being silent, they were immobile. They were his personal guard, but he was not extremely familiar with their personal views on the mayakari. All that they knew was that Ashoka was not his father.

'I don't like the mayakari,' one of his guards piped up, her expression somewhat timid as she sought his gaze. 'But I am loyal to you, Prince Ashoka, and I will trust your judgement.'

Around her, there were scattered murmurs of agreement. Ashoka saw Naila's face school itself into a mask of blank indifference.

His soldiers didn't need to trust the mayakari. They just needed to trust *him*. Trust garnered enough coin to buy loyalty, and loyalty was worth more than its weight in gold. More than anything else in this world, Ashoka needed loyalty for his grand plans to come to fruition without any commotion.

'Good,' he said, relaxing his rigid stance. 'Now that's settled – Naila, come with me.'

He led her to the study, still filled to the brim with his father's notes and maps. He'd cleared them into a corner, but even there, they took up space both physically and emotionally. The weight of their meaning was what scared him: that each cross on a map meant the discovery of a mayakari, that each slash across a portrait represented another undeserved death.

'There's something wrong here,' she remarked with a shudder.

'His maps?' Ashoka supplied, confused.

Naila shook her head. 'No, there's something *off* about this estate. I don't know how to explain it. Or perhaps I'm in a state of hyperawareness.'

She looked even more disturbed when they knelt to rifle through his father's materials. He saw the tears well up in her eyes when she pored through page after page of hand drawn portraits and regretted his offer to have her help him. For a long time, they sat in silence, reading, until Ashoka could stand his guilt no further.

'If you are unwilling to continue with this, I understand,' he began, but she firmly interrupted him.

'I am not so weak,' she scoffed and pushed a stack of half-torn pages towards him. 'Your father was simply depraved. Here he's described different methods of torture.'

Ashoka took the pages from her and read his father's sharp script, wincing at the orders to behead, to slash wrists to make a death look like suicide. 'As I said,' Ashoka remarked. 'My father was a monster.'

He threw the papers away like they were poisonous to the touch, and instead continued his perusal. There were a few mentions of the resistance leader here and there, with maps of the north-west marked all over with possible sightings, but nothing concrete. Ashoka found what appeared to be letters to Rahil's father, Adil's then-general, with cruel promises.

'*The witch deserves burial, not fire, Indran,*' he read aloud. '*Her treasures will be mine to keep.* How morbid. Have you found any mention as to when exactly the spirits' rampage began?'

'Not yet,' Naila replied, her eyes on the parchment she held between her hands. 'But from what I know, the Great Spirits began their rampage around a week after Usra disappeared.'

'So, she could very well have fled before enacting her curse?' he asked.

Naila tutted. 'Not exactly,' she said. 'As far as we understand them, curses work, but no one knows exactly *when* they do. It could be within minutes, days, months, or even years. There is no logic to their enactment. Usra could have cursed the spirits the day of her disappearance, or even the day when the rampages began. It's hard to say.'

'If a curse's enactment is unpredictable, does it mean their reversal is, too?' Ashoka asked, imagining a scenario where the Great Spirits continued their razing even after the curse had been discovered.

Naila shook her head. 'Reversing a curse is easy,' she said. 'The effect is instantaneous. Strange, isn't it?'

It was as if one puzzle piece slotted into place while having another piece removed at the same time. How frustrating.

'Do you think she fled?' he asked Naila. She paused for a moment, considering his question before ultimately shaking her head.

'No mayakari would leave their land unprotected,' she replied. 'What Usra did in cursing the spirits will no doubt bring her karmic retribution, but I do not think that she would have cursed them unless it was a last resort. You should know how I think by now, Prince Ashoka: I think that your father had everything to do with her disappearance.'

Naila stayed where she was, assessing him with a knowing glint in her eye. Even before she could open her mouth, he sensed that she was about to say something chaotic.

'What is it now?' he asked her, impatient.

'Nayani's request to you was reasonable,' Naila said, her tone oddly light. 'But I would like for you to consider another angle, Prince Ashoka.'

He thought of her alone, standing beside the severed head of her friend. 'Go on.'

'I think we all know that you will be unable to ban mayakari killings under Governor Kosala,' she said. 'And even if you do, he will reinstate them the moment you leave. Deposal is the answer, and it should be accomplished in a more . . . permanent manner.'

'Permanent in what way?' he asked.

A malicious smile split Naila's lips. 'A deceptively simple task, Prince Ashoka,' she replied. 'I want you to kill Governor Kosala. Now *that* is a permanent removal.'

CHAPTER THIRTY-FOUR
Ashoka

IT WAS LATE AFTERNOON WHEN NAILA FINALLY LEFT, HIS father's words hanging like a death sentence above them.

The witch deserves burial, not fire.

Her treasures will be mine to keep.

Vague words. Unclear meanings. What had he expected? Usra was likely murdered and buried somewhere only his father knew. That much Ashoka was willing to bet coin on.

If she was buried and not burned, perhaps a nature spirit can be tasked to help, he thought to himself. But if Usra's body was unable to be found, where did that leave him?

A pathetic child who thought to subvert me, his father's voice answered viciously.

Fatigue made it hard to dismiss his father. That, and Naila's additional request stuck to him like glue. *A permanent removal. Murder.*

He understood her logic, but his mind rejected the proposal almost immediately.

I won't kill. I would never kill.

That was his heated declaration to Rahil so many moons ago. Was that not a promise to himself? Was that not a loud pronouncement of himself as a person, of his guiding principles?

He can be deposed without killing, he reminded himself.

The dark, disbelieving corner of his mind refuted him. *Can you? One death to prevent many. Is that not justification enough? One life ordering the deaths of dozens, is that not an imbalance of power? For all the death he has presided over, is this not repayment in kind?*

Ashoka knew he was standing on a ledge with these thoughts, but he found that he was paralysed, unable to decide. To relieve his ever-growing anxiety, he took a short walk to the garden where the gold flowers were placed. It was as if he needed to see some kind of proof to tell him that his agreement with Arush was not in vain.

Like a ghost, Sachith followed him.

'Won't the minor spirit attack you again, Prince Ashoka?' he asked, worry clear in his voice.

'It didn't attack me,' Ashoka replied, 'it showed me something, that's all.'

He became lost in thought as they entered the garden feature, wondering again when Rahil would arrive. Since Sau's letter indicated that the deal was complete, surely he would have arrived in the Golden City's port by now? If he'd taken a winged serpent from the palace, it would have taken even less time to get here.

And the Ridi soldiers would take much longer. Just because an agreement was made did not mean that its terms were carried out in an instant. It could take days, or even weeks, till their arrival.

The flash of gold flowers against dying sunlight caught his attention. The moment he stepped past the neat hedges, a familiar face appeared next to him, with pale green and mismatched arms.

'You again,' he said. 'Hello, spirit.'

As usual, no human words came out of the minor spirit's mouth. It skittered around him, eyes wide, and engaged in steady chatter. It reminded him of when Sau was frustrated, moving about this way and that, arms flailing. Floating towards the gold flowers, it repeated the same motion he'd seen before; the human hand curled into a fist, pumping up and down.

Pity flooded him. Poor creature, habituating a garden where its main attraction had required death to achieve beauty.

'I'm sorry,' he told it. 'My father's cruelty has affected you, too.'

Behind him, Sachith was quiet. The nature spirit chittered and held out its tendril hand. Fascinated, Ashoka watched as it grew in length, curling like the very vines he had stepped on in his haste to descend from the balcony. The pale glow reminded him of glow worms in a cave.

The tendril snaked around his neck before its tip reared up in front of his eyes like a cobra and pressed against his forehead.

He felt nothing upon impact, but his mind shattered into a million pieces.

Pain. Fear. Earth. Lungs full, heaving with dirt. Manic laughter. Rubies. A circlet.

Ashoka clutched his head between his hands. He could barely feel Sachith's hand on his shoulder, could barely hear him shout for help.

A hand pushing through the ground, first flesh, then strips of muscle eroded away to reveal bone. Tendon.

Horror clawed through him as the images receded and he glanced up. The nature spirit watched him.

For such a small creature, it radiated so much rage. So much pain. Keeping such traumatic memories would cause it so much suffering. It did not need to ache all because of some ridiculous gold flowers.

'Do not be angry, little spirit,' he told it, face sombre. 'I will take away your pain.'

Wobbling slightly, he stood and turned to a panicked Sachith who grabbed his arm to offer support. 'You shouldn't come here, Prince Ashoka,' he chastised. 'This is the second time now.'

'It needs help,' Ashoka murmured. 'I need to remove it.'

'Remove it?'

Before Ashoka could respond, he heard commotion. Sachith's call for help had been answered in moments, for several soldiers burst through the garden entrance, weapons drawn. They stopped in surprise when they saw an unharmed Ashoka and a beleaguered Sachith.

'Excellent timing,' he said. 'I'd like you to remove these –' he pointed to the gold flowers '– immediately.'

One of his soldiers, Lalitha, cocked her head. 'You're unhurt, Prince Ashoka?' she asked, sounding baffled. Her eyes drifted to the minor spirit in suspicion.

'Very much so,' he replied. 'Fetch some shovels immediately – dig this eyesore up.'

At his command, they scattered. Thick gardening shovels were brought and, soon enough, the sound of metal slapping against soil filled the air. Only Sachith remained behind, as always.

'It was causing you distress, Prince Ashoka,' he began, 'why provide it aid?'

'You didn't see what I did,' Ashoka responded, keeping his eyes on the other guards. The process of removing the gold flowers did not seem to be as easy as he thought. They had been pinned to the ground by metal poles to achieve better retention. It made for a difficult removal. 'Imagine fighting to live, Sachith. Imagine your last thought before death being absolute fear. This little spirit lives on haunted ground; its unhappiness was a result of my father's cruelty. Is it not virtuous to relieve its sorrow?'

Sachith did not respond at first. Rather, he frowned. Following his gaze, Ashoka saw what had distracted him. Two of his guards were struggling to move the centrepiece, the largest gold flower. The minor spirit's flutelike chatter rose to a higher pitch as it wandered towards the guards who paid it no mind. Eventually, they managed to shovel enough dirt away to rip it out from the ground, a manmade weed. The ground around the pole caved in as it came away and then, he saw it.

Attached to the end of the pole was something long and thin and white.

The hair on his body stood on end. *Was that . . .*

'Step away!' he exclaimed, rushing towards the two guards who dropped the flower and its metal stem to the ground. It rolled towards his feet, and his stomach distended as he recognized the white-grey object.

Bones of a hand. A *human* hand.

No wonder the little nature spirit had been so distraught. All this time, it had been giving him an answer the only way it knew how. The flower patch hewn from stolen gold was not what caused it distress.

No, it was the grave beneath them.

CHAPTER THIRTY-FIVE
Shakti

A WEEK AFTER SHAKTI'S LAST DREAM INVASION, HARINI returned to the palace.

Shakti had never been so happy to see another mayakari in her life. Being surrounded by those who weren't, save for Ruchira who often inquired after her sanity whenever they met, had left her permanently on guard. There was a blessed relief in letting her walls down.

Both had acquired the same day of rest, and so Harini had elected to take them to the Marble Stupa that lay east of the Golden City, separated by the river that began as nothing but a stream from the misty points of the Mountain of Rebirth. Popular during the summer season, it attracted the masses like flies towards fruit. Early in the morning, it was utterly still, devoid of people.

Shakti was mesmerized by the quiet, the soft crunching of sand under her feet as she circled the white pagoda, and the fragrant incense sticks that permeated the air. Here was an ode to times past, when humans placed the heavy mantle of omniscient gods onto Great Spirits. They lived for hundreds, sometimes thousands of years after all, with much longer lifespans than humans, which made them divine. Once the mayakari had claimed the nature spirits to be yet another cog in the wheel of samsara, nature spirit worship had dwindled. Yet, the people still held a fondness for them, a deep-seated respect born from centuries of misguided prayer. Blessings and offerings in the form of flowers were often piled high into hollowed-out alcoves. Freshly picked lotuses and frangipanis with their iridescent petals sat atop the wilted mounds placed the day before, the stench of death and beauty intermingling in a glorious dance.

The stupas were an ode to peace. It made her feel safe.

A miniaturized version of this stupa existed in the grounds of the Maurya palace, but theirs was too stark, too sanitized, too sterile. Among the trees and the mountain looming above like a giant, the marble pagoda was sequestered in its own world.

'Were the mayakari receptive to Prince Ashoka?' Shakti whispered in Harini's ear as they took a leisurely stroll around the structure.

'Not initially,' Harini admitted. Nestled in her and Shakti's hands were frangipanis and freshly picked white lotuses they'd bought from a flower market in the city. They'd scattered water droplets over the petals to keep them fresh. 'He found one by accident and failed to convince her. It was only after he took me to the razed lands that we found members of the resistance. Having me there did help him. So did mentioning your friend – she's their *leader*, by the way. Thank you kindly for letting us know in advance.'

That information, even Shakti hadn't known. After all, Nayani hadn't divulged much about her time in Taksila. Ignoring Harini's sarcasm, she let out a contented hum as they turned towards an alcove hollowed into the pagoda. Sand turned to cold stone as they stepped onto the dais. The alcove's interior was carved with images of minor and Great Spirits, the latter of whom were depicted as leopards. 'I hope they're able to find a solution,' she remarked. 'The prince seemed quite determined.'

Placing their flowers onto the base of the alcove, both stood in silence for a moment.

'He seems more level-headed than his siblings,' Harini responded after a beat. 'Emperor Arush and his sudden fixation on the Frozen

Lands. Princess Aarya's *madness*. What on earth happened while I was gone?'

I happened, Shakti thought, but said nothing. Instead, she said, 'Two children in grief and one uncaring. That's what I think.'

Looking mystified, Harini stepped away from the dais. 'Such bouts of insanity from simple grief?' she mused. 'Well, I suppose it's not impossible.'

Bouts of insanity. After Shakti had drowned Princess Aarya in the dreamworld, she'd once again woken up in hysteria. This time, however, she hadn't cut herself. Instead, she'd caused a commotion in her chambers by toppling over her books and proceeding to beat herself over the head with them. From what Shakti had heard the next morning, the princess had also tried to submerge herself in a washbasin, refusing to come up for air until staff forcefully pulled her away, kicking and screaming Adil's name.

Shakti couldn't tell if her command to cease the hunt for the Ghost Queen had been obeyed. Princess Aarya had spoken no more of it since, but it had only been a short amount of time.

Safe to assume it worked, she told herself. *The invasions haven't let me down before.*

'They do seem somewhat . . . unsuited to lead,' Shakti replied to the mayakari's remark. 'Volatile. The young prince seems more viable in comparison.'

Harini didn't even blink at her overt treason. 'Yes and no,' she said. 'Prince Ashoka is idealistic, but he stumbles.'

Shakti imagined a young man staring out into the ocean, the sky pitch-black, figure only visible from the light of a full moon. 'What do you mean?' she asked.

In response, Harini cast her gaze to the sky, troubled. 'Your friend asked him one favour – to ban mayakari killings in Taksila. Anyone with half a brain knows that the only way that will happen is to depose the governor. And at this point, the only way to depose him . . .'

'Is to kill him,' Shakti finished. Ah, that was the problem. Of course, the prince would refuse to entertain such a thought.

'It's as if Prince Ashoka is standing on the edge of a cliff,' Harini said thoughtfully. 'Some semblance of cautiousness ties him to the ground. In this case, he needs to fall, but he won't, and it is no one's fault but his own.'

The following day, Shakti followed behind Princess Aarya as she attended an audience with Emperor Arush.

'You just missed Rahil, sister,' Arush said as they walked into the throne room. Soldiers surrounded the perimeter, expressions blank. When Princess Aarya shot him an inquisitive glance, he added, 'Arrived last night, spoke with myself and mother, and took a serpent to Taksila.'

Clicking her tongue, the princess shook her head, almost bemused. 'Straight to Ashoka,' she said. 'I wonder how long those two could possibly stay apart.'

Already looking uninterested, Arush shrugged. 'It's more a matter of how long it will take for them to return to each other again,' he replied. 'Perhaps Rahil's absence is causing our little brother to make rash decisions.'

Shakti could almost pinpoint the moment that Princess Aarya's hackles were raised at the mention of Prince Ashoka. 'Rash decisions such as . . .?' she inquired pointedly.

'Kosala informed me some time ago that Ashoka attempted to halt ironwood procurement,' Arush began, 'but not to worry, sister. He put a stop to it immediately.'

In a very un-Aarya-like manner, the princess wandered towards the steps of the throne and sat there, her back to her brother, the soft blue pallu cascading down her right arm. Quietly, Shakti made herself scarce by standing off to the side, watching their exchange.

'Ashoka knows that is a foolhardy choice,' Aarya said, scowling. 'What is he up to?'

Arush chuckled. 'Why must you always assume he has an ulterior motive,' he replied. 'Ashoka cannot fix Taksila. He will lose our bet, sister. Or have your bouts of insanity resulted in a distinct lack of judgement?'

'Nightmares are a relatively common occurrence, brother,' Aarya replied, nary an emotion across her haughty face.

The emperor turned away from his sister and focused on Shakti. She hated when he did, rather preferring to be like a minor spirit observing its surroundings, undisturbed. 'Would you call my sister's *affliction* bad dreams?' he asked.

In her periphery, she saw the princess open her mouth and beat her to it. 'I would, emperor,' Shakti replied carefully. 'Madness it is not.'

'*Ha*. It seems you've found yourself a loyal dog, sister,' Arush replied. 'Perhaps she will entertain your journey to the deadlands.'

Shakti observed the princess's reaction at the mention of deadlands. Though she was loath to admit it, part of her was too timid to simply ask Aarya about it to see if her command had worked. The other part was pure paranoia.

'Fortunately for you, brother, I have decided to let that go,' Aarya replied coolly. 'I was chasing an imaginary tail.'

It worked. A wave of relief washed over Shakti.

The princess's answer seemed to satisfy not only her but also the emperor, as he relaxed and began to wax poetic about the recent arrival of Taksilan soldiers into the Golden City. There were still some remaining under Prince Ashoka's control, but most had been redeployed. There were reports that the queen of Kalinga and the crown prince of the Ridi Kingdom were meeting on their own, the reason for conferring undisclosed, a statement that Arush didn't appear too bothered about, but Aarya was. It led to an argument about strengthening better ties with the latter's new monarch.

When the siblings' conversation finally ended, and they exited the throne room, the princess stopped and latched onto Shakti's wrist, gripping hard enough for it to hurt.

'Do not be so reactive,' Aarya snapped.

Wincing at the pressure, Shakti tried to tug back her hand. 'Princess?'

'Arush seeks to goad, and you fell for it,' the princess replied.

'Soldiers have their loyalties, I'm sure, but see to it that you do not so overtly side with me over the *emperor*. Don't be so foolish, Shakti.'

Shakti wanted to snap, *I favour neither of you. I simply thought I was doing what I had to.*

'What would you have me say then?' she blurted out in frustration before realizing her mistake, adding, 'princess,' to avoid a mercurial response.

Aarya didn't respond. She stared at Shakti impassively, and for long enough that she began to feel uncomfortable. 'You're uncouth,' she replied. 'Were manners not taught in your household?'

Calm yourself, little bird.

Clenching her jaw hard enough to fracture, Shakti nodded. 'My apologies, princess.'

'I'm unsurprised,' Aarya said slowly. 'From memory, Mathura's native language did not have a distinction between polite and informal speech as we do, no?'

Fuck. She didn't know the answer. Scrambling for an inconspicuous response, Shakti managed to stutter, 'No, princess,' hating the insecurity in her voice. Spirits, she should've sounded more confident.

'Hmm.' Shakti couldn't never unsee it: Adil's scrutinizing eyes behind the princess. Searching. Looting. Trying to swoop in and steal something precious. 'In the future, Shakti, you will use your sword, not your words.'

CHAPTER THIRTY-SIX

Shakti

THE SMELL OF FRYING CHILLI PEPPERS FROM A NEARBY
vendor almost made Shakti sneeze, but the scent of a roasting
human carcass threatened to drip tears from her eyes.

Use your sword, not your words.

The princess's command came rushing like a hot wind, and at
that moment, Shakti wished she could use both.

Just in front of her, Princess Aarya stood in a vibrant, shimmering blue blouse and a long skirt that cascaded around her like
a waterfall. Her eyes, lined with her usual sharp and upturned
wing of kohl, were alight with glee.

Up on a podium, tied to a wooden pole and burning the same
shade of blue as Princess Aarya's dress, was a mayakari who had
been captured by the palace soldiers in the outskirts of the Golden
City. Her features were hardly visible now, only half-blackened
crisps and melted bits of fat. The enormous crowd that had initially
gathered to view the burning was now petering off into handfuls,
uninterested once the screams had ceased and the body had burned.

As she made to conceal a poorly executed sniffle, Princess Aarya
turned her lively, malicious eyes on Shakti.

'Are you *crying*, Shakti?' the princess asked her.

'The pepper smell is a bit strong, Princess Aarya,' Shakti lied.

At least she could blame her tears on chillies instead of the mayakari.

'Oh.' There it was again, that dubious silence before the princess wrinkled her nose. 'I thought you were crying. The last time I saw someone weep over the witches was when father took us to witness a burning and Ashoka cried for days. Weak.'

Shakti tamped down the low growl. As far as she was concerned, the prince's response had been the correct one.

The mayakari who was burning in the city square looked to be around her aunt's age. When Shakti first laid eyes on the frightened-looking woman, her chest had constricted. Weeks of repressed pain had flooded her consciousness; her heart had hurt so badly that she was sure she would collapse at any moment.

Briefly, she'd entertained the thought of sprinting up to the podium, freeing the mayakari and cursing anyone within sight. The urge had been so strong that it had taken her a moment to realize her hand had drifted to the sword by her side, but she'd forced it down unhappily. As heartless as it was, it would do her no good to risk her life with the sure chance that both would die if she created a ruckus. Instead, she had to fight against the raging storm in her heart and watch the poor mayakari burn to death, her screams an eerie sound against the stillness of the square.

Princess Aarya's gaze looked a lot like sympathy. 'The smell takes a while to get used to,' she agreed.

I want to carve out your heart and feed it to the crocodiles, Shakti thought viciously.

Why the princess had jumped at the chance to witness such a gruesome spectacle, Shakti would never understand. Emperor Arush had been unavailable but had agreed to his little sister's request that she go in his stead. It was not as if Princess Aarya needed permission. Shakti knew that she would have gone with or without the order of the emperor.

'The people will see me as an advocate for the removal of the mayakari population from our empire,' she'd told Shakti as she had been standing utterly still in her chambers while her maids were flurrying about like a flock of birds in a rush to dress her.

Removal. The word sounded so clean, so sanitized. It completely erased the blood and screams altogether. Arush and Aarya never used the word *murder* to describe their targeted attacks. Shakti's blood boiled at the injustice of it all. Sometimes, as she slept, she dreamed of nothing more than the death of the monarchy under her hands.

'Leave it to Ashoka to try and *save* them.' Shakti was wrenched away from her thoughts by the sound of Aarya's scathing tone. 'Attempting to ban mayakari burnings – *hah*. Thank the spirits that the governor stopped him. It would subject our family to ridicule.'

The princess seemed to be lost in her own world when she continued her rant. 'Ashoka doesn't fight with fists,' she muttered. 'He plays with words. Predetermined plans. He suggested that to Arush for a reason, and that idiot can't see it. Sometimes, I wonder if he is fit to rule. Do you think *I* would be a more fitting monarch?'

Gobsmacked, Shakti found it difficult to respond. 'That sounds like treason, princess,' she managed to croak out.

The princess stiffened, then smiled. 'Entertain a hypothetical,' she ordered. 'Would I not rule better than my brother?'

Which one, Shakti almost wanted to say. *My answer differs for each brother.*

'I think you'd be more ruthless, princess,' she answered instead. Aarya would like that answer.

Observing her like she was a newly mined jewel, Princess Aarya cocked her head. 'Ruthless? Yes, well, that would be one way of describing me.'

'There are many ways to describe you,' Shakti replied.

Aarya arched an eyebrow. 'Your formal speech still needs work,' she retorted. 'There are times you miss my title when addressing me. But go on – what are these descriptions? I'm sure the common people have their own opinions.'

Shakti made to roll her eyes openly but stopped herself in time.

'Confident. Cunning,' she replied. 'Then there are the not-so-polite ones. Volatile. Mad princess. That if you were the empress, you'd only be a little girl playing make believe.' The last three were her own descriptors, and she relished seeing the outward confusion morph into a prominent frown upon the princess's face.

For a moment, she said nothing, and Shakti was sure that she would be castigated for her brazenness. But it never came. '*Mad. Make believe.* A bold choice of words.'

'Do you think I'm a liar, princess?'

An unreadable look flitted across Aarya's face before it quickly turned dangerous. 'Are you attempting to test my patience, Shakti?' Her voice was quiet. Lethal.

Nearing castigation, then. Shakti decided to rein herself in. 'That was not my intention, princess,' she replied.

'Hmm.' Princess Aarya turned her head away so that Shakti couldn't see her expression. 'Do not think me to be so oblivious,' she said slowly. 'My nightmares affected me in the real world, yes. I know, in part, it painted me as a lunatic. It was part of the reason why I decided to halt the search for the Ghost Queen. I have an image to upkeep, and *mad princess* is not one of them.'

CHAPTER THIRTY-SEVEN
Ashoka

The morning after his gruesome discovery, Ashoka had flown to the resistance stronghold and brought back Nayani and Naila with him.

The mayakari had been surprised to see him barge into the cave without notice, with some grabbing nearby pots and vases as weapons when he ran in. But in that moment, Ashoka had no care for his safety. All that ran through his head was the stray letter he and Naila had read, and the ever-growing inkling of whose bones were buried in the gardens:

The witch deserves burial, not fire.
Her treasures will be mine to keep.
The witch deserves burial, not fire . . .

Usra. Though he had no concrete evidence, intuition bore the full brunt of his reasoning. Sometimes, intuition had to be enough.

Nayani had listened in disbelief, appearing only half-convinced. He understood her perspective, knew what she feared. Though his theory could very well be true, and it really could be Usra's body that had been buried, there was also the chance that it wasn't her. That it was simply another mayakari who had succumbed to such a cruel form of death. It was why Nayani had been hesitant to send out a group of them to investigate. Instead, she had only volunteered herself and Naila for the job.

'I will not take too great a risk, Prince Ashoka,' she'd told him. 'I have hope, but too much of it is dangerous.'

Naila's skin was tinged with green when she slid from Sahry's back once they landed on the estate grounds but appeared otherwise unharmed. Nayani showed no signs of weariness.

'Beautiful animals, these serpents,' Naila coughed, 'but suffice to say I will not travel on one again.'

Despite the gravity of the situation, Ashoka smiled. 'They are not for everyone,' he agreed.

Once he made sure that Sahry was safely enclosed in her pen, he took the two mayakari to the ravaged garden. Gold flowers were ripped and scattered across the ground, soil was upended and covered the grass in large mounds. In the centre, exactly where he had ordered them to be left, were the bones.

Well, not *just* bones. Digging out the complete skeleton had unearthed something entirely impossible, but when it came to the mayakari, impossibilities were to be expected.

Attached to the bones were dark strips of muscle, yellowed knee-bone cartilage, still-white teeth and strands of black hair. The moment the body had been pulled out, it underwent further change. Sprouts with pale blue buds grew out from the ribcage and half-decomposed skin, a pretty garden grown out of a horrendous bed.

Every time Ashoka looked at the body, his stomach rolled. It was so grotesque. It had been several years since the burial; all the flesh should have decomposed but parts still remained. Magic was at play here.

'Spirits.' Nayani appeared appalled as they came closer to inspect it. 'This is . . . you think that this is her? How did you know to dig this up, Prince Ashoka?'

'I didn't,' he replied. 'There is a minor spirit who resides here. It approached me twice and forced me to feel such disturbing sensations that I thought it was recalling the way in which the mayakari had had their treasures removed.'

'Treasures?' Naila asked.

Ashoka flinched. He shouldn't have said that, but the damage was done. 'These flowers were made from melted gold that belonged to the murdered mayakari of Taksila. My father had it . . . commissioned.'

The two witches went still at his words.

'*Commissioned*,' Nayani spat. Her hands curled into fists. 'Their treasures were not an exhibition piece!'

'They were to him,' Naila murmured.

Nayani swore out loud. 'He buried her *alive*, that monster. He deserved to die the way he did,' she said. Each word out of her mouth was more bitter than the last. When she turned to look at him, Ashoka was perturbed to see the sheer loathing on her face. 'And you,' she said bitterly, 'are the monster's son.'

'Yes,' he agreed, 'but that does not mean I am one.'

'Your father burned my hometown,' Nayani snarled, all composure lost. Tears glistened in her eyes. 'Emperor Adil took my *mother* from me.' He could hear it in her tone; though her words blamed his father, there was still distrust aimed at *him*.

Ashoka snapped.

'Do *not* accuse me as if I am my father!' he roared. He was oil to a flame; a reaction that was fundamentally more his father than himself. It was maddening to realize that he'd reacted this way but patience, it seemed, was elusive.

Before he could discover the effects of overt, sustained fury, Ashoka forced it down. The crocodile that slowly rose to the surface stopped, frustrated by the lack of a kill, desiring nothing more than to taste a bloody confection.

'This is no time to indict me for my father's crimes,' he said, pinching the bridge of his nose. 'Rather, how about we bring justice to one of his victims instead?'

'Gladly.' Nayani palmed her face with a sigh and stepped towards the grave.

Glancing at the ground for a moment, Ashoka tried to alleviate the tension by changing the subject. 'Shakti once told me that mayakari don't know what they're bringing back,' he remarked. 'Not a soul but not nothing.' *Soul* was not a concept that was accepted in the Ran Empire any more. It hadn't been for thousands of years.

Thankfully, Nayani seemed to accept his attempt at a white flag. 'She's right,' she replied. 'We prefer to call it a "not-self". *Anatta.* Even then, the concept is hard to rationalize. Have you heard of the flame analogy, then?'

Ashoka nodded. He was familiar with the idea that all beings were akin to a flame on a dying candle. Just before it flickered and died, leaving nothing but the heavy smell of smoke lingering in the air, the flame was saved by transferring it onto a new, untouched candle. And so, the flame continued to live its short and bitter life until it descended onto the cusp of death and the process began anew.

'The flame that died is not the same one that burns anew on the next wick,' Nayani said. 'We can bring back what once was, but it will not be the same. Not quite. Nothing is static, after all. The world is ever-changing. To be honest, we don't know what it is we're bringing back. It was never fully understood.'

'Why not?' he asked.

'Surely you would know,' she replied. 'Your father was the culprit. He burned down the library where mayakari philosophers conducted their studies.'

'You know, I was always under the impression that it was the human philosophers of old that coined such thought until I learned otherwise,' he admitted sheepishly, but Nayani showed him no malice.

'The mayakari were scholars, Prince Ashoka,' she said. 'They understood the world before those without abilities ever did. They used their powers to expand the boundaries of knowledge, and the common people accepted it. Did you know that there was also a library in the north?'

He nodded. The Taksilan library, home to manuscript upon manuscript about magic, spirits, advancements in medicine and architecture. Everything that his world was built upon, again burned away into ashes under his father's command.

No more senseless destruction.

'Please,' he gestured towards the grave, 'begin when you are ready.'

Raising the dead was a dreary business.

Ashoka had never seen the process undertaken in front of his own eyes. Some part of him had always wondered how it was done. From what he'd read, it sounded unsettling, but interest buried the apprehension.

He stood outside the perimeter of the patch with his guards who watched as horrified but interested observers. It was Nayani and Naila who stood at opposite ends of the skeleton with their eyes closed, hands by their sides.

Tipping their palms upward, the two mayakari began to chant in a language that was indecipherable. Listening to it, Ashoka felt the strangest sensation. His spine prickled, causing him to shiver in discomfort. It felt unnatural, but then again, raising the dead was an unnatural business.

As Nayani and Naila continued to chant, the half-decayed skeleton rose into the air with all the lightness of a feather. Bits of grass and soil came with it, while slivers of muscle dropped to the ground in tiny strips. He found it macabre, by any definition, and it looked as if his guards felt the same.

'Speak,' Nayani's voice had suddenly become hoarse as she switched to their native tongue. 'The one who has cursed the land – speak.'

The skeleton said nothing.

'Usra,' he heard Nayani say again, louder this time. 'Curse-maker. Raise your hand.'

For an agonizingly long time, the body did not respond, and he thought it would not work. Ashoka was ready to kick himself for his failure when, suddenly, the skeleton raised one hand.

It *was* her.

'Spirits,' his voice came out strangled. Despite himself, his feet wandered of their own accord towards the body, ignoring the yells behind him. He couldn't believe what he was seeing.

Nayani continued her line of questioning. 'What did you curse?' Ashoka heard her voice rise an octave.

Again, there was no response, but the arm that was raised stayed up. Clearly frustrated, Naila turned her head towards him. 'She is unwilling.'

Ashoka grimaced. 'How long will she be silent?'

'We don't know. She isn't very responsive,' Nayani added. She appeared to be more composed. 'Odd. We are told that the dead are not usually cryptic.'

'What are they usually?' he asked her. His knowledge of the dialect of the dead was slim to non-existent.

'Blunt,' she answered. 'Emotion overpowers them when they're brought back to life, so they'll say anything. This one, strangely enough, *won't*.'

Emotion. Maybe they were leading with the wrong statements. Cupping his hands around his mouth, Ashoka raised his voice so that it was loud enough to carry towards Nayani. 'Usra, you were killed by Emperor Adil.'

The response was instantaneous. The bones shifted. They clattered together like a jar of teeth. Usra's mandible dislocated from its hinge. And then, suddenly, a low, disembodied voice boomed around them:

'*Murderer.*'

There it was. 'I thought that my father's name might overpower her emotions enough,' he called out.

'Good thinking,' Nayani replied, albeit begrudgingly, before shouting, 'Usra, Emperor Adil killed you, and you retaliated, didn't you?'

'*Yes,*' said the mayakari, her voice ascending to a dull screech. '*Yes. Yes!*'

This was good. Now, they had to keep Usra talking. 'Did you curse the Great Spirits, Usra?' he asked her.

'*Yes. No.*'

Strange. Ashoka shot Nayani a perplexed glance, and the mayakari took it as a hint to continue their line of questioning. 'Did you curse the emperor?'

'*Yes. No.*'

'These aren't answers,' Naila exclaimed. She sounded like she was struggling. 'Get her to answer, quickly! I can't keep this up much longer.'

Quick. Ashoka scrambled his brain for something, anything, to make Usra speak in a manner that was not so cryptic. 'Tell me your curse, Usra?'

She responded immediately in a language that Ashoka did not understand. All he knew was that it was not the soft, melodic tongue of the nature spirits,

He saw Nayani's face go slack, and an anguished yell escape Naila's lips. Ashoka watched in horror as Naila's raised hands dropped, causing the skeleton to follow. Whatever bones had been joined separated with dull cracks.

Immediately, Ashoka made his way to the fatigued-looking mayakari. Naila's clammy hands gripped onto his tightly as she sat herself down, breath heavy. Meanwhile, Nayani waved away any attempts to calm her down.

'She was confused at first,' she said after a long while. Her breaths were still irregular. 'And then she became angry. When she heard Adil's name . . . it was like a spark turning into a wildfire.'

'Understandable,' murmured Ashoka. 'Before the body collapsed . . . what did she say?'

He saw the witches exchange an indecipherable look. 'It was her curse, wasn't it?'

'Correct,' Nayani said. Biting her lip, she stretched out her hand to lightly touch one of Usra's bones. '*As the emperor stands true, none will stand with him. As the emperor stands true, you will lie with him.* That was what she said.'

Ashoka frowned. 'Are curses usually so riddlelike?'

'The curses aren't supposed to be specific,' said Nayani quietly.

'Otherwise, they will not work. Such is their nature. Here, though, it is comprehensible enough.'

Murmurs erupted from the soldiers behind him, but Ashoka paid them no mind. His mind raced, repeating Usra's last words:

As the emperor stands true, none will stand with him. As the emperor stands true, you will lie with him.

But his father was dead. The answer continued to evade him, and he felt foolish for it.

Where does my father stand, Ashoka wondered. *Nowhere, except—*

Lightning struck. A lotus bloomed from muddy water. The dead awoke. Understanding came as fast as his father's taunts.

'The statue,' he whispered, dumbstruck. 'The only emperor that stands true is his *statue*, isn't it?'

'Not once have the Great Spirits destroyed that abomination,' Naila replied. Sorrow tinged every word. 'We didn't know why, but it makes sense now. Why else would they circle that statue every night? Why else would they sing their sad songs and destroy what has already been destroyed?'

You will lie with him.

Impossible. Unbelievable, but . . .

'Usra trapped a Great Spirit into that statue, didn't she?' Ashoka asked. The crestfallen looks of the two mayakari were all he needed for confirmation. *Spirits.* 'That is . . .'

'No,' Nayani interrupted him, standing up. 'She was buried *alive*, Prince Ashoka. We will withhold judgement for now.'

Thinking of the trapped spirit, Ashoka found it hard to agree, but then berated himself. Who was he to cast judgement? It was not him who had been buried. It was not him who had to breathe dirt into his lungs. It was not him who had reacted out of fear, or anger, or both.

'Now that we know the curse, we can undo it,' Naila said. 'The Great Spirits can be at peace. The trapped spirit will be free. Thank you.'

'I . . . it was nothing,' he said, still rather taken aback.

Naila gestured to the remains scattered on the ground. 'May we take this back?' she asked, her voice soft and sad. 'Usra deserves a proper cremation.'

'By all means.' Keeping the witch's remains here would only give him more nightmares and a deep, deep sense of unease.

Bowing, Naila and Nayani moved towards Usra's remains. Directing some of his guards to assist the witches, Ashoka stood back and pondered.

He was one step closer to stopping the Great Spirits. One step closer to leading the war council. One step closer to proving the voice in his head wrong. Now, he had to keep his end of the bargain. As if by coincidence, he caught Naila's eye, and her request came rushing back:

Kill Governor Kosala.

Kill, and you become just like me, his father's voice taunted. *Will you do it?*

The Ashoka he was before Taksila would have let out an ear-splitting *no*. That Ashoka would be revulsed that his current self even paused at the question. Considered it.

I don't want to, father, he responded, *but I don't know.*

CHAPTER THIRTY-EIGHT
Ashoka

Shielding his eyes from the afternoon sun, Ashoka returned to the royal estate on Sahry after flying Naila and Nayani back to the razed lands. They'd agreed to meet him the next day with a handful more mayakari in front of his father's statue to undo Usra's curse. He didn't want to dally any longer now that they had found an answer. Once the Great Spirits were pacified, his main concern was resolved, and he needed to move towards deposing Governor Kosala without killing him.

Stupid boy. Violence comes easier than any convoluted plan you will think of.

When he entered his study, Ashoka found that he couldn't breathe. It was not due to his father's voice, but rather from the intimately recognizable pair of broadswords that sat atop his table.

Suddenly, a pair of arms latched around his neck and Ashoka was pushed headfirst onto the ground as the intruder gave the back of his knees a swift kick. The unexpected attack caught him off-guard, but only for a split second. Before his stomach hit the ground, Ashoka's training came rushing back and he swivelled around with just enough time to grip onto the muscled arms with as much force as he could muster. His eyes found a pair of familiar umber ones shining in the light that filtered through the windows, and he felt his grip loosen immediately.

Rahil.

Was he dreaming?

'You're here,' Ashoka said, feeling idiotic.

Rahil's smirk played across his heartstrings. 'I'm here,' he said.

Blood and heat were rushing everywhere as Ashoka felt his heartbeat pound in a way that he'd never noticed before. He'd dreamed of Rahil for what had felt like aeons, felt the pangs of loneliness at the distance between them. Now, here he was, so close that he could just—

Just what?

The answer came rushing at him like a heatwave. This had not been a loneliness born from being apart from someone he considered family. This was lovesickness.

Rahil was so close that he could just kiss him.

The realization hit Ashoka harder than he expected.

There it was – the reason a part of him had felt so impossibly alone without Rahil. Spirits knew if Rahil had ever reciprocated his feelings. Ashoka was too scared to ask. He wasn't like Arush, who was confident of himself. He wasn't like Aarya, who made her feelings as clear as glass to the men or women she desired.

The thought of ever asking Rahil only for him to say that he did not return his feelings was too unpalatable. Not taking a chance was better than taking one that ultimately led to failure. At this point, their friendship was far more important than his feelings.

'When did you arrive?' The voice was his, and he very much wanted to kick himself. Rampant emotions like this needed to be controlled. He could never, he would never. At every possible moment of expectation and longing, he would pull himself away. It was one of most cruel forms of self-inflicted torture imaginable, but he had to.

The moment lingered in the air as Rahil let him go, pushing himself up before pulling Ashoka with him.

'An hour ago,' Rahil said nonchalantly. 'But I was informed

that the prince was out on official business. Were you trying to expand the irrigation system here, or something as equally yawn-inducing?'

'I returned from the razed lands,' he told Rahil nervously. 'We finally found out why the Great Spirits were destroying it.'

'We?' Rahil raised a curious eyebrow. Ashoka quickly informed him of the events that had transpired mere hours ago.

'I'm glad that the mayakari were able to aid you,' Rahil said appreciatively, but he seemed rather doubtful. 'And they trusted you, too? That's surprising.'

'I found a way to earn their trust.'

Rahil's lips quirked up into a wry smile. 'Through successful diplomatic relations?' he asked, teasing.

Sighing, Ashoka picked at his ear. 'Through a promise,' he replied. 'To cease mayakari killings in Taksila.'

He stilled as Rahil reached out a hand to ruffle his hair and said, 'To think Arush doubted you.'

'I doubt myself,' Ashoka said. Admitting it aloud seemed like a weight off his shoulders. Admitting it to Rahil eased his conscience even more. 'Don't forget the governor. With him present, my hands are tied. Any semblance of sympathy for the mayakari enshrined into law will be repealed. Realistically, there is only one way to achieve their request.'

'Which is . . .?'

'A murder,' Ashoka replied.

For a split second, Rahil's expression became endearingly confused.

'Murder?' Rahil narrowed his eyes. '*Killing* murder? Or are you talking about a murder of crows?'

'What about this conversation makes you think I'd be talking about a murder of crows?'

'It makes more sense than you considering killing someone,' Rahil said, crossing his arms defensively.

'It wasn't my initial idea,' Ashoka said. His whole body was tense. 'One of the mayakari inferred it to me and – what?'

Rahil's whole posture had gone rigid, as if he had just heard something truly unbelievable. Something in his eyes shifted, as if he were watching Ashoka in a way that he hadn't seen before.

'A *mayakari* asked you to do this, and you're *considering* it?' he asked slowly. Ashoka knew that he found both statements to be contradictory.

'It's a matter for later,' he said. 'First, the Great Spirits need to be pacified.'

'You're hedging, and you know it,' Rahil pointed out. 'Once that is done, it leaves you with the governor and a promise you made. What will you do then?'

Ashoka wanted to argue. Wanted to respond with a clever idea in which he could achieve his promise without murder, but he couldn't. Mind blank, the only thing that reverberated was that insistent voice in his head; himself and not himself all at once:

To bring about peace, you must enact justice in whatever form it requires, it purred. *You think yourself to be above your father, but let me tell you otherwise, little prince. When you have the power to change the world for the better, your duty to the weak must override your duty to the self.*

CHAPTER THIRTY-NINE
Shakti

WATCHING THAT MAYAKARI BURN TO DEATH HAD GIVEN
her daymares.

Shakti could smell nothing but burned flesh for the rest of the
day. It lingered around her like a curse, clung to her clothes like
leeches against wet skin, sucking any form of happiness from her
tired body.

She didn't *want* to feel drained. She wanted to feel happy. But
by some cruel directive, one of the few people who had made her
happy was dead, and the only way to feel any sort of joy again
was to find some semblance of calmness in a place that welcomed
the quiet. Unfortunately for her, peace had come in the form of
The Collective, as she lay in her bed at night, meditating.

'You're too attached to The Collective, girl,' Adil remarked as
Shakti appeared in the throne room. 'It is an affliction.'

'You're an affliction,' she muttered.

Her comment didn't go unnoticed. 'Must you reply so childishly?'
Adil asked, his tone belittling. 'Why are you here?'

Because he's standing on a ledge and refusing to fall.

Harini's assessment of Prince Ashoka in Taksila nagged at her.
The knowledge that he had promised to ban mayakari killings was
all well and good, but it sounded as if the governor was a hindrance.

She found it unlikely that Arush would remove the governor from his position. Neither did Prince Ashoka have the authority to demote him, not when his older brother outranked him. Not when the governor only listened to the emperor.

To her, the answer was simple: *kill*. Though it could be done by a soldier's hand, there was more impact in a Maurya killing for a witch. In this case, it sounded as if the young prince needed a reason.

Like anyone else, he could be pushed. But unlike anyone else, she had better means to push him.

Leaving Adil's question unanswered, Shakti thought of Prince Ashoka, and entered his dream.

Out of all the dreams she'd visited, his was by far the most peaceful.

Two boys sat on a grassy plain, watching the sun rise as it bled bright yellow and red into a night sky that refused to recede. One was Prince Ashoka, the other was Rahil, oddly free of the broadswords he always carried. The young prince, meanwhile, held a dagger in his right hand while the left clasped Rahil's.

'Drop your dagger, Ashoka,' she heard Rahil say in muted tones. 'You are not cruel.'

Ashoka complied.

It appeared so *innocent*. Ashoka was innocent. Everything in this dream, from the brown hands clasped together to the drop of the dagger – Shakti was looking at a prince repulsed by cruelty. And yet, there was something underneath that harmless façade. The dagger that he'd dropped bled shadows onto the grass in an endless, contained smog. She couldn't quite understand it, couldn't quite place the gnawing unease erupting from the pit of her stomach.

Forcing herself into Emperor Arush's dreams had been easy, and Aarya's more difficult. Prince Ashoka's, however, had required three times the effort of his sister's. The feeling of pushing past a thick cloud of cotton was not present. Rather, it was as though she were pushing against a heavy brass door that refused to budge. It took a great deal of strength to get beyond it.

His mental fortitude was strong.

What else should I expect, Shakti thought, *from a prince who was burned and yet continued to push back against his father?*

Gut feeling told her to transform herself into Emperor Adil. Gut feeling also told her it would be a terrible idea, but she did it anyway.

'Son,' she called out, watching Ashoka's shoulders stiffen before he turned. Immediately, she was caught off-guard by his innocent eyes that threatened to spill tears, and was rendered mute, unsure for the first time about what to say to a child of Adil. 'I . . . I've come to speak to you.'

What are you doing, her mind was screaming. *Aggravate him, push him. Make him cruel.*

'Father?' Ashoka asked as he scrambled to his feet. Dream Rahil, meanwhile, sat perfectly still with his back to the commotion.

'Ashoka, I . . .' Shakti began hesitantly, marvelling at how it translated into Adil's voice. How unusual it was to hear uncertainty through his voice. She didn't realize that Ashoka's dagger had reappeared in his right hand until she saw the gleam of silver against the light.

'Get out,' he said emotionlessly.

'Ashoka, you cannot speak to your father this way,' she replied. She saw nothing but emptiness in his eyes.

'Get. *Out,*' he repeated. 'Or I will kill you.'

Shakti startled. *Soft* seemed to be the most inaccurate descriptor of Prince Ashoka Maurya at that moment.

'You won't kill me,' she said. For once, she was unsure. 'You can't bring yourself to do it.'

Ashoka laughed, the sound clipped and bitter. 'Don't test me,' he said. 'I can kill – I just choose not to. I always choose not to do what you do.'

Dreams held truths. She wondered how far she could push him, the prince who was whispered to abhor violence. He had a weakness and, just like his siblings, it was his father. Only, where his siblings were determined to gain affection, Ashoka was determined to keep away from it. He had anger in him, too, but it was rarely seen.

She *wanted* to see it. Wanted to see his anger in full force.

'Then you are weak,' she hissed, Adil's resulting baritone an icy tundra.

Ashoka's dagger was at her heart before she could even blink. Shakti could only watch as the prince's silver blade nicked Adil's – *her* – chest. There was no pain in the dreamscape, and yet she felt nothing but dread as she gazed upon Ashoka's eyes. At that moment, they were without mercy.

'I am not weak,' he said. 'I am the answer to your problems, father. I am the one saving the land in Taksila when you left it to rot.'

'And yet you cannot save its mayakari,' she responded, 'because I am right – you are *weak*, Ashoka. The governor must be removed, and you know it. To destroy me is to destroy my empire, and you will not do it.'

The weapon in the prince's hand retracted. The dreamscape turned grey. 'I-I can,' he replied.

'*To destroy me is to destroy my empire*,' Shakti repeated. 'To save many, you must harm one. Will you do it?'

Prince Ashoka wavered; she could see it in his eyes, in the way his shoulders hunched inward. Grey clouds wafted from his body like steam. His dagger began to crack until he started. In an instant, colour returned to the dream, and the weapon mended itself.

'Leave me, father,' he said, looking up to meet her gaze. Nothing but hatred was nestled behind those eyes. 'The dead should not haunt the living.'

Answer me, she thought, frustrated.

He charged again. Just before his dagger drove into her heart, Shakti leapt out of his dreams, pulse racing and her skin slicked with sweat. The Obsidian Throne reappeared once more with Emperor Adil upon it.

'Whom have you terrorized this time?' he asked her blandly. 'What my children have done to receive your vengeance is beyond me, witch.'

'I went in hopes of putting some sense into your youngest,' Shakti replied. 'It worked. He was quite violent, in fact.'

Adil let out a bark of laughter. 'Ashoka?' he chuckled. 'Violent? Well, I suppose he could only be so in his dreams.'

'You clearly show no favouritism to him,' Shakti commented, 'and yet you've named him after the emperor himself. How perplexing.'

Adil narrowed his eyes. 'Ashoka's name was not of my choosing,' he said. 'It was his mother's decision, and I do not wish to alter it. Such tradition must be respected.'

What an infuriating paradox this man was. She couldn't understand what he deemed followable and what he did not.

'It's a pity you don't believe in your son,' she told him. 'Dreams tend to tell us truths, Adil. Despite you not believing in Ashoka's inclination towards brutality, *I* do. That dream was proof enough.'

Adil scoffed. 'You think you can force Ashoka to be cruel?'

'It's not a question of force,' Shakti said, smiling confidently enough that the emperor's smug expression vanished. 'Ashoka wavers. I think he has *always* wavered. All he needed was a little push.'

CHAPTER FORTY
Ashoka

ASHOKA HAD NEVER BEEN SO GLAD TO SEE RIDI SOLDIERS in his life.

They arrived at dawn, around two hundred dressed in all-black armour, the insignia of the Ridi Kingdom – a sun bear – stamped upon the breastplates of their armour, carrying swords and bows of terrifying size.

He'd set them up immediately, and with an ease that he had never felt with the Ran soldiers. His command of the Ridi language was middling at best, and certainly not as polished as Sau's, but he had relayed his plans to the leading general to have them stationed in the poorer communities to safeguard the people – and the mayakari – susceptible to violent attacks by the old governor's soldiers.

Knowing that these men and women were unlikely to report back to his brother was a huge relief. Kosala could raise his concerns to Arush all he wanted, but here was an instance that his older brother would not care. Not when he'd approved the order himself. Ashoka reminded himself to thank Prince Ryu for his goodwill if he ever had the chance.

Goodwill, and yet the man was keeping his friend in Makon as part of the deal. He could only hope that Saudamini was working as quickly as she could to help with Prince Ryu's concerns regarding the mayakari disappearances before she came back to him.

The sun was beginning to set, bringing with it the colours of a bruise, when Ashoka arrived at the razed lands with Rahil and his soldiers. Rani, his longsword, hung at his side, passed down from Arush. They were met by a group of women, their saris, shifts, skirts, and trousers in varying shades of black. Dark, shimmering cloth obscured their noses and mouths, leaving only their eyes visible. A protective mechanism, he realized, to avoid being recognized.

'Try not to attack the mayakari, please,' he reminded his guards dryly as they approached the wary-looking bunch. He did not have to relay this message to the Ridi men and women – they understood that the mayakari were not to be harmed. 'Set up a perimeter around the area and keep watch. Do not let any civilians pass through, and do *not* let any other Ran soldier past this point. I will not have Kosala's men disrupt me tonight.' He expected townspeople to wander in. The noise and the rumours would make them flock here like crows to food scraps, and he wanted them to see without getting themselves killed.

The guards nodded before a majority dispersed, leaving Rahil, Sachith, and a handful of his own Ran soldiers behind.

'Prince Ashoka.' He recognized Nayani's voice immediately. The mayakari removed herself from the others and made her way towards him.

'Thank you for coming,' he said, nodding towards the dozen or so witches milling around the statue, speaking in whispers alone.

Nayani shook her head. 'Thank you for finding Usra,' she said. 'The spirit inside that statue has waited a long time, but don't forget your end of the bargain. Halt the killings.'

'I won't,' he promised, thinking of Naila and her more insidious addition to her leader's original request.

Kill him. You can. You have the ability.

It was getting harder and harder to refute the voice that always fought back against his peaceful side. After all, he'd nearly killed his father in his dream, and it had felt so oddly anticlimactic when he hadn't.

Sacrifice your beliefs to help the oppressed. It is the only way.

But to kill would be impossible. It would throw his morals away.

Last night's dream resurfaced again, along with his father's remark: *To save many, you must harm one.*

Is violence not necessary to protect the weak? That insistent, echoey part of his mind came running to him like a dog called to its master. *Can violence not be righteous?*

He didn't know. For once, he did not have the confidence to justify his thoughts.

'I will uphold my end of the bargain,' he said through gritted teeth, seeing Rahil's raised eyebrows at his comment. 'You have my word. For now, free that nature spirit.'

Nayani's eyes widened in surprise, her lips parting in a soft 'o' before they settled into a grim smile.

'Of course,' she said with a bow. The first one she had given him, he realized. Stepping away, she raised her voice to get the attention of his soldiers. 'I'd suggest you order your soldiers to disperse and guard the perimeters. Wouldn't want an unsuspecting citizen to wander in and lose their life, would we?'

'You heard her,' Ashoka said, turning to the remainder of his guards. 'Watch the perimeters.' Sachith gave him the tiniest of nods.

'As you wish, Prince Ashoka,' he remarked, signalling the men and women around him to separate, leaving him alone with Rahil, the mayakari, and the statue for company.

He glanced up and his father's face stared down at him, all burnished, untouched gold. Spirits, he wanted to tear it to pieces.

He watched as Rahil reached out to touch it in wonder. 'The spirit is trapped in here?' he asked. Disbelief clouded his voice, and Ashoka didn't blame him.

Nayani, too, strode forward and placed a hand against the metal. 'Yes, I can feel it,' she muttered after a few seconds. 'A little spark of energy. It's difficult to sense it, even like this.'

'What is your plan of action?' Ashoka inquired.

'Awakening and coaxing it out will attract the nature spirits from the forestland, princeling,' Nayani said gruffly. 'They'll be as destructive and dangerous as they were before, so no – I'd highly suggest that you keep yourself a safe distance from us. Or don't, if you have a death wish.'

Ashoka glanced at Rahil, who rolled his eyes. 'I fear Ashoka has a death wish,' he replied. 'We'll stay with you.'

With clinical fascination, Ashoka stayed to observe as the mayakari gathered in a half-moon formation around the statue. Their hands stretched out towards his father's marble face, palms facing upward as they began chanting in the eerie mayakari language of curses. Nayani began first before the others followed. For a few moments, nothing happened. But then, something in the air changed.

He heard the distant wail of nature spirits in the forestland and shivered. They were awake.

'Stay by my side,' Nayani hissed as she stopped her chanting momentarily. 'Do *not* leave this formation.'

'It's waking!' Nayani shouted in the din as a pale reddish glow began to appear from within the sculpture. A cloud of greyish dust appeared, the hazy mist enlarging so that it covered his father's statue completely.

'PRINCE ASHOKA!'

His stomach turned. *No. Not now.*

'*Stop this immediately!*'

Some of the mayakari faltered at the sound of Governor Kosala's voice, fear painting their faces. Turning around, Ashoka saw the governor straining to push past his soldiers who blocked him with bodies and swords. Undeterred, the governor's own guards pushed back, causing a scuffle.

'Keep going,' he called out to an anxious-looking Nayani. 'We'll take care of this. Rahil, with me.'

Meeting the governor's eyes, Ashoka stepped in front of him, gesturing for his soldiers to fall back but stand ready. 'Governor,' he greeted. 'A fine day, is it not?'

'Do not be smart with me,' the governor roared. 'Under the command of Emperor Arush, I order you to cease this nonsense. Your title will not protect you, *Prince* Ashoka.'

Tightening the grip on the hilt of his sword, Ashoka stepped forward. The governor only had a handful of soldiers; his own could easily override them. 'No, governor,' he ordered. 'You should leave, before you hurt yourself.'

Kosala laughed, the sound as grating as metal serrating against metal. 'I think not, Prince Ashoka,' he replied, throwing up a free hand. At his gesture, two soldiers charged at him.

Rahil moved like a wraith.

On moment, he was beside Ashoka, and the next, he vanished, appearing like lightning in front of Kosala's soldiers before attacking them with his broadswords. There was no hesitation; one sword sliced clean across a soldier's chest while the other defended and disarmed another.

While Rahil was occupied, Ashoka focused his attention on Kosala. 'Leave them be,' he ordered.

'Mayakari sympathizer!' the governor spat, reaching for his side. Thinking he was about to brandish his sword, Ashoka moved forward with his own drawn. Too late, he realized that Kosala had not reached for his sword. Too slow, he was unable to disarm the governor in time as he pulled out a gleaming silver chakram and flung it towards Nayani.

'No!' Ashoka yelled. A bloodcurdling scream was the confirmation he needed that the governor had hit his target. Sure enough, Nayani dropped to the ground, the chakram embedded in her calf.

Fury like he had never known coursed through him like wildfire.

Duty to the weak calls you to sacrifice your beliefs of peace.

To save many, you must harm one. Will you do it?

It was his father's voice that taunted him. For a split second, Ashoka hesitated. Killing would make him like Adil. But then came the crushing reality: mayakari burned, lands destroyed, more kingdoms annexed, and for what?

To achieve peace, you must accept violence.

His decision would cost him, but purpose overrode any sense of doubt. He did not want to see another mayakari dead.

Ashoka positioned himself with his sword.

The governor seemed to guess his intent, for he too drew his own. Steeling himself, Ashoka charged, and met the governor's weapon with his own, the *clang* piercing his ears.

Kosala was slow with his sword, but his precision was startlingly accurate. He struck – once, twice, thrice, four times with unrelenting fervour. Years of unforgiving practice kicking in, Ashoka obstructed all attempts at a strike to his chest. Kosala was surprisingly strong.

His fifth attempt at Ashoka's chest was blocked again, but Kosala pivoted quickly enough to slice into Ashoka's left arm. Gritting his teeth, Ashoka felt the sting of an open wound against air, felt the agonizing drip of blood sliding against skin. It wasn't deep enough to scream murder, but the blade had cut enough to hurt.

Wincing, Ashoka kept his mouth shut. Screaming would only distract Rahil and spur Kosala to victory and he wanted to show no sign of fear.

He parried, dodging, ducking, and diving. He needed to get Kosala on the ground, without his sword. Their weapons clashed together again, as Ashoka stumbled back but held his footing against the sudden and unexpected force that had come from the governor.

Instinct kicked in, as Ashoka fought like he had back in the Maurya palace with Rahil. Hard, swift, agile, unrelenting. The only thing that had changed was his goal. When he fought with Rahil, the aim had always been to get him to yield. Admittedly, it had also prevented Ashoka from truly causing any pain – he could never hurt Rahil.

Here, however, he had a target. A target he felt no empathy for, and it was all too easy to banish any thoughts of guilt from his mind, any sense of decorum.

Ashoka yelled, and forced Kosala's sword out of his grip, tackling the governor to the ground with him. Admirably, the governor put up an impressive struggle. Kosala rammed his forehead into Ashoka's, forcing him to lose his grip on his sword. It gave enough leeway for the governor to knock it away from him.

Letting out a grunt of frustration, Ashoka aimed the crook of his elbow into Kosala's throat, forcing a wretched gasp from him. He scrambled towards his sword, victory overwhelming him as his fingers gripped the hilt. Turning, he found that Kosala was attempting to stand up, his breathing severely affected by Ashoka's blow.

'No more,' Ashoka panted heavily, sprinting towards the governor, and tackling him down again, grappling to avoid Kosala's teeth from biting into his flesh.

'You. Can't. Win,' Kosala huffed, lifting an arm to block Ashoka's free hand. 'Weakling.'

Angrily, Ashoka wrenched the man's hand away from him, and forced it back, ignoring Kosala's yelp.

'Do you know why I'm going to kill you?' He leaned down to whisper in the governor's ear. 'I want the mayakari to trust me more than I ever want you to, and trust me when I say, governor, that I will feel *nothing*.'

Kosala's whole body went limp as he stared, dumbfounded. He'd got him. However, his momentary lapse of control was replaced by his furious hiss.

'You traitorous *scum*,' spat Kosala. 'You could never be the ruler your father was.'

Ashoka felt his senses snap. Red was all he saw, and rage was all he could hear. Again and again – he hated this. He hated people telling him that he would never be his father, as if he wanted to be.

He tightened his grasp on Rani's hilt.

'No,' he growled, 'I will be better.'

With that, he drove the sword between Kosala's ribs. Maliciousness overtaking him, Ashoka watched as Kosala screamed in pain, the blood pooling thick and fast around him. Darkness began to spread across the dirt.

Kosala sputtered, blood dripping from his mouth.

It's not killing him fast enough, Ashoka thought. Although he'd have liked to watch the governor die an agonizing death, he couldn't bring himself to watch any more.

Taking the dagger from his belt, Ashoka watched the blood trickle from Kosala's mouth.

'I want to watch you suffer slowly,' he spat, 'but I'm no monster, and I am *not* my father.'

Kosala attempted to speak but, with the speed of a leopard, Ashoka swiped downwards, aiming the tip of the knife at the bulging artery on the side of Kosala's neck, releasing a gushing torrent of red. Kosala burbled, wheezed, strained for what felt like an eternity, until his whole body became still. His eyes lay open, frozen with fear and disbelief, like prey trapped before its hunter.

The governor was dead.

Ashoka knew he was covered both in Kosala's blood and his own. The silk of his shirt was coloured an atrocious metallic russet. This death should have humbled some part of him, made him realize the weight of a life taken, but it did not. It only made him feel powerful. Immortal.

Untouchable.

His eyes sought Rahil's immediately. He stood surrounded by fallen soldiers, covered in blood like he was. Ashoka felt his own heart pang at Rahil's face. He knew that some part of him had been sullied for good in Rahil's mind. The young Ashoka who had denounced slaughter burned like mayakari in the night.

Disgust forced his throat to heave. Before he could stop himself, Ashoka fell to his hands and knees, and vomited onto the ground.

CHAPTER FORTY-ONE

Ashoka

THANK THE SPIRITS, NAYANI WAS NOT COMPLETELY incapacitated.

The group of mayakari had halted their chanting when Nayani fell and Ashoka fought Kosala, tending to her injuries. One had ripped fabric from her skirt and tied it around Nayani's leg to create pressure and halt the bleeding.

Dropping to one knee in front of her, Ashoka assessed the mayakari in concern. 'Are you all right?' he asked.

Wincing, Nayani nodded. 'I'll survive, Prince Ashoka,' she said. Her eyes flickered somewhere behind him. 'Will you?'

He didn't turn, didn't *want* to turn. Otherwise, Kosala's dead body would greet him.

He responded with a one-armed shrug. 'I suppose I can halt the mayakari killings without opposition, now,' he replied, then glanced up at the statue. 'Are you able to continue?'

Stretching her lips into a thin line, Nayani nodded. Using Naila's arm for assistance, she hauled herself up. 'Injury won't stop me,' she said, releasing a heavy breath. 'Let's return to formation.'

The mayakari followed her instructions and repositioned themselves around his father's statue.

Ashoka watched them. He smelled sandalwood and metal and knew instinctively who had approached.

'You took a life,' Rahil said, coming to stand beside him. There was an emotion there that Ashoka could not identify. What was it – anger? Surprise? Disappointment?

But why?

'Did you not think I could?' Ashoka responded. 'I trained under your watch. If you had no faith in me, I would have no faith in myself.'

'This isn't about faith, Ashoka,' Rahil said. 'I only worry.'

Before Ashoka could ask Rahil what he meant by his comment, the mayakari resumed their chanting. Smog emanated from the statue once more. A gentle rumble from the earth caught him off-guard as the statue began to glow.

Rubble on the ground skittered and bounced, stones clattered, and dust kicked up into the air as a bluish-white glow emanated from the greenery beyond the wasteland. One by one, giant spectral faces began to appear through the trees. A single-tusked elephant spirit, a tiger with dangerously elongated fangs, a leopard with eyes of rubies.

The Great Spirits.

With each heavy step, the wind whooshed around them, fast and then faster still. Like they did before, the spirits circled the statue, careful not to come near, careful not to get in the way of the mayakari chanting their horrific melody. Ashoka watched the spirits, breathless and transfixed, as they howled and groaned in their miserable song, until suddenly, the pressure dropped, and he found it difficult to breathe.

'Spirits help me,' Ashoka whispered to himself.

The being that emerged from Emperor Adil's statue was some sort of hybrid monstrosity. It held both the black eyes and oblong shape of a nature spirit at peace, and the enlarged, gaunt features of a mutated tiger, glowing an eerie reddish white under the dying daylight. The mayakari kept chanting, their eyes fixated on the newly awakened spirit as it stumbled outside like a newborn lamb on its thick legs.

Around them, the parade of nature spirits ceased their wailing, quietening down as the hybrid spirit let out a rusted, sorrowful moan.

The mayakari shifted from the cursed tongue to the language of the spirits. Their voices created a wondrous, harmonic melody as the air around them seemed to soften. The newly emerged nature spirit cocked its head like a dog listening to a master's command before it made a vigorous swipe with its paw. The first swipe sliced the head of Emperor Adil's statue clean off, dropping it to the ground with a loud metallic *thunk*. The second attack was harder, more forceful. It toppled the statue onto the mud and dirt where it rightfully belonged.

The spirit shook itself, as if awakening from a dream. In that moment, it was beautiful, a majestic creature of the natural world; a phenomenon. But thanks to his father, thanks to the useless governor – its voice had been trampled for years without so much as a scream allowed out.

Ashoka understood then that humanity was a horror beyond anything else he could imagine, and the nature spirits suffered because of it.

The creature's pitiful wails dulled, ceased, and mutated into the gentle birdlike song that was typical of a passive nature spirit until it sauntered towards its brethren. Lamentations shifted into song, much like the silent peace of the aftermath after a monsoon flood. As they had done every night before, the Great Spirits ambled back into the forest, but with a lighter air in their step. The freed spirit followed behind like the runt of the litter, but not before it turned its strange little head towards the mayakari, cooing out their unintelligible language, and disappeared.

It was over.

Ashoka stared in alarm at the mayakari who broke their formation, all in various degrees of spent. Nayani held a hand to her chest while Naila's shoulders were strung tight as she fought to regain control of her breath.

'It's gone!' a voice behind them shouted.

Ashoka and the mayakari turned around, the witches visibly shocked at the sight of a mass of townspeople gathered around the edges of the razed lands. They had seen the mayakari banish the spirits – good. He could barely hear the hushed whispers and murmurs that were carried by the wind but didn't have time to guess their assumptions. Instead, he strode forward purposefully towards them, watching with some amount of satisfaction as they bowed when they noticed him. Others, however, had their attention on the bodies of the slain soldiers and the governor. Alarm tore through the crowd, their voices getting louder as he approached.

'That's the governor.'

'Spirits, he's dead? Those witches . . .'

'. . . death magic. Cursed him too, I bet.'

'Isu, is that . . . the prince?'

More bows. More murmurs. More stares.

'The nature spirits will rampage this land no more,' Ashoka shouted out, forcing his voice to sound louder and bolder in the silence. He'd never found himself speaking to a crowd of this size. 'I planned to right Taksila in my governorship, and this has been one of the many steps that I've intended to take. The nature spirits have destroyed this township out of anger and sorrow. They had lost one of their own, and tonight, it has been found.'

Hushed whispers ran like wildfire through the large throng.

Feeling emboldened, Ashoka spurred himself on. 'My father may have conquered Taksila, but he made many grave mistakes,' he continued. 'His prejudice was what caused the spirit to be trapped inside his statue, and it was his greed that destroyed this community. But tonight, the destruction is gone. And tonight, I've been aided by the unlikeliest of sources. Sources that you've been told are far too dangerous to live.' He gestured towards the mayakari with a flourish, hearing the buzzing of conversation grow louder with every passing moment.

'You might call them curses, but I call them heroes.' Ashoka caught Nayani's impressed eye. 'Remember who it was who saved you from the nature spirits and their ruin.'

Belatedly, he hoped they *wouldn't* remember how the Great Spirits started to destroy the communities in the first place. That would only set him back a thousand steps, and he had neither the time nor the patience to regain that ground.

He had one last thing to say. 'You see the governor,' he said boldly. 'He attempted to stop me. Attempted to stop the Great Spirits from being pacified. Understand that I will do anything to see Taksila at peace once more, and he stood in my way. And under my governorship, there will be no more mayakari killings conducted. Anyone who aids and abets in the murder of the mayakari will be dealt with, because understand this – as long as I govern Taksila, innocents will not suffer.'

The crowd didn't clap, but he hadn't expected any sort of standing ovation. All Ashoka wanted was for the seeds of doubt to be sowed against his father's propaganda that had been ingrained into their minds for years.

'Guards,' he called his soldiers forward. 'Disperse the crowds without force.'

As he watched the soldiers move the horde along, he felt a firm hand on his shoulder. Nayani.

'Quite the bold play,' she told him. 'Trying to change their minds in a matter of minutes. I'm afraid it'll take some time to undo.'

'As expected,' Ashoka said. 'Change arrives when we're sick and tired of waiting for it.'

Even as he said it, doubt plagued him. Taksila could be changed, yes, but temporarily. Banning mayakari killings would only hold for so long before Arush intervened.

The governor was the root of Taksila's problem, but not the empire's. You know who is responsible for that, don't you?

An intrusive thought struck him again, crawling out like an earthworm from the ground. Images came, of his father, riding atop a leopard, the ground burning blue. Of his brother, young and reckless, failing to create a legacy but continuing a trail of carnage. Of his sister, taking that destruction and astutely multiplying it tenfold.

Your family is not your enemy, foolish boy.

Correct. They were not *his* enemy, but they were a hindrance. A barrier against peace.

I would do it better, he thought. *I can be better than them. This change isn't enough; I need more.*

Something in him felt different, then. Assuredness, perhaps, he couldn't quite tell, but he felt convinced. Determined. Realistically, what could he have achieved by leading the war council? How often would he have had to compromise with his brother's ideas? That was not change. That would continue to perpetuate violence.

Change in this empire could only come from revolution. From power.

And where else does that change begin but from the Obsidian Throne?

CHAPTER FORTY-TWO

Shakti

'THERE IS A MAYAKARI IN THE PALACE.'

Shakti stilled, her sword mere inches from Princess Aarya's throat.

The princess simply moved the tip of Shakti's sword away with her own, seemingly unfazed. They were practising combat on their own. Master Kudha had retired to her quarters briefly to place a healing balm over her injured leg, the nasty cut a result of duelling both the princess and Shakti at once. Distracted throughout the entire session, Shakti had hardly registered the sword-master's departure. She was still preoccupied by her invasion of Prince Ashoka's dream the night before where he seemed to have resisted her command.

'How do you know, princess?' she asked slowly, intent on presenting herself as casually as she could. She watched Aarya scratch her bandaged arm irately. It was covered in dust, little pinpricks of blood staining the cloud-white wrappings.

Images of the princess carving out the endless knot on her arm replayed itself in Shakti's head. Spirits, she shouldn't have played with fire, but there had been no room for forethought once the intoxicating mixture of mischief and vengeance had engulfed her very being.

'Deduction,' said the princess. 'I thought that first nightmare to be a ghastly anomaly, the result of weeks of stress after Arush ascended. But after the second time, I refuse to believe this fault is my own. This cannot be anything other than mayakari magic and when I find the damned witch, I will punish them accordingly.'

Punish them accordingly. There was an uncomfortable clawing in the pit of Shakti's stomach. Punishment for her would be death.

'Are you sure about this, princess?' she asked, ignoring the rapid beating of her heart as she sheathed her sword and feigned concern. 'Perhaps you are feeling overworked. Troubled.'

Princess Aarya's face was stony. She did not move to put aside her sword. 'Troubled?' she repeated, her tone indecipherable.

Not sensing any ire, Shakti continued. 'You have lost your father. You have been appointed to the council. You are attempting to work with your brother. It is understandable that this work can disturb your sleep.'

'Oh,' said the princess. 'You think the cause isn't magic.'

Shakti nodded. 'As far as I know, mayakari cannot control dreams,' she replied. 'I was told their powers were limited to three. What you suggest is rather impossible – *argh!*'

Her back hit the ground in an undignified *thud*, winded. A dull ache began to throb where Princess Aarya's foot had contacted her chest. Shakti had no time to scramble back up. Within seconds, the princess's foot pressed against her ribs as she towered over her. Her usually tamed hair was unkempt from the fight, sweat shining against her skin, that thin line of kohl bleeding black around her eyes.

In that moment, the princess looked just like an enraged spirit.

'Princess Aarya, what are you—' Shakti began to say, but was silenced when the tip of a blade hovered right against her throat.

'Stop talking,' Princess Aarya ordered, her previously blank expression lit up with fury. 'How *dare* you doubt me. Do you think I am a liar?'

No, Shakti thought. That the princess had guessed her affliction was what scared her.

Her brief silence seemed to have incensed the princess more.

Short, sharp pain exploded at the base of her throat: Aarya had dug the blade in, sliced the delicate skin. Goosepimples began to erupt all over her body, hairs standing on end despite the heat.

'Am. I. A. Liar. Shakti?' Each word from the princess was crisp. Pronounced. Sharp, just like her sword.

Shakti let out a ragged breath. 'No, princess,' she replied. 'I apologize.'

It was a relief when Aarya retracted her sword and stepped back, allowing Shakti to get back on her feet and press at her throat. The blood created an uncomfortable slickness and intermingled with her sweat. While she couldn't physically see the cut, she could pull the separated skin with her finger. The action resulted in deep, deep pain. When she removed her hand, her palm came away streaked with red.

Meanwhile, the princess watched her without shame. 'Have that cut bandaged in the infirmary.'

'Yes, princess,' Shakti replied tonelessly.

'And never, *ever* doubt me,' the princess added. 'Those who do tend to end up like those mayakari pests.' Having the mayakari referred to as *pests* was infuriating. For a blessed moment, Shakti imagined the Maurya empire in flames, meteors crashing down on the palace and its city in an unrelenting attack, the screams of the Maurya family as they suffocated under a dense blanket of smoke, crushed to death by their own statues, and relaxed. The thought of death brought her peace.

'How will you ever find the mayakari, princess?' Shakti asked instead, keeping a straight face. Princess Aarya seemed to have forgotten that she had caused her grave distress. And of course, she would forget. If she could leave marks on her lovers without guilt, she could hurt her guards without mercy.

'Interrogation. One cannot outwardly identify a mayakari unless you see them performing magic,' Aarya said as she shrugged listlessly like the impending death of a witch cost her no pain. 'It's quite a hindrance. I don't want any innocent women in the palace to be burned.'

Shakti almost made a point about how the mayakari *were* inno-cent women, but kept her mouth shut. She did not want another cut.

Motioning for Shakti to follow, Aarya made her way towards the edge of the courtyard. Weeks of training underneath the sun had darkened her rich brown skin even more. It had only resulted in twitters among the staff of the princess's relentless beauty, like the harshness of lightning in the rain.

'I will have my soldiers question the women of the palace,' Aarya stated noncommittally. 'I'm sure they will crumble soon enough, given that they've been threatened appropriately. After all, what is more fearsome than the threat of losing one's place in the royal palace?'

'Dying,' Shakti said without thinking. Immediately, she snapped her mouth shut.

Princess Aarya only laughed. 'Death isn't as terrible as losing one's livelihood,' she replied. 'It's simple logic; the powerful must take power from the weak.'

Shakti's hands were tremoring, palms damp. Her body was flushed, heat like the summer droughts coursing throughout her body to an uncomfortable degree. Some part of her wondered if she could ever have been friends with the princess in another life.

Perhaps. Or perhaps not. Maybe Aarya would be the same wherever she was.

I will kill you, she thought. *I will kill you and I will watch you burn instead.*

Her thoughts of vengeance were snuffed out by a sudden and horrific reminder. She wasn't the only mayakari residing in the palace.

Shakti had someone else to worry about.

Night fell when Shakti eventually found Harini was in the kitchens, eating a slice of milk rice with Ruchira. She'd initially gone looking for the mayakari in her sleeping quarters but had not found her there. This late, the kitchen was quiet. Pots and pans hung on hooks cast a long shadow on the floor.

'Shakti,' Harini said, before pushing the plate of milk rice towards her. 'Are you hungry?'

Shaking her head, Shakti dropped her voice to a whisper. 'I wasn't sure if you heard yet,' she said. 'The princess wants to burn test the women in the palace.'

By their dejected expressions, she guessed that the whispers had reached them, too. Ruchira's eyes were bleak. 'Spirits know how many women will burn in the following days.' She hung her head sadly. 'The cycle remains unbroken. What reason does Princess Aarya have, I wonder?'

'Her . . . unusual dreams,' Shakti replied. After all, was a truth, albeit one surrounded by shadows. 'She told me that she thinks it is mayakari magic.'

Ruchira cast her eyes skyward in response. 'The princess truly is going mad.'

Harini, meanwhile, remained silent, chewing painstakingly slowly on her food.

'Harini,' she hissed, grabbing onto the mayakari's hand firmly. 'You need to leave the palace for a few days.'

Harini's eyes were still as she swallowed her last bite. Guilt etched itself around Shakti's heart. This was all her fault.

'I'm sorry,' she said quietly.

Harini frowned. 'For what?'

'Nothing.' The existence of The Collective was a secret between two. She couldn't afford to let anyone else know. 'But please, you must leave before the princess orders the testing to begin.'

Rubbing the back of her head, the other mayakari sighed. 'I will,' she said. 'Returning from Taksila with a modicum of hope to be smacked by this – what else can I expect?'

Prince Ashoka and her command came to mind. 'Expect something good, at least,' Shakti replied.

Letting out a noncommittal hum, Harini stood, brushing stray bits of rice from her skirt. 'I have to help some of the staff unload some new produce,' she said. 'A late delivery. Some delicacies from the south that the princess had asked for, and then I'll leave. You should too, Shakti.'

She was right. Staying posed an enormous risk. Leaving, too, would cast suspicion on her. Vanishing without a trace just as the princess ordered the women of the palace to be tested for witch blood? Shakti may as well scream her identity from the palace rooftops.

I should go to Taksila, she realized. *I have the money. I have safety.*

Her existence was compromised. She needed to find Prince Ashoka. If her dream invasion hadn't pushed him enough to dispose of the governor, perhaps she could use her abilities to force the governor into submission. That way, her goal remained unaltered. It was, after all, her original plan to travel to Taksila with the prince. Pushing him to go against his siblings would be easier; she wouldn't have to fear for her life so much.

'Don't worry about me,' she found herself telling Harini. 'I'll leave the palace when I'm ready. I won't get caught.'

CHAPTER FORTY-THREE

Shakti

DESPITE BEING RELIEVED OF HER DUTIES EARLY THE following night, Shakti wandered through the palace corridors, unable to get an early sleep. Her mind was abuzz with what seemed to be an endless cascade of thoughts: escaping the palace, departing for Taksila. And she couldn't forget Harini. Despite her promise, the other mayakari had yet to leave the palace, and her lack of action made worry to spear into Shakti's chest. Part of her guessed that Harini didn't want to leave without her, a sentiment that was both brave and foolish. It wouldn't be long before Princess Aarya began burn-testing the women in the palace, and only one of them knew how to fight.

Shakti hurried through the squared yellow-stone pillars, engraved with naturistic designs and images of Great Spirits, her slipper-clad feet soundless against the marble floors. Only a few guards patrolled the corridors and hallways, making it easier for her to meander without being questioned.

Her keen ears picked up a soft sound of voices as she passed the throne room and dived behind one of the thick stone pillars. The night aided her, shrouding her shadow from view. Blocking out all other sounds from her senses, she focused on the voices that grew louder the more she concentrated.

'How *dare* you, Aarya!' she heard Arush's voice, loud like thunder.

'I'm helping you, brother.' It was Aarya's voice, the condescension vividly palpable. 'Imagine harbouring a mayakari under your nose. How shameful it would be.'

'What mayakari? The one you think exists because you succumbed into a psychotic fit?' Arush's voice was derisive. 'Little sister, that problem lies within you, not anyone else. Depravity has always been your speciality. You're undermining my authority by behaving like this.'

'But it's here,' the princess's voice was hard as glass. 'I told you it'll *work*—'

'And I said that you were delusional, because those are folk tales, sister. I should have you locked in your chambers – you truly are mad. You're not fit to *lead*. Spirits, when Ashoka returns, I should hand the reins of the war council over to him effective immediately.'

There was a profound silence after Arush's accusation. Shakti could almost imagine the vindictive glimmer in the princess's eyes as she fought to regain her composure.

'Brother, you're the poorest leader of us all,' Aarya's hard voice floated into Shakti's ears. 'Ashoka is in Taksila with Ridi soldiers under his command and you do nothing. He *kills* the governor, bans burnings, and you do nothing. What use are you?'

Arush's answer was frosty, capable of piercing through skin. 'I do not have any sway on another monarch's whims. If Crown Prince Ryu has decided to send soldiers to both the Frozen Lands and Taksila, that is his choice. Whatever Sau told him, he has acted upon, and if I remember correctly, *you* were the one who suggested she be sent. That is entirely your fault, Aarya.'

'Ashoka has banned mayakari killings,' Aarya's voice came out stilted. Likely the incident with Sau had hurt her pride. 'He has *killed* the governor. Are you not the emperor, brother? You can have him punished.'

'Ashoka told me the governor threatened his life. Would you not react the same in his shoes?'

'You are a fool for believing him.' Princess Aarya's tone was mocking. Shakti knew that tone well, and she knew that Arush would be feeling the same level of indignation as she was. Soon enough, she was proven correct. 'You and your senseless desire for the Frozen Lands. Whatever legacy you want to build, you'll destroy it all on your own.'

'Get *out*,' Arush bellowed. 'Out! Immediately, sister. Leave the ruling to the capable, not the mad.'

There was the sound of scuffling and a frustrated shout, as the throne room doors creaked open.

Aarya slipped out of the throne room like a shadow. From her vantage position, Shakti saw Princess Aarya pause at the entrance and rub her left cheek vigorously. She ducked when she saw the princess twist towards her direction. For six painful heartbeats, Shakti held her breath, her back pressed against the pillar.

When she opened her eyes and peeked out, Princess Aarya was gone.

CHAPTER FORTY-FOUR
Ashoka

ASHOKA LAY ON HIS BED, STARING AT THE CEILING without purpose.

His mind was scattered, landing at one thought before moving on to another as quick as a squirrel scampering for nuts. Three days had passed since the Great Spirit was freed from his father's statue. Keeping his promise to the resistance, he'd banned mayakari killings outright.

He'd learned from his staff that public sentiment was mixed. Frustrating news, but something he had to fix. People had spent so long living under the ideals of his father that such sudden change was incomprehensible. Likely they thought him a fool, a madman.

Arush would come knocking on his door soon enough, but Ashoka hoped that his brother was too preoccupied with his plans for the north. An illogical manoeuvre on his part; he was still unsure what exactly had pushed Arush to declare his intentions to annex the Frozen Lands.

His thoughts jumped again, this time to Governor Kosala. His soldiers had carried the bodies of the governor and his guards away on stretchers. He'd only taken one life but, at that moment, Ashoka felt like he had taken them all.

Change comes from the seat of power, repeated the small voice in his head. It had been prodding him for days. *Why don't you take it?*

'*Ashoka?*'

He started. Rahil stood by the doorway, observing him with worry. 'I called out your name three times. What's wrong?'

'Nothing,' Ashoka said quickly.

Letting out a disbelieving snort, Rahil stepped inside and closed the door behind him. 'Lies. You've spent an entire day in your quarters. The staff are whispering – some wonder if you're keeping someone hidden in this room.' The playful, teasing way in which he said it made Ashoka laugh and catch his eyes, holding them for a moment. Everything he wanted to say remained unsaid.

I want you, Ashoka thought, *but I'm too afraid of ruining what we have.*

Instead, he smothered a sigh and resumed gazing out his window, watching the midday sky. 'You've caught me,' he confessed. 'I am hopelessly suffocated by a thousand different thoughts. They won't leave me alone.'

Slowly, Rahil approached closer until he stood by his bed. For a moment, he stalled before sitting down on the edge, leaning over to tap Ashoka's forehead. 'Relieve them,' he said. 'Tell me – what are you thinking about?'

Thoughts scattered once more: *the royal circlet. The Obsidian Throne. Him, seated upon it.*

'When you said I would make a terrible emperor,' Ashoka began, 'did you mean it?'

His question seemed to catch Rahil off-guard. 'It was mostly in jest,' he replied. 'Why?'

'*Mostly*,' he repeated. 'Do you think I'm lacking?'

If anything, Rahil appeared mortally offended. 'Of course not,' he exclaimed. 'But people adapt, Ashoka, and they've adapted to your father over time. I was merely inferring that you may have a harder time being taken seriously.'

Do you doubt me?

He repeated his thought out loud, and Rahil denied it immediately.

Feeling bold, Ashoka beckoned Rahil closer until they were a hairbreadth apart. 'Can I tell you something?' he whispered. 'A want?'

Rahil's eyes fluttered closed, and Ashoka took it as an opportunity to briefly ghost his hands over the underside of his jaw. Mesmerized, he watched Rahil's breath hitch at their contact, and nod.

To destroy me is to destroy my empire.

Will you do it?

'The Obsidian Throne,' Ashoka said. 'I want it, and I'm taking it.'

The moment the words escaped his lips, he felt like a mayakari uttering a curse. Spoken aloud into the world, it was like a breath of relief and a heavy burden all at once.

Rahil's eyes flew open. 'You *what?*'

'I think you heard me well enough the first time,' Ashoka replied. 'Thinking I could change anything by leading the war council – what a stupid idea. It *won't* change anything because I must answer to the monarch. I must submit to my siblings. I've seen just how much my father's laws have destroyed the land and the lives of the mayakari here. You know as well as I do that the only way things can change is if I can force it, because spirits help us, this empire needs it.'

'I agree with you,' Rahil's voice sounded pained. 'But in saying this, you're risking your life.'

'I made a promise to the mayakari,' Ashoka said quietly. 'To stop their persecution is to rip the problem at the very root, and that root is my family. You can either disagree with me or stay with me.'

'I won't abandon you.'

Good. Straightening, Ashoka dropped his hand. The warmth vanished with it. 'Thank you,' he replied. 'Now, I need to meet with the resistance – I have a plan.'

*

When he and Rahil flew into the resistance's base of operations on Sahry, Ashoka was not greeted with suspicion like last time. Around him, mayakari continued to work and chatter among themselves. He was no longer a dangerous object.

'Prince Ashoka,' Naila greeted them, her demeanour much more relaxed than the last time he saw her. 'What brings you here?'

'I come bearing another request,' he said. 'One that you may not like.'

He must have spoken too loudly, for the witches in the cave fell silent, and suddenly all eyes were on him.

'What is it?' a middle-aged mayakari asked from the back.

'I'm sure you all are aware that this ban I've instated can only last for so long,' he told them, 'before my brother comes knocking at the door. I only ask that you help make this period more permanent.'

Behind him, Rahil gently bumped his shoulder to hurry his speech. He'd relayed it to him during their flight. Despite Rahil having listened, Ashoka suspected that he thought him to be drunk on false hope and delusion.

'To make certain that mayakari are allowed to live in peace, a change in power is needed in this empire,' he proclaimed. Palms clenched, he ignored their dampness. 'I am that change, and I need your help to take the Obsidian Throne.'

A stunned silence followed his announcement. Some of the witches stood frozen in place, others blinking rapidly as if they had experienced an auditory hallucination.

'Mutiny?'

That was Nayani's voice. Craning his neck, Ashoka spotted the tell-tale shadows under her eyes and the permanent scowl as she emerged from the throng of mayakari.

'Rebellion,' he said.

Another witch let out a strained laugh. 'Respectfully, you must be mad, Prince Ashoka.' A prominent burn was visible across her left arm. Like his ear, it had left scarred tissue behind. 'Are you even capable of leading an army? Spirits know your siblings aren't –

I hear from family that the princess has gone mad, and the new emperor is reckless. Who's to say you won't turn out the same?'

'Because,' he stressed, 'they aim to continue my father's legacy while I wish to burn it to the ground, and I will do anything to make sure I do.'

He knew how vehement and sure he sounded. Though his harsh words did not surprise Rahil, it gave the questioning mayakari pause, and that was all he needed. A pause in thinking was good; it meant that there was a conflict somewhere. A perceived fact needed to be reviewed. A set of ideals could be changed.

The charged disquiet was broken by Nayani. 'What is your plan of action, Prince Ashoka?' she asked. 'We cannot cause minor disruption and expect a revolution. It has been tried.'

'I agree. I cannot simply march into the Golden City and claim the Obsidian Throne,' Ashoka shook his head, 'otherwise, I'd be as idiotic as my brother. No, I need more power before I can attempt such a thing. I need an army, I need supplies.'

'The Ran Empire's army is one of the largest in the known world, Ashoka,' Naila jumped in, eyebrows raised. 'You'd need something double the size. That sounds rather impossible.'

'Not necessarily,' Ashoka said with a smile. 'If I can find myself an infantry where one person would amount to approximately three Ran soldiers, there would be no need to search exhaustively for more troops.'

Silent understanding dawned on both mayakari, but it was Naila who voiced their collective thoughts.

'You want to use the mayakari as soldiers,' she remarked, astonished. 'Destroyers.'

'Correct,' he affirmed. 'I know the mayakari have a strict moral code of pacifism but think of the power they could unleash on the battlefield. Communicating with spirits, raising the dead, cursing the living . . . they're powers that could topple an empire.'

'It's because of the damage we could inflict that the mayakari have always sided with non-violence, Prince Ashoka,' Nayani said with a grimace. 'Admittedly, us younger generations aren't too invested in that code, but you'd then be teaching mere children how to fight.'

'Child soldiers are not uncommon in war,' Rahil added quietly.

Naila scoffed. 'And we aren't Great Spirits, Prince Ashoka,' she said. 'We live and die as any human does. How then, do you propose this works? Our numbers pale in comparison to your brother's army.'

'The Ran Empire still hasn't taken full control of the south,' he said. 'There are still unconquered kingdoms like Mahvo where mayakari live without persecution. We can convince them to join our cause, train them, and have them fight.'

'So, you want to kill more of us?' Naila's eyes were stony at his proposal.

'Death is unavoidable,' he agreed, 'and I cannot guarantee that the entire army of mayakari will survive unscathed. But this would be for the good of the empire and the mayakari population. Your people will not have to live in fear any more.'

'I want the killings to stop more than you do,' Nayani growled. 'The mayakari here are willing to fight, but I cannot say the same of those who remain unharmed in the far south.'

'You're a natural leader,' Ashoka attempted to persuade her, 'it would be all too easy for you to send envoys to the unconquered kingdoms – to ask them to join us. We will train them here, equip them with better weapons.'

'But we aren't *enough.*'

'I understand, and I have a plan.'

'I'm sure you do,' she muttered.

'We will journey to Kalinga,' Ashoka said. 'There, I will request an audience with Queen Kalyani. If I can convince her to fight with us – *for* us – we have a chance to debilitate Arush's troops.'

'You want to use the *Kalingan* army?' Nayani's eyes widened. 'Prince Ashoka, I highly doubt that Queen Kalyani will waste her precious army in a siege. How will it benefit her? That is unthinkable.'

He knew that. He would have to bleed himself dry before Queen Kalyani would ever accept such a proposal. Still, he had to try.

'Queen Kalyani would want her kingdom preserved, unaffected by our empire's expansion. This would simply be the best way for her to achieve it, for I certainly will not continue the conquests once I claim the throne,' he argued.

'Prince Ashoka, has anyone ever informed you, that you are perhaps too staunch of an idealist?' Nayani jutted out her chin.

Ashoka shrugged. 'Many times,' he said. 'My older sister often reminded me that political idealism is a path primed for failure. I would like to believe otherwise.'

'She may not be entirely incorrect,' Nayani replied.

'Will you and the mayakari join me? Help me topple my brother from his throne?' he asked.

For a long time, she said nothing, and Ashoka was careful not to prod her any further. The mayakari was deep in thought. Finally, she turned to the witches behind her.

'Are we willing?'

At first, there was no response. Then, a few tentative hands were raised. Whispers of death and cursed speech ran through the group as more and more put up their hands.

This pleased him. How unlike his father he would be, to gain the assistance of the very women he'd scorned and burned. He would rewrite the Maurya legacy and create a new one out of the ashes of his father's defeat.

Finally, Nayani turned back to him and Rahil.

'To ensure the safety of our kind in the future, blood will have to be lost in the present,' she said, baring her rouged lips to reveal unusually pointed canines. 'You have your wish, Prince Ashoka. The mayakari will fight by your side.'

CHAPTER FORTY-FIVE

Shakti

SHAKTI WAS SUMMONED TO PRINCESS AARYA'S CHAMBERS at midnight.

When she opened the door, the scent of cinnamon overwhelmed her senses immediately. In front of her, Princess Aarya sat on a rich red cushion, legs tucked beneath her, face partially hidden by a shimmery red veil. She was still in the same white clothing Shakti had seen her in before, her under eyes notably shadowed. Surrounding her were several maidservants, all deathly quiet.

'Tea?' the princess asked when she noticed Shakti step in, gesturing to a steaming pot and array of cups laid before them. Her tone was nonchalant. Shakti observed her wryly; nothing about Aarya suggested that she was here to interrogate. Not yet at least.

'I'm all right, Princess Aarya,' she said carefully, greeting the royal with a bow. 'I do not drink tea so late into the night. It does not calm me.'

'I see,' was all the princess said at first. With a delicate shrug, she grasped the teapot and poured herself a cup, ignoring the startled looks of the staff behind her. The princess was not meant to do anything herself, it seemed. 'I find that it calms *me.*'

Remaining silent, Shakti stood there wondering what on earth she had been called here for. Unease pricked at her; her innards felt like twisted rope.

Did the princess know who Harini was?

Did the princess know who *she* was?

'Sit.' The order was soft. Swift. Maintaining a calm, unaffected expression, Shakti sat down across from Aarya so that only a low mahogany table separated them.

Shakti could not help but think of potential danger. Was the princess hiding a knife? Were there additional guards outside the door? Were the maidservants trained killers?

Instinct drove her to clutch at her bandaged throat. Her thoughts were threatening to fracture the serene mask she had so carefully put on. It did not help her frazzled nerves when Princess Aarya made a shooing motion towards the remainder of the staff.

'Leave us,' she ordered. Heads bowed, the remaining staff obeyed, exiting quickly. One young girl shot Shakti a furtive glance as if to say, *good luck*, before she left.

As the doors slammed shut behind her, Shakti grasped her kneecaps tightly. If the silence had been obvious before, it was now excruciating. If only she could torture Aarya's mind in that moment. If only she could force the princess into a hysteria.

The thought of death was the only thing that obstructed her from doing so.

'What is it you wish to speak to me about, princess?' Shakti asked.

Aarya's perfect face was illuminated with unadulterated mania. 'You saw me,' she said.

Shakti could almost feel her heart stop. *Betray nothing*, she told herself.

'I beg your pardon, princess?' she asked, politeness bleeding like an open wound into every word.

'Do not attempt to trifle with me, Shakti,' Aarya scoffed. The teacup clattered as she placed it atop the saucer and leaned forward. Determined not to crack, Shakti stayed put. 'The throne room.

You saw me. You heard my argument with Arush, and I saw *you* before I left.'

Shakti almost relaxed from sheer relief. This was not related to the mayakari. This was related to what she had heard. Thank the spirits.

Her throat was parched, and the tea appeared rather inviting. It had an interesting smell too, she thought. Green tea, jasmine, and some sort of earthy scent wafted from the cup she poured it into.

Taking a small sip, she allowed herself to appear guilty. 'Forgive me, princess.' She angled her head downward. 'I did not mean to. I was simply passing through and I heard the fight.'

A sharp nail dug into the underside of her jaw. Forced her head up. Princess Aarya appeared emotionless as she withdrew her index finger, warmed from holding the teacup, from Shakti's chin.

'Fight?' Aarya replied coolly. 'It was nothing but a harmless quarrel. Relationships between siblings are not always so good that we get along without trouble. Arush and I were simply discussing a matter of high importance for the Ran Empire. You do not need to make such outlandish assumptions.'

Slowly, it dawned on Shakti that Aarya was attempting to alter the version of events that she'd heard.

She must think that I will gossip to the staff about it, Shakti thought, suppressing a tickle at the back of her throat. *Even now, the princess aims to keep the disagreements between her family hidden.*

Pathetic.

'If you believe that I would gossip about what I have heard, you need not fear, Princess Aarya,' she replied candidly. 'You are allowed your privacy.'

The princess coughed. It sounded as if the tea she had been drinking had entered her windpipe. Then, the cough turned into a cynical laugh.

'Ah, you have caught on,' Aarya said as she pressed her hand against her throat. 'You are either smarter than the rest of the servants here or have no regrets in speaking your mind when others stay silent.'

'I would like to think it is the latter, princess.'

Aarya appraised her slowly. 'No wonder my brother took a liking to you. He does not care when his staff voice their thoughts. I find it quite unbecoming of a royal.'

This was no surprise. Aarya seemed the most likely of the Maurya siblings to distinguish herself from the common people, to let them know that she was of a different class.

In her vexation, Shakti remarked, 'It has the makings of a good ruler.'

She saw the way Aarya's shoulders tightened, the way her lips pursed as if she had insulted her very being. 'As expected by commoners who see a sliver of kindness as the makings of a great ruler,' she remarked, her voice stiff.

Leave it, urged the rational side of Shakti's mind. *It is wise to not incense the princess any further.*

The tickle in the back of her throat turned unbearably irritating, and Shakti coughed. Her body reacted of its own accord. Before she could stop herself, she heaved and dredged up spit and green tea all over the table. Mortified, she gasped, apologized profusely, and grabbed a nearby towel to soak up her mess. Her throat was still dry. The room felt hot. Spirits, her anxiety must have been sky-high. She needed to calm herself down.

The princess looked disgusted as she leaned away, but she didn't seem deterred. Instead, she appeared intrigued. 'Are you . . . all right?' she inquired softly as she tossed another cloth Shakti's way. 'Here. You seem anxious.'

'No, I . . .' Shakti struggled to form the words. '. . . I thought you called me here to be reprimanded for doubting you that day.'

'I think I made my point clear enough,' the princess replied, pointedly staring at Shakti's throat. 'Next time, do not doubt me.'

'Of course. And I apologize for my earlier comment,' she said. 'The mention of your younger brother appears to bring you to irritation, princess.'

Aarya scoffed, but it lacked force. 'All brothers exist to irritate,' she said. 'All brothers exist to not listen to reason. Not even when logic slaps them across the face. Not even when it is for the good of the empire.'

She knew that the princess was talking about Emperor Arush. *Leave the ruling to the capable, not the mad.* Shakti could not imagine the way in which the prideful princess would have seethed, would have imagined a world of bedlam descending upon her brother for his comments.

'Of course,' she murmured. 'For the good of the empire.'

'Yes,' Aarya replied, her tone flat. 'One can only hope my dear brother can overcome the challenges that will soon befall him.' She poured herself more tea, the colour of the brown liquid reminding Shakti of the same earth that her aunt's body was burned upon. The steam rose, obscuring half of the princess's face as it danced upward, dark eyes alight with barely checked chaos.

CHAPTER FORTY-SIX

Shakti

SHAKTI WAS STARTLED FROM SLEEP BY THE SOUND of bells ringing in the silence. Loud and insistent, they beat thrice at a deep, steady rhythm. A pause, and they rang thrice once more.

Death.

Heart beating in rapid-fire, Shakti scrambled out of bed. Sleep hadn't clouded her mind yet: it hadn't been long since she left Princess Aarya's chambers for her own. Staff who had been sound asleep had awoken with her and were opening their doors dazedly. The commotion had robbed them of their sleep as well.

Her mind was racing. *What was going on?*

Bumping shoulders against the crowd of staff who were muttering and whispering as they rushed out into the crisp night air, Shakti decided to race straight to the Obsidian Throne room. It seemed that she wasn't the only one with such an idea, because by the time she had arrived in front of the great wooden doors, a throng of staff and guards were huddled around it.

Shakti found Ruchira in the crowd instantly, dressed in a light grey sleeping shift, her eyes still heavy from sleep.

'Ruchira!' she exclaimed, coughing as she did. Her throat was still sore.

'Shakti!' the older woman exclaimed as she made her way to her. 'Spirits help us, there's been another death.'

Shakti blanched. Perhaps it *was* Aarya. She was about to ask which of the Maurya brood had succumbed to death this time, but her question was answered by the giant *bang* of the throne room doors opening. One of the royal physicians walked out, his face long and drawn before he gently closed the doors behind him.

'A false alarm!' He turned to the awaiting onlookers gravely. 'The emperor is not dead. He has, however, been rendered unconscious. Comatose.'

Shakti's sleep-addled brain thought first of Adil, before remembering that he was *not* alive. There was only one emperor, and that was—

'Arush!' the screams were coming from inside the Obsidian throne room, '*Arush!*'

A voice made frail by months of sorrow. It could only be Empress Manali.

Shakti turned her stunned gaze to Ruchira. 'What happened?' she hissed.

Ruchira appeared equally befuddled. 'I . . . I don't know,' she murmured. 'The bell rang thrice, and I assumed it was a death. It *always* means death.'

Shakti cast her mind back some hours ago, before she had been summoned to the princess's chambers. Back to the argument she'd heard between Aarya and Emperor Arush. Though she had seen the Maurya siblings quarrel before, that one had seemed particularly inflammatory. There had been an undercurrent of insidiousness in their exchange.

The emperor rendered comatose. Who would think to attempt it? Or better yet, who would stand to gain from it?

Aarya, her mind whispered delightedly. *Aarya, Aarya, Aarya.*

'What's the cause of the emperor's condition?' she asked loudly to the physician.

'A series of seizures,' he replied solemnly, eliciting a gasp from the crowd. 'Frankly, it's quite unexpected considering that his health had been excellent. Now, I don't want to cause any alarm, but the likeliest cause is poison.'

His statement only served to escalate the tension of the crowd who had now begun to speculate about the perpetrator, the true cause of the emperor's comatose condition. Meanwhile, Shakti's head was echoing that damned name over and over again in an endless, torturous cycle:

Aarya, Aarya, Aarya.

Her head was telling her that this was connected to the princess. Who else could Emperor Arush have seen so late into the night? The princess was the royal child who most lusted after power and glory. Shakti wouldn't have been surprised if Aarya had mustered enough depravity within herself to slip a vial of poison into her older brother's drink. The subsequent guilt would be nothing compared to the jubilation of claiming the Obsidian Throne.

As the head physician made to enter the throne room once more, the great doors opened to reveal Princess Aarya, wearing the same white clothes she had met Shakti in. She gazed upon the crowd, her face unusually bare considering her staunch addiction to maintaining her vanity. But that did not matter. The princess's eyes were bright, her posture erect, her expression haughty. It was as if Shakti were gazing upon Adil's face. As if he had not died at all.

Dozens of the palace staff fell silent at the sight of the princess as they dropped into deep bows and hasty murmurs.

'I'm sure you have heard that my dear brother is comatose,' she said loudly, her voice firm, clear, and without any inflection. Her eyes found Shakti's, and she felt an unpleasant heave in her stomach. The princess stared at her for a beat longer than necessary before she resumed her speech. 'Rest assured, we will uncover the cause of my brother's untimely condition, be it poison as the physicians claim, or what *I* believe to be wretched mayakari magic.'

At the mention of mayakari magic, the crowd tittered. Some

appeared confused, others disbelieving. Shakti caught hushed whispers that questioned the princess's sanity.

'Oh yes,' Princess Aarya replied. 'No one leaves until I find the witch. From this point on, the palace will be in lockdown.'

CHAPTER FORTY-SEVEN
Ashoka

RAHIL WAS UNUSUALLY QUIET AS HE SPARRED WITH Ashoka. Only his pants and grunts rung in the humid air as he ducked and attacked him with precise, lethal parries. Ashoka let Rahil dwell in his silence. He knew better than to pounce on him during these moments of quietude. However, the silence eventually became so suffocating that he stopped mid-spar, dropped his sword, and stared Rahil down, eye-to-eye.

'What's the matter?' he asked, voice softening. It always did when it came to Rahil.

'Nothing,' Rahil said.

'I can tell when you're lying too, you know.'

Rahil sighed. His voice was tinged with concern. 'Ashoka, don't you worry?'

'About what?'

'That in trying to reverse everything your father has done, you're becoming more and more like him in the process.'

That stung Ashoka more than it should have. Especially since it had come out of Rahil's mouth.

'Do you not support me, Rahil?' he asked him.

'My memory isn't so far addled that I've forgotten where my loyalties lie, Ashoka. I'm still on your side, and I always will be,'

Rahil shot him a frustrated look, 'but I hope you don't destroy the best part of you in mutinying and trying to take the throne.'

'You think I'll lose myself,' Ashoka remarked. It hadn't been a question.

'No, I—' Gingerly, Rahil stepped closer to him, a hand outstretched as if to grasp his. After a moment of hesitation, he let it fall limply to his side. Ashoka closed his eyes, infuriated. He wanted Rahil to hold his hand, but he didn't. He wanted Rahil to embrace him. He wouldn't.

'Don't,' he said quietly. 'Don't hurt me by comparing me to a man who built his life on hate and killed the mayakari. I am not him; I will never *be* him. Never, *never* compare me to him, do you understand?'

Rahil said nothing and threw his sword onto the ground.

'Spar without weapons,' he ordered. Ashoka followed and, before he could make any objection, Rahil charged at him with determined ferocity.

Ashoka grappled Rahil the first chance he got. He attempted to pin Rahil's arms above him, but Rahil was stronger. He elbowed Ashoka's chest, catching him off-guard and making him wheeze. Before he could blink, Rahil had turned the tide, latching onto Ashoka's shoulders and rolling on the ground so that he lay above him, chest pressing against his.

Ashoka couldn't breathe. There it was again – wrath and desire. The need to claim victory, and the need to kiss Rahil senseless. But all those thoughts were shattered and rendered mute when Rahil next spoke:

'A cruel Ashoka is not the Ashoka I know,' he said quietly. 'Do not become him.'

Underneath Rahil, Ashoka stilled.

'I will not be *cruel*,' he frowned, pushing Rahil off him, 'but I will not be soft. I don't need you to judge me for what I do, only to follow me without question like the soldier you are and keep your opinions to yourself. You are not my moral compass, so don't pretend to be.'

Rahil's expression shuttered, and Ashoka regretted his words immediately. He wanted to rewind time, to take back what he'd said, but the world did not work that way.

He stood up quickly. 'Rahil, I—' he began, but Rahil was already picking himself up, brushing the dust from his upper body.

'No need, Prince Ashoka,' he said. The use of his title as an address hurt him more than anything else. Rahil hadn't referred to him as Prince Ashoka when they were alone for a long time. 'I'll return to the soldiers and oversee their patrols.'

'Rahil—' Ashoka tried again, but to no avail, as Rahil picked up his scattered broadsword and strapped it to his back.

'Your offensive punches still need refinement,' Rahil advised him flatly. 'Sometimes your aim is off, so I suggest you work on that. Is there anything else you need, Prince Ashoka?'

Ashoka felt his shoulders drop. He wanted to argue, but he respected Rahil enough to let him go.

'No, Rahil,' he said. 'You're free to go.'

As Rahil left him standing on the grass, face streaked with dirt and dust, Ashoka felt his heart crack in two.

CHAPTER FORTY-EIGHT
Shakti

SHAKTI WALKED ALONE ALONG ONE OF THE PALACE'S corridors that looked out onto one of its long pools. Busts of past Maurya royals were placed on pillars between each column, their names etched into the granite.

She stopped by the sculpture of Emperor Adil. Even immortalized in stone, his features were made to be cruel. Shaking her head, she moved away from it. She could hear his taunts in her head, his noisy complaints of her wretchedness and unjustified anger engulfing her like a tidal wave. The palace was under lockdown, with no one able to leave. The only good news she'd heard from Ruchira was that Harini had left for the city some time before the announcement.

'Your family is a scourge, Adil,' she muttered. 'I hope that mayakari curses litter your bloodline for generations to come.'

Adil's bust, of course, said nothing.

'Your children will tear each other apart and I will watch,' she said heatedly. 'And then I will taunt you until I die.'

Adil's bust remained silent.

Releasing a high-pitched squeal of exasperation, Shakti aimed a swift kick at the pillar that held Adil's bust. However, it was so firmly melded into the ground that it made barely a wobble.

Frustrated out of her wits, Shakti took out her dagger and threw it at the bust. The dagger landed squarely between his eyes, right on the bridge of his nose. The material cracked upon impact, fissures travelling from the centre point before slowing to a stop.

She was so tempted to cast herself into The Collective, and order Aarya to drop dead.

Do it.

Was that her voice, or was it Jaya's? At this point, Shakti could not differentiate between her own volatility and the distorted echo of her aunt's voice that did not sound like her aunt at all. Maybe she was going mad, too.

'*Little witch.*'

She startled and looked down. At first, she could barely see anything, but her eyes adjusted to spot an ant-sized, moon-white nature spirit peering at her from behind the column.

'*Spirit?*' she asked, stunned. How did this creature exist here?

She glanced at the pool reflecting the moonlight with perfect clarity. Ah – the water.

This minor spirit could not communicate well, perhaps affected by its own surroundings. When it came forward to ghost against her feet, Shakti sensed a question:

Angry?

'*I am not mad, nature spirit,*' Shakti replied. '*It is the world around me that refuses to stay sane.*'

The nature spirit cooed, and a chill crept up her spine. *Fuck.* It had been so instinctual; she shouldn't have answered it. What if someone had seen her? What if someone had—

'I found you.'

It took all of Shakti's strength not to jump out of her skin. She knew that voice well. Dulcet tones, a demeanour of innocence that belied a tempest of hunger and wickedness. As she turned, Princess Aarya seemingly melted out of the shadows behind her, dressed in fighting gear.

The world around her constricted. It became hard to breathe. Clasped in Aarya's right hand was a sword, the very same one she used in combat practice. Before, it had been aimed at Shakti without proper intent. Now, with the silver blade shining beneath the moon, its intent was all too clear.

'Princess Aarya,' she said. Her heartbeat thumped against her ribs.

The princess's eyes were flat. Dull. 'You,' she said softly, taking a step towards her. The tip of the sword dragged along the ground in an unceremonious *screech*. 'It was always *you*.'

Shakti thought she saw a flash of disappointment, an under-current of sadness beneath her downturned lips. Something close to betrayal. But that couldn't be. That was not who Aarya was.

'I don't know what you mean,' Shakti replied, purposefully keeping her voice slow. Discreetly, she shifted her eyes to her own dagger that was lodged into the bust. There was enough time to wrench it out and defend herself. A dagger against a sword was no fair match, but she had the advantage of cursed speech.

'Don't lie to me, *mayakari*,' Aarya said as her pretty face twisted into a sneer. 'There was no need to see you speaking to that nature spirit. I already knew it was you.'

'Princess,' Shakti said slowly. Her heart was struggling to keep a regular rhythm. 'Are you feeling all right? I can get the ph—'

'You reacted to the tea, mayakari,' the princess growled. 'You cannot talk your way out of this.'

Tea?

Shakti's mind flashed back to the conversation she'd had with the princess in her chambers. Did she put in some kind of poison? No, that couldn't be it. So then, what was she possibly talking about?

Princess Aarya watched her with a devious grin. 'The stories are true,' she laughed, 'the Ghost Queen really does reveal a witch.'

The Ghost Queen?

No, she thought frantically, *that can't be. I made her stop. She couldn't have.*

'The Ghost Queen is a rarity,' Shakti sputtered, 'its claims are a lie.'

'*Really?*' The way in which the princess feigned shock would have been almost comical had the situation not been so dire. 'Then tell me why the staff who I had drink the tea did not cough it up like you did? They found the taste to be rather pleasant.'

Emperor Adil's voice surfaced in a haunting echo.

Listen carefully, witch – the Ghost Queen is purported to reveal a mayakari if they come into contact with it.

Magic harms magic.

Spirits. Her reaction to the tea made sense, then. The princess had really, truly found a Ghost Queen. Of all the bad karma Shakti could have received, and this was it?

'A foreign body reaction,' she lied.

'You know, I'm surprised you didn't see it yourself – I made the order to have one sent to the palace if the flower was found, and mayakari, they found *one*. One measly Ghost Queen on the cusp of death, and it was brought to me. One *fucking* flower, and I used it on you. Want to know why? Because I dreamed. Of *you.*'

The princess was ranting now, becoming more agitated with each passing moment. Shakti surveyed her surroundings, looking for a suitable port of escape. *Nothing.* Running was doable, but useless. Aarya would catch up to her.

Shakti found herself focusing on one remark during her assessment. Aarya had dreamed of her – when? She had remained as Adil for each dream she'd invaded. When had she—

Oh.

'Until the Ghost Queen was brought to me, I'd suddenly lost all desire to find it. I thought it was strange,' Aarya continued. 'Then, I remembered the nightmares. In one of them, my father drowned me beneath moss, and for a moment in that dream, I saw you. He turned into you. It made no sense to me why you would appear, why I would dream of *you*. But then I entertained that curiosity. Asked about Mathura's native language, and you told me a falsehood despite claiming it was your birth state. Remember it?'

A vague recollection surfaced, of Aarya asking her if there was a polite and informal level to the state's native tongue. She'd said no.

Fuck.

'What a shame it'd be to burn you,' Aarya mused. 'I trusted you to guard my life, you know. I liked you; I thought we were similar.'

Suddenly, an image of Jaya flashed in Shakti's mind. Her burned corpse, her emerald necklace, her laughter, her kindness. Everything good and terrible came rushing into Shakti's consciousness at once, and all she could determine was that she would not meet her doom like her aunt had done.

No, she would live, by any means possible.

'Please!' Shakti exclaimed, putting her hands up. 'Don't hurt me.'

Aarya stopped in the middle of her tracks, head tilting to the side like a curious dog's. 'And why not?' she asked.

'You once told me you desired power above anything else.' Her mind racing, Shakti said the only thing she could in a desperate attempt to save herself. 'You seem to be willing enough to poison your own brother for it.'

Aarya made no attempt to defend herself. 'How else could I take power and right what he'd wronged?' she remarked. 'Yes, I slipped in crushed sea mango into his drink. What of it?'

The careless, unconcerned way she admitted to attempted fratricide threw Shakti. Arush was Aarya's family. She could not imagine having such callous disregard for it.

'You've hurt your own family,' she said. 'Would your father not have been disappointed?'

'I did not mix enough to kill – I am not so heartless,' the princess replied as if Shakti's accusations had hurt her deeply. 'Only enough to incapacitate. And do not *dare* speak my father's name.'

Without another word, she charged at Shakti. Adil's name seemed to have spurred the princess to action. Swiftly, Shakti jumped back, her hand reaching out to grasp the hilt of her embedded dagger. Bad luck was playing against her; the dagger refused to budge. Shakti turned just as Aarya tackled her to the ground. She landed face-first, and felt her arms being pulled back roughly, secured by Aarya's own. She heard metal clatter on the ground and realized that the princess had dropped her sword. The fear returned stronger when she turned her head up, only to see the gleam of a small dagger instead.

'I carved my skin like it was a canvas,' Princess Aarya hissed against her ear. As much as Shakti struggled, she couldn't break away from the princess's iron grip.

'No,' Shakti rasped out. 'No. Let me go!'

'*Tch*. Such lies against a princess – you should be punished,' Princess Aarya's voice rose to a fervent pitch.

Shakti heaved. '*Fuck you*,' she spat.

An incredulous laugh. Then, 'An eye for an eye,' the princess remarked. The next thing Shakti knew, the back of her tunic was being cut open before the dagger's blade dug into her skin.

Shakti screamed.

It was as if her arm were being sawn off; the pain was excruciating. Aarya did not cut once and leave it at that. Instead, she went back in, scoring repeatedly over the same cut she had made, making the incision deeper and deeper as she went. If she kept going, she would soon pass the muscle and hit bone.

'Do you know what I'll do?' the princess asked softly, 'I'll pin my brother's affliction on you, mayakari. They'll believe me, too, when your body burns blue.'

In that moment, Shakti wondered if it was better to burn. She could only scream, struggle, and grit her teeth as Princess Aarya carved something on her back. What was it – an endless knot? The word *traitor*? *Mayakari*?

Her vision turned hazy. She was going into shock. If Shakti didn't react soon, she would faint then and there, and the murderous princess would carve a sculpture out of her body.

Do you want to die like this, Shakti?

It was Emperor Ashoka's voice. Faraway, but insistent. Was this how her life would end? Would this mean she would be free from The Collective? Or would she be stuck with it for eternity?

Shakti did not want to find out.

With an immense heave, she twisted to her side. It disturbed the princess for a split second, enough that Shakti rolled over and tried to sit up. Scramble away. Alas, Aarya recovered from the sudden motion and lunged, trapping her again. The newly cut skin on Shakti's back dug into the ground and she grimaced.

Before she could aim a kick at the princess's chest, Aarya's hands went around her throat.

Shakti gasped, her arms reaching up to claw the princess's hands, but she only squeezed tighter. Pain raged as she felt the soft cartilage of her throat contort. She couldn't breathe. She could only let out pathetic gasps like a fish out of water. Black spots began to cloud her vision.

While she struggled, Princess Aarya watched her with a manic expression. 'You've embarrassed me, Shakti,' she whispered. 'A mayakari working *for* me all this time and I did not realize. Did Ashoka know about you? I wouldn't be surprised if he did. You don't deserve to burn. No, I should kill you myself.'

I can't die like this.

A sudden burst of inhuman energy overtook her as she dug her nails into Aarya's hands and spat the saliva that had been pooling in her mouth directly at her face. The princess screamed, like her spit was something infected. The grip against her throat loosened.

Shakti moved quickly. She used Aarya's disconcertion to push away her hands and aim a hard kick at her abdomen. Letting out a pained grunt, Princess Aarya lurched back, still wiping her eyes.

Getting back on her feet, Shakti clutched her left shoulder. Her mind was racing. There was a sure way out of this. Quickly, she backed away when Aarya stood up, dropping the dagger and reclaiming her sword. Whatever the princess planned to do, she would show her no mercy.

Stall, Jaya's mind whispered. *Save yourself.*

'I have something that may be useful to you,' Shakti said, panting. 'A power. An ability. You could change the world with it.'

Aarya scoffed but thankfully made no move to lift her sword. Shakti let her approach, aware that one wrong word could cost her life. 'Like what?'

'Your father's memories,' Shakti replied, watching Aarya's eyes widen first in surprise before shifting to outrage. 'His voice, his *consciousness* – they were transferred to me upon his death.'

The princess had been so close to her, but once Adil was mentioned, she jumped back like Shakti was poison. Disbelief marred her eyes, along with a spark of disgust.

'His death? You lie,' said Aarya, her voice a torturous grate. 'That is impossible. How . . .'

A dark cloud descended over Aarya as she narrowed her eyes at Shakti in understanding. 'You – the poison. The curse . . . *you* killed—'

'I can speak to your father,' Shakti interrupted her, 'and I'm the only one who can.'

'Liar,' Aarya growled. 'You're trying to save your own skin. You seem like the type to fight death just to steal back the chance to live.'

She raised her sword.

Shakti wouldn't peter out like this. Not when she had one more trick left to try.

Just before the hilt of Aarya's sword made contact against her temple, Shakti made one last-ditch attempt. 'You want to know how I appeared in your dreams?' she gasped. 'It's because I can enter them, command them. I have powers that no other mayakari have. I can speak to your father; invade *dreams. I* gave you the order.'

Aarya stilled. 'What order?'

'*Cut yourself,*' Shakti repeated her old directive, '*for you deserve to bleed, daughter.* That was me.'

She saw the moment Aarya recognized it, saw the mixture of disgust, horror, and fascination in her calculating eyes.

'You want to rule the Ran Empire in its entirety, princess?' Shakti asked. One last chance. 'Keep me alive and I can help you conquer the world.'

CHAPTER FORTY-NINE
Ashoka

'Is that . . . a winged serpent?' Sachith asked, his hands shielding his eyes as he stared up at the sky.

From his seat on the balcony of his father's study, Ashoka trained his eyes towards the clouds. Sure enough, the silhouette of a giant winged beast was flying closer and closer to them. Its body twisted and swirled in the sky before the serpent changed direction and began to descend.

'A royal messenger,' Ashoka told Sachith. Rahil was not with them; he was still hurt by Ashoka's words and had gruffly informed him that he would be patrolling the streets that morning. He was yet to return.

If this was what love was, to be made happy before he was broken, Ashoka wished he had never realized it. Hurting Rahil was to hurt himself, and it was akin to a shard of glass wedged into the sole of his foot that he could not remove. Being empires apart had been lonely enough but having Rahil here and actively avoiding him was even lonelier.

'There must be some sort of urgent news, Prince Ashoka,' Sachith remarked. 'Do you want one of the staff to greet the messenger and relay the news to you?'

Ashoka stood from his chair. 'No need,' he replied. 'I will meet with the messenger myself.'

By the time he exited the royal estate, the winged serpent and its rider were still descending. Its wings created a welcome gust of wind as it slowed to land. This was a dark brown winged serpent, its scales the colour of damp earth. Unlike Sahry, the creature was more docile. It allowed one of the soldiers to remove its saddle after its rider slid off its back and proceeded to curl into itself on the courtyard. Poor thing: it would have been tired from its long flight to Taksila. Beneath the hot sun, it could rest.

Ashoka focused his gaze on the royal messenger. A tall woman with windswept black hair and a brown satchel attached to her side came towards him, her stride long and purposeful. When she stopped in front of him at the estate steps, she bowed.

'Prince Ashoka,' she greeted him. She sounded breathless. Anticipatory. 'My name is Samiha. I bring a message. From Empress Aarya.'

At first, her words did not register. Only after he reviewed the word 'empress' did shock finally hit him like a ton of bricks.

'*Empress* Aarya?' he repeated. This was a dream; he was hallucinating – he had to be. Had he been transported into that terrifying dreamworld again?

'Yes, Prince Ashoka,' Samiha replied. Her mouth tilted downward. 'The emperor has succumbed to a state of deep sleep. He has been rendered comatose, either from poison or mayakari magic. The physicians think it is the former. Your sister tells the latter.'

He could hear the birds, feel the warmth of his sun on his skin. This was the real world.

It couldn't be. Arush, succumbed to a comatose state? How had it happened, and who was responsible for it? Ashoka could not imagine his impetuous older brother lying on his bed, asleep and unable to be awakened. And now Aarya had taken his place . . .

'Give me the letter, Samiha,' he instructed. Dutifully, the woman reached into her satchel and produced a rolled-up piece of parchment that was sealed with wax. It bore the insignia of his family. If Arush was unable to wake, it meant that Ashoka was now the second-in-line to the throne.

Spirits, *so close.*

His hands were shaking. It had felt like aeons ago when he had stated that the throne was too far away to reach. Now, it was achingly near.

But Aarya was on the throne. Knowing her, the letter could only spell trouble. He could only imagine what this could be about. The seal cracked in half as he prised the letter open. Aarya's neat, loopy scrawl stared back at him. It felt like a threat.

Steeling himself, Ashoka pored over the contents of the letter:

Little brother,

You may have heard the news by now – our dear Arush has been rendered comatose. In his absence, I have been made acting regent. The empress, until he wakes, that is. I do not know when I will give up my tenure.

Or perhaps, I never will. Only time can tell.

As the new regent, I will be making swift changes to Arush's previously laid plans. I am relocating our soldiers to the south as father meant to do. Additionally, I aim to clean whatever messes you have made in your governorship.

As your new monarch, my command to you is this:

Remove the Ridi soldiers from Taksila. Lift the ban on mayakari killings. I do not understand why you attempt to destroy father's legacy, but I will not let you. You are not the emperor, little brother, and you never will be. Heed my warning. Obey my command. You may be my family, but when it comes to the empire, I shall choose its glory over you. This is your final warning.

If you fail to comply, rest assured, Ashoka – I will bring war to you.

When he finished reading it, Ashoka scrunched up the parchment and threw it onto the ground, much to the messenger's surprise.

Aarya still thought he was malleable, that he would try to resolve their disagreement with peace. She thought that his idealism was some errant-born rebelliousness that needed tempering. And, in true Aarya fashion, she was trying to repress it with a threat with the idea that Ashoka would fold and walk away and nurse his injuries alone.

Father's replica indeed.

Samiha's face was expressionless. Ashoka waited till her gaze travelled back to him, made sure that she could see his hard-set appearance. 'What message should I give the empress, Prince Ashoka?' she asked.

Empress. Hah.

'Tell my sister that I refuse her commands,' he told Samiha. From his periphery, he saw Sachith's eyes widen. Ashoka could only imagine what Rahil would say – or not say. But this was not his decision to make. To reverse his father's bloody legacy would be to spill his own. He wasn't afraid of his siblings the way he had been afraid of Adil. He was not the same Ashoka Maurya who had left the Golden City. This Ashoka Maurya had learned to be different.

If his sister wanted a war, he would give her one. And then he would claim the Obsidian Throne.

THE STORY CONTINUES. . .

ACKNOWLEDGEMENTS

To have an unthinkable dream become realized is a strange feeling. If I travelled back in time and told 14-year-old Maithree that she would one day become an author, she'd probably curse me for lying. I'd probably curse her back, too, but I digress.

So much work goes into publishing a book. The process is gargantuan, and I'd like to thank those who've helped get *The Prince Without Sorrow* to where it is today.

The first and biggest thank you goes to my wonderful agent, Maddy Belton. Thank you for taking a chance on Ashoka, Shakti, and myself at a time when doubt plagued me endlessly. Your dedication and support are nothing short of extraordinary. Here's to creating many more gremlin characters in the future. Thank you also to the wider team at the Madeleine Milburn Literary Agency.

To my editor, Natasha Bardon. The moment you said that you understood *The Prince Without Sorrow* to be about family infighting, I was sold. Thank you for your guidance and general editorial wizardry to elevate the story to become what it is today. An additional thank you to editor Kate Fogg. It was an absolute pleasure to work with you for the last year. To David Pomerico, thank you for bringing Ashoka and Shakti's story to North American readers.

To the wider HarperVoyager UK, US, and Australia teams: I may not know everything that goes on behind the scenes, but I know you guys do a lot, and that doesn't go unappreciated. For all that goes noticed and unnoticed – *thank you*. To my copyeditor and proofreader, amazing work. Your eagle eyes were much appreciated. Thank you also to the brilliant cover artists. I will never not be in awe of the work you've produced.

To Scarlett and Sophie – you two chaotic neutrals were there when *The Prince Without Sorrow* was still a lump of clay waiting to be moulded. Thank you for always cheering me on. I'm very lucky to call you two my friends (I will never say something this mushy again). In fact, thank you to all my wider friends and family for all your excitement and support. *Writers Block* – you guys were the first to make me feel like I was really part of a writing community. Our consistent sprinting sessions were the reason I was able to finish *The Prince Without Sorrow* in the first place. May all your writing dreams come true.

Ashoka might dislike his siblings, but I don't (unless there's a good reason to). So, to my younger brothers – *you're welcome*. I pay for you and subsequently pay for it with my sanity. Thank you both for existing, I guess, and for both roasting and supporting me. ILY.

Ammi and Thathi, there are a lot of things I could say, but I need to be concise. Thank you for deciding to stick me in the community library after school while I waited for you to pick me up after work. As a result, a good chunk of my adolescence was spent surrounded by books, and this eventually inspired me to write ones of my own on that block of cement we called a laptop. Thank you for all your sacrifices, for funding my reading obsession, and for never dulling my love of stories. I appreciate these little things more than you know.

This book is dedicated to Comet, my family's rambunctious, food-stealing Labrador. Oftentimes, I sat next to her and typed away on my laptop because her presence made my stress magically disappear, as dogs are often known to do. Sadly, she passed away

ACKNOWLEDGEMENTS

while I was working on *The Prince Without Sorrow*, but I associate her so strongly with the memory of writing this book that it made sense to immortalize her in the only way I knew how.

And finally, dear reader, thank *you* for picking up this book. I'm ever grateful.